THE IYNNDYRE BORN

Book One of The Book of Legends

by

ANNE SOSTMAN

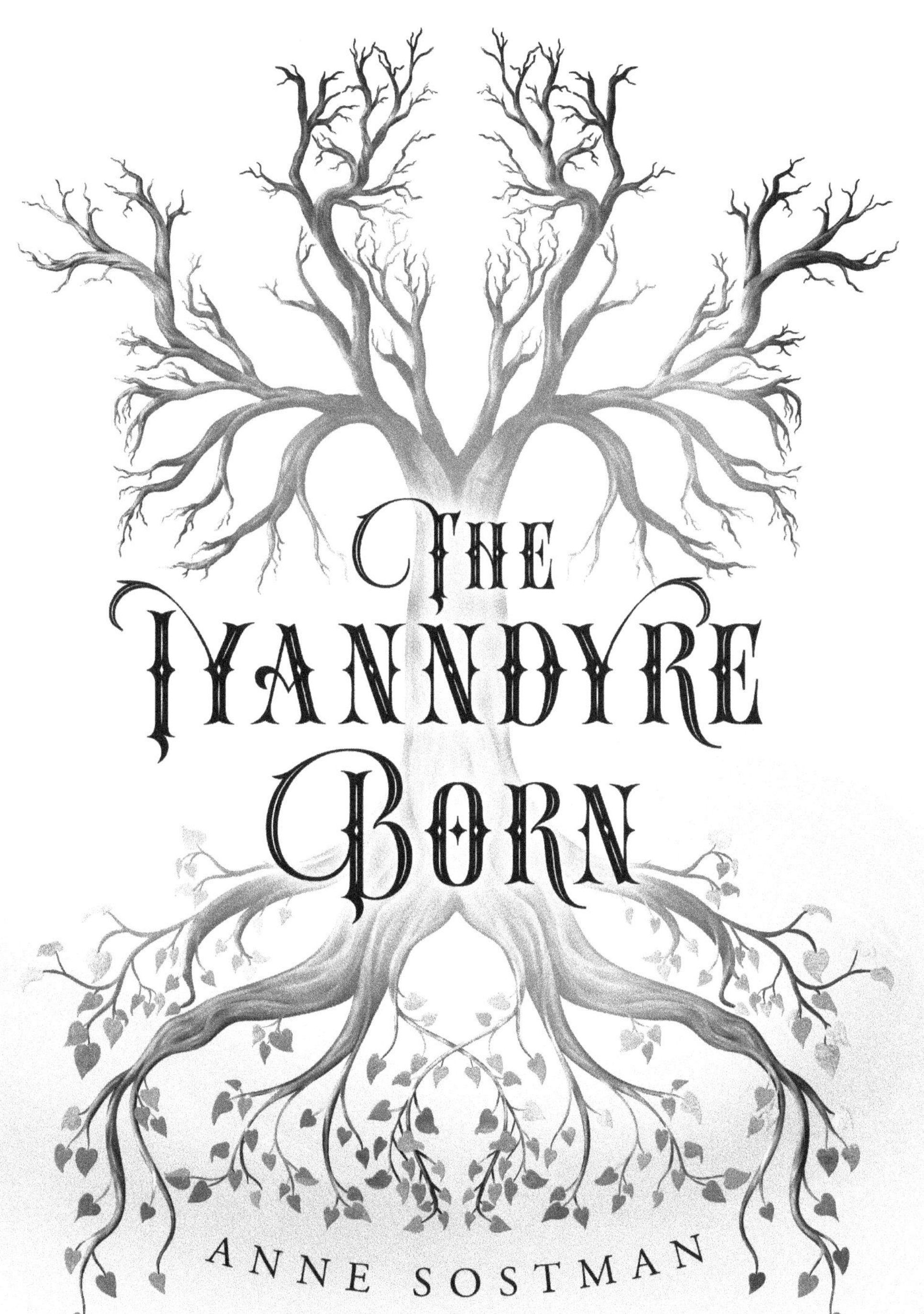

The Iyanndyre Born

ANNE SOSTMAN

Cover design by Rena Violet.
Map design by Rena Violet.
Interior design and format by Rena Violet

The Iyanndyre Born
Book One of The Book of Legend Series

ISBN Hardcover: 979-8-9921135-0-1
ISBN Paperback: 979-8-9921135-1-8
ISBN eBook: 979-8-9921135-2-5

For my parents.
Thank you for always believing in my wild ideas.

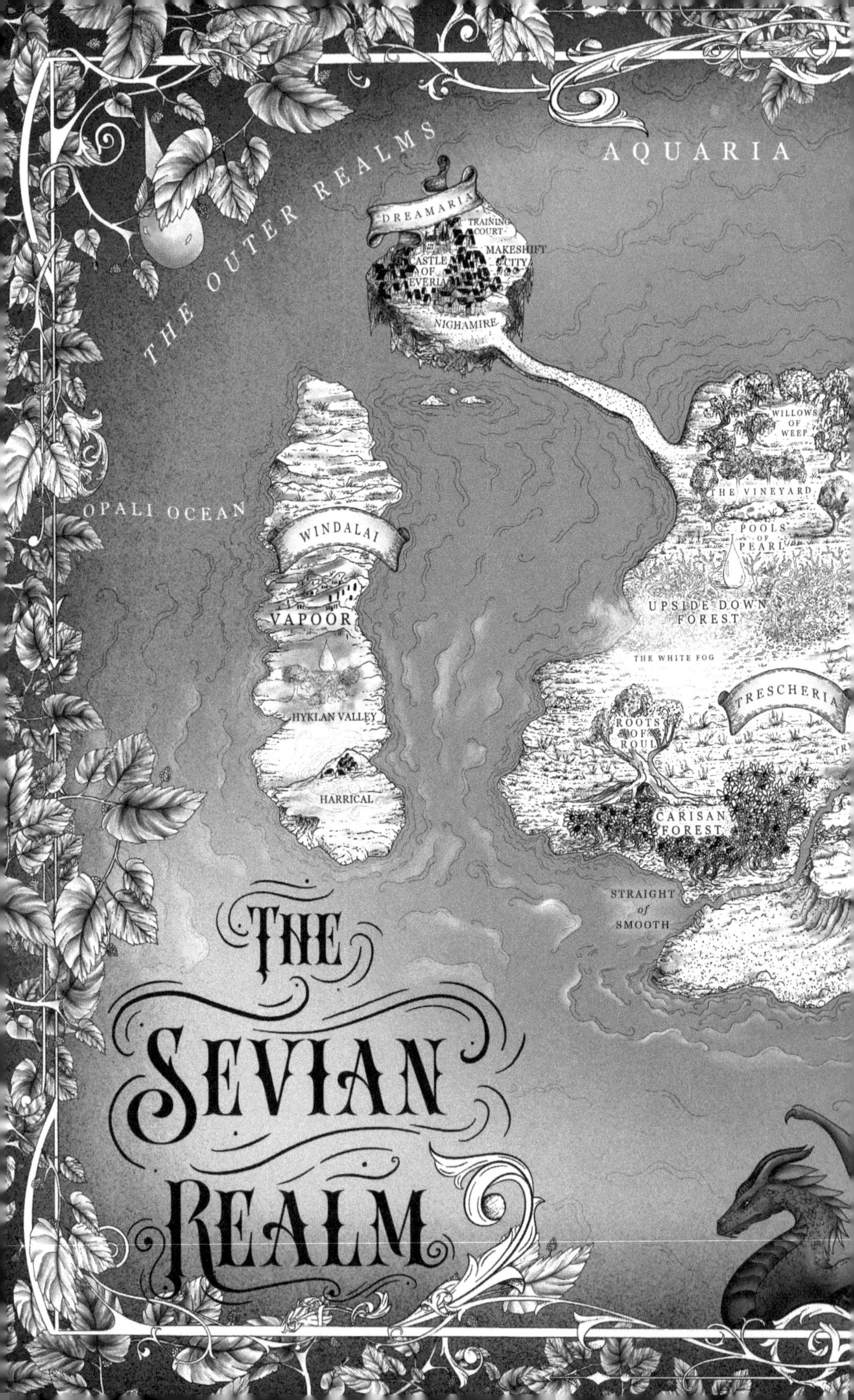
THE OUTER REALMS
AQUARIA
DREAMARIA
TRAINING COURT
MAKESHIFT CITY
CASTLE OF EVERIA
NIGHAMIRE
WILLOWS OF WEEP
THE VINEYARD
POOLS OF PEARL
OPALI OCEAN
WINDALAI
VAPOOR
UPSIDE DOWN FOREST
THE WHITE FOG
TRESCHERIA
ROOTS OF ROUL
HYKLAN VALLEY
HARRICAL
CARISAN FOREST
STRAIGHT of SMOOTH
THE SEVIAN REALM

ER OCEAN
INFINITE VOID
THE WAVES OF OMAURO
EZMARAD OCEAN
THE IYANNDYRE
IYANN VALLEY
DRONE MOUNTAINS
TURQUOISE RIVER
SANS CASTLE OF PRZYM
CAMARELHEAD
ROCCALI
SANS OF SAI
VALLEY OF SCORCH
SINKING DUNES
MAVERAI
GRYNNDYRE
FARMLAND
CANYON GORGE
CLIFFS OF PALIA
SEYKAHARA PEAKS
GRAND MEADOW
BRYAR BRIDGE
CAVANAVAS
PLATEAU OF BLISS
BRIDGE
CASSTELI
CLIFF OF CASTEEL
CIRCLE PARK
CLIFF OF MAU
THOUSAND STAIR SUMMIT
ECHOLYN
THE DAIYAMAN OCEAN
XAERIA
INFINITE VOID

XAERIA
Monnaire Lore
General of the Xaerian Fleet
Arro Lore
Leader of Xaeria
Scribe of Echolyn
High Archivant

ROCCALI
Xylar Aurn
Cadet in the Order of Soldiers
Kain Orro
General of the Roccali Legion

WINDALAI
Mikel Valkor
Cadet in the Order of Soldiers

GRYNNDYRE
ORRO FAMILY
Durran Orro
General of Grynndyre Command
Alora Orro
High Ascendant of Grynndyre
Rioyn Orro
Potential Cadet in the Order of Soldiers
Ayva Orro
Cadet in the Order of Galilei
Bair Orro
Graduate of the Order of Voyants

TRESCHERIA
RISOR FAMILY
Jaxyon Risor
Cadet in the Order of Soldiers
Cyanda Risor
High Voyant
KAI FAMILY
Falla Kai
FirstElite: Order of Soldiers
Xi Kai
General of the Trescherian Defense
Xan Kai
High Rank

DREMARIA
Zianli Wren
Ruler of Dremaria
GREYEA FAMILY
Evon Greyea
General of the Dremarian Army
Daun Greyea
General of the Dremarian Army
Shivane Greyea
Cadet in the Order of Healants
Sylon Greyea
Cadet in the Order of Soldiers
Caya Fakanery
Solider in the Dremarian Army
Coren Fakanery
Solider in the Dremarian Army

PRONUNCIATIONS

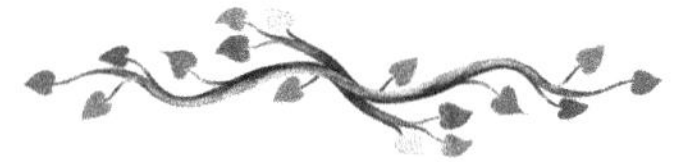

Iyanndyre: EYEY-AN-dy-er

Rioyn Orro: Ry-onn OR-oh

Ayva Orro: ay-vuh OR-oh

Durran Orro: duh-RAN OR-oh

Alora Orro: ALOR-uh OR-oh

Daun Greyea: Da-wn Greh-yay-a

Evon Greyea: ih-VON Greh-yay-a

Shivane Greyea: shih-VAYN Greh-yay-a

Sylon Greyea: SY-lawn Greh-yay-a

Arro Lore: AIR-oh

Monnaire Lore: MOH-nuh-REE

Jaxyon Risor: JAK-sun RY-zer

Mikel Valkor: mih-KEL val-KOR

Xylar Aurn: zy-LAR OR-en

Caya Fakanery: KAH-yuh Fah-KAH-nuh-ree

Coren Fakanery: KOR-en Fah-KAH-nuh-ree

Hanri Yonyx: ah-N-ree YO-niks

Heilana Nicor: HAY-LAH-nuh Ni-KOR

Bair Orro: BEar OR-oh

Atheyl: AY-th-a-EYEEEL

Zoura: ZOR-uh

Lord Zaxion: Lord ZAH-jen

Jyan Cour: WAHN KOR

Ixo Shen: IK-soh Shen

Grynndyre: GRY-AN-dy-er

Trescheria: TREH-sheeree-uh

Roccali: RO-kuh-LY

Windalai: WIN-duh-LY

Dremaria: DR-mah-REEAH

Xaeria: ZEE-REE-uh

Xall: ZAWL

Ecolyn: EH-koh-lin

Dragolyon: DRA-goh-LEE-own

Casstell: kuh-S-TEL

Sansyre: SAN-sy-er

Drycour: DRY-kor

Assihilator: uh-SY-uh-LAY-ter

PROLOGUE

"THEY ABANDONED US AND left us to die on this foreign planet." A tearful Everia forces her chopped words out.

The fierce, rip-roaring winds stir up fine golden red dust.

Not a single structure, mountain, or even faint hill is in sight to shield them from the brutality of this harsh, unforgiving environment—an environment considered a reprieve to these two sisters, Warriem and Everia Ryer.

Warriem cups Everia's damp cheeks in her calloused hands, wiping the flaming red strands of hair from both of their wind beaten faces. "They deserted us here but look around." *Warriem watches Everia gazing into the horizon.*

"There's nothing here. We won't survive. We have a few days at best. How could they leave us—their children—behind?"

Warriem collects the fallen tear from Everia's cheek, then looks around at the forgotten wasteland, at the potential they've been granted. "Unless we do something about it. We aren't kids anymore, Everia," she says, thinking. "We create our world. We can make it beautiful, magical, and peaceful just like our dreams. A place free from the death, destruction, and suffocation we've endured. We'll be free from evil, hate—raw injustice."

Warriem pours her whole heart into her convicted words.

"Will people come?"

"If you build it . . ." *Warriem's smile crinkles as Everia snorts a relieved chuckle.*

"You and your stupid ancient movies from that wretched planet called Earth." *Everia and Warriem hold each other in a strong embrace.*

Warriem's gaze falls upon a sand-laced sinkhole. "Do you feel that pull? As if gravity itself is pulling us into the depths of its heart."

Everia shakes her head and Warriem stoops, Everia following. They touch their fingertips to the ground to feel the vibrating tug.

They stand. Curiosity … fear … hope … tangled together.

Everia takes Warriem's outstretched hand in hers as their bodies become consumed by a magnificent force, enrapturing them in a golden whirlwind of fire which dissipates as quickly as it came. Their once hazel eyes glow with a fierce golden hue.

Warriem raises her arms with vigor and purpose as if lifting immeasurable weights from the ground.

Everia gawks, seeing Warriem erect walls of sand, creating a barrier from the destructive winds.

Everia looks at her hands, then shoots a bruised and bloody palm to the sky.

Dark tendrils of black smoke swallow her body whole. She disappears into it, reappearing behind Warriem who whirls to face an enthralled Everia.

Warriem whispers to Everia's mind, "We're home."

PART I

FESTIVITIES of MENDACITY

CHAPTER 1

THE CAVE OF CAIN

4,031 Years Later

RIOYN

ANY DAY, MY TIME will come. It must. It will be my chance to prove to everyone in the Grynndyre Command that I'm worthy to fight for them, not merely the son of a legacy.

They need to know I will be the best man, the best soldier, ever to enter Sansyre University's Order of Soldiers. I am an adult now…well almost!

Though I am but seventeen years old—soon to be eighteen—my hope is for my father to take me seriously, that he'll understand I am ready to learn, to train, to fight at his side. I rake my fingers through my wild, red spiked hair wondering if my father will ever respect me. Will he see me as an equal, or will he continue to hold me under his iron thumb?

At least this is what I try to convince myself of, hoping one day, it will become the truth. However, there's no time for wishful thinking right now. If Father won't let me enter the Order of Soldiers at the university, I'll simply have to find another way in.

Since being a kid, my dream has always been to fight for our realm, Seivan. The greatest of all the realms.

Thoughts collide in my mind as my eyes fixate on the fresh-faced cadets eagerly awaiting the commanders of the Grynndyre Command to announce the grand match to close out the final training camp before classes begin at Sansyre University in a few weeks.

I already know I will be in the final match, having outscored every competitor by almost double, very few coming close to my scores.

As we all wait in the unneeded suspense the commanders take pleasure in putting us through, our surroundings sink into my mind slowly. It's an area which so few are allowed to freely venture.

I, however, have risked coming down here a few times in the past. The waves of the Daiyaman Ocean roar behind us, clawing at its crystal sand beach leading into the mouth of the Cave of Caino, known for its treacherous, unpredictable nature. However, today the waves roar at the cave walls with an intense vigor that in uncharacteristic of this area.

It's surprising the commanders didn't make us fight each other while dodging falling rocks. My gaze locks on the crest just beyond the cave. Many times have my feet secretly trodden this same route, yet never have they dared venture beyond the crest's edge.

No one has.

My attention whips back into focus, hearing my name increasing in octaves.

"RIOYN ORRO!" Commander Goren shouts. "Thank you for your attention. You and Jaxyon Risor will be facing off in the grand match to close out our final training camp. Its winner has succeeded in also becoming the victor in the Tournament of Spar for the last two decades. We don't expect this year to be any different. The tournament will commence at the Festival of Seivan in two weeks, the winner being crowned FirstElite."

My nonchalant reaction earns a few head shakes and eye rolls, the many hands of fellow cadets shaking and jostling me with encouragement. But what they don't realize is that while their enthused support is welcome, the match already lies in my clutches.

To lose is impossible.

"Jax," I bluntly say. His muscular build is intimidating to the average person, but I match him in every way, except his height. He stands a few inches taller than me, always has.

"Rioyn. I'll go easy on you, old friend," he taunts with his charming grin.

We both enter the makeshift fighting ring at the very edge of the last sliver of dry sand before the waves begin their violent retreat into the ocean.

Jax shakes out his legs and arms in traditional pre-fight preparation, eyeing me dancing lightly on the balls of my feet, ready to spar.

"We will remind our final fighters that all rules still apply, and you are expected to adhere to all of them. This will be a fair fight," Commander Goren says.

Jax takes the immediate offense. However, his early, aggressive attack is straightforward to read, offering me the chance to defend it easily.

We trained together, he and I, for over a decade and have been best friends for longer. Does this fool really think he can beat me, that his every move cannot be anticipated?

But then the thought comes that likewise, he knows my every move too.

We go around and around for what feels like an hour; though we've each scored our fair share of points, neither of us is on the verge of giving in just yet.

The soreness of my muscles and tendons rises through my arches, radiating shingles of pain through my legs and into my back. The pain is welcome, a needed distraction from otherwise racing thoughts. It helps me stay focused, unwilling to lose this fight.

"You're not going to win this one, Rioyn." Jax's overly confident tone needs to lower an octave. He has never been able to best me, not even when we were small.

No one has managed it! I've proven myself throughout the years and now when it matters most, I will do so once again. It will be my pleasure.

Losing is not an option, not to him or anyone.

It's not in me to come in second, ever, and these are my busy thoughts as my shins scream in pain for me to stop, but there's no chance of that.

Jax is swift, cunning, and light on his feet.

I will give him that as he pushes me onto the jagged crystal sands of the crystal Daiyaman Ocean; the taste of foamy water soon fizzes on my tongue, the waves pawing at my sore ankles providing salty relief, albeit for the shortest time.

My eyes dart around the edges of our makeshift fighting ring.

The entire training camp has stopped to watch me … me. All two hundred future cadets training here—who hope to vie for the title of FirstElite—are rapt, observing.

Their attention gives me the fuel my body needs to best Jax.

But not just to best him, no. I must conquer him and show everyone my prowess, my mastery and place in the lead position, making clear that this does not belong to him.

However, my attention is fixed on the commanders of the Grynndyre Command.

They also need to know my name.

The Grynndyre Command being the premiere branch of Seivan's military, to become a soldier for Grynndyre is the ultimate accomplishment.

But first, a man must enter the Order of Soldiers, earning his way in.

With the same eager grin, I crack my knuckles and curl my fingers into tightly wound fists. Jax's hands stay open, his fighting style exemplifying the signature maneuvers of his home province, Trescheria—light, open, but deadly.

I bait him with an eager jab. He's too skilled to fall for such an amateur move. Do better if you want to win, I demand of myself.

He's light-footed, his stance perfect, balanced, and all his attacks swift and calculated. His jabs are smooth and fluid. He lands several punches to my ribs, scoring a few more points. Jax isn't deterred by the volatility of this cave and keeps his focus sharp.

How far he's come in his abilities!

I'd hoped these waves would give me the edge to weaken his confidence, but it's quite the opposite, so I'll have to figure out another tactic to crush him.

I dance on the balls of my feet, releasing tense fists, shaking out my nerves. I mirror Jax's stance then drop to my hands and sweep his feet. He leaps in the air but doesn't pick his back foot up high enough, letting me snag him. He slams down on his back, hard.

With one smooth, fluid movement, Jax hurls his legs in the air to propel him forward and lands on the balls of his feet, yet again in a ready stance. He unleashes several rounds of punches, jabs and uppercuts, a few landing, and hard. He's been training outside of our group sessions. He must have been. Sure, he is good but has never been this good.

Echoes of cheers designed for him ripple through me.

Time to stop this charade and win. I take the offense and charge at him, seeing him deflect as anticipated, and I catch him off guard, sending him to his back. His large, muscular frame lands hard, frustration appearing to saturate his emotions.

The crowd cheers louder for me, my arms raising, welcoming and enticing my fans to holler yet louder encouragement. I turn back to face my fierce competitor when he sweeps my feet out from under me, a sudden sharp whistle sounding.

"Cadet Risor, that is an intentional, illegal move. One more and you will be disqualified from training," Commander Goren says.

"All's fair in love and war, right, Commander?" Jax's arms raise high, searching for validation.

"Play by the rules, cadet. If you can't win honorably, then it's not a win worth gaining," Commander Goren continues in clear admonishment of my tactics.

Jax focuses his red-faced frustration back toward me, throwing reckless punch after reckless punch as I bait him with taunts and heckles, enticing the crowd for more cheers and applause at Jax's demise. Aha! I've got him now.

Jax forgets that I can read him like a book and whenever he feels he's losing control, he allows his emotions to gain the upper hand. It's a weakness I have tried to help him strengthen but his impulse and constant drive of the rush to win still conquer him.

This match has dragged out long enough. So, I seize my moment to go in for the winning shot, yet pull back for one more second of glory with this raucous crowd.

Jax fumes at the seams, seeing me finish the match with a roundhouse jab hook combo that isn't exactly illegal in the rules of the ring, though it isn't exactly favored either.

I see it as a chance worth taking, a combination move to highlight my skills as a fighter.

Jax cannot defend himself now, my moves flawless, rendering him quite defenseless, thus claiming for me a much-deserved victory. Once I knew I'd win.

The crowd rip roars with cheers, letting me revel in their praise and adoration. Some of the commanders shake their heads. What, were they betting against me?

My victory is short lived when the final training session of the camp gets under way.

The commanders train all the other cadets on the strategies of the winning one.

As the man who won, my attention diverts elsewhere. It snaps back on hearing a faint voice calling after me. "Rioyn! Hey, Rioyn!" Upon whipping my head around, there he is… Mikel, squeezing his way through the cadets with a clutch of battle notes in his knuckled hand.

I wave back, though this is not the ideal time for a conversation. Still, he persists.

"Rioyn! Rioyn! Wait up. I have notes," he eagerly says, delivering a big hug with his thick, short arms. His stocky body doesn't aid him well in endeavors of athleticism.

Even with his physical shortcomings, he's a soldier through and through but not one who fights on the battlefield; his battlefield and strategic knowledge are unmatched by anyone entering Sansyre or who has graduated in the last decade.

We all have our talents and gifts, and this happens to be Mikel's.

"I wouldn't expect anything less from you. Tell me, what do you have?"

Just as Mikel gets his notes organized, Xylar makes a grand show of his arrival.

"What? No notes for me?" He wraps Mikel's head in a bear hold and rustles his thick, chopped hair. Mikel pushes Xylar off him.

These two can go for multiple boring rounds, but before I can tear Xylar off Mikel, Jax does it for me. He's never been one for their antics either.

"You two never know when to stop," Jax huffs. I'm waiting to see what type of mood he's in before making my approach. Sometimes with Jax, he can be temperamental when he loses. This time, however, he reaches out his hand. "Great fight."

We shake hands. "You've always been a tough competitor to beat."

Before Jax can say anything else, the commanders nab our attention.

I strain to listen from the back of the crowd when a massive wave crashes into the side of the Cave of Caino, stealing away my focus.

The commanders march everyone out and back to Casstell, so almost without thinking, my head ducks below the crowd. They can't see me this far out. I need to go into the Cave of Caino. This is the only chance to gain access to this area.

Time to figure out if my long thought theory is correct!

Jax, Xylar and Mikel are in the back with me, and they can't possibly know how desperately I need them to accompany me.

"Hey, let's go explore the Cave of Caino before we head back," I suggest.

"For what reason?" Mikel inquires.

"Because it's a great terrain for sparring. Unpredictable, challenging, and forces you to think quickly. What better way to get the edge we need than to train there?"

Hm, good ploy, well-stated. My entire body buys into my own conviction. Is that agreement in their eyes? My head whips around and slowly, my feet begin walking toward the cave as if my body has a mind of its own.

Thankfully, Jax, Mikel, and Xylar follow, seeing me glancing back.

"Why do we ever listen to you?" Xylar retorts.

Fair point. They shake their heads in unison but receive no comment from me.

We make the half-mile trek that leads us into the mouth of the Cave of Caino, each of our curious eyes raising at the magnitude of this cavernous black marvel.

Xylar and Jax are the first to face off, going around and around, their footwork stumbling a few times while learning to pick up their feet.

They become lighter, swifter, nimbler. Mikel and I study their movements for review later when a massive wave crashes into us. Instinctively, my hand grabs hold of Mikel, hoisting him above water. We dredge through the strong pull returning to sea.

As more threatening waves crash onto the shore, we race into the back of the cave. Something other than logic is guiding my direction into this place.

"Rioyn, why are you risking going deep into it? The most unpredictable and dangerous cave there is in Seivan!" Jax inquires.

"There's something here. I feel it."

"What could you possibly be looking for here?" Mikel insists with his inquisitive stare.

"Whatever it is they're hiding from us, I have a hunch it has something to do with this cave. It's a risk …"

"A risk indeed, Rioyn, but you know Grynndyre better than anyone. If you weren't such a fierce fighter, I'd have pegged you as a voyant, charting the provinces of our realm instead of training to be a soldier. You've never given me a reason to doubt you." A wave of relief crescendos through me at Jax's sentiment, along with a bitter pain of grief.

"Move, now!"

We run to the back of the cave, scrambling our way to higher ground.

The waves force us into the highest, rearmost part of the cave, our backs plastered hard against its splintering wall.

"The moon's gravity is too strong this time of year. It makes these shores unpredictably fierce, you know. They'll rip us out to sea!" Mikel shouts.

Desperately scouring the cave, my eyes are seeking any way out when the waves retreat into the crystal ocean as quickly as they entered. "Is everyone okay?" I ask.

We peel ourselves off the wall as large, black rocks rip from the ceiling, their trajectory aiming directly at the four of us. Instincts overtaking logic, my body flings itself over Xylar and Mikel in an automatic protective mode.

Jax commands his Ascendance and traps the rocks in a cocoon of energy. His face is reddened, amber light swirling around him as he whips the rocks into the black ocean waves, saving us. The amber light fades as he quells his Ascendance.

Back to my feet again, my head snaps to my three friends. We narrowly escaped the crumbling rocks but now, everyone is clawing at their heads in excruciating pain.

"Make it stop."

"I can't see straight."

"My head's going to explode."

After a quick glance at them, I look upwards through a hole in the cave. "Move now!"

Jax and Xylar rise to their feet and dash from the cave while I grab Mikel under his thick arm to usher him out. As soon as they're outside, their pain ceases. I, however, am mere seconds from their scowls of betrayal as soon as they realize where we really are.

Xylar snarls, charging ahead, "Lies, Rioyn. You tricked us by coming here. We are not supposed to be here, not supposed to be this close to the Infinite Void. I'm going to report this immediately."

But I race to block him.

"Xylar, wait. Please!" Jax is able to get to him first, blocking Xylar with his strong arm as they lock hardened stares. Xylar's jaw flexes, his angular chin lifting toward Jax.

"Didn't know what was here," I plead, guilt-laden at my lie. "I've never been here, and wanted to help you guys do your best for the tournament."

Aside from wanting to train for the sparring, I've brought them here to help me determine if my voyant charting is right. Is the Infinite Void here, beyond the cave?

I've never suffered the effects of the Infinite Void like everyone else, needing to experience it up close alongside 'normal' friends, to understand if I have immunity to it. Turns out I do.

Xylar eases but the rigid tone of his body holds true, his searing crimson stare burning into me. "Another plot concocted by the captain of his island of one. You of all … citizens should know better." His words land with a brutal sting.

Citizen. Not a cadet in the Order of Soldiers like him, Jax, and Mikel. He chose that word knowing it would crush me, regardless of the fact that we all went to the same training camps as kids or that we've all trained together over the years. I've bested them every year, including the final match of our training camp today. None of that matters to them.

They're each enrolled in the Order of Soldiers and I am not.

Mikel puts his patronizing hand on my shoulder. "You may have meant well. You always think you do but …" His trailing but isn't beyond my understanding. They feel betrayed, and why wouldn't they?

I knew what I was doing. Now, they do too, but it was necessary to know.

Xylar chimes in, "You always have ulterior motives rooted in your selfish, self-interest. What reason could you possibly have to bring us to the Infinite Void? Are you trying to get us all disqualified?"

A shameful smile flashes, my thoughts ripping my mind apart.

When are you going to learn to make better choices?

I can't tell him, any of them, why, so I change the subject.

"Your Ascendance is getting better. Have you been training to hone it?" I ask Jax with sincerity, hoping to break the tension.

"I've put a lot of effort into it, yes." He flashes a coy smile.

Incompetence ripples through me.

Despite practicing my Ascendance daily, it hasn't manifested as it should.

It's sporadic and unpredictable, worthless. My mother prides us on being true descendants of Warriem but I've yet to see the fruits of that heritage, having only proved to be a failure once again. My father is right, then.

Jax insists, "It'll come. It's different for everyone, so we can practice if you want. I've picked up new techniques from Ascendants in Trescheria, and I'll have some free time in the morning after orientation." Jax reaches his arm for my tense shoulders.

It's a welcomed comfort, my shoulders easing.

"Orientation is tomorrow?" Panic squeezes all the air from my lungs.

"Why don't you enroll in another order? You'll turn eighteen next week. Then once you're enrolled, you can switch orders. Simple!"

Mikel's voice rises with excitement as though he's solved the quandary of the day.

"I wish but then, I'd be stuck in that order. I can't enter the Order of Soldiers without my father's permission, unlike you all. And the Order of Soldiers is the only one I care about. I want to follow in my father's footsteps and become Leader of the Grynndyre Command. So, I need to be in that Order to achieve my goals … dreams."

Xylar scoffs, "We won't see another battle in our lifetime. Why even bother?"

"You don't know that," Jax retorts. "Dremaria attacked Trescheria less than a decade ago. Who says they won't do it again? Or Roccali for that matter. A new battle among the provinces can happen any day and you know that. Especially since Shivane and Sylon Greyea are still alive."

"I can't believe they're still allowed their freedom after their role in the last battle. There's always the hope that the legend of the Iyanndyre Born is true," Mikel offers.

I can't mask my surprise. "You believe in The Book of Legends?"

"Who knows? Maybe? It's just a legend and we've never seen any of the legends from that book come true, have we? Maybe they're just to intimidate people from starting a war and nothing more."

"I've had enough fun for one afternoon," Xylar sneers as he walks off.

Jax, Xylar, and Mikel start their ascent up the cliff through the carved-out path. Jax whips back around. "You aren't coming back with us?"

I fumble for any excuse that doesn't arouse more suspicions about the real reason to have brought them here. "Think I dropped something in the cave. But don't let me hold you all up. You're almost at curfew."

Jax nods, accepting the lie he undoubtedly suspects.

Then, as usual, I'm alone.

CHAPTER 2

THE INFINITE VOID

MY MIND RACES WITH the same thoughts that have been plaguing me for months, convincing me every day that Father will come around and allow me to join the Order of Soldiers.

I've been studying and training for this for years, dedicating all of my time outside of school and chores to become the best.

Despite passing all of my skill, written, and oral tests with the highest marks of my year, still, he holds me down, constantly regurgitating how I'm not ready to become a soldier, to be a leader. It's ridiculous; no one could ever be more ready than this.

If Father sees my unique ability to be close to the Infinite Void without being affected by it, maybe he'll reconsider, or maybe it'll be the spike in my death throne. It's hard to anticipate since he never reveals the entire truth of his ever-changing motives.

Having lied to my closest friends today for my own selfish reasons, I can't stop myself from wondering … Is he right about me not being ready to be a leader?

Back in the cave, the waves have settled to their evening glass-like shimmer.

Stomping through the diamond sands scrapes my shoes, yet I don't stop before getting to the other side.

Rounding the rocky curved opening, coming out on its outer side, I'm searching for the Infinite Void, pondering into the horizon of the Daiyaman Ocean where the sun is ready to fold into its violent grasp. Light-footed, I go traipsing through the sparkling sand with gentle waves pawing at my feet until I feel it.

This is a reverberation so profound, every bone inside of me vibrates, sending me lurching back out of the grasp of what can only be the Infinite Void's elusive boundary.

No one has any explanation—at least not that they'll honestly give—of what the Infinite Void actually is. The simple answer is that it's the force protecting us from the Outer Realms, from the people who want to extinguish us from this planet. Finding the Infinite Void gets me one step closer to figuring out what happened to my brother.

Did he somehow figure out how to outsmart the Infinite Void to slip past its grasp? Or maybe he was consumed by it. Either way, only half-baked theories remain.

The golden glow of the sun deepens into an orange and red hue, emphasizing how I've stayed well past my permitted time. My absence from home will not go unnoticed.

Turning on the balls of my feet, they sink into the thick sand, wading through the cave and up the path carved into the cliffside. The pain in my legs is burning with each stride, but there is no time to lose to scale the cliffs faster than ever before.

Finally at the top, my lungs are searing from the salty sea-misted air.

I pause, looking back at the Cave of Caino for one last glimpse, almost expecting to see a dark miasma or some other evidence of the void. Instead, all that's there is black stone and the glimmering sea.

Ahead lies the stone wall surrounding Casstell, my home and capital city of the Grynndyre Province. I squeeze through the small, hidden hole where a series of stones has worked loose, then turn to patch up the opening, home just a few minutes away.

I'd have to run my heart out to make it almost in time.

Racing through the thick forest, my feet pound the fallen debris, soon to emerge from the foliage and quickly blend into the crowded streets. As I round the last corner to escape this neighborhood—the one called Lystaene, lovingly known as the stain, through which I have been forbidden to wander given the history of its surly residents and their defiant attitudes toward my father and his orders—I turn and slam straight into a tall hard body. Hanri Yonyx is glaring down at me.

He's a cadet in the Order of Soldiers, ranked ThirdElite.

The gold flecks in his hazel eyes burn with judgment, and with his spiked amber hair catching the remaining slivers of the sun, he almost looks like some kind of demon.

A demon ready to condemn me.

My heart pounds, adrenaline flooding my veins.

He shoves his hands into my chest, forcing me to stumble backwards. Though only a couple of years older than me, his strength has quadrupled over the last twelve months.

"Do my eyes deceive me or is the perfect Rioyn Orro in direct defiance of his father's orders to be out in the stain?" The thrill of catching me where I'm not supposed to be dances in Hanri's wicked grin. He closes the gap between us with a large step, raising his hand to my chest. I push his hand away and step to pass him. He doesn't relent.

"I was out for a walk and got lost in my thoughts, that's all. Anyway, I'm headed home, so thanks for your concern, cousin."

Hanri studies my face, waiting for me to give away my lie. I don't flinch.

"Oh, is that all? Well, silly me. Please, continue your lovely promenade."

Hanri extends his large arm, sweeping it in front of him. He can't possibly be letting me go this easily? There's no choice but to walk past him and hope for the best.

The alternative is to be even later in facing Father, a far scarier proposition.

Walking past Hanri, hoping to be in the clear, he pushes me hard from behind.

Surely, it's a move too low even for him, but apparently not when it comes to my deranged cousin. Stumbling forward, my adrenaline shifts from fear to rage in a split second. Hanri's lips have curled into a snarl, his fingers clenching into a fist, anticipating what comes next. Not this time, cousin.

With a clenched fist, my arm pulls back in a swift, straight swing that grazes his chin as he bends backwards in avoidance.

Before I'm able to reset my stance, his own knuckles are able to crush my cheekbone, making me fall back and palm my face.

"Good thing your father has the foresight to hold you back this year," he spits. "Pathetic." Hanri's cackle echoes, even as he turns to walk away.

A burning rage deep in my chest erases all rational thoughts.

Racing after him, shoving him to the ground from behind, it's a cheap move but who even cares? He rolls over, quick to defend the kicks to his ribs, but they aren't over until a brave bystander grabs me from behind, pulling me away.

Another bystander attends to Hanri as if he deserves a shred of anyone's kindness.

"Get off me." Wrestling out of the bystander's arms, I'm poised to charge after Hanri when the bystander whips me around to face him like a rag doll in the wind.

The rage drains from my body, leaving me staring into the angered eyes of General Durran Orro. My father.

CHAPTER 3

ASCENDENCE

AYVA

"Parallel lines intersect at a point of infinity. Two points at infinity have the circle in common. Find another point of symmetry. Four plus 3i where i is the square root of minus one. Need four points: A plus Bi, and C plus Di, and," … and … and!"

The notebook plunges down off my lap, shoved away, leaving me staring at the pages strewn across the smooth dark gray stone floors of the room. My head falls to my hands.

I have to win. Failure means I'm just the nerdy book girl everyone already thinks I am, destined to be a nobody for life. Too much is riding on this tournament.

So, examining the notes, what is the answer?

If I can't solve this, then the Tournament of Galilei will not be mine at the festival, losing me the chance to become FirstElite for the Order of Galilei.

The descending sun splinters through the sheer curtains with an orange and pink glow, bouncing off medals and trophies lining the floor-to-ceiling bookshelves. They represent wins in every competition for the past eleven years at our training camps, ever since I was six. Everyone is eager to assert that I'll easily win the tournament in the upcoming weeks.

So, why do I feel like a complete and utter failure?

Even though their sentiments bring a glimmer of confidence, it's impossible to rely on their praise. These formulas and equations need internalizing inside and out, backward and forward. Seivan needs to see, to know who I am.

"Never fall back on your talent. It will only take you so far. Study, learn, and understand the Order of Galilei, then you will become a master. Mastering this order could one day prove beneficial in ways you never thought possible."

My first-ever teacher told me something at training camp eleven years ago; at the point of wanting to take a break from studying, her words return.

However, my wandering mind desperately wants to drift to my passion project, that of understanding a world between worlds, one which is rumored to hide within our realm. This mysterious place of which no one has a solid grasp is the Labyrinth Brick.

It doesn't seem to follow the logic of science, astounding even to me; rather, it captivates my intrigue. How can this place exist?

What is it really? How to go about studying its mystical properties?

I shake off the thought of investigating it any further in this moment, needing to focus on my studies. I'll have time after the tournament is over in a few weeks to dive into that mystery but for now, there's a need to focus on what's important in the moment.

Mother's incessant instructions soon follow. "Whenever your mind is overwhelmed, stop and practice your Ascendance. With patience comes mastery."

Despite my obvious reluctance, Mother insists that Rioyn and I both practice our Ascendance whenever possible. I'd rather focus on my studies in the Order of Galilei, but is clearing my mind—focusing on something other than equations—really the worst idea?

The small, treasured piece of smooth tungstenore in my grasp focuses the mind. My Ascendance is in the field of mental energy, to be exact.

If strong enough with my Ascendance, I should be able to visualize Mother's emotions as she feels them right now. Yet is it possible to achieve such mastery without causing her a great headache?

I sit on the stone floor, legs crossed.

With the tungstenore in my hand at waist level, I close my eyes.

"Clear your mind. Envision what you want to happen. Feel it occurring with every fiber in your body. Transfer your energy to the matter you wish to control."

After reciting Mother's instructions a few times, my mind slips into the deep, hidden trench where my power awaits. There, I find myself sitting just like now, yet I'm in the middle of the Upside Down Forest in the northern part of Trescheria.

I've been to this place only once before but have studied its variant ways extensively. Leaves attached to the branches cover most of the ground except for a few walking trails where the trees' roots flow in the wind, absorbing the nutrients they need to thrive. The trees by nature are upside down.

Of the forests I've studied, this one is by far my favorite, so it is not surprising that my mind has transported me here. Calm, my focus shifts from the Upside Down forest's trees to my mother who stands in the kitchen, preparing our dinner. Her feelings absorb into me as my own, perhaps becoming mine, sending a profound sense of happiness and peace washing over me. Never before has my mind been so serene, a feeling immediately bringing jealousy of her; what generates these feelings inside her? How can she feel this way?

Then it comes. Her head starts splintering into excruciating pain, serenity and calmness gone by the wayside, lost in torment and agony, and in abject misery. My connection with her fractures, sent away by my unwilling mind, making my eyes shoot open. Instead of feeling her incredible emotions now, my confidence melts into my shrunken shoulders.

My excitement, along with the ashen purple glow around me, evaporates.

I should listen to Mother more and balance out my studies.

As the daughter of a great general, it will never be enough to be good at certain things but fail at others. Perfection is needed, and in the absence of this, a person needs to strive to attain it. So, with this in mind, my conflicted gaze shifts to the empty wooden boxes tucked in the corner of my room, my hand automatically reaching for the adornment received after enrolling at university. The medallion that hangs from the chain around my neck becomes twisted in my hand, fractiously. Cadets return this week to move into the dorms at Sansyre University, a whole two weeks before classes are due to begin.

First-year students must share a room with three other girls; it seems doubtful that anyone would choose me as their first or even second choice to bunk with, so my roommates will be strangers. Of this, I am sure.

It already feels awkward, perhaps even painful, to be forced to converse with strangers eager to get acquainted with their new dorm partner for the next ten months.

These are the types of conversations I have loathed and avoided at all costs.

Mother, though, is embarrassingly ecstatic for me to have new friends even though they're forced upon me by no choice of my own … or theirs for that matter.

Also, this will separate Rioyn and me for the first time in our lives.

Sure, I'll come home on the week's end and for holidays, especially since it's a short walk to the university, but the thought of him not being close is a little scary. Sad too.

I will be there alone, without him.

Without my twin brother.

Our father's stubborn stance on wanting to hold him back seems understandable, especially since Rioyn hasn't heeded any of his warnings, having an incredible talent for becoming a soldier and holding tight to his dream to protect our realm.

It's protection we seem to need now more than ever.

Why must Father be so hard on him all the time? But that's not my decision, even though it's one that impacts us both, not just Rioyn.

In the corner of my room, I find peace and comfort from the world around, huddling in my safe space, my little alcove, a corner of this world that's wholly mine, surrounded by all my books. I love the old musty smell of their spines and parchment.

There must be hundreds of the books by now, mostly about the subjects taught in the Order of Galilei. All day I could sit here on my plush lilac-colored pillows, watching the citizens going about; isn't there just something so peaceful and calming about watching the busy world pass you by? The cicadas are humming in the background, drowning out the noise from the bustling street.

The sun is so beautiful this time of year, summer drawing to an end.

Autumn in Casstell has always been my second favorite time of year behind spring. Now, the leaves turn from their vibrant green to golden brown, red, and yellow, day by day methodically changing into their muted yet evocative fall hues.

As the side of my head lies against the crested window, the slight chill of the evening begins to claim me. With a sudden breath, my lungs are forced to steal a deep inhale of the refreshing air, both eyes shutting to absorb the many fragrances.

Pine and cedar fires burn, and a faint hint of roasting nuts tickles my hunger. That delectable aroma emanates from my favorite candy shop tucked away around the corner. My senses linger in the blissful coziness of the city known as home—Casstell.

Finally, my gaze takes in the distant horizon, then lowers.

He is standing there, staring up from the street. Immediately, I freeze. I must look like a mess and that he finds me so weird, just like all the others do.

He smiles up through his mesmerizing blue eyes with flecks of purple sparkling throughout, his hands digging into his pockets for warmth as the frigid wind wrestles with his chestnut hair. His broad shoulders curve in, accentuating subtle muscles that seem to have suddenly taken over his body.

Only a summer or two ago, he was boyish. But now …

I bite my lower lip as if that'll tame the heat flushing my cheeks. The shirt he's wearing is familiar from camp, but it fits a bit tighter these days.

Stop staring and wave.

My hand juts up with a mind of its own, waving with an awkward stiffness. I don't need a mirror to know my face has turned beet red, something I've never been able to hide, especially whenever I see him. He's always made me feel … different.

Jax offers his perfect, charming smile, a hand lifting to wave, and he mimics opening the window. I follow his instruction with a rush of wobbly enthusiasm.

"Are you going to be at the Cadet Ceremony tonight?" he shouts up.

My mouth suddenly turns dry. Why does he care if I'm going? The words don't come, so I smile and nod. What's wrong with me? I'm so weird. Speak!

"Yes, are you going?"

"No, I have to go back to Trescheria tonight, but I'll be back in the morning. We'll see each other at the opening ceremony of the Festival of Seivan! Right?"

I nod with an overexcited smile. Rein it in, Ayva! Hopefully, the distance hides most of my amateur excitement, if I'm lucky. How is it possible to forget? He's enrolled in the Order of Soldiers and must be walking back to his dorm at the university.

Where was he coming from if he's taking this route back? It's almost curfew.

"See you later then," he shouts, continuing on his way.

My smile beams from ear to ear. I somehow succeed in reining it in.

Surely, he's just being nice because he's Rioyn's best friend.

Best to not get my hopes up.

Jax and Rioyn met at the Tenderfoot Camp when we were six. Eleven years later, they're still as close as ever. Now, we're all going to be at Sansyre University together. That is if Rioyn behaves and if our father loosens the reins and allows him to enroll.

Rioyn should enter another order, but he won't. He's a soldier.

My eyes stalk Jax, admiring the way his pants hug the back of him as he walks up the hill with ease. I can't help but stare at his new—rather, new to me—muscular form. What would it be like to feel those strong arms wrap around me? What is wrong with me! I've morphed into a sappy, drooling romantic girl who pines after a guy taking pity on his best friend's twin sister. Boys like him aren't interested in nerds like me anyway, so I'll save my fluttering heart for the characters in my favorite books.

A few minutes later, a door slams downstairs, ripping me from my reverie. I close the window, shuffling from my alcove to see what's going on, making it as far as the upstairs hallway before stopping to peer over the banister.

In the entry below stands Rioyn, and behind him, our father.

Rioyn's eyes are red, making my heart stutter in my chest.

What has my overly competitive and headstrong brother done now?

CHAPTER 4

DREMARIA

SHIVANE

Curdled milky light seeps into the room as it does every day, and just the same as on those days, I'm up before its rays can lurch across the stone floor and reach my bed.

Here in Dremaria, the pants and jacket in which I've dressed look as if they are black and stitched with white threads, though they're actually navy blue with gold and ivory accents. Everything is monochromatic.

The fastened brassore buttons go all the way to my neck, leaving no exposed skin, then I strap on thick, black boots, lacing them halfway up my calves.

I stare at my reflection, shuddering at this costume, taking one last look in the mirror then around the room. Its barren walls have been dusted with a soft gray paint.

Mother never fails to remind me that only the weak-souled crave lofty possessions, hence few are in my name, only a solitary indulgence for which I will never apologize, my bookshelf. It's filled to the brim, overflowing with books from all over Seivan. Volumes about our realm, the Outer Realms, and world history.

Their spines scream out titles on subjects such as herbs, healing tonics, and remedies. Stealing a sharp inhale of the crisp parchment and ink satiates my urge to cling to them.

These are possessions to be proud of, even if Mother thinks they're a dreadful hindrance to a girl's growing soul. Perhaps mine's already fled this existence in any case.

It would've been smart to do so long ago.

Two already packed duffle bags languish on the floor by the mirror, waiting for me to take them today since we're due to leave anytime now. Two half-empty black duffel bags, all my worldly goods. Sadly, most of the books must stay behind.

Soon inside the stone-wrapped hallway accessed off a light-smeared kitchen, the sound of an enthused, "Congratulations!" makes me stumble backwards.

Congratulations for what?

My eyes bulge. Sylon, my twin, mocks my shocked demeanor with his pleasure.

"What is all this?" My blustering heartbeat thunders on, spotting that Mother seems to have baked a round white cake with Congratulations written in black icing on top.

"We wanted to wish you off today," she proclaims with her clasped hands centered over her heart. "We're excited for you both to begin your first day at Sansyre."

"You just want us out of the house," Sylon chips in through his huff of a laugh. "You're not even coming with us to Casstell."

"I do wish I could join you both this week's end; however, Zianli has ordered everyone within the Dremarian Army to stay here and guard Dremaria this year." That would be Zianli Wren, our uncle and ruler of Dremaria, a shrewd and somewhat frightening man.

"Oh." It's all that slips through my tight thin lips.

"You have to move into the dorms before the festival starts. The rest of the cadets moved in weeks ago," our mother continues.

"Don't worry, sis." Sylon wraps his muscular arm around my shoulder. "If anyone so much as lays a finger on you, I'll gladly remind them where it belongs. With a few adjustments, of course." His wink tugs at the invisible string curling his lips.

Sylon stands a few inches taller than me, boasting a broad muscular chest and strong grip that digs into the side of my shoulder. The black curls of his hair fall on his face. With a mere flick of his head, he flings those unruly locks back in line, the light catching his devious deep purple eyes. In the shadow, his eyes are so dark, they're almost black.

He spares me a wink then helps himself to the cake, sending a waft of spiced sugar—my favorite flavor—to tickle my nose. The distracted look on his face is mesmerizing, as if something plagues him, harassing his soul. Is a piece of him missing? Is he in perpetual search for something he probably wouldn't recognize, even if he found it?

This is exactly how he appears.

"Your father is down at the market. He should be back soon."

My eyes perk up at Mother's absent-minded disclosure.

"I have to grab some things there too. I'll find him!" I whip around so fast that my own braid smacks me in my eyes. Sylon snickers through his cake-stuffed mouth.

"Careful," I snipe back. "Too much icing and those muscles of yours will go to fat." My brother's smeared face drops with utter annoyance, a nerve struck.

"You should wait for him. He—"

Mother's voice trails off as I dart out the front door and down the ashen cobblestone pathway where the black leaves sway in the wind, ready to take flight and pepper the yard below. My boots crunch on fallen leaves, turning them to charcoal dust.

Around the corner, I fly through the black wrought ironore gates separating the confines of Nighamaire and the Castle of Everia from the rest of Dremaria.

The white and black tents of the market are obvious, and this sight will be my last for a while. Where is Father? My eyes scan the crowds. He's a tall, lean yet muscular man with black-peppered white hair. His eyes are different from Sylon's and mine, being light violet and when the sun hits them exactly right, they almost look translucent.

Finally, there he is, hard to miss. People say I'm tall, but Father stands a whole head above me. He helps an elderly lady with her bags, then hoists her onto her wooden carriage drawn by two sickly steeds. He's well-favored within Dremaria. Since he and Mother took their positions within the

Dremarian Army, this province has flourished like never before. But still, so much improvement is desperately needed.

The stallholders and townspeople watch my father with clear admiration.

"Thank you, General. You are a hero in battle, and in the aid of an old woman with achy joints," the elderly lady quips.

My father takes her crinkled hand in both of his. "There are few heroes in war," he says, smiling. "But in the marketplace, it's a different matter."

The elderly lady smiles, commanding her exhausted steeds forward.

I slink over to him and stand right behind him, head lowered.

"Excuse me, General Greyea, but could you spare a coin for a poor child?" My grin is wide, sensing him shift toward me.

"Of course, my child …" I can't help but laugh, eventually looking him in his eyes at the heavy sigh following his recognition.

"Shi, you swindler! Please tell me your mother knows you're out here."

"Yes, sir!" I salute like a true soldier.

He snorts a chuckle, putting his arm around my shoulder and we walk together, taking in the various vendors and goods from chutney to jewelry and intricately carved wood pieces to the delectable homemade breads. I breathe in their sweet, doughy aroma and pull toward the bread maker to buy two loaves, a small indulgence to hoard in my dorm.

Father is studying me, seeing me indulging my senses in the sweet aroma of home and my ever-growing nostalgia for all the things to which I will be saying goodbye.

He squeezes my shoulder. "You and your brother tested the highest out of every cadet who enrolled this year. I'm proud to have two kids in the Order of Soldiers at Sansyre University." My heart skips a beat. How can I possibly summon the nerve to say that I don't even desire to be in the Order of Soldiers?

Yet his admiration is welcome all the same.

"Ah, this is what I came down here for."

My father leads me to a vendor's booth bursting with patrons, an unholy commotion if ever there was one. What's it all about? Father's arm slides down from my shoulders.

I wait at the front of the booth while he meets the vendor in the back.

As the crowd parts, I make my way to the table and find beautiful neck-laces, rings, bracelets and exquisitely crafted jewelry. A steelore pendant with black and white crystal jewels carefully inlaid is stunning, but what are its true gem colors?

"Need any help, dear?" A man, who I assume is the jeweler's husband, startles me from my haze. A hint of purple shines through light blue eyes as he turns his head slightly, a silvered streak on the left of his head in stark contrast to jet-black hair.

"No thank you, sir. I'm just waiting for Father." I turn back to the jewelry.

"You will have a profound choice before you one day. Choose wisely because if you don't, your heart will darken and suffer the consequences, your choice becoming the death of your soul," the vendor says.

What? Who is he talking to? There's no one else in earshot!

"Do you address me, sir?"

"You're Shivane Greyea, are you not? Daughter of Evon and Daun Greyea? First and Second General of the Dremarian Army?"

"Indeed, but what do you know of me?"

The vendor peers into my eyes. "Your soul sways in the balance, a fine balance. Choices, my dear. We all have them. You must choose wisely."

My gaze refuses to peel away from the vendor.

"Is this some kind of riddle? A joke?"

"Heed my warning, girl. For it is no joke."

Red-hot anger ignites at his impertinence, but I pause in my response upon hearing Father approaching.

"Shi, are you all right?"

My father putting his comforting hand back on my shoulder breaks the eye contact with the vendor, and now, he has gone.

"Yeah … I … Sorry. Did you get what you came for?"

My father's hand fumbles inside a black velvet pouch. "I did. Turn around."

My fingers lift to my chest as he drapes a beautiful silverore necklace around my neck, securing its fine clasp.

I can't help but get lost in my racing thoughts as to what the vendor meant by his menacing words, "Your soul sways in the balance …"

"Do you like it?" Father asks, breaking my trance.

The pendant feels cool and heavy in my hand, a black, translucent square stone laid in platinumore, intricately carved with tiny chrysanthemums. Impossibly detailed.

A kiddish smile has plastered itself across my face. "I love it. Thank you." I wrap my arms around him tightly.

"Don't tell your brother." He winks.

"You didn't get him anything?"

"What's there to give him? He'll hawk anything of value. I thought about getting him the sword he's always wanted but I figured—for the safety of everyone at the university—that it would be better once he's graduated."

My head bobs in agreement. My brother, I will love him forever but he lives with an angered heartache, never taking kindly to those who wrong him or those about whom he cares. He has a deep love for me, our family, and friends but whatever is missing inside of him, that pain he lives with is masked by an unrelenting fury.

At home, this is typically the root of his tension. But hopefully, in the cause of defending our homeland, his volatility will finally find its useful purpose.

Maybe then, he will find some degree of happiness.

Father and I walk arm in arm around the black wrought ironore gates back to the residents' entrance. On our way back, we pass by a group of people, dreamers. Their hollow stares drift to nothing. Their clothes match their faces, ripped and dirty.

"Please, sir. Might you have any coins to spare?" one of the bolder dreamers dares to ask. Cast in the light of reality, my feeble joke from earlier seems immature and foolish.

My father doesn't avoid or ignore them the way most people do.

He does hold me closer, tighter to him.

"There's a dreamsman in the market today. He will have what you seek for it is not coins." My father's voice is calm, strong but sends the message of dismissal.

Their bodies are deathly thin, their chapped lips craving the relief of fresh water. My heart steels to them, the dreamers, the lost souls of Dremaria. In an effort to be kinder, I reach into my cloth bag and pull out one of my beloved loaves of bread.

"Here, I have bread if you'd like some." I hand the dreamer the loaf, but he doesn't take it. Instead, he only stares at the necklace my father has only just gifted to me.

"Bread, girl?" The dreamer laughs in my face. "You offer bread when the necklace you wear could feed a man dreamium for a year?"

My nails dig crescent moons into my palms. In a split second, the snick of Father unsheathing the knife at his side becomes audible.

"Never mind. I didn't mean it." The dreamer and his group scuttle off in a hurry. My father whips his head behind him, nodding at the guards who stalk after the group.

What will become of them for their bold insolence?

"They should spend the rest of their lives in the Dungeon Lair," I spit.

My father's pale violet eyes follow the guards as they grab the ringleader by the back of the neck and swing him hard against a wall.

"That's a harsh punishment, Shi. They will answer for their disrespect but it's not a crime. They're suffering, struggling. Not everyone is as fortunate as we are."

"There are rules, and consequences for breaking said rules. If you let one go, then the rest will take advantage."

My father slants his gaze my way.

"You are correct. However, not everything is as black and white as our realm would have you believe," he says through his focused stare. "What is justice for one man might not be fair for another. All things you'll learn in your studies in the Order of Soldiers."

I understand his point, but still don't agree with it.

"Those dreamers don't deserve my sympathy."

"Then I hope you never have to walk in that man's shoes and find out."

We continue along the path and arrive at our house where he's summoned our usual square black steelore carriage helmed by six magnificently large black stallions.

Sylon and our mother patiently wait as we stroll up. "No, please, take your time. Shop." Sylon taps his foot as if it'll hurry me. He whips the carriage door open.

"Thank you. You make a great carriageman." There's no need to look at my brother to feel the roll of his eyes. I enjoy my chuckle.

Inside, the silken black drapes rustle in the dusty breeze.

Black velvet cushions line our seats and the walls. Home will be much missed, but it will be a long time before I'll start to miss all the black.

The people wave to us at the window as the carriage leaves Nighamaire.

We don't take the main route through the Black Hills, instead taking a separate, more secure one connecting to the shores of the Restful Isles.

Most of Dremaria is an open meadow filled with nothing but black blades of grass, gray skies, and that awful white-hot sun. Why bother looking out of the window?

All the trees look the same with their boring, dull colors. It will be good to be rid of this province for a few years, I think, sinking back against the plush cushions.

The words of that odd vendor still plague me, however.

"You will have a profound choice before you ..."

Was he high on dreamium? It's the only reasonable explanation.

After several hours, we make it to the sands of the Restful Isles that wash into the black waves of the Onyx Ocean, my tongue thick with the taste of salt in the heavy air.

This area has become the unofficial home of the dreamers.

They have taken to these shores when they dream at night. Something about the crashing waves and the sea-salted air heightens their dreams, so they say. I've never bothered to experience it for myself. To me, dreams are meaningless.

Our carriage crosses the isthmus connecting Dremaria to Trescheria, a rocky and rough strip of land where the carriage rocks side to side on this bumpy crossing that will lead us to the Trescherian Growla Station.

"Why doesn't Dremaria have its own Growla Station?" Sylon barks through his frustration at our rocky travels.

"When they were created, centuries ago, Everia didn't want the disturbance of them bringing people in and out of Dremaria like tourists." Our father reminds him of our province's history, one that Sylon already knows.

"New ones should be built," Sylon grumbles as he glares out of the carriage.

I can't argue with him, though. The Growlas are beautiful crystal teardrop-shaped glass globes that sail high through the air, attached to thick ironore cables. They are the fastest way to travel between provinces and their view from above is nothing short of breathtaking. I can't wait to sail over Trescheria to the Grynndyre Station.

Another hour passes and we've finally crossed the isthmus, entering Trescheria, a province beaming with lush green trees and rich, vibrant colors unlike in Dremaria.

My face is plastered to the window.

Ever since Dremaria became the only province where one is able to dream, the color scheme of the world became the monotonous monochromatic shade it still is today.

I eagerly look forward to living a life in vibrant color.

The pathway to the Growla Station takes us through one of my favorite places, the Upside Down Forest, making me marvel at how the rest of the realm is painted in a rich variety of vivid hues, green, gold, and plum-colored leaves coloring the forest floor. The burgundy tree trunks curve as if formed by the winds themselves over time.

Ivory roots glitter in the air, spritzed with a musky cedar scent.

Inside, the carriage remains a black void, my family gazing from the windows, and suddenly, it is striking that Father's silver-streaked hair is actually amber brown with silver peppered throughout. These are the things we do not see, not usually.

Then, there is Mother; her hair is light brown with stranded blonde highlights, while her pale violet eyes shimmer in the light softly kissing her through the window.

She's regal and poised, even while traveling. What an elegant beauty she is!

Next to Mother, however, there he is, my brother, sitting slumped in his seat as if every second of the trip is a grievous hardship. His hair is still jet black and his deep purple eyes have not welcomed a single, colored speck. His features are fitting for him, strands of dark curls tickling sharp cheekbones, his hard jaw flexing with every bump.

Do many women still chase after him? There was only one that he bothered to entertain for a few months, but he grew tired of her quicker than she did him.

Not one for casual encounters, his heart runs deep, and it's worrisome; will he ever let a woman get close enough to find the love he's sheathed deep within himself?

But these should not be my worries. Why fret for him?

We pass the fork in the road. The path on which we continue leads to the Trescherian Growla Station, and the other to the Pools of Pearl, the capital city of Trescheria. I've never had the pleasure of visiting the capital city, but stories of its beauty abound.

After another few hours, we finally make it to the Growla Station that sits on the edge of a grassy cliff soaring ten stories into the sky. Its intricately carved stone facade welcomes every visitor coming and going. My gawking is interrupted by a soldier snagging our luggage to haul it to the station's entrance. The Growlas come and go from high in the sky, and Mother stands at my side. "I will miss you."

I flash her a grin. "And I will miss you, too. Always."

I turn, wrapping my arms around her, laying my head on her shoulder.

"You'll do marvelous things, Shivane. Your father and I are beyond proud. Keep a sharp eye on your brother, though." Sylon flashes a wicked grin over his shoulder.

"You would banish us and have me be his keeper." My eyes narrow on her.

Sylon lifts his brow with a taunt. "You couldn't stop me if you tried." His voice is nearly audible in my head, undoubtedly a twin thing.

My mother hugs me farewell, Father next.

"Go show them what you're made of, Shi." He hugs me tight, murmuring, "And remember what we discussed. In the pursuit of justice and fairness, one must also hold empathy for experiences we do not understand. It's a choice."

Choice… That word is haunting me.

We say our final farewells, disappearing through the crystal-clear glass door windows separating us from the inner beauty of the Trescherian Growla Station.

Each station is different. Trescheria's is said to be the most colorful, artful mosaic tiles lining the walls from floor to ceiling, depicting the beautiful landscapes.

The Growla master beckons us aboard.

At this point, Sylon wraps his long, muscular arm around my shoulders, leading me to the Growla. "You didn't tell them, did you?" I recoil to look up at him.

He flashes a wicked grin. "You really think I don't know you want to join the Order of Healants? I wish you well, my sister, when they find out."

He stops me dead in my tracks, feeling his arm slink from around my shoulders as he boards the Growla. The Growla master waves me on, snapping me out of the daze in which my brother has left me. It seems my carefully guarded secret isn't so secret.

Has it been so obvious?

Aboard the Growla, I refuse to catch his eye, even when sensing Sylon's unflinching smirk taunting me to look at him. There's no point in discussing it with him. He won't understand. I am not the soldier he is. In the Order of Healants, I will learn how to craft tonics and potions both healing and deadly. I'll fight my battles differently, without a sword, more cunning and skillful than wielding a piece of sharpened metal at someone.

It feels as though hours have gone by without moving my head an inch.

Sylon hasn't bothered to say a word either, his head buried in one of his books of war, no doubt getting a head start on his classes.

The land over which the Growla sails is gorgeous. I admire the vast swath of colors and the newness of it all, having not spent much time outside of Dremaria as a teenager. We're almost at the Grynndyre Station; there is the Grand Meadow that separates the city of Casstell from the Fields of Garden to the north, where they grow produce for the realm.

The Growla makes its final descent into the station. These contraptions are quiet and do not sway in the wind or on their descent, magnificently designed and built.

We disembark from the Growla, our luggage awaiting us.

It transpires we have only a couple of duffel bags between us; I carry very little, but he has even less. A carriage stands waiting, to take cadets who aren't able to carry their own luggage or make the trek into Casstell on foot.

My arm nudges Sylon to opt for the carriage, but he snarls at the emerald cage.

"We've sat long enough."

The pathway to the Bryar Bridge is lined with people heading into Casstell for the opening ceremony. I already asked Sylon last night if he'd join me tonight. He gave me his infamous snarl of disdain before he

growled, "When I'm dead and cold." If he doesn't go with me, he could at least go with his fellow classmates, but he won't even do that!

We've finally made it to the Bryar Bridge, a massive, hand-carved wooden construct extending high over the treacherous Depths of Xall. Columns of intricately carved wood extend thirty feet into the air, while thick, tight rope connects the columns to each other to ensure people don't fall over the death bridge's side.

My eyes dart to the Depths of Xall below, threatening everyone.

The deep ravine boasts a high concentration of sharp, jagged granite gray slate rocks, so sharp they will shred and kill anyone instantly falling from the bridge. The Depths of Xall guard the Prison of Xall that hides deep in the cave system beneath Casstell.

We wind through the entrance of Casstell, faced with a barrage of vendors just like at the market earlier today in Nighamaire. Handmade, handcrafted, artisan finds from all over Seivan seem to spill from every surface—on stalls, in tall baskets, and hanging from storefronts. Sylon tugs my arm, pulling me from stopping at every vendor's table.

We walk through the central business district, lined with various establishments open and bustling with patrons. I spot a modest apothecary and take note of it for later, my jaw agape with the stark differences between here and Nighamaire.

We don't have a street dedicated to businesses such as bakeries, bookstores, clothiers, and jewelers. We have our little market and that's all that is allowed.

To be able to shop whenever and wherever you dream is surreal.

I stop to gawk at a sprawling restaurant with patrons dining outside, enjoying the gentle weather, divine food spicing the air with fresh herbs and hearty aromatics.

My mouth waters at the delectable food adorning the diners' plates.

Sylon, for once, is being kind, allowing me to absorb this new city we'll call home for the next three years. A foreign city we will be free to explore.

We find our way to Sansyre University, marveling at the size and magnificence of the first and only university to have been erected in the entire realm.

Cadets flow in and out of the large front gates, jostling for space, book bags banging against one another, each cadet lost in a dizzy conversation with two or three others.

Sylon shoves into my side as he finds himself shoved from behind by another cadet.

The arrogant cadet dares a glance back at my brother with his icy blue eyes and goldenore cuffs wrapped around his wrists. He's obviously from Trescheria, a province known for being curt and cold. The cadet flicks his choppy, chocolate brown hair from his eyes to match Sylon's twisted, taunting snarl.

I place my hand on his forearm. "Come on. Let's find the registrar's office." Sylon's stare tracks the odd-looking young man as we weave through the throng.

CHAPTER 5

The Stars Above

RIOYN

SLINKING INTO THE DARK foyer of our home, my sandy shoes scratch against the stone floors but that's the least of my problems as the wooden door slams shut behind me.

A cold chill shoots down my upright spine.

At the top of the staircase, Ayva's crested brows peer over the banister.

She's quick to defend me and defuse our father but tonight is different. Tonight, I do not want her anywhere near the disaster I've not so cleverly created for myself. It's not fair to her. I shake my head, warning her to avoid getting mixed up in my clustered mess.

Father brushes past, bustling toward the kitchen with his silent yet burning anger radiating off him. I follow, our conversation far from over. It hasn't even started.

Our entire walk home is filled with nothing but a bitter, angered silence as hot tears slide down my cheeks. Not for fear of punishment, but more in fear of what he will likely take from me, or rather continue to withhold.

Gingerly leaning against the polished stone countertops, pain radiates through my legs from the training camp, but I don't dare sit, standing in silence as Father fills a glass with fresh water, swallowing it in a single gulp, turning for more.

I sit waiting like an obedient dog. Eventually, he places the glass down with a definitive clink, not bothering to turn around. "So, you found the Infinite Void?"

Damnit, Xylar. That sanctimonious jerk rushed back to the commanders to report me! I shouldn't be surprised.

"Was Xylar the one who reported me?"

When Father turns to face me, he appears genuinely taken back. "Your friends were with you? You dragged them into this?"

Ugh. My eyes fall to my feet, searching for an answer that isn't there.

"Answer me. Now. Who else was there? This is a serious matter of realm security."

My eyes close, head lolling forward. No way must my friends be punished for my decisions. I could lie and say I went alone, and that Xylar spotted me returning, but Father is a master of finding out—and hiding—the truth. Lying won't help. Once he finds out, it will be worse for them and for me. I bring my eyes to meet Father's glare.

"I veered from camp into the Cave of Caino. Jax, Xylar and Mikel followed my curiosity without any idea of where we were going. It was all my own idea, Father.

"While we were there, they felt the effects of the Infinite Void and immediately left. They had nothing to do with any of this."

He exhales a loud sigh, the tension in his shoulders easing.

"I'm glad they demonstrated good sense, even if it's sadly lacking in my own son. They will make great additions to the Order of Soldiers this year."

His unspoken words hang between us, implying so much. They hurt.

They will make great soldiers, but you will not. That is what he means.

"I suppose in your rush for adventure, you forgot all about the alarm," he continues.

The alarm! I almost groan aloud. When the vibration of the Infinite Void changes, it signals the Grynndyre Command. How could I have been so dense?

By taking friends there and deliberately exposing them and myself, it alerted Grynndyre Command to the interference.

Then it was pure luck that Father showed up to investigate and not a horde of angry guards. A lump forms in my throat in preparation for what to say next.

"I waited for the three of them to make it back up the Cliffs of Mau. Once they were out of sight, I went to the other side of the Cave of Caino and walked to the edge of the shores of the Daiyaman Ocean, and that's when I felt the vibration and knew I'd found the boundary of … the Void."

The anger in Father's eyes is obvious, but what is more troubling is the second emotion lingering beneath his frown, not something I've seen on him before.

Fear.

My father is a tall man of unrequited strength, his presence alone drives people to avoid walking in his direct path. I may be talented in the sparring ring—and my strength increases daily—but he will crush me without breaking a single bead of sweat.

These are skills I desire to learn from him.

"How were you even able to get close enough to feel the vibration of the void and not succumb to its effects?" He paces, rubbing his forehead. "I have to report this. I have no choice. You've put the entire realm in harm's way because your curiosity got the best of you, again."

Heat sears through my chest. "You're going to report me?" My body shakes with anger. "Right before I'm meant to enroll at Sansyre?"

Snatching his glass from the counter, I clutch it in my fist. If I don't focus my frustration, I might start punching something—or someone.

We both stare at the glass clenched in my trembling hand.

"Control your temper. Now," he commands.

"You can't just—"

"Now!"

With every bit of self-control possible, I refuse my impulse to hurl the glass at the wall, placing it back down.

"The Infinite Void protects us from outside threats. Don't be so naïve to think our enemies in the Outer Realms aren't monitoring the same vibrations we are, constantly looking for an opportunity to poke holes in our defenses. You didn't just brush up against the void today," he says, staring with fiery intensity. "You sent a shockwave through the whole network."

My mouth hangs open. A shockwave?

"I am the General of the Grynndyre Command," he continues. "It is my responsibility to protect this realm from all threats."

All threats. Including me. "I am not a threat."

"Really? Because what I see is a young man who can barely control his temper, and who seems to believe the rules were made for everyone else but him."

"How can I follow the rules if I don't understand them? Everything's kept a secret, and—"

"Shape up and stand down! That is an order. You don't determine what confidential information is disclosed or not disclosed to you. No citizen does."

Citizen. Not cadet. Not soldier. Everyone is quick to remind me of my status. I restrain my growing temper with a nod, the fire burning within me starting to drown in a cool, suffocating grief. There will be no university for me this year.

He doesn't even need to say the words for me to know the truth.

"If you ever want a chance of earning an Elite rank and wearing Grynndyre Green, then I suggest you never forget the Seivan Honor Code again. Doing so could cost you your life. Worse, it could cost the lives of those you have sworn to protect."

A lump forms in my throat. "Yes, sir."

He fills the glass with water and slides it across the counter, a sort of peace offering. My mouth is dry, but if I take a sip, I'll be sick.

Father asks once more, "So, son, why did you head to the void?" His eyes search mine, flitting from one to the other. "What were you really searching for?"

The words won't come, and instead, my lungs heave in a huge breath to prepare my nerves and force my voice to cooperate.

"I wanted to find the Infinite Void because … because I want to find Bair."

My tear-drenched eyes catch sight of Father walking slowly toward me. We stand facing one another, toe to toe. "Bair is gone."

"Until you show me his lifeless body, I refuse to believe it."

The bitter truth. My elder brother was—is—my world, my inspiration.

Can't he just hug me? The pain bites deep, merciless, and still, he stands there in pain too, his arms hanging limply at his sides, unwilling to be sensitive and to break.

Father, just show me one ounce of it! One ounce of the pain you must be in!

My heart begs him, pleads with him, yet here we are facing one another, both silent men. He is afraid to show me that he's human too, that I'm not the only one weakened by feelings. My hand reaches out, expecting what, I'm not sure.

A handshake? A hug?

He side steps me, then marches forward.

LATER THAT EVENING, I shuffle down to the kitchen to get something to eat, pausing as Mother's voice rings out from the door of Father's study.

"Don't you think you're being a bit too hard on him?"

"He needs to learn how to control his impulsivity."

"And from whom do you think he got that? Being at university will help him mature. He'll grow and become the man you know he's destined to be."

"You're right. He's like I was at his age, which is why I know how dangerous it can be. Rioyn will be under me in the Order of Soldiers and needs to learn that his actions have severe consequences. That way, he'll grow and learn."

"Ayva's starting in two weeks, and Bair had the same impulses, yet you didn't hold him back. And you also studied under your father."

"Bair was in the Order of Voyants. He didn't enter the Order of Soldiers, and neither will Ayva. They're different. The Order of Soldiers is for cadets who are ready to become protectors of our realm. Not ones who act alone and with selfish intentions."

My mother holds her pause.

"If you hold Rioyn back for a year, he might never forgive you," she ventures.

"Be it a week or a month, Rioyn needs my permission to enter the Order of Soldiers since I'm the General of the Grynndyre Command. He's free to enroll in any other order."

My breath catches in my chest at this injustice. How can he do this to me?

Even Mother, the one who faints at the idea of any harm coming to her children, can see how unfair this is.

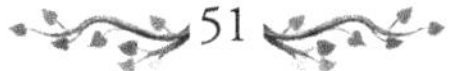

"Bair's disappearance was my fault," Father continues. "He's gone because of me. Because I couldn't protect him. I'll not let the same happen to Rioyn."

I ease back against the wall. It all makes sense now; I'd never realized he carried the weight of Bair's disappearance like a brand.

"You can't protect everyone. But what you can do is train him to be able to defend himself. Plus, Bair isn't gone. He's just lost. He'll come back to us. I feel it."

"You need to stop saying that. You've infected Rioyn with hope, and it could lead him into great trouble."

"Or hope will sustain him through dark times. You can't protect your children forever, my love. Eventually, you have to give them their freedom. In the end, hope is all we have."

As I stand there in the dark, a faint outline of my parents' reflection is visible in a window, Father holding his head in his hands, Mother comforting him in her embrace.

A great man bent over by grief and worry is now reduced to despair because of me.

CHAPTER 6

FIRSTELITE

RIOYN

I STARE AT THE WOODEN boxes in the corner of my room, the ones already packed, ready to move into the dorms. A waste of time. Time I could've spent training.

The awards accrued over the years are admirable, those that encouraged me to push myself further and to be better, to never give up.

Sparring Champion: Rioyn Orro

1st Place Obstacle Course: Rioyn Orro.

The awards go on and on. I've spent years striving to be the first in everything but neglected to refine the insatiable anger living and breathing fire inside of me.

My father is right. My impulsiveness is a problem, but it also makes me who I am, the very reason I've never wanted to change.

However, I do know better than to doubt my father. If learning to master my emotions is what I need to do, then I'll do it. I will not lose.

"Practice your Ascendance and it will help calm your mind, calm your temper." My mother has said this to me a thousand times. She's always right, especially when it comes to Ascendance. She is the High Ascendant of Grynndyre after all.

I sink to the cold stone floors, cross legged, placing my hands on my knees.

By focusing and concentrating hard enough, I can shroud myself in shadows, becoming one with the night.

"Clear your mind. Envision what you want to happen. Feel it with every fiber in your body. Transfer your energy to the energy around you that you wish to control."

Taking a deep breath, I tell my mind to go black, but instead, somehow see my brother's face and Father's immense disappointment. As frustration swells, the vision in my mind begins to flicker and wobble, then bursts into flames.

My mind rages in a fire so strong that my head radiates with heat. I run through the fire, searching for a dark corner of my mind that isn't consumed by the flames.

It's not there to be found, and the fire just burns brighter, stronger when a hand falls on my shoulder causing a visceral response, almost leaping out of my skin.

My eyes open, Ayva kneeling before me. Worry fills her eyes as she looks through me, trying to figure out what just happened. All of my books, notebooks, and papers are littered across the room as a faint black smoke fades.

"Finally. It feels good to have a room cleaner than yours after all these years," she says with a smug smile. I snort and we both burst into laughter. Words are never needed between us, a solitary glance able to tell me all I need to know and her the same.

Her eyes dance at my mess. She reaches for The Book of Legends lying upside down atop my boots. She squints at it with a dismissive chuckle.

The page has fallen open on the legend of the Iyanndyre Born. She shakes her head.

"What, you don't believe?" my voice mocks.

"Of course, I don't believe. It's a silly book of fables meant for kids. I can't believe you still believe in this stuff."

"This stuff is real. I know it. Even Bair knew it was real, see."

I turn to the page with his writing on it.

Ayva squints at his faded scribbles. My gaze shifts to a passage at the bottom, a new passage, recently added. Excitement shoots through me. Every now and then, the book magically updates itself, but it's been years since it's done so.

The Iyanndyre Born lives among you.
The Iyanndyre Born lives for peace.
The Iyanndyre Born conquers all.
The Iyanndyre Born embodies all three.
The Iyanndyre Born is born of the two.

"Just because the book is enchanted, it doesn't make it real," Ayva says. "Besides, why do we even need a savior? We live in a peaceful realm where nothing bad happens. Ever."

Even she knows that sentiment isn't true.

Who is she trying to convince, me or her?

"Then why do we have a university dedicated to war studies? A place that trains us how to fight and prepare for battle?"

I got her there but knowing her, she'll figure out an equally sharp reply. Instead, her smile fades.

"I'm sorry Dad won't let you join the Order of Soldiers this year," she says.

My head lowers, concealing my raw emotions.

There's no point in hiding them from her but I try to, anyway.

"I keep telling myself that it's for the best and he has his reasons but—"

A cough clears my throat to bury my feelings, but they stay right where they are. Ayva looks at me with heartfelt eyes, making it even harder to speak.

A soft knock on my door saves me. Our mother, a welcome sight, stands in the doorway, the light from the hallway shimmering off her golden-brown hair as she takes in the sight of us gathered over the book with a gentle smile. She has always known when warmth is needed, and how to fill the gaps our father seems unable to.

"The fireworks will be starting soon."

I release a heavy sigh. The fireworks are a celebration of the new year, and new recruits. The last thing I feel like doing is celebrating the death of my own dream. But a new future awaits Ayva, and it wouldn't be fair of me to dampen her excitement.

I stand up, take the book from her hands, and place it on the bed. "Come on sis, time to celebrate you."

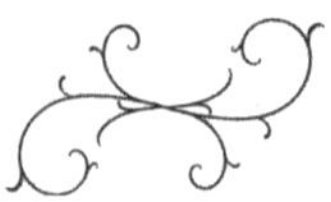

IN THE BACK GARDEN, our mother has laid out a picnic blanket. Father is lounging in his formal ceremonial military uniform in front of the crackling fire. He puffs on a thick cigar, staring at the night sky, reflective. The smell of tobacco and leather seeps into the house as I sheepishly hover at the back door.

"Ayva, help me with the dessert pouches." Whirling at our mother's attempt to save Ayva from this tense moment, I must enter the lion's den alone, not allowed to be mad.

Father is my hero, my mentor, and my friend. It's vital to make things right.

Sitting beside him, I avoid his glare, my shoulders slouching forward.

I study his perfectly pressed uniform, admiring the goldenore medallion holding his cape together at the top of his shoulder. In its center is the outline of the Iyanndyre, the one structure in all of Seivan that our militaries have sworn to protect.

Inhaling a crisp breath filled with remnants of pine, my mouth parts to apologize for the hundredth time but he breaks the silence first.

"Do you know what each of those stars represents?"

I shift my sight to the night sky. "Big, burning balls of fire in a galaxy far from ours?"

"Nonsense. Each star represents someone down here, and we represent a star up there. When someone's life ends here, one star's life ends up there."

"That's just a story they tell kids at camp," I dismiss.

"Like the rest of the stories in your Book of Legends?" Point well made. "Watch as each star sparkles. Then watch the twinkle on someone's face and tell me we are not all connected."

"Ayva would disagree with you and quote a line from one of her many books."

"Indeed, she would, my son, and I don't doubt any of the books of Galilei. However, I choose to believe that legend because I look up at those stars and know I'm protecting everyone down here. Protecting you."

His words strike a chord and resonate deeply.

"Father, look. I'm sorry about earlier. About everything." I eagerly or desperately wait for him to accept my apology, but instead, he sits in perfect silence.

It inflames my anxiety. He drags another long puff of his fragrant cigar.

"Son, you may think I'm being overly difficult and unfair. I expect this reaction from your young mind and do not disagree. However, I am not raising a boy to become a weak man. I am raising you to become strong, resilient," his words strike me with the right amount of realization and humbleness.

Before I'm able to inch my thoughts out, he continues. "To be a leader who will not indulge his emotions but lead with decisive fortitude and razor-sharp strength. I will not always be around to guide you. And it is in those moments that you will need to think for yourself. That is what I am training you for."

His poignant words resonate for the both of us. We sit in still silence.

"It may seem like we haven't seen a battle since the one at Trescheria and that there hasn't been a war since the Great War of the Realms. But we fight more battles than you know, ones about which no one reads."

My interest forces me to lean in, desiring more if he'll allow it.

"More and more battles are being waged through the provinces," he continues. "Most are thwarted by our swift actions before they reach the point of destruction, like the Battle of Trescheria. We must always be ready when the next one comes. It's no longer a matter of if but when." He turns to me. "What is the third order of the Seivan Honor Code?"

Without hesitation, I say, "We must be ready for battle even if one is not at our shores."

He nods, his gaze directed up at the stars, minuscule specks in the night sky. Balls of fire in the space beyond our world give him his reason to find purpose and peace.

Curiosity compels me to ask, "I thought our realm lived in peace and that our true and only threats were with the Outer Realms."

"Sansyre was created to train the next generation of soldiers, healants, sayers, voyants, archivants, Ascendants, and Galileis. Warriem and Everia created the university because they knew peace was a dream. It's an illusion we fight to preserve every day."

"So, more threats come from within than from the Outer Realms?"

My father's gaze doesn't shift as he offers a weary nod.

My sights turn to the night sky, longing for the same solace when he says, "I will make my decision by the week's end. If I decide you are ready to begin training, you will obviously miss the Tournament of Spar since registration closes tomorrow night. But you will have my permission to enroll in the Order of Soldiers."

My mouth drops, feeling beyond grateful for the change of heart but that means … "I won't be able to win FirstElite."

"Titles, trophies, and awards do not make a soldier. Nor do they make a man. You aren't ready to lead as a FirstElite cadet within the Elite Rank, yet. If granted entry this year, then next year, you may compete for SecondElite during your second year at Sansyre. When you are ready."

I study him, scouring for the words needed to convince him how important winning FirstElite is to me. "But I need to win Elite all three years."

I will not come in second, ever.

"No. You only need to place in the top four by the end of your third year to be able to choose the military branch you want to enter. Not competing the first year will make it harder, yes, but I'm confident you'll place in the top four by graduation. Adversity fuels perseverance—and discipline."

"But you were Elite all three years. How can you deny me the chance to follow?"

"Until you learn to master your weaknesses and humble yourself, filling my shoes should be the last of your concerns."

Consequences. He's trying to show me I must pay a price for my actions without destroying my dream altogether. I should be grateful, but I'm not.

He looks me square in my face. "That's how you become great, and unstoppable."

"Yes, sir. Thank you for considering me for enrollment this year." My emotions catch hold of my breath and my pulse, sending both into a magnified state.

The ripe tension breaks when Ayva and our mother bring trays of dessert pouches out. I'm relieved; even though I want to continue this conversation, my temper won't stay contained for much longer.

Ayva tosses the pouches onto the fire, then smacks me on my arm. We both turn to look at our father and mother staring into each other's eyes.

How much has Father conceded because he believes in me, versus simply wanting to make Mother happy?

"We should get going to the cadet welcoming ceremony," Ayva says, interrupting.

"Not until the fireworks start. You know the rules."

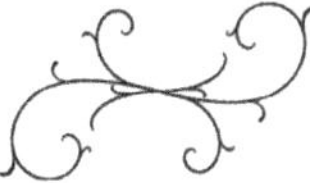

ONCE THE SHOW IS over, Ayva and I put on our coats, promising to meet our parents later. We're about to leave for the festivities when I pause.

"I forgot something upstairs. I'll catch up."

Racing upstairs, I charge into my room and look through the mess of papers on the floor, finding the enrollment form. There's a big bold heading at the top of the page:

SANSYRE UNIVERSITY — ORDER OF SOLDIERS

I check the box requesting admission, thinking, Father will grant me enrollment by week's end. But that's not enough. My entire life has been spent looking up to my father, dreaming of achieving the same glory, wanting my own son or daughter to see me in the same light one day. It's to be FirstElite or nothing.

It's just not in me to come in second. Not ever.

My hand moves to the signature line.

Underneath the line reads: Durran Orro, General, Grynndyre Command.

With a mighty flourish of the pen, I forge his signature, willing to accept the consequences after I win. Victory will be mine.

CHAPTER 7

SANSYRE UNIVERSITY

RIOYN

THE SUN PEEKS OVER the buildings to the east, casting a light amber hue over Casstell. Jogging, there's a light hop in my step, enrollment papers rolled in hand.

The smell of warm, fresh bread dusts the air, my stomach roiling in its delicacy.

I didn't dare indulge in breakfast, escaping the house before anyone could ask where I was headed so early. Plus, my squirming stomach is in knots.

Rounding a corner, I approach the thick ivy infested stone walls of Sansyre University. The walls soar into the sky on getting closer, until the large, green steelore front gates loom before me, already peeled open for the hundreds of cadets hauling bags and belongings to their dorms. Parents hover, dictating orders. Some have tears of joy, while others stand with stone faces, masking whatever they feel.

There are more people here than initially expected.

It will make it easier to hide among the crowd but if anyone recognizes me—many knowing my face as the great General Orro's son—then my chances of ever entering the university will wash out with the high tide.

Bringing the hood of my jacket over my head, I lower my eyes. For too many times in the past years have I wandered the halls of this university, on those occasions when Father would drag Ayva and me here, he and our mother having matters to attend to.

Within twenty feet of the registrar's office door, there's already a line.

Just my luck! I impatiently wait, a sitting duck, stretching my hood further over my face and hunching over. Anxiety electrifies my veins, and only after noticing the irritation of the others do I catch my relentless pacing back and forth. How aggravating!

The line moves quicker than expected, many people staring, trying to decipher who this idiot is who disturbs everyone. My head turns to the side, seeking to find refuge behind the only other tall man ahead. The line inches closer.

My conscience creeps into my chest, a fire rising from its birth. Is this the right thing to do? No! It's not right. Father will be disappointed yet again.

Should I really do this? Does FirstElite truly matter in the end? Then something grabs my attention. At the far corner of the university, there he is, Ixo Sheyn.

My father has told many stories of him, namely that he's considered one of the most talented cadets to ever enter Sansyre University in the Order of Soldiers.

This is the cadet who won First and SecondElite for his class year without so much as breaking a sweat. He competes tomorrow for ThirdElite. And of course, everyone who comments on the tournament believes he will sweep this year again—with ease, no less.

As he walks this way with other third-year cadets, I hide my face.

We've crossed paths a few times, so he knows who I am.

My decision to enroll is even more definitive after spotting him.

The winners of each enrollment year have the chance to face off. First year versus second year, then the winner faces the third year. Not only is it vital to win FirstElite, but I also want my chance to face Ixo and prove to everyone that I am the most talented cadet to ever enter the Order of Soldiers. I have to be the best, number one.

Generals and leaders have been recruiting Ixo since he won FirstElite two years ago. Normally, that doesn't happen until year three.

Missing my chance this year means it will be too late to fight him since he will graduate at the end of spring, receiving his first choice of any military branch. Then I'll never know if I am the best.

My harsh insecurities crack my confidence. Could I even beat Ixo? Do I even have what it takes? Is he really the best?

"Next … NEXT!" the registrar clerk yells, snapping me from my illusion. A single deep inhalation intends to calm my increasingly jumping nerves, hands shaking, handing over my enrollment form. The clerk analyzes it too closely for comfort.

"Good morning. I am enrolling in the Order of Soldiers," I say, trepidation seeping.

"Well, Rioyn Orro, it's about time we received your forms. We processed your sister's paperwork weeks ago. Glad to see you both will be joining us this year."

She slams her stamp on the forms, tossing them into an overflowing basket.

"Here is your ticket for your uniforms. There are only a few dorm slots left. Take this form to the dorm captain and he'll assign you a vacant bunk. Your books will be issued on your first day of lectures."

She looks up from her oversized glasses that hold back graying black hair.

"Lastly, here are your goldenore cuffs. You must wear these at the Festival of Seivan if you wish to compete in the Tournament of Spar in two weeks' time. Most already wear them. You are competing in the tournament?"

My overwhelmed stare gives way to a nod.

"Good. The uniform department closes in twenty minutes. I suggest you hurry."

And so, I do.

In the uniform department, a tall, thin and graying man with the tired motion of a tortoise moves indolently to the shelves with the Order of Soldiers' attire. He pushes the entire shelf back, another large one moving forward, permitting him to thumb through multiple sets of neatly folded uniforms. He plucks free a set of navy-blue pants with a jacket lined with accents of gold and ivory threads; it's decorated with brassore buttons.

He hands the items across, returning to his duties.

"Should I try them on to make sure they fit?"

"They will fit. Good day, cadet." His eyes shift to the next in line.

The uniforms in my pack, I rush from the department. By now, the sun has fully risen, shining bright on the crisp green grass of the courtyard filled with cadets and parents. In the courtyard, the cadets of the Order of Soldiers are filing out of the sparring gym. I stuff the remaining paperwork into my satchel, weaving my way over to them in the crowd.

"Jax. Hey!" I shout as he, Xylar, and Mikel head back to their dorms. They all stop.

"You're not supposed to be on university grounds unless you're enrolled."

Xylar is quick to remind me of the rules. As I open my satchel, it reveals the same goldenore cuffs that adorn each of their wrists, meeting with a range of reactions.

"There goes my chance at FirstElite," Xylar scoffs. His resentment shifts to a scowl. "How'd you convince your father, anyway?"

"Don't be too upset. You never had a shot. Even if Rioyn wasn't competing." Mikel is swift with the counter.

I shoot Jax a smirk that falls on his stiff arched brow. "Don't worry. I'll go easy on you in the tournament you must agree I'm fated to win."

Before he's able to retort, girls from the Order of Healants walk by us, immediately capturing Xylar's attention.

"Ladies. Need an escort back to your dorms?" Xylar offers with a huge smile.

"We can manage. Thank you." The girls giggle as they scurry off.

Mikel leans into Xylar. "Smooth." Xylar might very well punch Mikel today.

My gaze lifting from the girls, it catches Jax studying me.

"Speaking of women," Xylar says, turning to Jax, "how did your special visitor's pass go last night?" His brow arches as he smirks in anticipation of juicy gossip.

Jax is still staring. "You ready to train?"

My best friend's silence riles Xylar even more. He grabs Jax by the back of his shoulders, shaking him, and Jax shoots a dismissive glance. Visitor's pass? Surely, he didn't go home and entertain some random girl.

As Xylar and Mikel stalk off, Jax's stare meets with one of my own.

"A visitor's pass, huh?"

"I got that pass hoping my mother would be here," he says, sounding slightly hurt that I would even question him. "Stupid, I know."

"And did she show?"

Jax shakes his head, and suddenly, I feel like a fool. He's not the type of guy to doubt, possessing more integrity in one finger than I could ever hope to have.

"It was a stupid hope. If she were still alive, she would have found me." He shrugs. "It's just that she always encouraged me to enroll, and I had this weird vision of her suddenly appearing."

The emptiness inside of him is raw, unfiltered. What he's going through is evident; his mother disappeared without a trace a few years ago, just like Bair.

It's one horrible thing we share.

"I'm sorry. I didn't know, otherwise … Well, I never would've asked."

We walk past the main lecture hall and back through the courtyard. The different cadets from the various orders are distinguishable simply by their adornments.

We pass by a group from the Order of Sayers, each wearing a steelore cuff around their left ear, the end leading into the ear's center.

Sayers within each of the military branches communicate through these devices, able to alert others of any news being transmitted between provinces.

We all have sayer devices in our homes, but they don't compare to these.

The Order of Healants wear chains of goldenore with a medallion at the end to send a vibrational signal through the chain.

This then alerts the healant of injury or infection on their patient.

Mother studied under this order but then switched her concentration to the Order of Ascendants upon realizing she was better served where her powers were stronger.

She loves to tell us how our father was injured in the sparring ring one misty fall morning and how she was the healant assigned to his injury. He was stubborn about receiving treatment until his eyes met hers. Her soft hazel gaze eased him back on his stretcher. Never in his life had he lain so still as on the day my mother tended to him.

After that first meeting, he visited her almost daily for any cut, scrape, or bruise he collected, even going so far as to visit her over a week's end at the Dara'Ana Station, a place where healants travel to be with the High Healant.

There, those who cannot be healed by regular tonics and medicines go to seek a higher healing level. After their week's end, our father finally mustered up the courage to ask her on a proper date, and so their great love story began, a story I've heard far too many times.

We rush by the Order of Archivants, these recognizable by their stack of six silverore rings on their left pointer fingers. Their eyes dart around, taking everything in, no doubt in preparation for a long night of note taking.

Jax and I stop in our tracks as we come to a group from the Order of Voyants, the cadets who will travel and chart every inch of the Seivan realm, charting throughout the seasons and after major weather events. The bravest of them will venture into the areas within the realm that are considered the most dangerous.

Sometimes, soldiers must travel to these places also, but when we go, we do so as a group, packing a heavy arsenal. Therefore, these cadets also travel in small, inconspicuous groups and must face each challenge with limited support.

The blood rushes out of both of our faces as Jax and I stare with wide eyes at their copperore charting compass. Bair and Jax's mother, Cyanda were—are—both voyants. My stare is broken by Jax bullying his way into the center of the voyants' circle. Not a single cadet makes eye contact with him as he demands information.

Jax's arms flail through the cool air, demanding answers. Answers he—and everyone else—knows he will never gain. The Order of Voyants is the most secretive in the realm.

Never has one broken their silence, not even for my father.

I yank Jax away from the cadets who don't even flinch at his presence.

We both immediately shift from their quiet, noble group to avoid any more painful memories of us that they may be conjuring inside.

Last but not least, we pass a class from the Order of Galilei, the order Ayva will be joining. They are distinctive by the tungstenore necklaces, each with a magnet hanging from its chain. A member of the group glances up at us; her smile is bright and warm, suggesting she recognizes me.

"You're Ayva Orro's brother, right?" I nod and increase my pace, hoping to pass by without further conversation.

Jax grabs my arm. "Why don't you want to talk to cadets in your sister's order? She was only being friendly."

"I want to train and get back home. That's why."

I dare raise my eyes to meet Jax's in hopes my plea is enough for him to stop his questioning. Then comes his dawning realization.

"Your family doesn't know you're here, do they?" My shoulders sink and my head hangs. Jax forges ahead. I tug him to stop. He has always been able to read me.

"I can explain."

"You and your secrets, Rioyn! You put us at risk by leading us to the Cave of Caino yesterday, and now you're what, looking for more ways to infuriate your father?" Jax shoves my chest. "Do you ever think about how your choices to always be the best impact others? Do you? Because from my perspective, you just do what suits you."

The full weight of Jax's frustration sears through me. There's no decent answer to give to this, nothing that would sound credible to both me and him.

Sure, there are many arguments to make but he has already formed his opinion, and not a particularly good one. Of course, I certainly do consider the fallout from my choices, but I forge ahead anyway, because of hating how Father willfully holds me back.

Isn't that just the way things go in life, that we fight especially hard for the things we're told we mustn't do?

It starts when we're learning to crawl, and we never give it up.

Because I want to be the most respected soldier in our order, is that really so bad? Is it a sinful thing I should be trying to curb? I don't think so! Because ultimately, every reason I have is rooted in what I want for myself. That's all I've ever really cared about. It's the only thing that matters, and that won't change for anyone.

Jax shakes his head at my silence, charging ahead of me.

"Promise I'll make it up to you," I say, striding after him, ebullient. "Tell me what to do. I'm ready to listen." But he still races ahead, unwilling to stop or talk.

Jax doesn't even turn to look at me, to the point I might as well not be there.

We walk past the dorms and through the sparring arena. He heads to a side exit gate and swings the heavy steelore gates open.

"I have to prepare for training." Jax's gaze falls to the stone pathway.

"Jax, I'm sorry."

He huffs, shaking his head. "Save all your apologies for your father. You're gonna need them."

With heavy shoulders, I leave through the gate, and he lets it slam behind me. Turning back to plead my case again, my eyes scan around. But he's gone, not a sign he was there.

I trudge up the steep hill to the rear of the Garden Theater, the roiling entanglement of emotions inside of me forcing me to stop. Stoping, I brace myself, soon down on my knees, hands shaking. I fight the acrid bile desperate to flee my gut; even the meager contents of my stomach are eager to abandon me.

As the nausea passes, I'm finally able to right myself and stare down into the Garden Theater. How can you be so stupid? My anger at myself rises along with my temperature.

Right now, I could scream until my screams have had enough of me as well.

Anything to stop the guilt and regret torching through my body.

"Clear your mind. Envision what you want to happen. Feel it with every fiber in your body. Transfer your energy to the energy around you that you wish to control."

As I collapse to the ground, my legs pull into a rough sitting position, my mind showing me the assorted colors of the energy surrounding Casstell. Blue, coral, purple and turquoise, the colors are vibrant, joyful, while simultaneously, the radiant energy from the citizens below is soothing. My mind turns dark, conveying me to the Bryar Bridge.

A heavy, dark energy surrounds me now, unlike any force encountered before.

My eyes open, and with that, a gasp escapes my lips.

What aspect of my Ascendance did I just experience? It's far from my ability to control it. A soft blue light billows beneath me, then dissipates. What was that?

Off in the distance, dark storm clouds form over Trescheria. Storms are relatively normal this time of year, but these are the darkest, most hostile looking clouds I've ever seen. Am I still experiencing some kind of left-over vision?

But no. They're real, at least to me. Rising to my feet, I start running home.

CHAPTER 8

ORDER OF SOLDIERS

The Past

S Y L O N

I SIDE-EYE MY SISTER, UNABLE to believe she did it. She registered to join the Order of Healants instead of the Order of Soldiers. She walks at my side but doesn't say a word. She could've studied with them through her auxiliary classes. Instead, she chose to waste her time here and go against our parents' wishes and our heritage.

"I convinced the dorm captain to have our rooms next to each other even though you're a healant."

"I don't need you watching everything I do."

I sense her narrow-eyed glare without even looking at her, huffing out a laugh.

"Trust me. I don't want you this close to me either, but I also won't let anything happen to you since you won't be learning how to defend yourself, sis."

She makes a dramatic show of her irritation, and I can't help but chuckle.

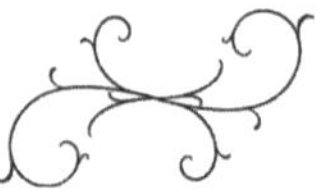

THE WEEK'S END FLIES by and thankfully, Shivane hasn't bothered dragging me to that ridiculous festival. She's already befriended her dorm mates. Thankfully, she has others to occupy her time. My dorm mates aren't interested in striking up any sort of conversation except to claim dominance over their designated areas.

They have left me to my own devices, just the way I like it.

The festival is over, and university has officially begun.

With my black duffel bag slung over my shoulder, I traipse through the buildings to the sparring ring, grateful the lectures I had to suffer through this morning are finally over.

Nothing of real value was taught, however.

Today will be the first day of sparring lessons, leaving me excited and eager, having been chomping at the opportunity to enter the ring.

Looking around, it's evident I am the first to arrive, perhaps too keen for my own good. For now, I drop my duffel bag on one of the wooden benches, impatient. In my guts, a whole battle seems to play out, every nerve and sinew on edge, dancing with urgency.

Warming up, I see him, the cadet from a few days ago who felt it necessary to taunt me before we'd even begun sparring. His icy blue eyes singe my stare.

Pray we're allowed to choose who we fight first; I'll gladly rip that smug Trescherian smirk right off his face.

He dares to take a few steps closer. At the same time, the rest of our sparring class floods in along with the rank commander who orders us to stand in a line, arranged by height. So, I take up position at the opposite end of the line from my new enemy, being the tallest in the class. As for him, he's somewhere in the shallow end.

The rank commander reviews our rules. There aren't many except for a few critical ones. My focus escapes the commander's instructions, for which I don't care much care for. I understand the rules. Instead, I size up each of my opponents. This class is going to be easier than I thought.

My focus snaps back to the commander as his voice bellows to a point where it's impossible to imagine he can speak normally. We all shout back, "Yes, Commander!"

We're each paired off with a partner matching our height. The rank commander calls out our names. I eagerly wait to learn the name of my Trescherian enemy and finally, the rank commander calls him forward. "Xi Kai." His name sears in my memory. I snap my focus back and await my opponent's name to be called.

BEADS OF SWEAT TRICKLE down my deep red face. I ignore the salty fluid seeping into my eyes as I lunge toward my opponent grabbing him by his slender waist and slamming him on his back onto the unforgiving mat. His burning red eyes give away his exhaustion.

My opponent props himself up to stand. His quick fist telegraphs his off-balance swing. I sidestep left and block him. He stumbles forward. Frustration consumes his better judgment.

My body is calm, poised. Exhaustion begins its saturation into my muscles, but I don't dare indulge. My sole focus is on my weakening opponent. I taunt him with a quick smirk. His emotions ignite and he lunges for me, again off balance.

I wait until the last second and reach for his leg. He's planted on his back again. I lock my knee into his neck and deflect his feeble attempt to kick me off him. He has no other options but to tap out.

Shocked expressions lace every cadet's face. The stench of fear emanates from each of them. I revel in their weaknesses. Instead of stepping up to the challenge of fighting a superior warrior, they all cower behind each other.

The commander adds another tally to my wins. That makes nine for the day. I stand undefeated, which is where I belong.

My curiosity gains the better of me as I watch Xi fight on the mat in the corner. He lunges for his opponent and is off balance. He is unable to deflect his opponent's rudimentary punches. I scoff at both of them. Xi arrogantly swings his fists hoping to land a punch. Defeating him will be easier than I initially thought.

Once training has ended, the rank commander comes to my side. "Cadet Greyea, a word." I finish tying my last boot before glancing up, his green eyes meeting mine.

I give him a slight nod and stand. He saunters to a corner away from prying ears. Grabbing my duffel, I follow.

"I congratulate you on your swift victories today, cadet," the rank commander says, a thinly veiled contempt slithering through his words.

"Thank you, sir. Expect this from every training session." I push my shoulders back, chin pointed high, but my announcement meets a heavy sigh. "Is there a problem, sir?"

"I feared you might say that." His forefinger taps his dented chin. "We need to build confidence in our cadets. No one benefits by being beaten up every day, which I sense you will be."

My posture straightens even more, but this time in indignation. Does he dare suggest I take it easy on other cadets, allowing them to best me?

"I do not follow … sir." In fact, never have I been so confused in all my life!

"Surely, you do. Though you fight like a brute, your scores speak otherwise. You've tested higher than any other cadet in the year. You're smart, Greyea. Arguably too smart."

My eyes narrow on him. "I will give everything I have every day. If someone wishes to best me, then I encourage them to step forward and try. If they do, then they will know they have earned their triumph fairly."

His chin lifts but he still stands several inches shorter.

"Anything else, sir?"

His green eyes wait for me to break his stare. I do not.

"Report directly back to your dorm, cadet." He sidesteps me and moves on. I don't bother looking back, swinging my duffel over my shoulder and commanding my exit.

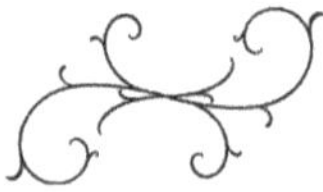

The next several months are more of the same. Classes and training. Ever since the first training day, cadets have been trying to weasel their way into my good graces. I don't bother acquiescing to their invitations to join them for whatever distraction they've concocted. That's not why I'm here.

Several girls loiter around after my training, offering to walk with me.

I pay them even less attention. Shivane seems to enjoy my newfound popularity, however, which has somehow overflowed to her.

Our rank commander hasn't assigned Xi as my sparring partner—yet. I've been studying his moves and advancements in every class, intent on having my moment and when I do, I'll make him regret ever stepping foot inside my awareness.

I'm fortunate to have one friend here aside from my busybody sister, not realizing he was even here until one day when we bumped into each other in the courtyard.

Since we were young, we've always had an effortless friendship, training together for years, honing our skills. He made the trip from Dremaria to Grynndyre at the last minute, so he was assigned to a lower-ranking training class that he has now dominated and from which he's moved on.

The sparse free time I do have, I spend with him. My only friend, Coren Fakanery.

We spend most of our time in the sparring ring after hours.

Tonight, however, we venture down the cobbled curved roads leading into the heart of Casstell from Sansyre. Rarely do we venture into Casstell but when we do, we make the most of our spare time and spend it well as any young men can.

As soon as we hit the first tavern, Coren is a moth to the flame when it comes to women. He's never satisfied with just one, insisting on commandeering every single girl he can. I, on the other hand, rarely meet one who can hold my attention.

Occasionally, my needs outweigh my better judgment, which is why I opt to avoid dabbling in the nighttime festivities Casstell has to abundantly offer.

Tonight is no different, leaving me standing back and watching Coren dancing to the rhythm of the night when a seemingly ragged man approaches.

My attention is diverted by a voice bellowing behind me. "Your quest for love has been long and arduous but will soon return the other half you've longed to seek."

My brows push into my hairline at this man's odd and random comment. A stark silver streak cuts through his jet-black hair.

As my mouth rushes to inquire about his ridiculous comment, my attention is diverted back to Coren. I rush to his aid as he's once again instigated another bar fight.

Between him and me, we sequester our opponents almost immediately. I drag his intoxicated ass out of the tavern, and we make the trek back to Sansyre. A couple of times, my gaze filters behind us, wondering who that odd man was and what his random message means

CHAPTER 9

THE OUTER REALMER

The Passt

SHIVANE

IT'S BEEN ALMOST SIX months since my brother and I left Dremaria to study at Sansyre University and I've loved every moment of it, especially when I ran into my best friend Caya Fakanery. She and I became quick friends when we were six because we had annoying brothers. She's a year ahead, so she's given me the lay of the land.

Another friend, Heiliana, is one of my dorm mates.

Both in the Order of Healants, we have the same classes together. Never have I met anyone as gifted with the art of healing as she is.

Her Ascendance is strong, much stronger than mine, but she's been teaching me her ways, always pushing me to become better, greater, and I'm grateful for her.

Her great-grandparents were originally from Seivan but left for Drycour with promises of a better world. Her family returned and sought refuge here not too long ago. Even though her heritage is here in Seivan, she's still considered an Outer Realmer.

Caya, Heiliana, and I bask in the warm sun on a frigid winter's day in the courtyard, waiting for our next class.

"When our time at university is done, I want to find a wealthy Lord and become his Lordess," Heiliana proclaims while dismissing her wind-taken strands of hair.

"Your title would be lady," Caya says.

"Lady is too … dainty. I am anything but. Lordess will be my title."

"You have to first find a Lord who can stand you for longer than a few moments," I chuckle.

Heiliana throws the remains her of lunch at me when suddenly, a group of girls from the Order of Soldiers—Caya's order—saunter over. They take hold of Heiliana's duffel bag and throw it in the trash.

Caya and I launch to our feet.

I may not be in the Order of Soldiers, but I've spent many summers fighting and training with Caya, my brother, and his friend—her brother—Coren.

"Pick it up!" I bark at the crimson-eyed girl.

She shoves me but startles when I don't stumble back. I flick her a greedy snarl and step forward, Caya at my side. Heiliana stands behind us.

"So, you're a sympathizer?" The girl looks me up and down. I knew there were some who feared and disliked people such as Heiliana, Outer Realmers, but this is the first time I've seen such hatred shared so openly.

"Pick it up," I grit a second time, hoping my expression clarifies I'll not ask again.

"You should be ashamed," the girl snarls, spitting at my feet. Wrong move.

Heiliana grabs my arm to pull me back. Caya's focus doesn't deviate from the girl.

I've been practicing my Ascendance, deciding to send my new friend a little message. Focusing on her twisted face, familiar words ripple through my mind. "Choices, my dear. We all have them. You must choose wisely."

Choices indeed. I've made mine.

"Bother us again, and you'll be sorry." I force the words from my mind, squeezing them into hers. "You've been warned."

The girl stumbles backward and rubs her temples. Her friends, staring as if I'm some monster from the deep, pull her away from our group. They leave, but not before she has the last word. "Typical Dremarian trash."

Before I can curl my fingers into a fist, Caya unleashes on the girl.

There's a sharp crack as bone meets bone, blood spilling down the bully's face.

Caya lunges once more but the other girls step in to pry away their crimson-eyed friend. It's too bad. They wanted a fight, and now, they have one.

Heiliana and I shove them back as Caya satisfies herself with a final, brutal punch.

We leave the girls huddled over their bloodied comrade as we gather our belongings, including Heiliana's bag from the trash, and strut off.

"No one has ever stood up for me like that. Thank you both," Heiliana confides.

Caya leans forward. "Oh, it was my pleasure." She sounds too enthusiastic about it.

We three head back to our dorms with pride smeared across our faces, attracting bold stares from the people we pass. We remain in our dorm the rest of the day, hearing scandalized whispers through the door, tales of what we've done.

No one has the gall to poke their head inside and ask us outright.

We don't care. If people want to attack us with their hateful words, assuming there will be no repercussions, they now know that we will retaliate. Let them try and seek revenge.

The day grows long, and we keep our noses buried in our studies when a loud knock raps on the door. Curious glances dance between us as Caya answers it.

Rank Commander Tau Sheyn of the Order of Soldiers—Caya's training rank commander—stands before us along with Healant Reblair, Heiliana's and my command healant. Several soldiers of the Grynndyre Command stand in line behind them.

"Caya Fakanery. Shivane Greyea and Heiliana Nicor. Follow us." We stare back, shocked by the small army that's shown up. "Now."

Rank Commander Sheyn turns sideways, motioning for us to exit our room.

Caya storms out, head held high, followed by Heiliana and me.

The three of us follow Healant Reblair with our shoulders back and chins raised as we're escorted through the university. All eyes are on us, yet again.

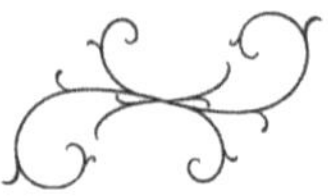

SYLON

Being escorted to the office of the principal, I'm accompanied by all six rank commanders of the Order of Soldiers. They side-eye me, afraid of me or for me, I'm unsure which. But I know the drill, having seen it with Father and those he's escorted to appear before Ruler Zianli. There are those who keep their heads held high and those who sink defeated into themselves. It rarely ends well for the latter.

A gurney carrying Xi suddenly appears from a hallway in front, cutting off our path. My glare snaps up to meet the bruised and bloody swollen eyes of Xi, the man who dared play with fire, now barely clinging on to his pathetic life.

I was only too happy to watch his life slip from him, clenching his neck in my hands. It took ten men to pull me off him, saving his pitiful life just in time.

Every eye is on me as my escorts drive me forward. I don't falter. Until …

A small hand touches my leg, my eyes widening upon finding a young girl staring up with large hazel eyes. The last thing I expect to see in this brutal place is a tiny child. Confused, I find myself kneeling to face her.

She places her small hand on my shoulder. "Good luck." She says it with a big, innocent smile, as if she already knows all will be fine.

I stare into her captivating hazel eyes, wise beyond their years.

"How old are you?" I manage to squeeze out.

"Eight."

Before I can speak, a man appears ahead, beckoning her.

"Ayva. Come, now." I whip my eyes up to meet Durran Orro, General of the Grynndyre Command. The child must be his daughter. It certainly explains how she is not cowed by powerful, dangerous men. The man's steeled gaze catches mine as the girl skips to his side, tossing a light and cheery "goodbye" over her shoulder.

Her father reaches for her hand as one of the rank commanders takes my arm, hoisting me back up. I push my shoulders back, raising my chin again as the girl and her father disappear around a corner. Walking, I can't seem to shake the child from my head almost as if I've met her before, though I'm sure it's impossible.

It takes effort to push her from my mind, though there are much bigger concerns to face. The rank commander parades me through the university, straight into General Orro's office. The mahogany wooden door opens to a large room overlooking the university's courtyard. On one side of the office, a fire roars in a large stone hearth, four empty leather-bound chairs sitting before it. It looks like a comfortable place to rest, but I'm instead led to the large table in the room's center where the general—and judgment—await.

Perched in a chair before the desk, I'm surprised.

Why is my sister Shivane here?

Why has she been drawn into my mess? Regardless, I take the empty seat next to her, though her focused stare doesn't flinch from the general. I can't help darting a glance around the room, in search of his puzzling little daughter, but it seems she's gone.

A fourth person joins us, High Ascendant Alora Orro, the highest-level Ascendant in all of Seivan, and General Orro's wife.

"My sister had nothing to do with what I did. She doesn't belong here," I snap before either member of the Orro family may speak.

"Your sister is here because she used her Ascendance to crawl through the mind of another cadet, barking orders through the open channel she forced open."

I huff in awed pride at General Orro's accusation.

If Shivane harmed another student, they likely deserved it.

"Is something funny, Cadet Greyea?" My head shakes. "Then wipe that smirk from your face at once." My stare captures his as my smirk hardens to one of disdain.

"I was defending a friend," Shivane offers, probably trying to spare me from escalating the situation. "Someone who suffered an unsolicited attack. I believe the Seivan Honor code states we must protect all cadets from such injustice."

Both Orros shift in their place. "Injustice must be rectified," High Ascendant Orro says with admirable calm. "But not at the cost of an even greater injustice."

Her bright blue eyes laser in on my sister.

"I accept the repercussions of my actions, but also stand by them."

Although not privy to what happened, I can't help but feel proud of my sister.

"Well then, there isn't a need to drag this out. Shivane Greyea, you are expelled and your belongings have been packed. A carriage will take you to the Grynndyre Growla Station. Your parents have been notified. You are dismissed."

Shivane looks at me, her violet eyes dry of any tears.

My head remains held high.

"I'll see you when this is over. My fate will be the same as yours," I whisper to her internally. "Hold your head high—don't give them the satisfaction of your disappointment."

Shivane is quick to her feet, leaving, not looking back.

My gaze settles on General and High Ascendant Orro.

He pontificates about honor and integrity at this backward university, my thoughts drifting to his strange daughter.

I almost sense her presence standing on the outside of the heavy timber walls. Leaning forward, I see her through the tall, thin glass window on the outside of the office.

How could such stern, insufferable parents have created that sweet little girl?

"Sylon." She speaks my name in a faint whisper, then louder until it bellows through the halls, snapping me from my trance.

"Cadet Greyea. Do you understand?"

I turn, facing General Orro and High Ascendant Orro, my white knuckles gripping the wooden armrest of the leather-bound chair. I lean back, my ankle resting on my knee.

"Say that again, sorry?" I won't back down now, giving them what they want.

"You are also expelled." The general looks ready to explode.

His wife places a calming hand on his rigid arm. Good call.

"We expect better from the children of fellow generals," she says. "From what I've been told, you have immense potential, more so than anyone who has ever come before you. But all that talent is worth little if you can't master your temper first."

I mull the decision to continue this thrilling debate or to be done with it. In my brief time here, I've realized that anyone who questions the rules of Sansyre is an immediate enemy of the university. This is not the place for new thinking, or even excellence, and it's not an organization with which I wish to be associated anymore.

"Anything else, General Orro?" The general's fierce glare doesn't waver, and I'll be damned if mine will either.

Standing, I'm ready to take off this pitiful uniform, dumping it in the trash.

"You're dismissed."

Outside the mahogany door, Shivane's friend, Heiliana, is waiting so I move to the side, allowing her to enter. The door doesn't fully close.

I hover there to listen, curious if what Shivane did was to protect her.

"Cadet Nicor. Do you have anything to say for yourself?" General Orro starts.

Seeing her through the sliver of the door, she sits tall, strong. "I would like to know what will become of the girl who harassed me with no provocation today."

"We haven't decided her punishment at this time."

"But you're quick to judge my friends. Your honor code states that such words are condemned here, yet the instigator remains."

"You are a foreigner here. Your amnesty from the outer realms is a fine balance."

"So, you'll have me shipped out because I was attacked on your university grounds."

She is impressive. The general and High Ascendant Orro are at a loss for words. High Ascendant Orro catches my hulking shadow just beyond the door.

With a flick of her wrist, it slams shut.

Shivane sits beside Caya; my only friend, Coren—Caya's brother—is pale faced, leaning against the wall. Of everyone, I feel sorry for him the most.

"I assume we reprobates are all in the same boat?" I offer.

"I was expelled first," Caya grunts. "They kept me in another office until they broke the news to you two." She crosses her arms over her chest, exposing scabbed knuckles. "I will not stay here a second longer."

"I'm going with you," Coren says. "I refuse to follow the orders of these people."

"Are you sure?" I ask. We don't have a choice, but he does.

He shrugs. "I'd rather walk away than remain on my knees for a bunch of fools."

"Well, no point in dragging this out any longer." Each of them is grim-faced but determined. "Let's go."

We're escorted out of the university and to our carriage, which drops us off at Grynndyre Growla Station. As we float away, I once more feel the pull of the child, Ayva, as she sends out a mental tendril, inviting me to communicate. But what would be the point? I don't allow her into my mind. Instead, I block her out, settling into my cushioned seat. However, her presence still has a hold on me. Odd. There's no reason to converse with a child. Can her Ascendance be that strong? But her mother is the High Ascendant.

It'll be late by the time we reach the Trescherian Growla Station and an even longer ride in that miserable carriage back to Dremaria.

I close my eyes, praying for sleep, ready to forget the miserable fools left in our wake.

CHAPTER 10

THE NIGHT BEFORE

AYVA

I PERCH ATOP THE STOOP, stealing glances of our neighbors' homes, wondering who's staying in and who's going to the opening ceremony. Our home sits midway up a hill, allowing me to see over some of the homes in our rolling hill city.

Neighbors, visitors, and citizens of Casstell weave through the streets, heading toward Circle Park. Smiles caress every person strolling by.

My lips curl, matching their excitement. The opening ceremony for the Festival of Seivan at the start of every fall equinox is my favorite event, always two long weeks after the cadet welcoming ceremony. This time of year is my absolute favorite, especially now since I'll be competing in the Tournament of Galilei.

Waiting for Rioyn, I decipher the color of each passerby's eyes, discerning from which province each person hails. Regardless of where a person's family originates, where they are born determines their eye color. It's just another small but magically wonderful detail about our realm, that our people connect to their birthplaces in deep and mysterious ways.

No one has been able to understand with absolute scientific certainty.

According to research, their pigmentation is due to the soil and air of the province of their birthplace. But if that is the case, you would think that colors might change with time as people move to new places, but they don't.

It is a theory to which many cling, but no one has any answer.

People born in Grynndyre have green eyes. Occasionally, there's a pair of red, however, from Roccali. A couple strolls by with gray eyes, hailing from Windalai.

I sense Rioyn behind me, shutting the front door quietly.

He has a tight lip and a conflicted gaze. My brow crinkles at him.

"You've been weird these past few weeks. What's going on with you?"

He startles out of his stare. "What? Nothing. Let's go."

"Whatever it is, it's not nothing. You've barely spoken to me over these last few weeks, and you've avoided Dad as if he had the Seivan fever. What's going on?"

"Didn't say anything. Can we please not ruin this night with your incessant questions?"

My brother's sharp tongue appalls me.

Whatever's bothering him must be important for him to not even tell me!

"There are a lot more people here for the opening ceremony than last year." Will there be any response from Rioyn? It seems his mind is still wandering.

We make our way to one of the openings leading to Circle Park, where a group of people gathers around a large portrait made entirely of flowers.

Casstell is known for many things but one of its most famed attractions is its unique blooms. The flowers that grow here are large, bright, and some have hundreds of little petals on their heads. Flower vendors rank among the top-selling attractions.

Moving closer to the portrait, I make out that it's of our former Leader of Grynndyre, Jyan Cour. Several citizens of Casstell and Grynndyre kneel before it and noticeably, a few find themselves overtaken by their emotions.

Cour was a great leader from what everyone says, one our province misses to this day.

Rioyn and I were kids playing in the sandbox way back then, when he was our leader.

He's remembered in many ways, but this memorial is a fitting tribute.

Rioyn and I make our way to the top of the Garden Theater where the bright moon shines down on the burgundy clay rows carved into the hillside, giving the center platform the perfect stage for acoustics.

Rioyn is looking around for someone, his neck craning back and forth.

"Who are you searching for?"

Then it hits me. Rioyn looks down at his shoes, kicking a few lonely rocks off the path. Before his words are able to form, he's saved by his friends.

"Orro! Over here." Our eyes shoot up.

Off in the distance are Xylar, Mikel, and Jax, all waving him over.

I steal a glance at Jax, his perfect chestnut hair tangling with the soft breeze. My stare is broken when Rioyn mentions he's going to hang out with his friends and for me to find mine, pointing to some girls in the distance.

"Have a new date for tonight? I don't recognize that one," I poke.

Rioyn shoots me a dismissive smile. Does he actually like all these girls that he dates or is he just burying his heartbreak in their company?

I don't want to hang out with the girls with whom he thinks I'm friends.

My true friends are my books. They are kind, informative, and non-judgmental.

The group of girls sees me, and I can't hide in the way I hoped. These girls pretend to be my friends, thinking it will get them closer to Rioyn and his friends.

They stare at him as he trots over to his group.

Kalli is the only one not watching my brother. Instead, she smiles with her golden hair bouncing in the breeze and stands on her toes, waving for my attention.

A grin forms on my face as she waves me over and then there she is, Zoura, her perfect rusty brown hair matched with polished hazel eyes shining under the moon's light.

Her deep golden skin sparkles under the stars; this woman is absolutely stunning, but the look is deceptive since she is also wickedly cruel.

Pushing through the ever-moving crowd, I say, "Hey Kalli."

"I'm so glad you came out tonight," she replies. "It's been so long since we've seen you."

"I've been studying," I say, unnecessarily as if believing I have to excuse myself for not being around so much. "I have the Tournament of Galilei tomorrow."

That information I should never have divulged.

"You are so going to win—FirstElite all the way! We'll be there cheering you on tomorrow, right, Zoura?" Kalli's smile is genuine, and she'll be cheering for me.

Zoura just shrugs. "Don't you think it's a little odd that you've decided on the Order of Galilei, instead of the Order of Healers or Archivants like the rest of the girls at the university? Aren't you worried about being bored and lonely?" Her beautiful eyes flick up and down as if taking my measure and finding me decidedly lacking. "Or perhaps not."

Stupid me for thinking she'd be so kind and happy for me.

"I wish I were as smart as you, Ayva." Kalli flashes her sweetest smile.

Zoura's hazel eyes roll.

Kalli has always been nice to me; everything about her is as sweet as she first appears, and it's disappointing to know there's no chance to get closer to her, not now. If only we could have been better friends. But she and Zoura are inseparable.

They've been that way their whole lives, so it won't change now.

"I'm bored." Zoura pouts.

Then her face changes from one of utter annoyance to pure delight. I whirl around to see what has changed her mood. Turns out it's not what, but who.

"Jaxyon Risor!"

As Jax walks up to us, Zoura darts forward, reaching for his arm and stepping in between me and him, hanging off him as if they are already an item. It certainly prevents anyone else trying to get close. She almost wears him like a garment of clothing.

"Hey, girls. Hi, Ayva." He nods.

Jax's glowing smile soars over Zoura's head, landing on my flushed face.

My heart skips a beat, or twenty to be honest. My grin aims his way but just as predicted, before there's a chance to say anything, Zoura chimes in.

"Jax, will you dance with me later tonight?"

I break Jax's stare and tune out, he and Zoura chatting about the festival and their plans for the evening. In the distance, my gaze catches my brother watching me through the crowd, seeing me standing on the outside of the circle.

Zoura's back is to me as she chats excitedly with Jax. My brother probably sent Jax over here to be friendly. But once more, there I am on the periphery, the forgotten extra. It must be embarrassing to have me as his twin. My cheeks flush with guilt at the wasted opportunity he's tried to give me, one of many over the years.

"Hey, Ayva. How have you been?" Xylar slicks back his blond hair, his eyes charting the dirt at the front of his shoes. Finally, his crimson eyes meet mine, inquiring.

"I've been good. It's good to see you too. How was your summer?"

"It was … um, it was good. I'm glad you came out tonight, by the way. Would you—"

The moment as well as Xylar's lost thought are both disrupted when more girls swarm my brother and his popular friends, including Xylar. Especially Xylar.

These girls are all familiar. We all went to the same camp every summer, and each of those summers, they'd flock to my brother, ignoring me. Recognizing my exit, I take it, quickly ducking through the moving crowd until they're far behind.

Soon, there is distance between us, and I watch Zoura effortlessly standing next to Jax with her arm entwined in his. It's so natural for her to command the attention of those around her, something begrudgingly admirable.

Jax laughs at some joke, pain lancing through my chest. Could I not make his face light up like that? But what does a girl like me have to offer someone like him? Interesting facts about Seivan invertebrates?

Oh, please.

In Circle Park, the vendors are already set up, some open for business tonight, but others not due to open until the festival officially starts tomorrow.

People meander past, going about their night, not a frown among them—all except for mine. There's a sense of resentment, something deeply abhorrent in me, wishing Zoura didn't bother me so much when she really does. Why do people gravitate toward her like she's a beacon of light, leaving me living on the outskirts of life, watching from the outside in? Hope all changes tomorrow at the Tournament of Galilei. That's if I win.

I've almost made a complete circle by this time, finally getting to see what I've hoped to find. Crème bowls! I rush over to the vendor, hoping he hasn't run out for the night.

"One crème bowl, please," I ask the vendor. "Oh, will you add a dash of merrisweets, please?" The tang of the buttery sweet crème flirts in the breeze, watering my mouth.

"How much do I owe you?"

The vendor looks at me with his light blue eyes flecked with purple. He's from Trescheria, I think? His lips crinkle, and he lifts his brow into silver-lined hair.

"Why, Ayva Orro, master of Galilei! This crème bowl is yours, with my compliments."

My cheeks flush at the fact he knows my name. Perhaps I'm not as invisible as I imagine, I think with a flush of pride. "Please, take the money. It's wrong to expect to get something for free; you have a living to earn."

He waves me off as I fumble for my wallet. "Ayva Orro," he says in the softest tone, "I gave it to you as a gift. You were not expecting anything. That's how gifts work."

And he is right, of course, and a warm smile spreads across my lips. "Thank you."

"Instead of payment," he adds tantalizingly. Should have known there'd be a catch! But I am grinning as if I just won the grand prize, barely able to focus on what he's saying.

Then he asks, "Might you indulge a humble vendor for a moment?"

I shrug non-committedly. What does he want?

"The quest that lies before you will end in failure," he says. "But within that failure lies the quest." Then he simply stands there, looking at me, waiting for a response.

Huh, what? All I can do at first is stare at him, clutching my crème bowl, waiting for the punchline. It never comes. "Is that it? What do you mean?"

At that moment, a forgotten firework explodes in the sky. People jump in shock, then all around me are giggles, everyone laughing in relief as the market is bathed in bright gold, orange and red light. "Sir, I—" My words stutter to a stop.

The man has gone.

The crème bowl is melting in my hand, so I scurry off to stake residence on an empty stone wall, enjoying my dessert away from the bustling crowd.

His rhyme repeats in my head like an addictive musical lyric.

The quest that lies before you will end in failure. But within that failure lies the quest.

As I sit there mulling, two plump, colorfully dressed women take up a resting seat on the wall nearby, entwined in conversation, not even noticing me lingering near.

Nothing new for me. I'm but a shadow in this bright world. Get used to it, Ayva …

"Everything must be at least double the price of last year," the woman in the vibrant green, blue, and gold dress huffs. "Coin is the new religion. No one ever cared for such things when Jyan Cour was our leader. Now that each province has its own coin, it's created a division among the people. It's a hideous thing. Don't you think?"

"Yes! It's true," laments the friend beside her, a large pink ribbon in her hair. "Once upon a time, an apple here had the same value as an apple anywhere. But not anymore."

The other woman leans in. "Have you heard about the betrayers?"

My ears perk up at the foreign word. Betrayers? I inch closer, eavesdropping.

"No one seems to know what to think about them. Or if the rumors are even true."

"Things are changing around here," murmurs the one in the green dress, conspiratorially. "And maybe some resistance would be a good thing."

"Be careful with that talk," pink ribbon woman hisses. "I warned you about my neighbor who disappeared in Trescheria. The High Voyant. It's been such a long time of looking after her place, hoping she'd return but it's been two years now, you know. Her poor boy. She was all he had left after his father was killed in the Battle of Trescheria."

My gaze locks on the women. Did she just say the High Voyant was her neighbor?

I need to get closer still, beginning to edge my way off the wall, but it's at that moment the crème bowl slips from my hands, clattering down against the stones.

The chatty women whirl at the sound, wide-eyed at my innocent but awkward smile at my ungainly moves. In return, they nod before standing, continuing on their way.

That was stupid. Why can't I be less clumsy? Now I've scared them off.

The crowd thins out, everyone taking their seat in the Garden Theater.

As I reach it, there is my brother in the distance along with his friends, and mine if you can call them that. Zoura's still right by Jax, while lingering off to the side is Mikel, as terrible at socializing as I am. It's good to know Jax looks out for him.

Like a stray dog, Xylar saunters up to Zoura as if searching for little scraps of her attention. She flashes him her typical polite yet playful grin; when he doesn't take the hint, she ignores him, focusing back on Jax.

"Why aren't you with your friends?" comes a familiar voice right by me.

Rioyn hovers at my side, worrying about me as usual.

"I am," I say and smile, pointing to a random spot beside me. He studies the empty gap then rolls his eyes. "Ayva. There's no one there."

"I don't have real friends as you well know," I huff. "Besides, I wanted a crème bowl."

Rioyn slips his arm through mine. "Twins," is all he says as our hands connect.

"Maybe you'll meet some new people who share similar interests once you start studying," Rioyn begins, only to pause as Jax strides up, saving me from another well-intentioned but hopelessly embarrassing pep talk.

"Do you want to sit with us?" he asks, Mikel appearing at his side.

"Your intelligent conversation would be most welcome," Mikel says sniffily.

Has my brother put them up to this? Even so, I can't help but smile with a slight blush.

Jax extends his elbow, and suddenly, I drop my brother like a hot pan.

Rioyn scoffs, watching us with intrigue. But I barely take note of my brother. A surge of electricity palpitates through me the second I touch Jax's arm.

He tucks me into his side. Is he just treating me like a cherished younger sister in front of Rioyn, or is it potentially something more?

His eyes don't deviate from mine.

My smile falls to panic, then … what's that? I feel a slight stickiness between our arms.

Please no. Damn it; there's a mess all over my clothes! When the crème bowl dropped earlier, it must have targeted its contents down both my sleeve and dress!

And now, it's smearing all over Jax's impeccable uniform.

"Oh no! Jax, I'm so sorry! I'll clean it up."

Is there any way to clean the mess I've made? Mortified, I feel myself attempting to slink away … but Jax tugs me back. We're inches away from each other at this point, my breath intensifying. Our eyes meet, and he smiles, holding a handkerchief he must have pulled from his pocket.

He holds my hand in his, gently wiping my arm with the fine white fabric.

"We're going to lose our seats if we don't hurry," Xylar scoffs with his long muscular arms folded across his chest, his impatience getting the better of him. "Hey, Ayva. Happy festival." His lip curls into his high cheekbones, flashing me a genuine, interested smirk.

Jax rips his glare from Xylar, turning to me. "Ready?"

I smile, the five of us heading toward the front rows of the Garden Theater.

Family members of the leaders and generals have reserved seating up front, one of the many perks of our father being General of the Grynndyre Command, the strongest of the military branches, according to him.

Rioyn leads the way followed by Xylar and Mikel.

I follow behind them. Jax has now made it a point to walk beside me.

Xylar and Mikel sit a row behind, my position sandwiched between my brother and his best friend, painfully aware of Jax's leg pressing against mine from hip to thigh.

It takes all my self-control to avoid squirming.

Zoura and Kalli walk to the front, looking at our row. Rioyn looks around, seeing if we can make room. "It looks like the row is full," Jax sternly states.

How I would love to smile smugly at Zoura in that moment, but for all my triumph, she still terrifies me. I turn away, staring down the row instead.

"Ladies, I have a seat right here for you both." Xylar smacks the bench, enticing them to join his side but Zoura dismisses his invitation with a flick of her wrist. "We have other seating arrangements. Happy festival." Her snarkiness sends Xylar's crimson eyes rolling.

"I think she likes you," Mikel whispers.

I make an audible snort, then blush with embarrassment. Jax smirks down at me. I glance back at Rioyn, watching him still searching for someone.

"Have you seen her yet?" I ask, seeing his eyes roving the crowd.

He doesn't need to say who; I understand what he's talking about.

"Not yet." He shakes his head.

"I'm sure she'll be here. She loves the festival too much not to come. If not tonight, then tomorrow. Have you talked to her since—"

"Oh, believe me, I've tried. She keeps rejecting my calls over the sayer line. Her mother's also great at making up excuses for her."

"Why don't you go to Trescheria and talk to her?"

"Did that, too. She slammed the door in my face, refusing to come out. It was a complete waste of a day, which is why I'm not holding out hope that she'll show up."

CHAPTER 11

THE OPENING CEREMONY

RIOYN

I SWIVEL FROM AYVA, CUTTING her off before she can pry anymore. She knows all too well what happened between me and Falla and it's not a memory on which I wish to dwell, having replayed it a thousand times in my head since last winter's break.

The awkwardness in the air lingers. Finally, a man takes the stage, and it seems the ceremony may finally be about to begin. Caught up in the excitement, Xylar clamps his hand on mine and Jax's shoulders. Out of the corner of my eye, I notice Jax fall forward slightly, bracing himself on Ayva's leg.

He murmurs an apology. She nods in silence, fiddling with her dress.

Is there really something going on between them?

I narrow my eyes on Jax, never considering overly flirtatious like Xylar, but many girls do favor and chase him—although he's known Ayva as long as he's known me.

Surely, she must be like a sister to him! It would have to feel quite strange.

"Ladies and gentlemen," booms the announcer. "Welcome to the opening ceremony of the Festival of Seivan. Many of you have traveled from across the provinces to be here at what has become a grand ceremony to celebrate the peace and prosperity of our realm. Tomorrow and the day after next, we have the Tournaments of Orders where first, second, and third-year cadets will vie for the title of Elite."

A pit forms in my stomach as I hunch forward. Saliva overwhelms my mouth. Did I make the best choice?

Finally, he sweeps his arms wide. "Now, without further delay, I'm proud to introduce our first Leader of Windalai."

Mikel launches to his feet, sending a swift and painful knee to my back as he cheers with pride for his home province. Wincing, I manage to let it go.

"She is escorted by the General of the Windalai Force."

They move to the center platform to take their bow.

Mikel speaks highly of his leader's generosity and kindness throughout their province.

The general is dressed in his formal ceremonial military uniform, as is every general here, but his includes the Windalai province crest, a medallion of silverore inscribed with a cyclone.

"Typical. Still no women as generals," a woman quips behind me.

"The top general of the realm is a woman, in case you forgot," the man next to her counters. I feel her huff of hot air tingling the hairs on the back of my neck. I chuckle.

"We thank you for your leadership and service," continues the announcer. "Next in line, the Leader of the Roccali province, escorted by the—"

Ayva and I leap to our feet, beginning to cheer proudly for Uncle Kain Orro.

He flashes us a thankful grin.

"—General of the Roccali Legion."

Uncle Kain's medallion is made of sansone, inscribed with the outline of Camarelhead.

Our uncle blows a kiss our way, smiling to see Ayva pretending to grab it from the air, pressing it to her heart. My eyes roll.

The kiss was something Uncle did whenever he left our home when we were kids.

Ayva loves it. It still means something to her even now, even if it's nothing more than a childish memory to me.

Uncle Kain used to visit us four times a year but now, his visits have been reduced to only one. No matter how pressing matters were with his military meetings, missions, and obligations, he always spared time for us.

He was the first to teach me about sparring footwork, and about anticipating an opponent's next move.

They were instructions I took to heart and practiced consistently, just as he instructed.

His visits were always a joyous time of the year until he and our father—his older brother—got into a heated argument. Now, we rarely see him.

Tonight, and during the festival, is the only time we're able to spend with him.

"Next up is the Leader of Trescheria." Jax stands, loudly clapping to celebrate his home province. Ayva claps with him as she gazes up at Jax with an excited smile. My mind grapples with whatever this new and slightly disturbing thing is, blooming between them.

"He is escorted by the General of the Trescherian Defense …"

General Xi Kai has his family's icy blue eyes, while his chocolate hair is long in the front, covering his patched left eye and the scar running from his hairline to the opposite side of his chin. He fought in the battle for Trescheria, the place he received that scar.

General Kai wears the circular copperore medallion with an outline of the Roots of Roul. Past General Kai, I'm dearly hoping to see Falla Kai, his niece.

This will be her second year in the Order of Soldiers.

She won FirstElite last year, the first woman ever to champion the title.

"Maybe their family's stationed to watch Trescheria this year?" Ayva offers.

"Yeah … maybe." I crack a small, thankful smile but my nerves are anything but eased. They won't be until I can see Falla and tell her how deeply sorry I am, again, for the pain caused and the damage wrought upon our decade-plus friendship.

She didn't deserve what I did.

"Swimming all the way from the northwestern part of the Ezmarad Ocean, the Leader of Aquaria, escorted by the General of the Aquarian Maritine."

The general's medallion is centered just below his chest, and it's made of coral spun by the ocean to create its wavelike shape. They take their bow and instead of clapping, people glide their hands to emulate waves rippling through the ocean.

The announcer takes his place at center stage.

He looks to his cue card, then whips around to his squire, forgetting to cover his mouth as he's still in acoustic range. "What do you mean Zianli Wren is here?"

Whispers and gasps erupt among the audience, and mortified, the announcer turns back.

His audible swallow alarms the frantic crowd, cries booming through the stadium.

Zianli is not allowed out of Dremaria. There's no sight of the unpopular leader.

"He doesn't deserve to grace this theater's stage!" comes a shout a few rows away.

"How dare he show his face here!" a woman shrieks.

Ayva, Jax, Mikel, Xylar, and I exchange glances, listening to the grumbles of the crowd. The announcer fumbles to find his words.

"Um, ladies and gentlemen, please, let's maintain our decorum …"

It's at that moment Zianli, apparently unconcerned with everyone's disdain for him, appears from behind the stage, walking into the center spotlight. 'Boos' reverberate in a flood of anger and disapproval as the leader raises his hands.

"I'm here not as the Leader of Dremaria, but as its ruler. You might hate me, but I am a true descendant of Everia. I, along with my kin, carry her true and pure bloodline."

The announcer leans into Zianli, demanding to know, "Where are your generals?"

Zianli turns to the announcer, looking him dead in the eyes. "What generals?" A smirk cuts across Zianli's long, dark face, his purple eyes boring into the announcer.

Every general launches to their feet. Zianli is quick to threaten them with his elemental Ascendance that is stronger than most give him credit for.

"I will be on my best behavior tonight. I promise." A devilish grin plasters across Zianli's face as the Generals think better than to create fight in front of the entire realm.

Zianli turns back to the audience with his hands raised, absorbing his self-imposed glory.

Mikel leans in. "Dremaria stopped sending cadets to the university nine years ago. Why would he even want to attend the festival? No one from there is to compete."

The announcer composes himself, looking to his next cue card, his hands visibly shaking. "One moment, ladies and gentlemen."

The announcer runs off stage as the already raucous grumbles from the audience grow louder. "This is the best opening ceremony ever," Xylar says, leaning back and soaking up the drama. Jax and I can only glare back.

The announcer races back to the stage. "My apologies again. Arro Lore, Leader of Xaeria and Monnaire Lore, General of the Xaerian Fleet are regrettably absent tonight."

Ayva and I turn to each other in unison. Zianli's appearance is undoubtedly a shock but Arro and Monnaire not being in attendance is even more alarming. This festival was created by them over a century ago. They have never missed a single year. Why now?

"Taking their place and giving the opening ceremony speech is the Leader of Grynndyre, Emmil Rytche." Everyone in the audience rises to their feet with applause. "He is escorted by the General of the Grynndyre Command, Durran Orro."

Ayva and I clap until our hands spark red, then Emmil and our father walk past the other generals and leaders seated at the back of the stage.

Emmil moves to center stage as our father takes his leave. He tilts a proud smile directed at Ayva and me and I swallow hard, thinking about how I forged his signature on my enrollment forms a couple weeks past. I can only hope I'm in the clear since he hasn't found out yet. If he had, then I'd have been dead by now. It doesn't matter anymore anyway. I've made my bed. By the time he finds out, it will be too late; I will undoubtedly endure the full wrath of his anger and can only hope he understands.

I had to find another way to compete in the Tournament of Spar.

"Fellow Seivanians. Thank you all who have traveled from afar to be here tonight. A personal welcome to all first-year cadets who will be entering Sansyre University after this week's end and to the parents who will be saying goodbye to their children. This night is bittersweet for so many of us."

If only you knew.

My sister squeezes my arm in sympathy, but I haven't the heart to tell her what I've done. If she knew the truth, she'd kill me before our father ever got the chance to.

I keep telling myself it's my future, not theirs.

"This festival is a time when every citizen comes together to celebrate each province and how much Seivan has grown since Warriem and Everia created this beautiful world for us all to enjoy." Emmil's gaze rakes over the crowd.

He directs a look in Zianli's direction. "It's a time for unity and peace."

"We have a week's end full of great entertainment, fun, and the part everyone looks forward to, the Tournaments of Orders. We are fortunate to watch and celebrate our children becoming adults as they compete for the esteemed honor of winning the title of Elite. To the cadets current and past, remember your honor. Remember your code, for the Laws of Seivan govern us all. Enjoy your best night's rest and I look forward to seeing everyone tomorrow at the Festival of Seivan."

The crowd erupts in cheers. I catch Jax's furrowed brow and Xylar's crossed arms, Mikel's arched brow. They are as suspicious of Emmil's closing remarks as I am. He has been a vocal harsh critic of the Seivan Honor, yet he pontificates about it now?

The audience disperses, disappearing into the night.

Ayva walks ahead with Jax while Xylar and Mikel fill in beside me.

"Are you sure you're eligible to compete with us tomorrow? I was looking forward to taking home the title of FirstElite." Xylar can't help but rub it in.

"If Rioyn doesn't compete, my coins are on Jax," Mikel snaps.

"Traitor!" Xylar cuffs Mikel over the back of the head. As the two scuffle beside me, I search for Ayva, finding her walking ahead with Jax. I jog up to them.

"What are you two chatting about?" I flash a grin at my intentional interruption.

Jax ignores my inquisition, focusing his smile on Ayva instead of heeding me.

"He was telling me how he starts class tomorrow. A few days ahead of the rest of us," Ayva explains.

"Shouldn't you be headed back to the dorms with Xylar and Mikel?" Jax finally takes his eyes off Ayva to address me.

"I'm walking Ayva home."

"That's okay. We're both headed in the same direction. The university's the opposite way." I put my arm around my sister's shoulder to walk her home since I didn't dare move into the dorms yet. If I had done, then it would've been a dead giveaway.

Ayva whips around, her furrowed brow showing she is anything but happy with my sudden protectiveness. Until Jax's true intentions are clear, all I dare do is maintain my stance, analyzing the understanding in his eyes.

He nods then stops, taking Ayva's hand in his. I shrink my arm back and give them a moment, watching as he leans in close to say something, making her laugh.

As my best friend kisses my twin sister on the cheek, I try not to hurl in disgust.

"See you both at the festival tomorrow, Orro," Jax says, flinging his goodbye at me.

"Sure."

Jax's jaw flexes at my rebuff, but he nods, turning to catch up with Mikel and Xylar. Ayva whips around, irritation searing from those bright hazel eyes.

"So, you and Jax, eh?"

Ayva rolls her eyes, speeding up.

I can't help but let a chuckle roll, my smile fading to take one last look around.

"Are you coming or what? You said you'd walk me home."

I did indeed. Pressing forward, my face still hangs.

"Just because you screwed things up with the one you love, doesn't mean you have to rain on my parade," she says. I only need to wait a few beats before her sympathy kicks in, and she turns to me with an apology in her eyes. My sister is as kind as she is predictable. "Sorry. Have you thought about what you're going to say to Falla when you see her?"

"That depends on how mad she still is at me."

My chuckle sounds hollow, even to me.

Ayva wraps her arm around mine, staying close. Her hands are cold even through the sleeve of my shirt, so icy that it elicits a natural wish to warm her. I put my arm around her, hoping it helps. Soon walking through the vibrant streets, Ayva stops suddenly.

"What is it?"

"Do you hear that?" She asks.

I listen, confused. "Hear what?"

"Exactly. It's quiet. Too quiet."

"I can hear people in the distance," I offer.

"Yes, me too, but something's not right. The cicadas should be humming this time of year. Crickets and owls. It's like a hush has fallen over everything."

I wave off her concerns, thinking she needs to spend less time with her head buried in her books, and more time with friends.

"Come on. We better get home." I walk, assuming she'll follow but she doesn't, still stuck there, listening to the night. "Ayva! Let's go."

She just huffs at my demand.

CHAPTER 12

THE FESTIVAL OF SEIVAN

AYVA

"ARE YOU READY FOR your big day?" My mother is more excited than I am.

I nod, still clutching to my nervous smile staring back at me in my fogged mirror. Mother checks over my uniform, pulling at my jacket's end, brushing out the shoulders.

"I hope you find time to enjoy the festival this morning with your friends before you head to the tournament."

I grimace. What's with everyone's obsession around my social life?

"That Kalli girl is sweet," Mother presses.

"She's Zoura's best friend, and Zoura is …"

"Zoura is a brat."

"Ma!" I'm scandalized. It might be the first time I've heard her bad-mouth someone ever—and at my defense.

"Just promise me you'll have some fun this week's end before classes start."

"I will. I promise."

"And promise me that you'll make time for your Ascendance training."

"Of course." I turn away, fiddling with my buttons.

"Sweetheart, you have an exceedingly rare gift. One both you and your brother are truly fortunate to possess."

"It doesn't seem fair that some have abilities, and others don't."

103

Mother cups my cheeks in her warm hands. "Warriem and Everia gave their people the gift of their own powers but people from the Outer Realms, and even some who fled their planet in distant galaxies, have gifts of their own. But Ascendance grows weaker with each new generation, and those who still possess it must try to preserve it." She flashes a rosy smile. "You're a true descendant of Warriem. Soon, your power will burn inside you, itching to be released."

"You say Rioyn and I are true descendants, but my Ascendance is weak at best. Even when I do practice."

My mother's eyes dart around the room. She's calculating what to tell me.

"Will you please just tell me what's wrong with me!"

Her eyes whip to meet mine. "Nothing is wrong with you."

"Then why am I not as strong as I should be?"

She releases a deep inhalation. "Remember when you and your brother were so sick?"

My thoughts race. "Barely, but yes, I remember him and me spending an entire winter's break cooped up in our rooms."

"That was because you'd both been poisoned."

This news sends me stumbling backwards, searching for my bed on which to plop down. "What? Why have you never mentioned this? Can it happen again?"

"No. No, my dear. The Assihilator has been taken to a place where he can no longer hurt you or anyone ever again,"

"The Assihilator? He's real?"

By the look in Mother's eyes, she's told me more than she intended. She cups my flushed cheeks in her hands, pulls me in, kissing my forehead.

"Don't worry yourself about him. He can't hurt you. Just focus on practicing your Ascendance, and you'll regain your powers. You'll see."

But training and using my Ascendance scares me, already feeling other people's emotions stronger than I'd like.

Sometimes, they become mine, then I'm an emotional wreck for no reason. I'd rather read, study, and never have to deal with emotions ever again.

My mother leaves me to my tangled thoughts, closing the door behind her. I've barely started braiding my hair when the door whips open again, revealing none other than my twin brother with his hands spread wide.

"What do you think?" He turns to show off his eccentric yellow outfit.

"Is that what you're wearing?"

"Er, yeah! Why else would I have it on? Anyway, what do you think?"

"I know they say to dress with colors and to use your imagination, but wow!"

"I look good!"

"You look like a drunken bumble bee."

Rioyn turns in front of my mirror, checking out his outfit, turning his body this way and that as if he is vain. The garments are a shade of yellow brighter than the sun, while various other colors are splattered throughout in no particular pattern from what I can tell.

"No wonder why the paint store sayered a message; they said you forgot a few colors."

Rioyn whips his taunting eyes at me, his arched brow telling me that my joke landed badly, and I can't help but smirk. "Where's your outfit?" he wants to know.

"I'm in uniform today, for the tournament."

"You can change before you compete. Today is about having fun!"

He stands before the mirror, turning yet again one way, then the other, doubt beginning to cloud his features. My heart twists.

"I'm joking, brother. You look good. Like … a sun king."

"Really?" He looks at me hopefully. "Twins?"

"Twins." My hand reaches and takes his, our fingertips enmeshing for a moment. Now, I'm forgetting all about my pesky braid which would only irritate me anyway. My hair can flow free; I don't need fancy braid work to perform well.

"Did you see that storm a few weeks back just before the fireworks?" Rioyn asks.

"I remember seeing dark clouds, but didn't think anything of it because they never made their way here. They were centered over Dremaria."

"Dremaria? Thought it was Trescheria?"

"The cloud structures indicated they were more centered to the northwest with some cloud cells spidering to Trescheria. Why do you ask?"

Rioyn hesitates, then says, "Because there was a tingle in the air. I've never felt it before, but it was there again today. Didn't see any clouds, but I felt it."

Rioyn looks at me with trepidation, wondering if I'm going to dismiss what he felt.

"I didn't feel it but believe what you're saying." Rioyn perks up, lowering his shoulders from his unassuming hunched position.

We head out, winding through our neighborhood and up to the center of Circle Park. Most of the festival goers wear bold outfits.

I sneak a glance at Rioyn, who seems pleased to be the brightest of them all.

Every pathway entrance leading to Circle Park has a different musician or band playing. You can't move anywhere in the center of Casstell without being serenaded by music. People dance in the park without a care in the world.

Our boots crunch the tiny rocks on the gravel pathway leading to the center, the sun again bright overhead. We meander down the pathway.

In the center of Casstell sits a single home surrounded by a plethora of businesses operating within the confines of Circle Park. The abode was once Warriem and Everia's, over four centuries ago, the first house ever built in Seivan.

But it isn't a regular house; this one has been constructed out of an ironwood tree of a reddish hue that's turned violet over the years.

Rioyn and I stand in front of the old timber door. I've always wondered what their lives were like all those centuries ago. Their home is now a cherished part of our history, but never open to the public. The bronzeore cast plaque to the right of the door reads:

HOME OF WARRIEM AND EVERIA RYER:
CONSTRUCTED IN YEAR 2

"I wish I could go inside one day," I huff, reaching for the elaborate door handle. It begins to rattle when Rioyn grabs my arm.

"Maybe one day."

He guides me to the vendors selling a variety of treats, books, handmade items from various provinces, musical instruments and accents to complement the various orders of the university. There's something here for everyone. Well, almost everyone.

I think back to the conversation on which I'd eavesdropped between two women the night prior. It's true that things have become more expensive in recent years.

It has a negligible effect on a family like ours, but there must be many others who can no longer afford to spoil themselves over the festival.

Children clamor around a group of people spinning sugar into a light and airy treat that looks like a cloud.

Farther along, a small crowd has gathered around a tall, slender woman with bright red eyes. She dances in an elaborate silk dress, her hair braided into a crown.

An amber light radiates around her and she snaps her fingers, a cloud of sparks flickering and snapping through the air.

Children and adults alike watch in awe, the bright sparks floating before them.

"Wow, her Ascendance is incredible. The way the sparks flitter through the air like sparkle bugs. It's beautiful."

"It's rudimentary." Rioyn dismisses her performance.

"She's able to channel and perform for people. I'd just love to have her control."

Rioyn rolls his eyes through his huff. "Just practice. You're infinitely more gifted than she is. Perform all the parlor tricks you want; become a festival act if that's your wish."

I punch him in the arm, knowing he'll never know what it's like to feel invisible at times. He's always the center of attention.

We continue past the woman, coming upon a word peddler.

"Dreams are not only to be found in Dremaria. Do you believe me? You should! You can dream here in Grynndyre. In Windalai. In Aquaria. Why should dreams only be for Dremaria? Because they have a hold on your minds. Free your minds, free your souls. Dream your dream. Not theirs."

I glance at Rioyn who's just as perplexed as I am. We weave through the crowd to see more of what the word peddler speaks of.

"When you control your dreams, you control your life. Get your dreams back today. Follow me to Dremaria and I will show you a path to capture your mind, capture your heart and allow you to re-capture your soul."

I study the crowd, wondering, what do other people think of this most peculiar speech? Is it supposed to mean something? Or do people just persuade themselves that it does to avoid looking foolish for not comprehending?

On the opposite side stands one of our neighbors living a few doors down. I poke Rioyn, pointing to Ms. Croush who stands listening with rapt attention. Well, she looks just as perplexed by the peddler's bizarre oratory, and she finally moves on.

We continue walking, passing yet another neighbor, walking with his daughter. "Well, Miss Ayva and Master Rioyn. How are my favorite twins of Casstell?"

"Fine today, thank you," I answer politely. "Are you enjoying the festival?"

"Oh, it's swell, my dear. Will you both be competing in the tournaments?"

"I will," I say, at the exact same time as Rioyn.

My brows nearly kiss my hairline, gasping at my brother's bold admission.

"We'll certainly be rooting for you both. Happy festival."

"Happy festival," I say with haste.

They continue walking but before I get a chance to interrogate Rioyn, we hear his daughter say, "If they're twins, then why does he have red hair and hers is blonde? Dirty, dull blonde no less. Red hair is the rarest of them all in Seivan. Almost no one has it."

"A mystery for another day, my dear," our neighbor politely says as I'm sure he knows we're still within earshot.

I launch my furious curiosity at Rioyn.

His hands immediately fly up in deference. He knows I'm ready to pounce.

"What do you mean you're competing? I thought our father made his decision two weeks ago. He said you could join the Order of Soldiers, but you couldn't compete."

"I know what it means and what you're thinking, and I'll explain everything after tomorrow. Promise."

"Why do you always do everything in direct defiance of our father? I can't imagine how you managed to enter yourself into the Tournament of

Spar without his permission, but you have to know this will not end well for you."

My pleading voice doesn't penetrate his hardened mind.

"I had to do what was best for my future. Our father is holding me back because of Bair and that's not fair."

"He's holding you back for good reason. Why can't you see that?"

He lurches back, dropping my arm as if I just said something heinous.

"You agree with him?" he asks.

"Of course I do!" I shake my head. "How can you join the military if you refuse to take orders?"

"Orders from our father. They're not really orders, are they? Not the same."

"Orders from anyone! You … you just don't like being told what to do!" How can he be so dense? "And need I remind you our father also happens to be the commander of this place? The very man you'll one day serve!"

He pauses, taking a deep breath. I believe the greatest enemy my brother faces is himself. I can't even imagine how it must be, constantly immersed in warring thoughts.

"Twins. Please don't say anything. I will handle this. I promise."

I sigh. He's invoked our sacred promise, so now I have to keep his secret, no matter what. I'm so furious with him right now, but it's his mess, his secret to bear.

Gently taking his hand, I nod.

"I hope you're making the right decision," I say, my voice cracking.

We stare into each other's eyes, searching for answers.

"Hey, Ayva!" Of all the people to interrupt a moment, it has to be Xylar. He wraps his arm around Rioyn's neck, flashing a big toothy grin. Rioyn elbows him in his ribs.

When I swivel to catch my breath, I'm swallowing my emotions, sure his other friends aren't far behind, including Jax. The last thing I need is everyone piling onto my brother, assuming they don't already know what he's done.

"Ready for a week's end of fun."

Xylar pretends they're in the sparring arena, trading air punches.

"I for one could use a good week's end of fun before our studies begin," Mikel says, standing upright in his stout frame.

"You wouldn't know what to do with fun if it fell before your feet," Xylar jabs.

"I'm sure fun falls at your feet often, Xylar," Mikel says. "Dead and mangled."

Their odd banter is a reprieve from the tense standoff Rioyn and I just had. I study my brother and can't help but wonder what's gotten into him that he is so bold to defy our father. I'm sure he has his reasons but are they justified?

"What are these stupid bracelets we've been told to wear?" Xylar blurts.

"They have something to do with the activities," I share, unsure what they mean as well, twirling mine around my wrist. The bangle is hammered metal, dyed green for Grynndyre. I glance at Xylar's. His is red for Roccali but isn't made of metal, only of simple twined rope. There are more red bracelets as a group of Roccalians walks by.

Some bracelets are like Xylar's, made of thick rope while others are barely a strand.

Are there different classifications within each bracelet as well?

"Help me, Orro. How is it that you were able to convince your father to allow you to enroll this year? From what my father says, he's not a man who changes his mind, ever."

Xylar's father is a head of rank in the Combat Division within Roccali Legion, which means his father is extremely familiar with ours.

I arch a brow at Rioyn, but my attention is pleasantly diverted upon spotting Jax in the distance. The boys' banter turns into a muffled background drone as the sun above Jax's head lights his confident step. He runs his hand through his wild hair, eyes softening as they meet mine. It's almost as if he's floating toward us, toward me and—

"Finally decided to join us!" Xylar opens his arms wide.

Jax clasps hands with Xylar and they wrap their other arms around each other's backs. Jax's stance is rigid. Mikel does the same but in a less aggressive way.

"Have you been working out? Your muscles are nice … Big. Strong, I mean." Mikel blushes as his word jumble, focusing hard on a nearby flower.

Jax and Rioyn seem to avoid acknowledging each other altogether. Does Jax know what Rioyn did? I wonder through slit eyes. Of course he does.

Eventually, they engage in a quick embrace as if to avoid raising suspicion.

Jax is quick to break contact with Rioyn, turning to me. His smile melts through the tension in my chest, but before any of us speaks, loud horns sound in the distance.

Everyone turns their focus to the center of Circle Park. Emmil emerges from the crowd with our father at his side and stands atop a large platform.

While admiring our father, I can't help but catch the fury in his eyes, directed at Rioyn. Does he know? Rioyn stands unwavering, regardless.

"Ladies and gentlemen, welcome to the annual Festival of Seivan. In celebration of this momentous occasion, our dessert vendors will be providing treats for all of you to enjoy, regardless of your coins."

A small cheer rises from the crowd, but many remain noticeably quiet.

"Everyone has received a band coordinated to their province. In addition to the scrumptious desserts available to you, you will find other activities and gatherings specific to your colored band. This year's festival is sure to be remembered through the ages."

Remembered indeed.

More cheers erupt from the crowd. Some have placed their hands on their hearts as a sign of great gratitude, one of the highest honors a citizen can bestow.

But amidst the happy people are many whose arms remain loose and limp at their sides, and others who seem to only feign gratitude with a sort of strained contempt.

"In an hour's time, the Tournaments of the Orders will commence. First up is the Tournament of Galilei in the northeast Galilei quadrant, followed by the Tournament of Archivants and then finally, though of course, no less exciting, the Tournament of Healers. Tomorrow, we will have the Tournament of Voyants and to finish off the festival, we will have the grand tournament everyone has been waiting for, the Tournament of Spar."

At this, the crowd hollers with more genuine, animated applause.

I glance at Rioyn, Jax, Xylar and Mikel as they clap with the crowd, but I'm not convinced they buy into Emmil's unexpected generosity either.

"He's quick to try and buy favor," Xylar scoffs, always ready to cast the first aspersion.

"I wonder what the activities are that he mentioned and why we're required to wear these colored bands," Jax adds.

"It's a nice gesture," Mikel offers.

Rioyn's gaze is elsewhere as Jax moves by my side. "Are you ready to win the Tournament of Galilei today?" His excited smile calms my nerves.

"Of course, she is," Xylar pipes up. "She'll win in no time. Everyone knows it, too." I can't help but smile a little brighter. Xylar's not one for heartfelt compliments but he's always been nice to me.

"May I walk you to the quadrant?" Jax asks.

I glance at Rioyn to see if he's going to interject or let us be.

He looks at me but is quick to turn his focus to Jax, giving him a flexed jaw nod. Then he turns, headed in the opposite direction.

Jax takes my hand in his, interlacing his fingers. He looks down at me, beaming a bright smile through those beautiful crystal blue eyes.

His thumb caresses the inside of my palm, sending a frisson of shivers up my spine.

Perhaps winning is not the only pleasure in life. The thought bolsters me, even as I quickly think that I will win—at all costs. Jax will be a support, not a distraction.

We walk, laughing together through the crowd.

C H A P T E R   1 3

THE VOYANTS' QUADRANT

RIOYN

I'M RELIEVED JAX IS distracted with Ayva and she with him, so I don't have to bear the weight of their judgments. There isn't much time before the start of Ayva's tournament.

I hustle to the northwest quadrant where the cadets—who will be competing tomorrow in the Tournament of Voyants—meet to rehearse their stories of voyage before presenting them to the judges.

"Aye, Rioyn Orro!" I stop, whirling on my heels to peer through the crowd, finding a lonely vendor waving me over to his movable cart. Curious, I weave through the festival goers to see why someone I don't recognize is summoning me.

"Good afternoon, sir. Do I know you?"

"Not that I recall. I wanted to wish you well on the journey that awaits you."

"Do you mean the Tournament of Spar tomorrow?

"Your journey is one of foremost importance. Forsake it not. Embark on it with a noble heart, for it will determine a future intertwining us all."

Gazing into the bright blue eyes of the vendor, beads of sweat are collecting on his golden skin. My mouth hangs open, struggling to find my words.

"What journey do you speak of?"

"A journey of humility and generosity. Happy festival, Rioyn Orro, master of warriors."

The blueish … maybe purple-eyed vendor skirts through the crowd with his wobbly cart, disappearing.

Without much thought of who it was and what that vendor had to say, I turn, light on my feet, sprinting to the Voyants' Quadrant. There's no time to spare and dwell on unimportant thoughts. I sprint, stealing glances of the crowd, hoping no one else recognizes me.

I've been trying to infiltrate this quadrant for the last two years, the order to which my brother Bair once belonged as if walking amidst his people somehow brings me closer to him, even if just for a moment. A moment is all I need, then I sharpen my focus, getting ever closer to this super-secret order.

Behind a large flower sculpture is the perfect place to hide my ridiculous bright yellow outfit, not the best choice for today. I need to find a voyant cloak if I have any shot at hiding among them and to get close enough to hear their stories. I scour each voyant, looking for any exploitable weakness to win a cloak from one of them.

Just as I'm about to give up hope, I spot an unsuspecting cadet off in the corner.

His back is turned as he engages with festival goers who do a wonderful job in aiding me with a distraction. Stealthily, I move from the vibrant flower sculpture to hide among the soft shadows billowing from the trees above. I approach the cadet's bag, carefully reaching my hand out to yank the cloak from his knapsack.

The festival goers continue their mind-numbing questions about the Order of Voyants.

This cadet is doing a wonderful job of dodging them.

My arm reaching over the small rock wall, I grab hold of the cloak when the unsuspecting cadet turns to grab his water canteen.

Adrenaline surges through my veins, holding expertly still. The cadet drinks several large quenching gulps, then returns his water canteen to his knapsack's side.

As soon as the cadet resumes his conversation with the festival goers, I rip the cloak from his knapsack, whip it over my shoulders and weave through the crowd to the northwest corner of the voyants' circle.

The main collective area is the southeast side. However, I figure this side will give me the best advantage to sneak in, avoiding all questioning eyes.

Right before I cross the boundary into the Voyants' Quadrant, I pull the hood of the cloak over my head, covering my eyes. Keeping my head down, I look for the others who use their cloaks as a hiding device as well. I must remember to blend in and stay out of the limelight, needing to hear their stories, convincing one of them that I am a trusted voyant.

A task easier said than done.

As usual, the quadrant overflows with cadets from the order, their faces aglow with excitement. But the groups stand huddled, locked in tense conversation.

Bair isn't the only voyant to have disappeared in recent times.

No doubt as the community comes together for the festival, the rumors and theories run rife. I need to get closer to those people.

The corner of my eye glimpses the silver streak of the lonely vendor from earlier, my eyes needling through the crowd to find him in this haystack.

"Your journey is one of foremost importance. Forsake it not."

I am accustomed to strangers reminding me of the importance of my family, and of our responsibility as leaders. But the vendor's words seemed to carry a greater weight, as if he knew something important, but secret.

Up ahead, an effervescent voice calls for everyone's attention. I squeeze my way to the front of the crowd as a gangly woman leaps on top of a bench.

"I'll happily spend many days exploring and adventuring any forest except the ones south of the White Fog. I, along with all of you, would be a fool to cross the White Fog and meet the judgment of the Sancaros. Even if I made it through the White Fog alive—and sane—I'd never dare to share a whispered breath with the Carisan Forest, turned evil by the Fayrilynds' cruel enchantment which sucks you deep into its forest's depths.

"Fayrilynds are said to leach their evil from the land, giving them their strength.

"So it is written in a brand-new passage recently appearing in The Book of Legends, a book I dare not question. No one will dare venture into its depths, saving those we've lost for their perils are lost to the forest forever."

"Cowards we are! No place is too dangerous for voyants. No area within Seivan will keep us away from our sworn oath to chart this land," a firecracker of a woman scorns.

"Maybe that is where our fellow voyants disappeared to?" one brave voyant shouts. An awkward hush befalls the Order of Voyants, eyes darting one to the other.

Does someone know something? Will they come forward?

Finally, I might be one step closer to finding an answer to where Bair is. I whip my head back to the gangly woman. She takes a dramatic pause to enjoy a sip of her lavandee, a bitter tea mixed with sweetened lavender tips. She wipes the drip from her bottom lip then takes her bow. My luck was too good to be true. I'll have to find another way.

I back out of the crowd, lingering on the outskirts looking for someone, anyone who might be loose-lipped. I haven't had much luck in the past but maybe I will today.

My focused eyes scope for the weak when whispers resonate behind.

I slink to the side, then slip behind a chubby cadet captivating his friends.

"I traveled through Roccali where I was ambushed by several soldiers of the anti-Iyanndyre regime, the Camarelians. Luckily, I was alerted to their presence by fellow Roccalians, able to flee down Camarelhead to the Jesper Ocean coast. It was the scariest encounter I've ever had as a voyant, but every bit worth the risk once I was able to behold the towering glory of the Iyanndyre."

Leaning in closer, I can't believe what I'm hearing, anger searing its path through my fiery veins. But I must be sure this isn't just a coincidence.

"I stood there for hours just marveling at the Iyanndyre's magnificence from a distance of no less than a mile by order of the Grynndyre Command and the Iyanndyre itself. Even from the distance at which I stood, the magnetism of the Iyanndyre was pushing me away.

"A surge of electricity ignited my body. It was a glorious sight, one to forever cherish."

"Liar! Story thief!" I shout. The chubby cadet and his audience turn their heads to face me, my finger jabbing in the cadet's chest, anger seething. "That is not your story."

The chubby cadet takes a quaking step toward me. "Do you dare question your fellow voyant? Voyants do not lie and lying I am not."

I shed the hood of my cloak, standing tall, revealing my identity. The chubby cadet along with his friends take a large step back, letting the spotlight shine on me. Their attention isn't why I came here, but I'll allow no one to steal from my brother.

"That is my brother's story. He traveled through Camarelhead and fought off the Camarelians. He didn't run from them but no doubt if you were faced with the same fate, then you would still be their prisoner."

"You have no business being here."

"What happened to my brother?" I demand.

"We do not speak of voyant matters with order outsiders. It is against our code of honor."

"Then you have no business stealing my brother's story. You have no honor."

I push toward the chubby cadet, his eyes wide.

Before I reach him, a thick, strong hand stops me in my tracks.

"Why Rioyn Orro. Brother of Voyant Bair Orro and son of High Ascendant Orro and General Orro. You're quite the legend in the making." I stand before the new High Voyant, Lair Yourn, who replaced Jax's mother when she disappeared.

Bair spoke highly of him when he was his commander. He has to know something.

"You knew my brother well. Please tell me what you know."

Lair doesn't break eye contact with me as rumbles from the crowd begin to echo in ripples. He raises his hand for silence, and once the crowd hushes, he escorts me to a restricted area of the Voyants' Quadrant.

"I knew someone had to have informa—"

My sentence dies at Lair's raised hand.

"Young Orro, you, more so than anyone else, knows that I will not nor am I able to divulge any information regarding any voyant. Family or not."

Red fury conquers my otherwise calm demeanor. "Please. If you have information that could help save my brother, you have to tell me."

Lair shakes his head, backing away when my name echoes through the crowd like a roar of thunder. I freeze as it comes again, crackling through the throng, splitting it down the middle as people begin stepping aside.

I slowly turn, discovering Father standing at the crowd's edge, Mother at his side. My throat bobs, my head falling to the path in front of me as I walk toward my parents.

My father's large strong hand grabs the back of my neck. "Why are you in the Voyants' Quadrant instead of with your sister?"

"I … you know why."

I glance his way, catching the white-hot anger in his eyes.

His grip around the back of my neck tightens, clasping me close to him as we walk through the crowd to the Galilei quadrant. As I glance back, there is Mother, her gaze focused on the gravel in front of her. My jaw clenches.

From the look in his eyes, it's evident that Father has reached the limit of his tolerance with me. Through his feigned smile to keep up appearances, he whispers, "Did you really think I wouldn't find out?"

His vise grip tightens around my neck, and I resist the urge to pull away even though his nails threaten to pierce my skin. I refuse to give him the satisfaction. When we escape the crowd, he stops dead in his tracks, releasing his grip. I turn to face him.

"You went behind my back, intentionally defying my orders."

His clipped tone commands every hair on my body to stand at attention.

I steal a deep inhale in the face of two choices. Own up to what I did and stand firm against my father or grovel for his mercy. I choose my words carefully.

"It's my life, my future. For that, I answer to no one."

My father leans back in shock, hearing me stand firm. "Is that what you think? You think this is about you?"

"What else could it possibly be about?"

"Look around." We stop. My eyes don't move from his. "I said look around."

His eyes direct mine to look at the people before us.

"Every single citizen in this realm depends on us. That is the true nature of leadership. You winning some title will not keep them safe. Satisfying your ego will not guide them to a better future. You may enjoy the indulgences of childhood, or the freedom and liberty of manhood, but you cannot demand both."

My head lowers, my jaw clenching shut. It's the only thing I can do to stop the tears of anger from flooding through me, admitting he's right again.

"Do I make myself clear?"

"Yes, sir." I yank my arm from his grasp.

My mother and father continue walking through the crowd, leaving me to trail behind, my head hiding behind his large stature. Mother glances at me out of the side of her eye but the damage I've done has ignited a rare anger in her. Who can blame her?

We've arrived at the Galilei quadrant where Ayva is set to compete in the Tournament of Galilei for FirstElite. I move to the back of the crowd away from Mother and Father. Away from everyone. I'd rather run, fleeing this town until this festival is over, but I will never abandon Ayva, no matter what issues I've crafted for myself.

The cadets take the stage. Ayva appears, waving heartily. Then, I see the question on her face. "Why are you standing way back there?"

My shoulders shrug just as the announcer lunges on stage to begin his speech.

I glance over my shoulder, seeing that the wretched storm about which I warned Ayva earlier, the one I predicted, is here. My gaze lowers from the ominously dark storm clouds lingering above to find teenagers destroying buildings in the distance.

Rushing over, my mind assesses the disturbing, out-of-place behavior.

Now I am running, running to stop children from throwing stones through the windows. Something catches in the corner of my eye, making me glance over at the Bryar Bridge as a young woman sprints across it. Blood drips down her face and arms.

She's dressed in blue Trescherian Defense-issued armor.

I sprint toward the woman. Reaching her as she collapses in my arms.

I sweep her jet-black hair caked in blood from her face.

My eyes dart wide, mouth dropping at the feeling of holding Falla Kai so close.

CHAPTER 14

THE STARLESS ARMY

AYVA

THE WIND JOSTLES MY hair, dancing in my face. I hold the restless hair back, sneaking a glance at the competition clock. An hour still remains. My focus locks onto my quiz. Only a few questions remain. Focus, Ayva. Focus!

Minutes melt by and finally, I finish, already aware of being the first but my better judgment glances around the competitors' table just to be sure. Leaping from my seat, I'm racing to ring the champions' bell when my accomplished and prideful gaze is broken.

Rioyn runs toward a woman caked in blood.

Did she injure herself somehow?

My mouth plummets to realize who he's running toward. It's Falla Kai.

Without conscious thought, my legs run to leap off the stage when someone cries out, "Congratulations, Ayva! You did it."

"We knew you were the champion!"

"You're an inspiration!"

My dumbfounded, indulgent gaze glances down to the crowd, searching for the people praising my accomplishment. Mother and Father break through, waving with pride.

Jax is in the front row, beaming with a supportive smile.

His presence—and that he's here to support me—brings a flush across my face. He supports me! Yet my heart-racing indulgence is quickly fractured, severely dark clouds colliding overhead. A storm has been brewing but these clouds don't seem to be any form I've ever studied. Black and gray, they swirl and roil into the eye of its center at a breakneck speed, my gaze whipping back to the crowd. Everyone's stares are captivated when a massive bolt of lightning crescendos from the eye of the storm.

Without hesitation, I leap from the stage, automatically running for my parents, a strong arm wrapping around my waist. Jax.

He is holding me close, refusing to release me from his tense grip. My father grabs Mother's hand, and together, they chance the fury of the lightning strikes as they scatter down from the clouds above us. With me tucked in tight to him, Jax follows my parents through the panicked crowd. My heart misses a beat. Where is Rioyn?

Citizens run for shelter as the lightning bolts relentlessly ripple across the ground.

Fire singes through the sky as if the clouds themselves are breathing fire.

Flames engulf the ancient trees lining Circle Park, amber flares quickly jump from tree to tree, lighting the entire pathway of the spindly canopy ablaze.

We reach my parents away from the crowds' frantic chaos, Father shielding Mother beneath his cloak, keeping her safe from the falling debris and burning embers.

"Take your mother and go home until you hear from me."

"What's happening? This isn't a typical storm!" Mother bellows, fear in her tone, something so new to me. Jax keeps his tight grip on my hand as if intent on breaking it.

"I don't know what this is. I'm going to Grynndyre Command. We'll figure out what's going on, and I'll sayer a message as soon as I know."

"I'll come with you." Jax stands tall, waiting for Father to size up his abilities to fight beside him.

"No. Get my wife and daughter to safety. That's an order, cadet."

"Yes, sir."

My father kisses Mother quickly, but with the intensity of a man who takes nothing for granted. All the while, like worker bees frantically seeking their queen, people race around us, cries of panic and fear drowning out the crackling of thunder and lightning overhead.

Jax interlaces his steady fingers with my trembling hand, yanking me forward. He's quick to dodge the panicked citizens. My mother keeps pace at my other side.

We race through the burning Circle Park, our shirts covering our mouths to breathe through the thick, billowing smoke. Where is Rioyn?

I fail to see him through the crowd, even in his bright yellow garb.

We reach the main street that will take us home when lightning explodes down in front of us, sending us flying onto our backs.

Jax hoists me up. I search for Mother. She landed a few feet ahead of us, lying perfectly still, spreadeagled in the middle of the street. "Ma. Ma! Get up!" I shake her but she doesn't move. In one swift action, Jax picks her up, carrying her in his arms.

"Stay close," he commands. We run the remaining few blocks back to my house. Looking out over the distance behind us, the dark clouds have traveled from north to south, covering all of Casstell and the city's outskirts.

I race up our front stoop, charging through our wooden door to enter the darkened home. Jax is right behind me when I race to turn on the lights.

"Until we know what this is, lock the windows and close the curtains," Jax instructs. I rush to follow Jax's instructions as he gently lays Mother down on the couch, propping her head up on a soft pillow. Her eyes open slightly, looking slightly dazed.

"It's okay, Ma. We're home now." She grabs my hand, forcing herself to sit up.

"Where's your bro—" Her question is interrupted when the front door flies open.

RIOYN

I HOLD FALLA IN MY arms and for a split second among this hellish chaos, I'm lost in the surreal, dreamlike quality of the moment. She's here, in my arms. A deafening thunder rumbles above as lightning floods the darkened sky, striking fires right across the city.

Falla's hand brushes my neck as she groans for us to keep moving. I stand her up, taking her arm around my shoulder, being as gentle with her as I can.

We move to find shelter away from the screams and frantic crowd.

"Out of nowhere, they attacked," she says as if I don't know it already.

Anyone watching the storm can see it is enchanted, but hearing her confirmation that we are under attack is chilling. Fires erupt in the skies through the lightning.

Is the lightning on fire or vice versa?

"What about the sayer alarms?"

Falla confirms, "They didn't work."

I prop Falla against a wall, seeking to wipe the blood and tears from her face with my ridiculous yellow silk handkerchief.

"They're all dead," she cries, her tiny voice so plaintive, so beaten.

In the twelve years I have known Falla, I've never, ever seen her cry. Never heard it either, and it's visceral, reaching my soul.

Everything inside me twists. "Who? The border guards?"

A sob wrenches from deep within her, and at once, the truth is apparent.

Her family.

My tears instantly match Falla's and her immense heartache. Her family was one of honor, every member enlisted in the Trescherian Defense, each one highly respected.

Anger fuels my body.

"Ma, Pa … Slaughtered right in front of me. No justice. Not an ounce of mercy or remorse. They were just … They were ripped away. They were—"

The more she speaks, the more the tears cascade until I can't stand it.

"Falla, who did this?" My rage is ready to rip the ones responsible apart. Our people haven't needed to face such evil or such fire power, not for eons.

"Shivane and Sylon. They're coming for us all."

Foreign soldiers cross the Bryar Bridge in droves, their black uniforms instantly setting them apart from our own forces. But what's more disturbing is their eyes—or more specifically, lack of them. Even from a distance, I can see that where each eye should be, there's nothing but a lacquered black void.

I hoist Falla up under her arm, pushing her to forge ahead.

Like this, we weave through the panicked crowd, dodging lightning strikes and attacks from battles that have broken out all over the city.

Falla and I stumble over bodies strewn across the streets and through gutters running red with blood. I've never seen such carnage and destruction.

Falla yanks her hand from my shoulder, my gaze whipping to her.

"I can manage. We need to find the generals."

"We need to clean you up, find somewhere safe to shelter. We should go to my house."

I pick up my pace, tugging Falla along behind me before she can argue—because argue she will. We round the corner to my street, stopping dead in our tracks.

"Halt!"

Hanri and his friends, Cartus and Niklon, are arranged there in a line, blocking the entrance to my house. But as much as they might be whole in body and uniform, the creatures standing before us are not the boys we know. We retreat a few steps.

With shock filling my veins, I stare into Hanri's black lacquered eyes, seeing two swirling pools of hate.

"Hanri, it's me, Rioyn. We can help you."

"You will bow to your new lords. Surrender now," Hanri cackles.

"Hanri! This isn't you. Don't do this."

My words fall on deaf ears as Hanri and his friends push toward us.

We have no choice but to fight. As Falla and I brace for the imminent attack, Hanri and his friends stand up straight, their stares rising over our heads. They march back toward Circle Park, joining others with the same lacquered black eyes heading in that direction.

I launch up the front stoop, then barrel into my house, hoping my family is inside. Jax kneels at Mother's side with Ayva, who rushes to us.

I meet her embrace, and Falla whips the door shut behind us, bolting the lock.

Ayva pulls away from me, aghast at Falla's injuries.

"What happened?"

Falla crumbles into Ayva's arms, something else I've never seen Falla do with anyone. In halting, broken sentences, she tells them what she has already told me. Upon hearing the names Shivane and Sylon, Mother's face pales further.

"Come upstairs. I'll dress your wounds." Ayva helps Falla up the stairs where they disappear down the dark hallway. I bend at Mother's side.

"Where's Dad?"

"At command. You two need to take your sister and Falla. The four of you need to leave town, now."

Jax turns to fully face my mother.

"I'm sorry, Mrs. Orro but our friends Mikel and Xylar are still out there. I need to find them and our commanders. We need to help defend the city."

My mother can see that it's no use trying to change his mind. Instead, she instructs Jax to go into our father's study and arm himself before leaving. She implores me to stay and defend the house, and though I'm filled with shame not to be joining Jax on the streets, I agree. I can't leave my mom, Ayva and an injured Falla alone.

I hug Jax before he goes. "Come back when you've found them," I tell him.

He promises me he will, then he's gone.

My mother groans as she sits up. "You, your sister and Falla need to leave town. There's no time to waste. They'll be here soon."

"Who will be here?" My wide eyes are searching Mother's for an answer.

"Shivane and Sylon." Her voice is grave.

"I'm not afraid of them. And besides, you are one of the greatest Ascendents we have. Let them come."

"No. You're but a child, Rioyn. For once in your life, you'll obey the orders you're given. These are not just two generals turned evil. They're much, much more than that."

My head shakes. The Orros are a powerful family, but she acts as if we are cowards who must flee at the first sign of trouble.

My whole life, I've been raised to be a fighter. Now I'm meant to run?

It's at that moment the front door slams open.

A gust of wind thrashes in through the foyer, bringing leaves and debris with it.

I hope to see my father, but instead, black-clouded wind billows inside, whistling shrieking wails of screaming, fetching death trails.

Shivane and Sylon take their death-snarled shape from their menacing black smoke tendrils. They're dressed in long black crystal cloaks. Shivane's sharp shoulder spikes soar upward, toward the thorny crown upon her head. Her hands drift freely from her cloak with long, razor-sharp black nails that look ready to claw our hearts out.

Sylon's cloak floats with the black air swirling around him.

Two black-stained swords hang at his sides. Their hoods shroud their faces, but death glows from within those deep purple eyes.

Sylon raises his arm, a long, thick scar branding his forearm. He holds out a single glass rod with a glowing molten orange substance running along its length.

My mother's gaze is focused on Shivane's, Mother's Ascendance being one of the mind. So now, she appears to be communicating with Shivane mind to mind.

I must know what they're saying.

I focus my energy, my Ascendance, to try and intercept the thoughts they lob back and forth. Powerful enough shadow Ascendants are sometimes able to intercept mental Ascendances. I can do this. Focus Rioyn. Focus!

"Leave now, and you might just live."

"Your threats are idle, High Ascendant Orro. We will leave once we have taken that which we seek."

The connection is severed when my mind is suddenly filled with a violent screech. My eyes clear to reveal a black crystal encrusted collar, locked around Mother's neck. Her eyes dim, her thoughts ceasing. Anger floods into my already searing veins.

I focus my anger toward Sylon, hoping to control my Ascendance enough to deliver a fatal strike. He sees the gray smoke of my Ascendance rising.

Before I release my wildly untrained Ascendance, his shadow Ascendance launches me into the unforgiving stone wall with a mere flick of his wrist.

I crumple to the ground, my burning eyes fighting to stay open. Sylon grabs hold of Mother, dragging her roughly from the house.

Shivane sashays over.

I struggle to prop myself up on my elbows. She bends down, searching for something in my eyes. "What do you want?" I whisper through a rasped voice.

"We want it all and we're here to take it." She raises her closed fist, the dark void of her purple eyes fixing on me as she opens it up, blowing black crystal dust in my face.

The room shifts suddenly, the world seemingly tilted on its axis.

"Welcome to the Starless Army, my darling," is the last thing I hear, my world sheering to black.

CHAPTER 15

GRYNNDYRE COMMAND

AYVA

I REMOVE FALLA'S ARMOR, BEGINNING to tend to her many cuts and bruises. She has lacerations on her neck, bruising all over her face as if she has fought a week-long battle.

She winces at my touch but doesn't stop me. So much pain oozes from her distant stare. How did they rip through the purportedly impenetrable fibers of her Trescherian Defense armor?

I take dried herbs from a series of bottles kept in my dresser, crushing them together with pestle and mortar. Upon adding a special serum, the leaves turn to a paste, which I apply slowly and carefully to each of Falla's deepest cuts.

By the time I am done, she has slumped onto her side, asleep. I don't dare wake her. She needs the rest, her awful journey here is written all over her body.

I finish bandaging her, laying a warm, soft blanket over her.

As I finish cleaning up the bloody clothes, a commotion rumbles from downstairs.

I move quietly down the hallway to listen, curling my head over the banister.

Downstairs, a tall, lanky figure dressed in a black cloak saunters down the hallway. Another person, dressed in all black but with a much larger, stronger frame, stands watching. The next thing, Rioyn is flying through the air, hitting the stone wall with a bone-cracking thump.

They drag Mother out of the house, a black collar around her neck.

No!

I feel myself lunging forward to race down the staircase when a hand wraps itself around my mouth and torso.

Falla whips me around to face her with a dire look in her eyes. She shakes her head and keeps her hand clamped over my mouth. Quiet, she mouths. But panic has me in its grip.

Falla folds me into her chest as I try to wrestle from her grasp, but she only pulls me tighter and even though she's injured, it's impossible to overcome her strength.

The intruders disappear from our house. Falla holds me a moment longer, then releases me. We race downstairs, finding Rioyn slouched against the wall, passed out.

Falla crouches down beside him. "Help me move him to the couch."

We tuck Rioyn's shoulders under our arms, hoisting him.

He's a lump of dead weight. I do my best to carry him, but my physical strength is almost non-existent compared to Falla's.

We lay him down on the couch and I grab a wet rag, dabbing at the cut on the side of his forehead. A sparkling black dust crusts the gash.

I dab at it, but the dark dust refuses to come off. Sweat beads form along his hairline.

I study Rioyn as he sleeps, his eyes fluttering under his eyelids. I lean in closer when his eyes fly open, solid black but quickly turning back to their normal hazel as if a smoke has just cleared from them. Then all of a sudden, the front door flies open.

Falla draws her short blade from by her side.

"Whoa! We're friendly!" Xylar shouts.

Falla sheaths her blade, rushing over to them.

They clasp hands and embrace. Mikel gives her a hug followed by Jax.

"I'm glad you are all okay." Falla exhales a sigh of relief.

"What happened to Rioyn and where's Mrs. Orro?" Jax presses.

"Shivane and Sylon were here. They're the ones behind this. They took Mrs. Orro," Falla explains as everyone's mouth drops with shock.

"We have to go after them," Jax proclaims.

"We have no way of knowing where they are. We must regroup and figure this out."

"What happened to you?" Mikel inquires, studying her bandages.

"Trescheria has been destroyed. A massive storm hit. The next thing we knew, an army with lacquered black eyes pillaged through the Pools of Pearl, capturing, killing and converting everyone into what Shivane calls her Starless Army."

Jax's crystal blue eyes go wide. He hugs her again, this time tighter.

Falla fights back her tears, though a single one smears the blood caked on her face.

"Is there anything left of our province?" Jax inquires.

Falla shakes her head. "Monnaire and Arro came to our rescue, and we all fought valiantly, but we were no match for the Starless Army. Their strength was … something more than human. I was held down by fellow Trescherians, neighbors entranced into the army as Shivane and Sylon slaughtered my family in battle."

Falla chokes on her words.

Xylar reaches out a comforting hand and rests it on her shoulder. Falla takes a deep breath. "I ran to Monnaire and Arro to fight with them, but they were captured. Black metal collars were slammed around their necks. They took Arro right away."

"They captured the mighty Arro? The man who is invincible and can save us all?" Mikel's mouth hangs open as does everyone else's.

"What about Monnaire? There's no way they were able to capture her as well. She and Arro are the two most powerful people in all of Seivan," I'm quick to add.

"She told me to flee to Casstell and sound the alarms, so I ran as fast as I could, escaping every member of that disgraceful army. I looked back just as she and the dragolyons were fleeing to the skies."

"She got away? That's great! We have to find her," I shout with a shred of hope.

"Those collars seemed to have rendered them powerless. Both tried to use their Ascendance, but neither could."

"They put the same one on our mother." Heads whip around to find a groggy Rioyn getting up from his injury. "I could see the Ascendance drain from our mother's eyes once they slammed that metal thing around her neck."

Falla grabs Rioyn by the shoulders. She peers into his groggy eyes.

"What are you looking for?" I question her inquisition.

"His eyes are clear. He's lucky."

"What do you mean lucky?" I stammer.

"He has the black crystal dust on his cut. It's what Shivane uses to convert people to her army, but it hasn't affected Rioyn, at least not yet." I'm stunned, realizing what I saw.

Rioyn's eyes were black. How did he fight it?

"What I don't understand is how did they even made it to Trescheria without the sayer alarms being triggered?" Xylar poses the question to the group.

"They appeared through a black portal. They didn't come by way of land, air or sea," Falla explains. "They also had their own sayer devices."

We shake our heads, in awe of their apparent powers.

"So, what do we do now?" I ask.

"We need to find the generals and the rank captains," Xylar says. "They all should be at Grynndyre Command, going over protocols."

"That means our father should be there, too." I hesitate. "Are we all going?" I'm worried about the answer.

"I can stay behind." Mikel is quick to avoid any sort of battle.

"No. We all go." Jax steps forward, looking directly at me. "We stay together. We're safer that way." Terror ripples through me, but he's right. We have no other choice.

"We take the back neighborhood trail," Rioyn says softly. "It'll bring us to the backside of command. Stick to the shadows and we should make it without being seen."

We nod in quiet agreement, then sit in a heavy silence with mulling thoughts.

All week we've been celebrating our newfound adulthood and independence, but in this moment, I've never felt so young and out of my league.

I'm almost grateful for the numbing shock that has dulled my senses.

Our mother is gone. Our city has fallen. Our father is leading a defense that appears to be failing. I try to understand how much our world has changed in just a few short hours, but I can't. The truth is just too great, too terrible to hold.

CHAPTER 16

THE STARS ABOVE

RIOYN

WE SLINK OUT OF the back door one by one, through the tall grass wall separating our property from the neighbors'. We slide down the stony embankment and into a storm drain in which we used to play as kids.

As I lead my friends, my head throbs with a malicious burn and tendrils that run deep inside my skull. It's a sensation I've never known before.

Part of it I recognize as my raging desire to win, driving me to find our enemies, making them suffer for what they've done.

But it's the other part of it that worries me more.

A soothing, quiet calm whispers promises of peace, calling for me to release every ounce of hatred ever known, to lay down my weapons, accepting what's inevitable.

Accept this promised life of hatred and cruelty. These feelings have something to do with the dust Shivane blew in my face, but I refuse to let her power gain another inch over my mind. I will kill her and her entire army before that has a chance to happen.

I peer ahead to take my mind off the throbbing thoughts, catching the vibrant light glistening off Falla's face through the mist. Her presence quells the thirst of my desire to conquer all. She's lost her entire family; how can I ever begin to imagine the pain she's suffering? Yet here she is, still pressing forward to help save everyone else.

We emerge from the grimy tunnel, clambering from the oily wash.

We hide behind mounds of fresh-stacked hay, surveilling our surroundings. I snake into the smoke-filled neighborhood, leading the way.

My hand reaches Falla's shoulder, but she slips away with a grimace. Even through the chaos, her feelings remain walled off towards me. Can't say I blame her.

"The path ahead will take us to the back of the university, up to command," I whisper. "The pathway was washed out last summer from the ten-day flood, so watch where you're going, otherwise, you'll catch a hole."

I make it to the edge of the house, staking a lookout while the others cross.

Shadows favor this path, aiding us back into the center of town undetected. We find the backside of a few businesses lining Circle Park. Many of the doors have been busted in, windows broken, their insides gutted. Who knows what has become of the people inside?

At the edge of the crumbling brick building, we peer through the open scorched field, the only area between us and the entrance to Grynndyre Command. There should be soldiers in front of the building, defending the people inside.

Instead, the area is eerily quiet.

"Does anyone have an Ascendance that can provide cover?" Falla looks to each of us, then her eyes settle on me. As does everyone else, I shake my head, not daring to use my Ascendance of shadow when I'm unable to control it and use it effectively. Jax's Ascendance is the strongest but his is within the field of energy, doing us no good in this moment.

Falla peers out at the still terrain. "We go one by one."

"I'll go first, then look out." I don't wait for her to stop me, staying low to the ground, moving quickly. After a few breathless minutes, I make it to the entrance of the building, hiding behind the smoothed brick wall. I wave to the next person.

Mikel runs straight across the field as if running a race and it seems he's forgotten everything from basic training.

Xylar is quick on his heels. They both make it. Falla is next, followed by Jax shielding Ayva from any possible attack. We each cling to the shadows like glue.

"Inside. Hurry." Xylar props the door to command open, waving us in. We stay below the openings in the wall, entering a place normally closed off to anyone not enlisted in a military order. We race through the dark hallways, looking through every window.

Each room is shrouded in darkness, no sign of anyone.

We round a sharp corner, fly down a set of stairs and find the doors to the inner intelligence room. Without even thinking, I reach for the latch, flinging open the door. We flood inside, met by the angered stares of the rank captains.

Xylar is quick to dismiss them, searching through them. "Where's my father?"

"None of you is allowed in here. Who are you?" a rank captain bellows.

"I'm Combat Rank Aurn's son, sir. Where's my father?"

The room falls to silence. High Rank Tau Sheyn of the Trescherian Defense steps forward, Ixo Sheyn's father. No wonder Ixo is regarded as the best cadet to ever enter Sansyre University; his father is highly regarded, and shrewd in his trainings.

High rank is a step below the generals and oversees the rank captains of the three divisions within the branch: Battle; Operations; and Intelligence.

"No one has seen your father. He wasn't at the opening ceremony watch and he also didn't show today," High Rank Sheyn explains. I glance at Xylar to see the blood drain from his face. What does he know about his father that we don't?

"Have any of you seen my son?" High Rank Sheyn asks, looking through us one by one.

I step forward. "No, sir. We have not seen anyone from Sansyre."

"And you are?"

"Rioyn Orro, sir. General Orro's son."

Sheyn stands up straight, saluting me with his right hand straight, angled over his heart.

"Where is our father? He said he was going to command," Ayva demands.

Sheyn looks side-eye to the other rank captains.

I study each of their eye movements. What are they hiding?

"We are not at liberty to disclose the location of Grynndyre Command's general," Sheyn barks.

"He's our father! Where is he?" As I close the distance to Sheyn, arms hold me safely away. Are they worried for his safety or mine?

"Our mother was captured by Shivane and Sylon. We need to speak with our father. We need to save her. We need to reach out to him through the sayer lines."

"That's not possible, cadet. Now stand down," High Rank Sheyn commands.

Tensions flare strong. I will not back down to anyone here, not when my parents' and everyone else's lives are at stake.

"If I might respectfully interject. I'm Mikel Vakor, no relation to anyone. Order of Soldiers first year, sir." Mikel squeezes his way between us to stand before the rank captains. "How is it that we had no warning of the attacks? The sayers should've been able to alert us at the first attack on Trescheria. Even before that when Zianli left Dremaria to come here to the festival."

"How do you know of the attack on Trescheria?" High Rank Sheyn looks at each of us. "All communications are down. We haven't been able to reach anyone in any of the provinces nor have we been able to reach anyone outside of this room."

"But how is that possible? Our communications lines are supposed to be war proof," Mikel continues as Sheyn's eyes dart down to him in dismissal.

"Any information relating to our communications system is classified, first year. If you'll excuse us, we have work to do." Sheyn whips on his heels.

Falla turns on her heels, storming out, slamming open the metal door so hard that it rebounds from the wall, almost breaking free of its hinges.

Ayva and Mikel file out. I wait for Xylar to march. He doesn't move.

"Xylar. Let's go."

"I'm staying. I need to find my father." He turns to look at Sheyn, who stares him down with a slight nod.

"You're not staying. Let's go, Xylar," Jax commands. Xylar squares up to him.

"I either wait here or head to Roccali."

"That's not why you're staying. Your father didn't come yesterday, and he's not coming today either. Maybe the rumors are true about him being a betrayer. When it comes time to step up for your realm, you're nowhere to be found. Just like all those years at camp when you chose to retreat instead of fight, you'd rather hide here."

"Watch yourself, Risor," Xylar warns.

Jax and Xylar stand nose to nose. I stand at Jax's side facing him, my back to Xylar. I grab his arm to pull him back, but Jax is a stone wall.

"It's not worth it," I whisper but Jax tenses in my grip. He turns to leave with me but not before getting one last jab.

"I knew you were nothing more than a coward. Once again, you've proved me right."

Xylar shoves Jax from behind.

Fist already balled, Jax winds around and lands a punch, sending Xylar flying backwards. I stand in front of him, chest to chest. Jax pushes me off him, making me snap.

"ENOUGH!" My sequestered temper explodes through me, encapsulating both of them in a shadowed energy stopping them in their tracks.

A newfound surge charges through me, bringing a sense of strength.

The rank captains move to seize me. I release the hold, grabbing on to Jax's upper arm. We turn to sprint from the room, running to the exit of Grynndyre Command where everyone else waits. "What's gotten into you?" I whisper to Jax.

"Me? What about you?" he snaps back. I hold his stare, unwilling to let him off the hook. "Let him stay. He's more of a distraction than a help, anyway."

We reach the others as they impatiently wait for us.

"Where's Xylar?" Mikel asks.

"Not coming." Jax is quick to answer.

"What do we do now?" Ayva inquires, fear catching in her voice.

"Why not?" Mikel continues.

"He wants to find his father," I share, studying Jax who's ready to attack. My gentle hand rests on his arm, urging him to stop.

"Where's our father?" Ayva asks, holding back tears.

"Yeah, why wasn't he at command?" Mikel wants to know.

"Do you think something happened to him? Did they capture him too?" There's no answer to Ayva's question. I wrap my arms around her to give her some sort of comfort.

"I've an idea where Dad might be," I say to Ayva.

"I'll go with you."

"No, Ayva. It's a treacherous hike in good times, let alone right now. It's better if I go alone."

"You're not going alone. I'm going with you."

My mouth drops at Falla's demand. I can't tell her no, but I'm also worried about her safety. "I can handle myself, Rioyn. Don't you dare tell me no."

My head and eyes dip in submission to her. This will give us a chance to clear the air, something I've been all too desperate to do.

"While you two search for your father, what should we do? Where do we go from here?" Jax asks.

"We should try and find some sayer devices," Mikel chimes. "If we continue on this mission, then we can at least communicate. Maybe get an edge on Shivane and Sylon and if not them, then maybe on their entranced army"

"The university's down that corridor. Is there anything there you think will help us?" I direct my ask to Mikel. He thinks about it.

"There are sayer communication devices in their order's wing. We could use those for comms if we separate."

"You heard them. Communications are down between provinces. They'll be useless," Falla retorts.

"No, the modern network is down. The old sayer devices, the ones they use for training at the university are run on an old analog wavelength. It's only to be used in backup situations. Wonder why they aren't using them now?" Mikel loses himself in thought.

"They may be but if they are, they won't tell us," I offer to Mikel.

"There's a way to access the network. We should grab whatever's available along with the tracking radar devices. I'll grab those. You guys find the devices."

"You're not going alone. I'll come with." Mikel nods. "Falla, with us! Ayva and Jax, you think you two can handle the sayer devices?"

Jax nods.

"What about our father?" Ayva tearfully asks.

My head lowers. "If he wasn't at command, then he's likely been captured."

I bear a glance; sadly, she knew the truth. "Get the sayer devices. We'll all meet at the main lecture hall in an hour."

CHAPTER 17

LORD SHI & LORD SY

AYVA

JAX LEADS ME THROUGH the narrow corridor.

We separate from the others, headed straight for the sayer wing. He's careful around each corner and opening, studying the shadows as if his vision can pierce its darkness.

Even in the midst of this attack, his steady grace and determination have to be admired.

He's cautious but never falters, leading me forward by the hand, even as I tremble and jump at every sound.

We reach the sayer wing, marked by the large silverore crest with its beaming circles reducing in size to the center. Jax forces the door open, pulling me in, quietly shutting the door behind us. We crouch to hide below the windows.

I survey the room, studying where the devices might be kept, frantically searching through drawers, cabinets and closets. Yet we're coming up empty handed.

A flash of black smoke tendrils causes puzzlement. Digging below the lip of the windowsill, I slip into the shadowed corner, watching the dagger-formed tendrils cruelly impaling people running for safety. Bodies crumple to the ground.

Tearful, yet unable to tear my gaze away from the gruesome sight, I see they each rise from their false death, their eyes gone, replaced with black voids.

Pushing into the wall, suddenly, my knees give out.

Jax catches me before I fall forward.

"Ayva, are you alright? What happened?"

His soft voice eases the horror of what lies outside these walls. I clasp on to him, hard, allowing him to hold me until my breathing regulates.

In the far corner, I spot a metal case, moving toward it, Jax following behind.

"The metal case keeps a kinetic charge with the devices so they should be operational," I whisper to Jax, lifting the lid to the intricately designed metal box.

Jax stands closer to me, the heat of his body comforting.

Inside are six sayer devices. Mikel was right, they're all the older models. Jax finds a beige cloth bag. We swipe all six.

Then, we wait at the main lecture hall behind a large stone pillar, Jax and I sitting huddled next to each other. I shiver in the cold, misty air. I curl into a ball trying to create warmth. Jax eyes me, no doubt feeling me tremble.

He takes off his uniform jacket and drapes it over me.

Chilled to the bone already, I accept it without asking if he'll be warm enough. His under shirt is tight and hugs his muscles, showing every line and curve of his arms.

I turn away before he can catch me staring. Instead, I simply say, "You didn't need to, but thanks."

Nodding in acknowledgment, Jax glances around the pillar, keeping watch. He turns back at my shiver, catching a stray hair and tucking it behind my ear, flashing a smile. "Everything is going to be okay, Ayva. We'll get through this." He sighs. "Somehow."

His eyes lift suddenly, making me tense as he looks at something beyond my shoulder.

"It's about time you got here," he whispers. "Did you find him?"

Mikel launches into a rambling account of their failure, but Jax cuts him off as Falla and Rioyn join us. He's white faced. "Follow us. You guys have to see this."

We are heading to the center of the university quadrangle when a commanding voice rings through the air. Fear and anger rise in Rioyn's face. "That's Shivane," he whispers to the boys. "She's addressing their prisoners. Let's get closer to hear what she's saying."

"How do we get close enough?" Falla asks.

"I know a place." Rioyn leads but I stop, frozen, but this time not due to the cold.

From behind one of the tall stone columns appears a man, his huge frame and obvious strength commanding attention. His broad shoulders are pushed back, his muscles bulging through a black armored suit. He wears the same black cloak that shrouded him as he walked through our house, but now the hood is pulled back.

He tosses back a wave of curls, revealing an arrogant smirk.

My eyes narrow. I've seen him before, but where? Something about him is strikingly familiar. The weight of his presence bears down as something inside me warms and awakens; feelings that have lain dormant for most of my life are now revived and somehow connected to him. They're feelings I've felt before, yet never knew were there.

Then it hits me like a flash. We met when I was young, didn't we?

The thought pervades my mind. I can't make sense of it, not even realizing that I've dropped my hand from Jax's grasp until he grabs it again, yanking me from my enchantment, pulling me forward. I blink in relief, steeling myself.

The man must use powerful spellwork to draw people to him. No doubt everyone in our group just experienced the same bizarre sensation. Right?

We climb up a steep hill that peers down onto the university's quadrangle, then lie prostrate on our bellies to hide among the charred long grass, listening in.

The acoustics from the university's quadrangle float all the way up here.

I keep my eyes glued to the dark enigma of Sylon, my heartbeat quickening.

"Look!" Falla whispers. "They have the generals and leaders chained together. There's your father."

"Where?" Rioyn stirs. My gaze intently searches for him as well.

Falla points to the man at the end of the line, the one who is beaten and bloody almost beyond recognition. Tears consume me, his pain coursing through my veins as if his suffering were entirely my own. He's barely holding on.

I focus with every ounce of strength I have, willing him not to give in, not give up. Not now when we need him the most. Every ounce of love and hope that stirs inside of me, I send to him. He needs it all even if it drains every bit from me, struggling to reach him.

My Ascendance isn't strong enough, failure consuming me. Negative emotions mustn't reach him. Rein it in, Ayva. My emotions must settle if I'm going to help him, so I take a deep calming breath after deep breath, settling enough to channel the love and hope I have for Father. He needs to free himself and find our mother.

He needs to save us, saving our realm from these horrible beings.

Finally, he eases, becomes calmer and his breathing less labored.

It worked. I did it! Keep it together, Ayva. I can't get too excited or ahead of myself.

But where is our mother? We have to find her.

The rest of the people line the theater, forming a circle.

There must be hundreds if not thousands standing tall, looking straight with the same fierce lacquered black eyes directed at Shivane.

"Citizens of Seivan. I am Shivane Greyea, and this is my brother Sylon Greyea of Dremaria. We are the niece and nephew of Zianli Wren and your new rulers of Seivan. You will refer to us as Lord Shi and Lord Sy, respectively."

Grumbles emanate from the captured crowd below, Sylon blasting them with a radiant energy rendering one man unconscious. I gasp, Jax covering my mouth just as Zianli wrestles with his cuffs, trying to break free. Why would they hold their own uncle captive?

"Do not speak my name after you have dared to defy me!" Zianli barks.

Shivane mocks him with a chuckle, lifting her taloned hand, and now, Zianli is on his knees. Sylon touches Shivane's arm, which she instantly drops, sparing her uncle at the final moment.

"We are the true descendants of Everia, here to take back what is rightfully ours."

What is rightfully theirs?

Rioyn and I raise our brows at one another. What is theirs? They aren't entitled to anything by way of Everia. Are they?

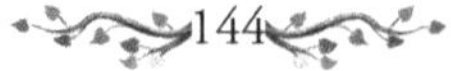

"We have seized all strongholds across the Seivan realm. Your communication systems belong to us. Ports have been destroyed and the trade routes are governed by us. We have every general and leader here before you." Shivane motions to the captured generals and leaders. Our father, our uncle, they rank among them.

Sylon, with a delighted grin, moves to the generals and leaders as they glower from beneath their dark hoods. He grabs one of the men under his arm, lifting him to his feet with ease. His strength is equal to ten strong men.

He rips the hood from the man's head to reveal Xi Kai, Falla's uncle.

I feel her tense beside me.

She held me back from throwing myself after Mother. Now, it is my turn to hold her hand, squeezing it as she trembles violently, fighting back tears.

Xi's one eye narrows on Sylon as if there's more to their story. Sylon foams at the mouth, gripping the air before Xi's neck, making Xi writhe in pain. Sylon chokes him without even touching him, sending Xi to his knees gasping for air. Sylon stalks closer but Xi is miraculously spared when one brave soul shouts through the crowd.

"Monnaire and Arro Lore are still free," comes the bold voice. "You don't have the two most powerful people in the realm. You are not our leaders. They will stop you!"

Cries ring among the crowd.

Shivane clenches her fist before her. "Silence!" Everyone in the crowd—except for the soldiers of the Starless Army—clutch their heads in pain. "Monnaire and Arro are in fact captured. They rot deep within our dungeon."

The crowd knows no fear, hurling objects toward the center stage.

Shivane seethes at the disrespect, raising her hands, stopping the objects in midair. She sends everything flying back at the crowd, injuring several people.

Her lips curl with a sinister grin of delight.

Shivane stares down at the crowd, searching for the fear within them all.

"We have the strongest Ascendance in the realm. There is no one more powerful than us." Shivane turns to the line of generals and stands before a woman kneeling at the end. Her hands are encased in black crystal cuffs with a black crystal collar wrapped around her neck, a jet-black cloak draped over her drooping head.

She reaches under her arm, dragging the woman to the platform.

We watch in silent anguish, recognizing the woman's form instantly.

"Kneeling before you is the one The Book of Legends hails as the Iyanndyre Born." The crowd gasps as Shivane parades our mother on stage. "She has been rendered powerless by the power of the black Iyann crystals. The power we now control."

"I thought the black Iyann crystals were a fable?" I whisper to Rioyn.

"Do you believe in The Book of Legends now?" he whispers back, eyes glued to our mother.

"For too long, the people of Dremaria have starved. For too long, you people have damned us to live a life of poverty while forcing us to beg for scraps. Now, you will taste your own injustice."

"Set her free!" a man shouts, the chant gaining momentum. "Set her free!"

Shivane's eyes flood with fury. "This is your savior," she says, laughing. "Behold her in all her power and glory." Shivane raises her hand then snaps her fingers. Our mother collapses on stage. "Your Iyanndyre Born is dead. You will submit to me, or I take everything you have left to fight for and destroy it."

"We must do something. We must stop them," Rioyn suggests.

I feel the weight of staring eyes. Quickly, I find them and identify them as our father's, connecting my mind to his.

"Ayva, you must stop Rioyn from wanting to fight. He will not win. No one will. Take your friends and flee Casstell. Find somewhere safe and stay there until this is all over. Please convince your brother. If there ever was a time for him to listen, that time is now."

Immediately, I break the connection, whispering to Rioyn, "Pa wants us all to flee Casstell. We cannot win."

Rioyn whips his frustrated glare to me.

I cut him off before he has the chance to speak. "Listen to our father for once in your life. Their lives, our lives, they all matter and your dedication to winning isn't what's important now. We need to get to safety if we want a chance to save anyone."

Miraculously, there's been a shift in Rioyn. Is he actually going to listen to our father for the first time in his life? My focus on him is broken.

Shivane saunters to the fear-stricken crowd, stopping in front of a woman hiding her face from hers. Shivane bends down to lift the chin of the crying woman.

She reaches into her pouch, pulling out a handful of the black Iyann crystal dust and blowing it in the woman's face. The woman's eyes roll back in her head.

When they return forward, they fill with black smoke, converting them to the darkest voids. I glance at Falla who is studying the black crusted cut on Rioyn's head.

Shivane rejoins Sylon on stage, saying, "You've seen what we can do. The choice is yours." Then she slams a glass orb with an onyx filament to the ground.

The glass shatters, the filament converting into a smoke that blankets the crowd, encapsulating them. When the billowed smoke clears, everyone has disappeared into thin air, the Starless Army are the only ones left to rain down terror and destruction across the entire realm as they see fit. We rise to our feet, sprinting back to our house.

CHAPTER 18

THE SPIRITS OF OLD

RIOYN

THE EERILY QUIET STREETS are blindingly dark, making it hard to recognize this city I once knew like the back of my hand. We wind through the desolate and destroyed streets, sticking as close to the shadows as possible. I take this moment to practice my Ascendance on the fly.

The shadows give me cover in case I'm not able to fully cloak myself.

My abilities are spotty at best, my Ascendance the one thing I have practiced the most, yet it's also my greatest failure. Our mother prides us on being natural Ascendants, yet my abilities still somehow remain weaker than of those of the ones who never even practice at all!

An electrifying cold hand grabs me by the elbow, spinning me.

"Why aren't we fighting? Why aren't we trying to figure out how and where they all disappeared to?" Falla questions.

All eyes land on me. I stop to address her hurt more than anything.

"We need to find somewhere safe first. Shivane and Sylon already kidnapped our mother right from under us back at our house. It's not safe there. None of us are safe there."

We need to find safety first before we can even think about saving anyone. "We need to regroup and figure out how to move forward. Together. Safely."

"You're a coward, Orro. You don't stand for anything except yourself."

Falla has stolen the air from my chest with her fatal blow of words, her tear-drenched blue eyes seething at me with an anger I have never seen before.

Is it because of me or is she still reeling from her family's death, or both?

I can't tell, and she still refuses to talk to me, at least in a real and meaningful way.

In the past, we've never gone more than a week without hearing from one another. Now, we face each other for the first time after nine months of stony silence.

I'm a fool to think I don't disappoint her with everything I do.

I inch toward her without regard for who is around and watching our every interaction. My shoulders crash, forehead leaning in to meet hers, something we always did as kids.

It was our way of saying I'm sorry. Except this time, her already elusive emotions harden, and she turns away with a long, stony face.

It seemed impossible for my heart to crack any more today, yet she stomps on its already shattered pieces, crushing them even more.

If only I could profess to blame her, but it wouldn't be true.

My head and vision remain fogged from whatever keeps trying to take hold. Whatever it was, the feeling with which it consumed me was abhorrent, so much evil and hate rolled in with it. So, staying a safe distance behind Falla, I take up the rear of our group, keeping an eye out on the strangely quiet streets.

Peering through two thin birch trees, a ripple in the air halts me dead.

It tears against itself, revealing a sliver of what appears to be a hidden world. Edging closer, it's clear this ripple isn't meant to be seen, isn't meant to be here, which means the Shrouded Veil cast down by Shivane and Sylon has weaknesses.

I summon my Ascendance, channeling shadows, reaching a tendril of smoke forward, able to pry open the ripple more to peer into the hidden world. My focus is quickly broken by a sense of astonishment at the depravity dwelling in this world beyond ours. My smoke tendril dissipates back into the form of my hand, the ripple searing closed.

Heading back through the air to where the ripple was, nothing's there.

Did it move? Is it somewhere else? My cold gaze rakes through the trees, analyzing every motion: nothing. Did I imagine it? Will I somehow find it again?

I glance ahead, everyone continuing forth without me, making me race to rejoin the group. Jax is the first to approach our house, then he surveys inside, waving us all in.

"We can't stay here!" Ayva warns.

"She's right. Let's split up and pack up whatever supplies we can find and carry. Ayva and Mikel, raid the kitchen for any food that will travel. Falla, grab our survival gear. It's still in the basement. Jax and I will comb through Father's arsenal of weapons."

Not waiting for anyone's rebuttal or questions, I yank Jax by his arm and we race up the stairs to collect every weapon Father keeps hidden.

He's been clever over the years with his hiding places, but he has never succeeded in concealing them from me. Not even a single one. Tonight will be no exception.

Together, Jax and I rummage through the arsenal room, quickly gathering every weapon we and the others will be able to carry.

Ayva comes bursting in through the door like a storm on a warpath of destruction.

"We have to go check on Gran'ama. If she's alive, we have to save her," Ayva blurts.

My stance freezes. She's absolutely right. If Gran hasn't been captured yet, then we must save her, protect her. Jax' own eyes agree.

"We've no way of knowing if she's been captured or she's still out there. It could put us right in the Starless Army's path," I say.

"So, we just leave her to be captured by them? We have to try. We can't leave her behind, Rioyn," Ayva pleads. "Plus, she may know something about what's going on. You know she has that ability."

I melt at her insistence, her eyes burrowing into me until I acquiesce.

Plus, if Ayva is right, Gran'ama just might be the person who can give us insight into what's going on and what we need to do.

"Rally everyone. If we're to make it to her village, then we must leave now while the night provides its cover."

Ayva nods, whipping around on her heels, then dashing out. Jax and I quickly gather every weapon we can carry so that each of us is armed to the hilt. To have any chance at survival and saving others, we desperately need every shred of hope available.

We unite with everyone in the foyer, dispersing all the weapons among us. None of us wants to fight but if we must, then we'll be ready for it.

"We're headed to Graalaston to find Gran'ama," I state.

"No, we don't have time to go visit your gran. We need to get out of town."

"And go where, Falla? We need to find Gran because if she's alive and safe, then she's the only one who could possibly know what's going on and what we need to do. If you have a better suggestion, then let's hear it!"

Falla snaps her neck back. My tone was pointed but at the same time, I'm tired of her second guessing everything I say just because she's still mad at me.

This is far bigger than the two of us.

THROUGH THE SHADOWY HILLS of the backside of Casstell, we wind our way through to come up at the back of Graalaston. There's something oddly calm about this village as if this little pocket of our realm is untouched by the destruction of Shivane and Sylon.

How can that be?

Racing through streets and alleyways, we come upon the oldest cottage in the village, Gran'ama's house. Faint lights flicker through the curtain-bedecked windows.

It looks so warm in there, so welcoming and cozy yet we daren't go inside, not yet.

We circle the cottage for any signs that danger might be lying in wait.

"I'll go first. See if she's there." But before I can stop her, Ayva whisks into Gran's house. I'm quick to follow her, the others all following suit. We barrel into Gran's foyer and find her sitting in the middle of her worn black leather couch.

"Glad you've finally shown up. We have work to do. All of you."

My face doesn't hide my flinch at her statement.

Did she know we were coming? I'll never be able to understand exactly what her true abilities are, but it's always frightened me how accurate she is with her words.

Ayva rushes to wrap her arms around her. "Gran'ama, I'm so glad you're safe."

"Thank the upper worlds you and your brother are okay and escaped harm's hand." Gran'ama turns her gray-blue eyes toward me. "Come here, my boy."

I skulk over to her. She takes my face in her aged hands, surveying my bloodstained cheeks. My emotions lump in my throat.

My gaze down, my body respectfully backing away, both of her hands fall to her heart.

"Where have you been the last few months?" Ayva asks.

"None of that matters right now, my dear." Gran'ama looks to each one of us. "What matters is figuring out how to get to the Iyanndyre." Wide eyes dart around.

"The Iyanndyre?" Falla sputters. "That's impossible. Even if we could somehow make it there, it's been restricted by the order of Grynndyre Command."

"No, not impossible—far from it—and restricted is more of a formality at this point."

"Is that where Shivane and Sylon took everyone who disappeared?"

Trepidation seeps into Falla's tone.

"I'm unable to get a whisper of their location. Wherever they are is heavily shrouded with a type of power I've never seen, only heard of."

"Could they be in the Labyrinth Brick?" All eyes dart to Ayva's speculatory question. What does she know of the Labyrinth Brick? She is dedicated to the laws of science.

The Labyrinth Brick is something else entirely.

"How do you know all of this?" Falla continues.

"My Ascendant speaks with the Spirits of Old. Your mother has some of my powers but refuses to use them. Had she embraced her gifts, she might've seen her capture coming. Your father's, too."

"You knew this would happen? That our mother and father were going to be captured, tortured, and killed?" Ayva frantically inquires. Her eyes are reddening, her tone breaking.

It's far too upsetting to consider this could have been prevented.

"I knew something was happening. What exactly was hard to say. I sought help from others who might know but no one was able to pinpoint it exactly."

"Not meaning to interrupt but time's not on our side right now. What's at the Iyanndyre that's so vital we need to risk going there?"

Gran cranes her neck to Falla. "You are right, Falla. No disrespect intended. And I'm deeply sorry for your loss." Gran's words hit Falla in a way that elicits immediate tears.

Falla ducks behind Jax to hide her burgeoning emotions.

Gran returns her focus to us.

"Our world hangs in a frail balance right now. To save it, you must travel to the Iyanndyre. There, you will find the most powerful weapon in the world, the only thing that can stop Shivane and Sylon. Without it, our world will fail and not just Seivan."

"The journey to the Iyanndyre is one very few people achieve. Most don't even make it, and the rest don't come back. How do you expect us to achieve it?" Mikel warns.

"Yes, you are correct, but people have made it, Bair being one of them. And the route everyone knows to take to travel to the Iyanndyre is not one you can take anymore. Trade routes, ports, and heavily traveled areas are seized and blocked off. War will do that."

Mikel says, "We've haven't seen a battle in a decade. How can this be happening?"

He's frantic.

"That you know of." Gran'ama's suggestive brow tells of the secrets she keeps.

"What about the Growlas? They would be the quickest method of travel?" I interject.

"I disabled the Growlas at the Grynndyre Station when fleeing Trescheria, not wanting Shivane and Sylon following me. But it didn't matter," Falla explains.

My stance sinks to hear it; the Growlas would've been our best bet as they're the fastest way to travel between provinces. But they're likely compromised as well.

"So then, how do we get there?" Ayva's voice falters.

Gran'ama moves everything off the ironore glass table in front of her, then reaches into her satchel to pluck a white scroll. As she unrolls it, it glimmers in the slivers of the night light slicing through crinkles in the curtains.

The scroll looks to be made of finely crushed white crystals. Everyone hovers over it.

Gran'ama traces her finger along a route leading into the Carisan Forest.

Mikel insists, "We can't go through it. Fayrilynds are very real, very evil creatures. If we were able to make it through, we'd be too close to the White Fog and risk being captured by its lure. We'd never make it. Even if we did, we wouldn't be able to cross the Cryar Bridge. Not to mention we'd have to pass through the supposedly 'impassable' Drone Mountains to even get to the Iyanndyre."

"Fayrilynds are a myth from The Book of Legends. They're not real," Ayva huffs.

"Those are the worst, most dangerous areas to ever travel through in all of Seivan," Mikel continues.

"Even worse now." All eyes dart to Gran'ama. "The evil unleashed by Shivane and Sylon has made our realm unpredictable. Anything that leaches evil or feeds off it will have … motivation to attack when the opportunity arises."

"Once we exit the Carisan Forest, can we cross the Tryar Bridge? It's the easiest bridge to cross and would be our best option," I suggest.

"If you can navigate properly through the Carisan Forest, then yes, the Tryar Bridge is a viable option," Gran'ama confirms.

"This is a dead man's mission." Mikel's anxiety boils over, becoming contagious.

"You must also avoid all towns, villages and any travelers. The Starless Army has infected the whole realm. You have to be cautious of everyone," Gran'ama continues.

Falla steps forward. "I'll do whatever it takes to exact justice for my family."

"Me too." Ayva and I both step forward.

"Count me in." Jax steps forward next to Ayva. Eyes all turn to Mikel, seeing the copious sweat beading down his forehead. His nerves are so tense, I feel them as my own.

Mikel steps forward, back straight at attention, attempting to hide his trembling voice.

"I … I'm in."

Gran'ama smiles brightly at the five of us. "Good."

Jax lunges forward, his finger in the air. "I have just one question. What is this so-called powerful weapon that we must find and why has no one else ever found it and kept it safe in case we needed it, like we're doing right now?"

All eyes dart back to Gran'ama. Her stoic eyes land on me. "The weapon you seek is the one legends hail as the Iyanndyre Born."

Mouths drop, eyes filling with shock.

Mikel plops down in a creaky and worn wooden chair.

"More puzzling idioms from The Book of Legends?" Ayva says. "Shivane and Sylon said that our mother is the Iyanndyre Born and that all hope is gone."

Gran'ama turns to face the window.

Her face contorts as she speaks with the Spirits of Old. After a silenced moment, she turns back. "I cannot confirm or deny that. Everything under the Shrouded Veil is hard to discern, you see, even for the Spirits. But one thing is true, which is that your mother is not the prophesied Iyanndyre Born, even as powerful as she is."

Relief settles into me, my shoulders relaxing.

"We now face the most powerful beings who've ever existed in our known world, including the Outer Realms. Somehow, they have found the black Iyann crystals containing the dark Ascendance of Everia and developed powers far greater than anything ever known. Powerful enough to bring a great woman like your mother to her knees."

I think back to a few hours earlier when the evil siblings had entered our house. Sylon had raised a long glass tube with a glowing orange substance, pointing it at Mother.

The substance within had glowed as it faced her. I tell the group what I witnessed, and that I wonder whether this was some test to see if my mother was the one they sought.

Gran'ama pauses, looking at me thoughtfully.

"It sounds possible, but if so, it was a false positive. Your mother has strong Ascendance as a true descendant of Warriem, like you two. That's why it got that reading." Gran holds my gaze. "As long as they think it's her, they won't look for the true Iyanndyre Born. We must use that to our advantage, and have you find them first."

"What about Monnaire and Arro? They're said to be the most powerful people in our realm," Falla interjects.

"Not anymore. Eventually, there'll always be someone who comes forward and dethrones the most powerful person. The struggle for power will never fade."

"Where is this Iyanndyre Born?" Ayva says. "Shouldn't he—or she—come forward on their own to help us, assuming they're so powerful? And why us of all people?"

Gran'ama smiles at Ayva. "The Iyanndyre Born can only be awoken by true descendants of Warriem—that's you two. And the Iyanndyre Born must only be awoken when the true need has arrived. That time is now."

Exhausted and famished, we leave Gran'ama to rest and prepare some simple fare in the kitchen. Once everyone has enjoyed their fill of bread and cheese, Jax, Mikel and Falla venture upstairs to rest. We have a long, arduous journey ahead.

Sleep calls to me, but I feel drawn back to Gran'ama's side. Who knows when I will see her again, if ever? The thought tears me apart. Ayva soon joins me, and we crowd at Gran'ama's knees like the children we were in years gone by, listening to her stories.

"Why's this happening, Gran'ama?" Ayva asks, yawning. "Our provinces have always been different, but they've managed to coexist in balance and peace, haven't they? Why risk so much in the invasion? It doesn't make sense to me at all."

"To understand the present, one must look at the past," Gran'ama says, stroking Ayva's head. "Everia was cold and bitter toward the end of her days. She grew tired of Warriem controlling what happened in the realm. So, she wrote a manifesto detailing what she believed was the correct way to lead the realms." Gran'ama's breathing grows labored.

How taxing was her journey to find out what happened?

"Zianli found the manifesto," she continues. "But his interpretation was one of total control and power, rather than independence and autonomy. He passed those beliefs to Shivane and Sylon's parents and then on to them. Their anger has intensified over the years as anger always tends to do, among other reasons. Now, the Iyanndyre Born is our only hope of restoring peace to our realm," Gran'ama continues, looking at us both.

"No! The Iyanndyre Born is just another fabled tale in The Book of Legends," Ayva corrects. "A myth, written by people hundreds of years ago. Just like a fairytale."

Ayva is the smartest person, but she believes only in science, mathematics, and things that can be proven. After all, even the powers of Ascendency can be measured and monitored. But my heart has always whispered of mysteries we don't understand. I can only hope Gran'ama is right, and the Iyanndyre Born is one of them.

"Warriem and Everia foretold of a person who'd take that mantle, bringing peace to the world."

"I can't believe this is what we have to do. Travel through our realm now filled with evil and hate to find some legend no one's seen in over four hundred years."

Falla shakes her head, going off upstairs.

Mikel follows her with fear-laced eyes. Jax sees me nodding for him to go along with them. We all need to stick together, not only for safety but also for support.

Gran'ama's eyes take on a sad light.

"The last thing I want is to send you into danger, but it's the only way. It's good and noble that your friends wish to help you but …" She sighs. "Sorry to say that if they join you, they'll not make it, and they may even end up holding you back."

Shock spills from my expression. "What? You want me and Ayva to go alone?"

"Not alone. With Falla," Gran'ama clarifies. "She knows Trescheria better than anyone, including you. And you'll need her to navigate you both through her province. The others will only prove to be a distraction."

Ayva and I catch each other's eyes.

Mikel will no doubt be relieved to stay back. But Jax?

It's hard to imagine him wanting to leave our sides.

As hard as her instructions might be, she has wisdom and knowledge few of us can understand. We would be fools to ignore her warning, which means we'll need to have a difficult conversation with our friends when we leave, shortly before dawn.

"I'll go break the news to Jax." Ayva rushes upstairs.

"Rioyn. My boy. Sit."

Gran'ama pats the puffed worn leather cushion, great clouds of dust polluting the air.

Gran'ama quickly rolls The Scroll of Alderon up, reaffixing the clasp. It's a platinumore medallion with the outline of an infinity symbol weaving through a star, Warriem and Everia's crest of honor. She hands me the scroll.

"Take this with you, but only use it if you absolutely must. The scroll emits an energy that will lead the enemy straight to you, and it would be a disaster for everyone if it were to fall into the wrong hands. But the time will come when you'll cross the path of a trusted person, and the scroll must change hands. You'll need to search your heart to recognize this ally, to avoid betrayal." Her eyes darken. "And to avoid catastrophe."

I nod, understanding her quick desire to put it away.

"Will we make it?" I ask.

Gran'ama undoubtedly senses the fear compromising my voice.

"I have faith in you, my grandson, but it will not be easy. You will encounter those who wish to betray you. And if you do succeed, your triumph will come with great sacrifice. You will no longer be the person you once were. There is the threat of physical death, but there are other forms of death too, such as the death of self."

Her words send a chill down my spine, but as always, they ring with truth.

CHAPTER 19

RETURN TO DREMARIA

The Past

SHIVAN

Our black, square carriage sits waiting for us at the Trescherian Growla Station. My nerves tense, knowing we still have to face the harshest critics, our parents.

Soldiers wait patiently by the side of the carriage, apparently ordered to escort the four of us back to Dremaria, but they don't step forward to assist us.

Bags in hand, we stop before the glowering men. A soldier opens the door and my heart drops, waiting for our parents to disembark.

Instead, the only thing before us is emptiness.

Caya and Coren enter the carriage, followed by Sylon.

It's a relief our parents didn't come, though the thought of what their absence means is terrifying. The soldier holding the door clears his throat, urging me to enter, and when I do, he slams it shut.

I sit next to Sylon as he exhales a large sigh, no doubt equally relieved. We have a few more hours before facing our parents' wrath, but this unknown limbo is somehow worse. I sleep as best I can.

We arrive in Nighamaire as the white sun slides over the Drone Mountains to the east, the carriage dropping us off at the Residents' Gate.

All four of us look as though we've been dragged the entire way here, our heavy eyes having difficulty staying open.

We say our goodbyes to Caya and Coren, wishing them luck with their parents, almost as fearful as ours. There's a slight warmth in the spring air, the black trees blossoming, their leaves itching to return and bask in the white-hot spring sun.

The streets in Nighamaire still sleep, only a few early rising souls wandering about enjoying a brisk morning walk through the sleepy neighborhood.

Sylon and I have not said one word to each other since departing the university. He doesn't wish to speak about what happened and neither do I. We will have enough time to explain our actions once we cross the threshold to the home before which we now stand.

Sylon opens the black ironore gate as our parents emerge at the front door, a surge of anxiety pooling in me. My shoulders curl forward in an involuntary slump as Sylon stands bolt upright like a sentry, pushing his shoulders back.

If only I had his confidence. What I'd give to be like that.

Our parents offer a silent stare, then turn into the house.

They seem to expect us to follow, to obey.

Sylon marches in, leaving me lingering just a few steps behind as we cross the dark threshold.

Sylon drops his duffel bags in the foyer. I place mine beside his, following him into the kitchen. There are Mother and Father, seated at the dining table with an array of breakfast pastries and beverages laid out before them like some grand and special feast.

The kindness is overwhelming, beyond anything imagined. The aroma of fresh-baked pastries eases my nerves, even if I'm too sick to eat.

Sylon stands, blocking the chairs for either of us to sit.

"It's been a long ride. I'd like to rest before—"

"Sit," our father barks with a cold stare. Not even Sylon can disobey that tone.

Sylon moves sideways and pulls out a chair for me. We take a seat.

Their icy gazes shift between us, the quiet anticipation slowly destroying my nerves, eating away at them. A glance to Sylon shows him sitting with his spine straight as a sword again, eyes forward, a battle soldier waiting for the enemy to make its first move.

Eventually, Mother breaks the icy tense silence.

"Would either of you care to explain why we should not expel you from this house at once? Why you feel entitled to bring your disgrace to our home?"

Sylon leaps into the fray without pause, undaunted. "I stand by what I did, and I'd do it again!" His voice is raised high as if he is ready to lead a charge into battle.

Our parents' eyes narrow on him. Then they shift their ice-cold glares to me.

"And what do you have to say for yourself?" Our father slithers his focus to me, spotting me sinking further into the chair, its wooden spindles digging into my back.

No words wish to come, Sylon's thoughts creeping into mine. "Don't let them intimidate you. Command their respect."

Our mother's eyes shoot to Sylon.

She evidently knows he's speaking to me through our special connection.

"Your impertinence knows no bounds." Her eyes narrow beneath age-heavy brows.

"That university is a corrupt cesspool of incompetent leaders," Sylon spits. "Shivane and I stood in defiance and refused to be cowed and humiliated. Just as you raised us to."

My brow arches, curious at our parents' response to Sylon's thesis.

"Beating a fellow cadet to almost an inch of his life is how we raised you? Would you care to elaborate on that? I have a quite different recollection."

Our father's face reddens, and now, he's turning his attention to me.

"And you … I don't even know where to begin with you. You used your Ascension to poison the mind of a fellow student?"

"I was defending my friend, who was being attacked for coming from an Outer Realm." My parents' faces soften slightly, almost indecipherably, which tells me they weren't informed of the full story.

"That doesn't give you the right to defy the rules and bend them to suit your needs. You are not the High Court that rules our realm. You are children. Arrogant and reckless."

Our father's words sink into both of us.

The truth is our father is right. But that doesn't mean we are wrong.

"You have little respect for the generals, commanders, and other high-ranking officers," I say. "You have little respect for anyone outside our province, yet you side with them over us."

Father leans forward. "We have our reasons to criticize the other provinces who keep our own in isolation and poverty. But by molding the law to suit your vengeance, it makes you become no better than them. It is the same aberration exposed in a different manner."

"Even so, I still stand by my actions," Sylon snaps. "If that offends you, so be it."

Anger is etched across my brother's face just as it is across our father's.

For the first time, my mind deigns to consider Sylon's actions more fully. It is true I acted recklessly, but I was defending an innocent friend. In contrast, Sylon attacked a cadet in training, the same boy who had accidentally bumped into him on the first day.

While I will always stand by Sylon, he delivered a brutal punishment simply because of feeling so disrespected. I watch him now, wondering, how can he truly defend his actions? Is there more to his story? There surely must be. He's not that reckless.

"And we had to discover that you joined the Order of Healants from General Orro, of all people." Our father turns his fury on me, disappointment radiating off his face. "We have never discouraged you from doing what you wanted, have we? So, why didn't you tell us?"

"I didn't want to disappoint you," I whisper.

"So, lying to us was the better option?" he is dismayed, then adds, "In seeking not to disappoint me, you have done ten times the damage. There is no logic to this madness."

I break our parents' relentless and unhappy stares, focusing on the center of the table to avoid their hurt-filled, reddened eyes and blotched skin. It's simply unbearable.

"I'm sorry, Mother, Father, truly sorry to have disappointed you both." In that moment, it is the truth of things, my heart sunken to the ground like a stone, robbed of self-belief.

They seem to ease in their chairs when a hand falls upon my shoulder. My head whips up to discover our uncle and ruler of Dremaria, Zianli. My eyes open wide.

This cannot be good.

"Your uncle has been very understanding of your transgressions," our mother says. "He's generously offered to allow you both to train with him and his soldiers of the Dremarian Army."

"Don't bother unpacking," Uncle Zianli says. "We're leaving now."

I analyze the punishment our father just issued, mainly to me.

For Sylon, this is excellent news. He would probably have preferred going straight into service over studying at Sansyre.

Rising from the table, I catch Mother's eye, but she looks away, her face unreadable. We both know my aspirations of graduating from Sansyre University have died, and along with them, so has all my hope of one day becoming a healant.

Instead of saving lives, I will be trained in how to take them.

CHAPTER 20

THE TRAINING COURT

The Past

S Y L O N

S HIVANE AND I HAVE been stationed at the training court on the far edge of Nighamaire for the last six months, kept separate from the rest of the city during our training. For this, I couldn't be happier. Everything for which our parents reprimanded us is incomprehensible, but training under Uncle is a dream come true.

If only I could say the same for my sister.

Even now, our parents' choice is puzzling, knowing there's usually more to the story than they choose to let on.

I wait outside Shivane's private quarters, one of only five apartments reserved for the top soldiers training in Zianli's army.

She emerges from her quarters right on schedule; her hardened face doesn't glow like it did when we were at Sansyre, but her eyes are fierce, menacing.

Being here has changed her. It has brought out the unrelenting warrior living and breathing deep inside of her. But is it really a good thing?

We've both gained unrequited strength and skills since training with the rank leader.

It has been a great honor to train and learn from him.

167

The rank leader works us from sunup until high noon, and after lunch, we train with the High Ascendant of Dremaria until dusk. Shivane and I have increased our Ascendance abilities tenfold, further affirming my belief that Sansyre was a waste of time, run by old instructors who haven't seen a battlefield in their lifetime.

The Ascendant has also trained us to unlock our powers so we're cross-Ascendants, no longer limited to our Ascendance of the mind. While she can also control nature, I can control energy. We have worked on controlling all three, only to be told it's impossible.

Working hard, we are fulfilling our potential, but can Shivane see that?

We traipse through the gray limestone walkway connecting our quarters to the training court. Now, Shivane no longer walks a few steps behind.

She leads the way into our private arena in the back, and as we round the limestone corner of the weightlifting room, we come face to face with Zianli.

His thin lips curl into a smirk as his pallid lilac eyes meet ours.

His tall thin frame is draped in a fine black cloak, his hawkish face jutting out atop curved shoulders. "Ah, my favorite niece and nephew. I've been receiving reports about your progress thus far."

Shivane arches her back, offering a slight bow. "Positive, I hope. It's been an honor to train at your court."

My smirk matches his as my brow arches, curious as to why we've been called here.

"If you both would be so inclined as to suspend your training for the moment and join me in my study chamber."

He doesn't wait for our answer as he turns and walks off ahead of us.

We follow him up the vast stone staircase, leading to the rear of the Castle of Everia where we disappear into the fifth level through a pointed stone archway.

It leads on to his chamber. The steelore door is wide open for us to enter, and soon, another surprise greets us: our parents, outfitted in their black Dremarian Army armor.

The threads are fabricated from impenetrable fabrics that mold to the curves of their bodies. There's no hint of color anywhere on their uniforms. The only insignia if of the Dremarian crest, that of the stars and moon in a circle.

Neither Shivane nor I greet our parents.

They haven't visited since banishing us here. I have it in me to thank them, but Shivane doesn't share my sentiment. Zianli motions for us to join him at his meeting table.

I step forward but Shivane doesn't budge.

"Let's see what they have to say before you rip them apart," I offer internally.

"After their betrayal, you expect me to meet them with warmth?"

"You know they care for us both. I can't just believe I am the one telling you to be nice." A chuckle ripples down our connection before I sever it.

It's doubtful our mother is able to detect our communications now, after so much training, but it's best to not to test that theory.

We sit in black leather-wrapped chairs, each large enough for two, me leaning back with my ankle resting atop my knee, hands gripping the thick sidearms.

Shivane sits with her back rigid, hands folded neatly in her lap. A little too proper for my comfort.

"I understand you might feel betrayed by our absence," Mother begins.

I shoot her a look, wondering if she is able to intercept our chatter after all. "But we've made it a point to watch your training from afar and give you space. There comes a time when every bird must leave the nest."

Father speaks up, taking the gauntlet from Mother. "On this day, you are both nineteen," he adds as if we might have forgotten this. "Old enough to stand alone."

"Is this meant to be some kind of Happy Birthday message?" Shivane snarks. "Because it's a pretty lame one."

"Please, there's no need to be hostile. We come here to say that we're proud of you, proud of how you have taken the challenge offered and met it with resolve."

Shivane stares through our father.

He's always been one to throw himself in the line of fire, no matter from where it comes, to protect her—all of us. But she's in no way inclined to accept his peace offering.

"You wanted me to learn to fight, so I did." Shivane lifts her chin in defiance. "But as you said, I am an adult now. So, let us consider our business complete."

Our father's eyes widen in hurt and rage. He angles his narrow-eyed glare toward Shivane, forcing her back into her chair. She claws at the force of his Ascendance locking her in while his amber energy wraps itself like a viper around her neck, forcing her to gasp for air. He's testing her abilities but she's too shocked to fight back.

"He's testing you," I hiss through our connection. "Fight!"

Shivane grunts in pain, gripping her chair with whitened knuckles.

She can't move or even breathe, but the resolve in her eyes is enough to overcome the panic. She glows amber, in return wrapping his energy into a ball, sending it back down the line connecting them. "Yes!"

Father struggles to hold her off. She senses his wavering power and intensifies her own, pushing his limits to the edge without any indication of relenting.

Her point has been made. She is now the stronger of the two.

I grip her forearm for her to stop, she doesn't and her formerly amber glow darkens to a blood red. Clamping down, I move to jerk her arm toward me.

She doesn't rein in her Ascendance, so it spills over to me, but I'm able to sequester it before she can reach me. While she's grown in strength, I am still the stronger one. I will always be the stronger one.

I keep my fingers wrapped around her forearm, growling at her in warning. She may still be frustrated with our parents, but they don't deserve this treatment.

It was our actions that landed us this fate. She snarls through her deep purple eyes, threatening me with her anger. My stern grip on her arm reminds her to check her anger.

"End this now. Or I will."

She lowers her eyes and sits back into her chair, releasing her tension. I steal a glance of our mother, horrified. She must have seen the red glow, too.

"I apologize," is all she whispers, her stare plastered to the floor.

"You've mastered your power," our father strains through his rasped voice, massaging his throat. "But not your temper." Rattled as he is, he's so obviously filled with pride. "Your Ascendance is impressive to say the least."

He speaks genuinely, but if he'd seen the red glow, he might not be quite so sporting.

Shivane blushes with shame. "I didn't mean to hurt you, Father. I … I'm still accepting what I did and where I am now. What I lost." Shivane's head lowers, heartbroken.

She hasn't opened up to anyone, not even me, about what happened and how she's been dealing with being here. She's been clinging to acerbic, dismissive comments as shields.

Now, I understand what she's buried deep inside of her.

Not the sense of guilt for what she did, not remorse. No, she's grasping to accept that her actions have had unfair and unfavorable consequences.

My glance dances to our parents, both of them nodding at Zianli.

"My dearest niece and nephew. We have great news."

He stands, then paces to his large metal desk.

"When the university dismissed you both, I was quick to recognize that their loss was our gain. That they had foolishly overlooked the potential in their hands."

Shivane and I don't peel our eyes off Zianli.

"The three of us have charted your impressive progress over the last six months and you both, in your own ways, are two of the strongest soldiers we've ever had. In fact, you are the missing pieces for which we've been waiting."

My head bows in thanks for his generous words, but what does all this mean?

We might be the missing pieces, but I'm struggling to see the larger picture.

Father leans forward. "What your uncle is trying to say is that the time has come to put our power to use."

"Defending Dreamaria …" I offer, "from attack?"

My father smiles. "Sure. But as I'm sure you've learned in training, the best form of defense is attack, my boy. The time has come to finally end the injustices we've endured, for no better reason than our place of origin, and the differences they despise as lesser."

Shivane and I look at each other, shocked. But that can only mean …

My uncle leans forward, his severe face twisted into a smile.

"We're going to war."

PART II

An ODYSSEY of RECHERCHÉ

CHAPTER 21

High Moon

AYVA

THE MOON SOFTLY ASCENDS to its highest peak in the night sky, meaning we need to leave soon, and I need to break the news to Jax. I tiptoe into my room where he lies sleeping on my bed. My bed! I wish the circumstances were better, but regardless, I'll cherish this prized memory for as long as I can.

Gently, I sit next to him. He jostles awake at my presence.

"Is it time to go?" Jax asks with bleary eyes.

"Almost. But you and Mikel must stay back and help everyone you can. We need someone to monitor and report what's going on here."

Jax leaps up out of bed. "Absolutely not. I will not leave you. I'm going."

I grab Jax's hand. He eases at my touch, gliding down next to me.

Our legs touching, my body ignites with an overwhelming frisson of electricity. He interlaces his hand into mine, piercing my eyes with his stare.

"I'm not letting you go without me."

As tempting as it is to embark on this journey with him, the dangers of going against Gran'ama's warning are all too clear.

I'll never go against them again and must convince Jax of it.

"If you go, you will not make it. We need to break up into smaller groups to cover more ground and protect everyone we can. Falla's going with us since she knows Trescheria better than anyone, including you." Jax deflates. I hope I was harsh enough for him to understand that he can't go, but not too harsh to crush his spirits.

Jax takes my other hand in his, leaning his forehead on mine, our breaths colliding.

"If that's so, promise me you will not do anything to get yourself hurt or captured. Promise me you'll return to me, safe."

My forehead peels back from his and I gaze into his beautiful crystal blue eyes.

He leans in close, our lips millimeters away from each other, the heat of them on mine.

"I can't bear the thought of losing you. I've cared for you since the day I met you at camp eleven years ago. I didn't know it then like I do now, but how I've felt for you all these years. I wish I told you sooner but now I have you, I'm not letting go. So, promise me, Ayva."

"I prom—"

Before I'm able to finish, his tender lips meet mine, and I'm enraptured in a rush of passionate emotions searing through every muscle and synapse. My body yearns and beckons for him, his hand cupping my face as he pulls me closer to his sweltering body.

Our lips part, immediately making me crave him more.

Yes, I crave more of him, more of this, inhaling his scent of sandalwood mixed with the taste of him melting onto my lips. It's a moment to remember forever.

As his hand slides to the small of my back, there's a knock at the door.

We both startle. Rioyn inches through the door, saying, "It's high moon. Time to go."

I nod and hint with my eyes for Rioyn to give us a moment. He slinks through the door. Jax lightly kisses me one more time, my hand still nestled in his.

We glide down the stairs where everyone waits for us.

Rioyn, Falla, and I stand at the front door, busily checking over our packs. We each wear thick, long brown coats that are tight along our chests but flowing along the legs, making it easier to move. With a steeled face, Jax adjusts my pack as Gran'ama strolls in.

"The high moon is upon us. It is time." She hands Rioyn a steelore sword. "This was your Gran'apa's sword from the Battle of Trescheria."

Rioyn accepts the sword with wide eyes, studying the intricate carvings on the hilt. "Use it when you must. It will serve you well."

"Thank you. I will take care of it with pride."

Gran'ama whirls to me, holding a smaller black dagger.

"This too belonged to your Gran'apa. It was his favorite dagger, and he always had it on him. Legend has it that this dagger alone was the weapon he used to save his entire cavalry of men. It became his good luck charm, so of course, it went with him everywhere. He always tried to convince me it was made of some sort of magic. Anyway, take care of it but never be afraid to use it should you need to."

"I will take care of it. Thank you, Gran." I accept the gracious gift.

Mikel pushes through the group clutching four copperore metal cuffs, one for each of us, wrapping around the backs of our ears with a single opaque gem to fit in the ear canal. Jax takes two cuffs from him. Mikel hands the other two to Falla and Rioyn.

I sweep my hair to one side as Jax tucks the cuff over my left earlobe. He adjusts it exactly right. "Does that fit?" I give him a slight nod. His hands fall to my shoulders.

"When you receive a transmission, tap the gem in your ear and then slide your finger from the top of your ear all the way down." Mikel demonstrates.

"That is the decryption pattern for our channel. To initiate a conversation, do the same pattern then tap twice on the gem. It will send a transmission to us. The communication lines run on the antiquated system, which means they're easier to intercept. If someone happens to be listening through those lines, we could be compromised. So, stay off the channel unless absolutely necessary, and always assume someone is listening in."

Falla hugs Mikel tightly, unsure how to receive affection from her.

She then grabs me by the arm and spins me to face her. She places her hands on both of my shoulders, her eyes boring into mine. "You don't have to come, Ayva."

My head lowers for a deep breath.

"I know. And I'm not as strong or skilled in combat as you and Rioyn. But there's something inside of me pulling me to go. I think I'll be able to help, somehow."

Falla's eyes study mine. "If you're sure. After the last few days, I'm not sure I can handle losing anyone else, especially you." She pulls me in for a tight embrace.

"Remember. Avoid populated areas. Stay off the main routes. Stay hidden. Do not use The Scroll of Alderon unless necessary. And trust no one."

Gran'ama hugs Rioyn and me, cupping Falla's face in her hands and kissing her cheek.

I hug Mikel goodbye. But before I'm able to say goodbye to Jax, my heart dives into my stomach, struggling against tears.

My eyes are terrified to meet his, all emotions running raw inside.

He adjusts my hood over my head and I look up at him. His own hood is up.

"Let's go." He takes my hand, and we follow Falla and Rioyn out the back door. "I'll walk you to the edge of Casstell. We can say goodbye there."

He should be safe enough heading back to Casstell.

Selfishly, I want him to stay with me as long as he can.

We jog through the moonlit field behind our house, weaving through the tall, skinny birch trees, hiding in the shadows we meet along the way. Leaves and sticks crunch beneath our boots before disintegrating into the hardened mud.

"Do you think your mom is out there?" I ask Jax, keeping my voice low.

"Maybe." He sighs. "Though if I couldn't find her in peaceful times, I'm not sure what luck I'll have now. It's weird. Everything suggests she's gone. But I've always sensed that she's out there, somewhere."

I'm glad Jax has that connection to sustain him. But his words make me feel ill. When I try to feel the presence of Mother, there's nothing there.

It really does feel as if she's gone.

We run through the back woods until we arrive at a row of businesses on the outskirts of town, and eventually, at the high stone wall that marks the edge of Casstell.

Rioyn pushes on a few of the stones to find his opening.

Jax adjusts my pack and checks the knife in my boot.

"So, I asked Mikel for a special favor," he says, looking down as if embarrassed.

"To go easier on the garlic?" I answer and laugh, attempting to lighten the mood.

"Ugh, the guy loves garlic as much as I love …" He pauses and chuckles. "Erm, crème bowls. Anyway, I asked him to program a communication channel, just for us."

My heart pitter patters in my chest. "Really?"

He carefully shows me how to add a special movement to either call or answer our line, specifically. Rioyn and Falla now stand at the open gap, watching us.

"Use it sparingly though," he says. "Like Mikel said, someone could intercept it."

I nod as he checks the straps of my pack again. His steeled face looks confident and strong; however, his clumsy hands betray his emotion.

I take them in mine, squeezing gently.

"If I don't come back …"

"You will come back."

"Take care of Rioyn. Please."

Jax's hand interlaces and tightens in mine. "Promise is a promise."

"I promise."

A smile curves his lips, his other hand gently gliding through my hair to the back of my neck. His forehead meets mine. Being with him even for a moment, I forget where we are, forgetting the evil we face and the death-bound journey on which we're about to depart. He interlaces his hand with mine again, his tender thumb caressing a line into my palm.

"I'll see you soon." He releases my hand and with a few silent steps, gracefully disappears into the night as if made of shadow himself.

I whip on my toes, breaking Rioyn and Falla's stare.

They quickly turn away, stumbling over themselves. A smile forms after touching my lips, the same ones that Jaxyon Risor kissed not long ago.

Falla flashes me a playful grin with intrigued brows. I blush as the warmth rises from my neck to my cheeks, lost in savoring the moment, trying to imprint it upon my heart.

I can only hope the promise of returning to Jax will sustain me through whatever we may face beyond that wall.

CHAPTER 22

THE CLIFFS OF MAU

RIOYN

IT'S IMPOSSIBLE NOT TO stare at Ayva. She beams like a glowing lighthouse on a moonless, foggy night. At first, it's unclear why her happiness bothers me so.

It's heartwarming to think that my sister is in receipt of some small bit of comfort in the midst of all this madness. I think of how I stood there dumbly, watching them together with Falla at my side. Just inches away, but miles apart.

The truth dawns bright and clear.

I'm jealous.

Of course, that's it. My chance came last winter break, and I screwed it up, like always. Now, Falla hates me. Her cold shoulders and snarled glares are what she gives me and what I deserve. She lost her entire family just days ago, and even with that gaping loss, she refuses to let me close.

But I tell myself hate is still something, an emotion like any other.

She isn't totally indifferent to me yet.

It's a small and bitter win to hold on to, but it's all I have.

"Where is this bridge?" Falla asks.

"Ahead on the right, the point where the ridge dips off."

I lead the way through the dry grass that scrapes against our shins.

The ground trembles the closer we get to the edge of the Cliffs of Mau. I raise my arm for Falla and Ayva to stop, and they each stand on either side of me as we peer down at the wooden bridge suspended with frayed rope. The wood planks creak in the wind as the bridge sways. The planks are weather worn, but intact.

"One step on that thing and it'll crumble into the strait."

Falla crouches for a better gander at just how high the drop is.

"Isn't there another way?" Ayva asks.

"Not one you'll survive crossing," I reply. Ayva's eyes reveal the fear I feel. "I've crossed it before. Just move with confidence and don't stop."

"Just move?" Falla chuckles to relieve her irritation.

"Move carefully, don't jerk the thing around, and you'll be fine. I'm the heaviest, so I'll go first." I'm about to take my first step when I freeze. In the distance behind, figures are moving through the hole in the wall. I was so consumed by my stupid thoughts and jealousy about Falla that I forgot to block it up behind us. We've been discovered!

"No time to be careful. Run!" I yell, shoving Falla onto the bridge.

Falla looks back at the soldiers then takes off at a sprint.

The wooden boards splinter and crack beneath her feet and the bridge sways but holds. As soon as she's made it across, I whip around to Ayva.

"Go now!" Her balance isn't as fluid as Falla's but she's almost there. I keep my eyes glued to Ayva.

Behind us, the soldiers are pointing, moving across the field like a pack of stealthy shadows. They move with a weird ease, almost as if they're floating.

A scream draws my attention back to Ayva, who's clinging to the left railing of the bridge. The right has broken loose.

"Keep going, Ayva!" Falla shouts.

Ayva is almost at the end when the second side snaps, and the wood planks fall through the air, slamming against the cliffs.

"AYVA!" I scream at the top of my lungs, expecting to see her hurtling toward the bottom of the river. Instead, she's wrenched over the lip of the cliff by Falla. They fall backwards onto sturdy land, and I whip my head around.

The Starless Army soldiers are but seconds away.

I run toward the pathway I carved into the side of the cliff.

The soldiers clip at my heels as I move side to side down jagged rocks, my movements swift and unpredictable. I risk glancing behind, filled with relief to see a few of the soldiers tripping behind me, finding their passage equally challenging. One of them, however, moves with fluid efficiency. With a jolt, I recognize that tall, heavy form.

My cousin Hanri is moving down the cliffside with a ferocity that shows he has no concern about harming himself. Hate fuels his every step.

The salt of the Daiyaman Ocean tangs the air. I'm close, my feet slapping into the soft sinking sand. I run on the balls of them to stay light, Hanri thumping close behind.

Too close. My pack weighs me down, but I can't let that be the reason Hanri catches me. The added weight cannot be used as an excuse.

Push, fight harder! I preach to myself.

Reaching the inside of the Cave of Caino, I head straight toward the jagged rocks at the back. If I can't outrun Hanri and his goons, the best I can do is hide.

I push with everything I can, hoping that the Infinite Void that hurt my friends so recently might help protect me now.

I grab a rock, finding it slick from the moist air and my hand slips. Hanri grabs my shoulder and tears me down, sending us both tumbling into the shard-like diamond sand. One moment, he's raising his fist above my face. A split second later, he's crouching, pressing the heel of his palms into his temples, groaning with pain.

"Go back, Hanri! You're too close to the Infinite Void." His black eyes sear mine, wild fury foaming at his twisted mouth. He lunges for me but falls to his knees again in scalding pain. I climb up the back of the cave, reaching for a small opening. "Turn back now!" Darkness clouds my eyes, and I slam them shut, shaking the dark from my head.

Hanri staggers backward to where the sand kisses the base of the cliffs, and his comrades wait. It seems they have accepted defeat, for now. But they aren't about to just let me walk back out of there. At least Falla and Ayva are safe, at least for a while.

I rush deep into the heart of the back of the cave to locate a narrow hole I remember being here a few weeks back. Ayva and Falla wait at the top, unable to get too close to the edge. I wiggle my shoulders through. The palms of my hands plant on top and I push myself up. My hips are stuck. There's no way to get through, after all.

"Rioyn! We're coming!" Ayva hollers.

"Stay back! Don't come any closer. We're too close to the Infinite Void."

Ayva and Falla stop dead in their tracks. They look up, searching for the invisible barrier that surrounds and protects our realm.

I push down on my palms harder, squirming to break free.

Finally, I push through but the rocks break and crumble beneath me. I hold onto the rock jutting out as tight as I can but my footing slips, my arms poised to slip from the rock when two sets of hands pull me up. I scramble to flat land.

Falla is crouched on the ground, grabbing her head. I latch on to Falla by her underarms and tug her up, dragging Ayva along with us. Together, we run out of the radius of the Infinite Void as fast as our feet can take us. Once we're clear of it, we fall to the ground.

"You're not affected by the void?" Falla strains to find her words between breaths.

I drop my head. "I am, but not like everyone else."

"How, Rioyn? How is that possible?" Falla's fierce stare demands an answer.

"I don't know, Falla. Just add it to my list of failings!" My fists are clenched so hard that when I release my grip, my nails have carved half-moons into each palm.

Falla seethes with frustration, and Ayva reaches down to help me to my feet.

"Up ahead, there's a hollowed-out tree," Falla spits. "It will give us shelter for the night. It's close to the boundary of the Carisan Forest. We should rest because we'll need our wits about us the moment we cross into it."

"Shouldn't we keep going to get as far into the forest as we can tonight? Won't the Starless Army come looking for us?" My eyes dart between Falla and Ayva.

"Be my guest but I won't dare enter that forest at night. Not when Fayrilynds are about, whether you choose to believe or not." Falla nods at Ayva's warning.

"So, you do believe in The Book of Legends?" I prod.

"I know the Fayrilynds are real, and their danger's not beyond me. Regardless of The Book of Legends. Hopefully, we'll be safe here for the rest of the night."

"The Starless Army won't be able to cross because of the void and there's no way they'll make it across the Ruby River. We're safe for the night," I say, soft-toned.

Ayva relaxes.

We quietly camp for the remainder of the night.

CHAPTER 23

The Carisan Forest

RIOYN

WE ARE AWAKE, SETTING off walking before the sun has risen. After a night of sleeping on the hard ground, we're too tired to bicker so we trudge along in silence, munching bitter apples we find along the way. An incoming message pings in my ear. I activate the decryption pattern.

Mikel's voice comes through, and a surge of guilt comes over me, wishing it were Jax's voice instead. I miss my best friend. No doubt Ayva would like to hear his voice as well.

Mikel and I exchange a few relieved words of greeting, then get straight to business, wanting to keep the call as short as possible.

"You want to head ten degrees northwest," Mikel broadcasts to us all. "I spotted activity to the far east side on the edge of the Carisan Forest and also at the shores of the Ruby River. You're best to steer clear but don't deviate too far from the ten degrees. I'll sayer in later as you get closer to the Tryar Bridge. Hopefully it's clear to cross."

We need to head east to get over the Tryar Bridge. We cannot take the chance of crossing at the Cryar Bridge further north.

I glance over to Falla who keeps her readied gaze on the Carisan Forest.

"How do you know there's activity to the far east?" Ayva inquires.

"I found a weakness in the Grynndyre's command mainframe and was able to infiltrate their radar detection platform. Yes, it's a highly illegal offense but given the circumstances, they'll surely forgive my intrusion."

We wrap it up and sign off, but not before Mikel tells Ayva that Jax sends his best wishes. Falla and I roll our eyes, and for a moment, not everything is pure hostility between us, a welcomed relief.

The transmission severs, and we continue.

Falla leads the way. "If we follow Mikel's bearing, it takes us closer to the center of the forest, which isn't ideal. We should be okay; we just have to stick together at all times."

Before we cross the boundary into the forest, Falla stops. "Keep your mind clear and be alert. This is not a kind forest. It will play tricks on you– if you allow it. Do not eat a single piece of fruit from this forest. Do not pick anything up or stop to study things. We need to keep a fast pace if we want to make it to the Tryar Bridge by sundown."

I remember studying the forest in school but nothing those books taught us prepares me for this reality.

The colors become vibrant and rich, us included.

The radical change is mesmerizing. Our arms sparkle like crystals among the rays of the bright yellow sun that pierces through the thick, deep green foliage above. I can't help but gaze upon it all in wonderment.

Falla claps her hands, snapping Ayva and me from our entrancement. We pick up our pace to a jog.

The fruits growing from these trees have colors I've never seen before. Swirls of multiple colors that come together to brighten each fruit, almost calling us to pluck one as we pass. My stomach grumbles at the memory of the bitter apples we finished, but I remember Falla's careful warning.

There are many stories of people who have ventured into this forest, never to have returned. The fruit is delicious, and addictive to the point of insanity. To Falla, there is nothing enticing or magical about this forest. Her conviction keeps her focused, and I find myself wishing I could approach life with her sense of focus and certainty.

I try a few times to tempt Falla into a conversation, but she's quick to shut me down. I slow my pace and fall behind Ayva to take up the rear. Ayva flashes me a pity grin and right now, I'll take it.

The bright yellow sun approaches its highest point in the sky. We've been traveling for several hours and come to the top of a steep hill.

"Why don't we take a break here for a moment?" I call out ahead to Falla.

She stops, looks around. "Fine. But just a moment." We dismount our packs and rest our feet. My stomach grumbles with hunger pains. I jump to my feet.

"I'll go look for something to eat."

"Not if you want to walk out of here," Falla snaps.

"Got it. I'll look for water." I walk off before she can deliver some other jab. I glance back to apologize but she's turned her back, tending to her seeping bandages. I shake it off and get my bearings.

CHAPTER 24

FAYRILYNDS

AYVA

THE TENSION BETWEEN FALLA and Rioyn is palpable. They make me feel like I'm intruding on awkward private moments, just by being in their presence. On top of everything else, it feels like just another reason to be down. If we're going to make it through this journey, we need to start working together.

As Rioyn wanders off I take my chance with Falla. She's always been like a sister to me. I hope she still feels that way. "He means well," I say, gently as Falla tends to her bandage. "He hates that he hurt you."

"I don't have anything to say to him, Ayva. And if you think I came along to mend things with him, you're wrong. I have one purpose, to kill Shivane and Sylon for killing my family. This is just the best way for me to achieve that goal." When I fail to respond to her words, she looks up and softens. "And to protect you, of course."

"I don't doubt your motives. But I'm not sure we'll make it if we don't start working together. Rioyn is—"

"He humiliated me in front of everyone. And for what? His stupid determination to always be the best." Falla's fingers massage her forehead.

"He didn't mean to…"

"I forgive him for his stupid antics time and time again, only for him to find another way to hurt me. Each time I hope he's changed. Maybe this time he has. I don't know. It's not that I don't care for him. You know I do, greatly. I just don't know how to forgive him anymore." Her throat bobs, but then she takes a deep inhale, shaking away her emotions that swell under her steel exterior. "I won't promise anything but I will try Ayva."

"That's all I can ask for," I say. "And he totally sucks. I get it."

She snorts a laugh, and it's the first smile I've seen her have since she joined us.

"So, you and Jax, huh? When did that happen?" A slight grin of intrigue tugs the corner of her mouth. I grin back and allow the abrupt change of topic.

"At the opening ceremony."

"That recent?" Falla ponders her own question. "Well, maybe not. He's always been very protective of you."

"Yeah, I guess."

Falla chuckles. "What do you mean you guess? You do like him, don't you?"

"I've had a crush on him since I first knew what a crush was," I sigh. "He has always been kind to me, but I assumed it was just because I'm Rioyn's twin. I never allowed myself to think it was anything more than Jax just fooling around."

"Jax isn't the kind of guy to fool around with that kind of thing. Feelings run deep in that boy."

"Maybe, but after everything that's happened, who knows what feelings are real right now? With all the stress and chaos, a person can experience heightened emotions and an increased rate of—"

"Ayva! Get out of your Galilean head. I've never seen him that way with any other girl. Not at camp. Not on holiday. Not even when we're home in the Pools of Pearls. Only you. So don't go breaking his heart by doing something foolish, like getting yourself killed, okay?"

My face glows. "I'll do my best."

"It doesn't hurt to have hope and something to fight for, you know?" Falla says. I pick at the grass, embarrassed by my own happiness. "I do miss him though."

Her exhale is noticeable.

"Who, Jax?"

Falla laughs. "No. Rioyn." Her smile falls. "I don't know how much more heartbreak my heart can take from him. Especially after—"

Branches crunch behind us. We both whip around to find Rioyn with full water sacks. "You two ready?" Rioyn looks to us both.

"Sure." Falla rises to her feet, shooting me a look as if to say, See? I'm trying.

If this is her trying, I shudder to imagine the journey ahead.

They are both so frustrating! I flash Rioyn a smile to ease some of the tension, but he's distracted, staring off into the woods.

Falla moves into a jog slightly ahead as Rioyn joins my side. "Did you two have a lovely little chit chat?" I roll my eyes and pick up my pace. "Twins!" he calls out after me.

I concentrate on my footsteps and ignore the many enchanting visions around me. As much as I'd love to broker peace talks, I can't insert myself into the middle of their battle. For now, I'll just have to remain uncomfortably sandwiched between the two.

THE GOLDEN SUN RISES past its highest point in the cloudless sky. We are a few hours deeper into the forest. Falla and I occasionally stop to drink, but Rioyn is growing increasingly quiet and withdrawn. Out of nowhere, he stops.

"What is it?" I whirl around to ask.

"Do you hear that?" Rioyn surveys the forest, listening for something. His pupils dilate as if he is inflicted with an entrancement of some sort.

"Hear what?" Falla whips around in a panic.

"Help. Someone's calling for help. The voice sounds like …"

"Whatever you hear isn't real, Rioyn. Don't give in to the temptation," Falla warns.

Rioyn doesn't listen. He takes off running in the direction of the voices.

"Rioyn, stop! RIOYN!" Falla screams. We chase after him, darting through the twisted tree trunks, leaping over fallen branches and racing down a steep hill.

Rioyn stops, looks around. "This way."

He keeps running as we catch up to him.

"Rioyn, stop! It's not real!" Falla shouts, desperate for him to stop.

Rioyn comes to a screeching halt, Falla pulls at him to turn back. He points to an area in front. "There they are!" Falla and I whip around, finding two figures off in the distance. Rioyn sprints toward them.

"No! They're not who you think they are. RIOYN, STOP!"

Rioyn rushes up to the two guys hunched over a fallen lone tree. "Bartolem! Divan!"

Falla and I stop dead in our tracks, mouths agape, and at the same time, my racing heartbeat plummets. "Is it really them?" Falla shakes her head. We sprint to stop Rioyn.

He reaches them before we do. "Guys, I'm here. I can help!"

Falla runs at an all-out sprint, while Rioyn is reaching out to touch one of them when Falla barrels into him, rolling a few times in the dirt. She draws her sword. Falla and the two figures circle each other, taunting each other to fight.

"Falla, stop! Put your sword down now," Rioyn screams.

"They're not Bartolem and Divan," Falla snaps. "Stay back."

"Yes, it is. They're our friends. We can save them. I have to save them this time."

The figures lunge toward Falla. She swings her sword again, pushing them back.

"Falla, stop!" Rioyn shouts with an angered pitch and a crazed look in his eye.

My heart slams into my chest.

Rioyn is losing himself; what can we do to save him?

Falla pushes forward, the two figures evading her attack with an uncanny swiftness gliding through the air. Quick to study their movements, she evades their attacks, the hilt of the sword dancing in her grip. In one swift move, she lunges with her sword straight towards them.

Whoever or whatever these figures are, they aren't who Rioyn thinks.

Falla lands a hit and slashes one of their arms. Rioyn screams at her but doesn't stop. I hold Rioyn back with every shred of strength I have but he's so strong, too strong.

Her attack is smooth with precision, and she lunges forward, piercing her sword into one of their shoulders. The figure falls back, stunned and cut badly, lurching. But it does not fall or stop the attack, instead rising to its feet. When it stands, its true form is revealed. My mouth drops. Shock riddles through me. *So, they're really real.*

I remember the passage in The Book of Legends depicting the Fayrilynds:
With pointed ears to hear your broken heart sing for them, they will come.
Eat their fruit, you will find their lair.
If you resist, their red, red eyes will find you and lure with a hiss.
Do not run. For it's just a little kiss.

Rioyn's eyes widen as they hiss for him through their multiple layers of razor-sharp yellow teeth. I reach for my dagger. Rioyn draws his sword, and we join Falla in the battle. "Stay behind me," Rioyn barks.

The Fayrilynds swing their long, sharp claws for us.

Rioyn and Falla attack the Fayrilynds with everything they have, but struggle to slice through their thick, calloused purple skin.

Rioyn and Falla are relentless, unwilling to give up, their swords striking again and again, finally drawing thick black blood.

The Fayrilynds screech in pain, a screech so shrill it's likely heard for several miles.

I'm useless in this battle with my lone dagger, also terrified of using my unfocused Ascendance on them for fear of hurting Rioyn or Falla. It's impossible to focus my mind to control a specific person to get them to do what I want.

More Fayrilynds emerge from the misty forest's trees. We're surrounded by several dozens of these lustful creatures.

"Ayva, help us! Use your Ascendance," Rioyn commands.

"Yours is stronger!"

"No, I only see the fire, not channel it. You can." Rioyn and Falla charge at the Fayrilynds lunging for us, hissing and spitting their revolting black blood.

"We can't fight them all," Falla cries. "We'll die in this forest."

I have no choice, driven to at least try; what would we do otherwise, just run like cowards? Metal crushes into scaled skin. More and more Fayrilynds emerge. I close my eyes, focusing on the fire as the battle rages around me.

I see the flames, feeling their burn.

Do it or they'll die.

My eyes rapidly opening, a purple glow beams from my hands. I lift them, focusing on the Fayrilynd closest to Rioyn.

The Fayrilynd doesn't shift from its desired path.

"Focus! Ayva," Rioyn shouts, narrowly missing the swipe of a jagged claw.

A Fayrilynd rushes toward me. I clutch my knife in my hands but trip over a tree root and fall backward. The Fayrilynd pounces on top of me. I push my dagger against its throat but it's strong, too strong, my meager strength waning.

Its black, split tongue slithers at me through jagged teeth, also glazing my cheek with its spittle while I choke on its rotten breath.

"Help!" I search for Rioyn and Falla, entangled with a fleet of Fayrilynds. The Fayrilynd Falla battles, proceeds to drag its heinously sharp claw deep into her back.

If I don't get this thing off me, I'll die. My knee jerks up, thumping into its stomach. This seems to only excite it more.

Falla screams, a flash passing by as Rioyn rushes to her aid.

Sharp, thin claws sheer down my cheek as the Fayrilynd toys with me. It rips its claws into my neck, and I screech in pain. Do something, Ayva!

Flames erupt in my mind, heat singeing through my veins. The red glow returns, brighter, and a high octave scream belts out of my throat.

With my palm pressed against the Fayrilynd's face, it enters my control, allowing me to whisper my command into its mind.

"Kill every last one of your kind. Don't stop until you're all dead."

Now that it's erected to standing and facing its kind, I command the entranced Fayrilynd to charge at the one attacking Rioyn, then Falla. The other Fayrilynds watch in a mystified stupor until the entranced one comes for them.

Eventually, the Fayrilynds retreat into the depths of the forest, their fiery purple hair streaking through the trees, hell bent on heading for their hidden caves.

Rioyn and Falla keep their swords drawn until the Fayrilynds are no longer in view.

Once they have all retreated, I sever my mental connection with the one.

It all leaves me shattered, thoroughly depleted, collapsing to my knees.

"Is everyone all right?" Rioyn asks.

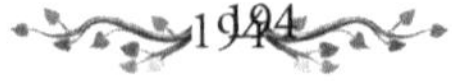

A sharp bolt of pain plagues my head and Rioyn rushes to kneel beside me.

"Ayva, are you all right? Talk to me."

My blurred vision begins to focus, the bolt of pain dissipating. I come to, and Rioyn offers me his water sack from which I drink hastily.

When I'm done, he carries it to Falla, but she brushes him away. "I told you to stop!" she snaps. "I told you to be careful. You almost got us all killed."

Rioyn falls back as if he's been slapped. "I'm sorry. I—"

"Enough of your apologies!" Falla shouts, stalking back toward the trail.

She's angry at Rioyn, but mostly spooked by the fact we almost died. She loves us, you idiot. She loves you. It's clear now, but Rioyn's pitiful eyes are glued to the dirt as he nods for me to follow her. Pain builds in his chest, his heart, is palpable.

He turns his gaze to me. "Believe in The Book of Legends now?"

I look at him, speechless. So much for, 'thank you for saving my life.'

Biting my tongue, I get up and stalk after Falla, leaving him to his own accord.

We only walk for a few miles before it becomes clear that Falla is struggling, moving her pack from one shoulder to the other, snapping at Rioyn when he offers to carry it for her.

As a large stain forms across her back, Rioyn takes her by the arm, forcing her to a halt at last. He sets her down, propping her up against a tree, then leans her forward and raises her shirt. Just below her shoulder blade is a blackened purple bruise, dark green toxins running outward from a deep scratch.

"It's nothing," Falla says, trying to push him away but lacks the strength.

"Falla, stop. I need to help you. Please don't make it any harder."

Falla doesn't respond, tears streaming down her cheek. "I can't lift my arms," she cries.

"Connect to Mikel. Figure out what this is and what to do," Rioyn commands.

I tap the pattern, activating the sayer transmission. "Iyanndyre Command. You have Mikel."

"Falla's injured. She was scratched by a Fayrilynd. It seems infected and spreading; she's struggling to move."

Mikel can be heard working furiously to find the information, but deep down, I already know the truth. Even if I always considered the Fayrilynds mostly legend, I've studied them at length. Few have survived encounters with them, so not many lived to report on their abilities. But records have spoken of poison, madness, delirium, and paralysis.

"Hold tight. Hold … got it!" I wait as Mikel fails to stifle a groan. "It's not good."

He lists off the symptoms I'd guessed, and worse. We have about half an hour before paralysis takes hold, and Falla suffocates to death.

My face turns white as my head whips to Falla, seeing tears consume her fear-ridden eyes. "Is there a remedy?" I ask.

"Already searching." More sounds. Another groan.

"It's a tea made from a rare root of coral flowers. You have to find the coral flowers hidden beneath bigger roots."

"I know what it is!" It's something I've studied. I'm not a healant, but love botany, knowing most of the primary healing plants, what they look like, where they grow.

When Mikel describes the root, it only takes a moment for me to pull it up from memory. The Roots of Roul has leaves of varying colors that sparkle on its branches that grow in the middle of the Carisan Forest. Thick, large white roots protruding from the ground that hide the coral flowers.

"Direct me where I need to go," I tell him.

"Head due north and look for the tree with a giant canopy of red flowers. The Roots of Roul is just beyond them. I'm closing the transmission."

"You go," Rioyn says. "We'll follow."

I take off at a sprint.

CHAPTER 25

The Roots of Roul

RIOYN

WITH THE LAST OF my strength, I hoist Falla into my arms, hurtling as fast as my legs will allow over the bumpy path and tangled roots.

Falla might be a girl, but she's solid muscle and far from light. Her eyes are open, staring straight at me. I smile, offering every ounce of comfort I'm able to.

"Ayva will save you. Just hold on."

My heart pounds out of my chest, sweat pouring down my face. Ayva was in my sights, but now she's gone. I hope I haven't lost her.

The salty sweat drips into my eyes, stinging and blurring my sight. I try to blink it away when my shin slams hard into a large rock, making me yelp in pain, tumbling forward, then crumpling to my knees, keeping Falla pressed to my chest.

I place her gently on the ground and rub my throbbing shin; have I fractured it? An angry bruise is forming, but there's no time to waste.

Hoisting Falla onto my back, I struggle forward, gripping her arms. But without her being able to hold on, it's hopeless. I murmur an apology and instead place my hands under her armpits, effectively dragging her, limping backwards.

Focus. Concentrate. A quick moment's pause manages to erase the doubt of my strength from my mind. One step at a time, pain shocks up my leg with every movement.

"Not much farther." The words are mostly to convince myself.

My strength is waning, but my determination is not.

Fight. Fight for Falla. You are the only one who can get her there.

The giant tree appears through the densely wooded path ahead, its massive canopy spreading across an expanse of forest, pierced by beams of sunlight.

Hope is near. Ayva has what she needs and is in the process of brewing up a miracle. She has to; the alternative is unthinkable.

Falla's story can't end here, in this beautiful but terrible place, her blood on my hands.

AYVA

THE TREE WITH THE giant red-hued canopy marks my entrance into where the Roots of Roul live. I come to a screeching halt, finding the tree standing at least three hundred feet high and fifty feet around. The roots protruding from the ground are as thick as I am, the leaves sparkling with a varied array of colors in the stagnant sun.

Without wasting another second, I'm off searching for the flower under the roots, the one with small, heart-shaped coral leaves.

From memory, it likes growing deep in the depths, far from the light.

Searching desperately, I scour every pocket and grove. How much time has passed? If I had to guess, at least ten minutes. At least, it's been around twenty minutes since Falla was first infected by the Fayrilynd's poison. So, we have about ten left. But even if I find the plant now, it will take time to build a fire, boil the water, steep the—

Hush, I instruct my scrambling inner thoughts. There's no point in falling prey to hopelessness. I have to find the plant; that's all that matters. I will figure out the rest.

Through sweat and tears, the vibrant wall of green blurs and clears before there, peeking out from under a stubbornly thick root, is the brightest coral flower I've ever seen.

Clearing away some leaves, I shout out, "Yes!" But the flower itself is small and young, no bigger than the small pots of herbs we grow on the kitchen windowsill at home.

I claw at the soil, revealing the roots while being careful not to break off segments and miss any of the bulbs below. My fingertip lightly taps at my earpiece. A moment later, Mikel's breathless voice comes on the line. "You found it?"

"Yes, but I don't think there's enough!"

Looking at the pale white roots in my hand; all up, it's about a mouthful.

"Time is up, so you'll have to work with what you have. The tincture needs to steep for at least three minutes to activate. You want to crush the roots—"

"But not go so far as to create a paste," I finish for him. Pulverize the root and you risk destroying the medicinal element. "I've got to go. Thanks, Mikel!"

I run, stumbling back toward the giant tree to see a small curl of smoke rising from behind the wide trunk. Rioyn has placed Falla against a fallen log, but from her awkward position, she's lost control of her body. If she can't swallow, then how is she meant to swallow hot tea? Don't think Ayva, just do.

Rioyn's groan resounds; he's struggling to get the flame to catch, pressing his lips close to blow on the embers. When he catches sight of me, he stands up and limps over to me, pulling a blade from his belt. "Hold still." With a jagged slash, he cuts off the end of my braid, then hobbles back to his fire. "No better kindling than hair," he grunts, and soon, bright yellow flames are licking up the sides of the slivers of kindling.

Crushing the roots against a flat stone, I hurl them—dirt and all—into my metal cup, my fingers burning to clasp it over the flames.

Then we watch for an agonizing eternity, small bubbles forming in the water.

"It needs to reach a simmer, then steep for three minutes."

We look at Falla, whose eyes are closed, her chest barely moving in shallow breaths.

"We don't have time," Rioyn says, going to her side and placing his fingers against her throat. "I can barely feel her pulse."

"Just one more minute."

"We don't have a minute!"

Rioyn lifts Falla's head slightly. We're out of time and can't wait for it to cool.

Rioyn places his sooty fingers against her lips which are usually rose pink, but now vaguely tinted blue. He opens her mouth, and I pour a sip of tea, wincing at the steam wafting from the cup. She coughs and whimpers, but the liquid stays down.

I empty the rest into her mouth, Rioyn holding her up.

Either we've helped her, or we've just poured a cup of water into her lungs, succeeding only in drowning her. But we're hopeful; she still doesn't cough.

We watch as her skin turns ashen, and her breathing slows even more.

As I clutch Rioyn's hand, we both take Falla's into our own. Then, we wait, our faces anguished and taut with anticipation, barely daring to breathe or to move.

She doesn't shift, doesn't seem to change at all.

"Falla? Can you hear me?" Rioyn says softly.

Nothing. Rioyn's face contorts.

Our special channeled twin connection isn't necessary to know he is struggling with the thought of losing Falla, and with the idea that it might be his fault.

"Come on Falla," he says, more urgently. "You're just going to give up? Let those monsters kill and destroy everything you love?" He squeezes her hand. "Whatever happened to the girl with the fire in her eyes? The girl who'd take on a pack of bullies with her bare knuckles, and leave them crying?" His voice falters, almost breaking down.

I hold Falla's hand tighter, calming my mind, calming my emotions.

My mind runs through memories of Falla, seeing her smiling and laughing when we were young together, tracking through the years until now, to this moment, this anguish.

I channel them all into her dark, clouded mind with no idea if this will work but I have to try, my mind awhirl with fear and anger. I breathe deeply, attempting to soothe the tempest with warmth and peace, channeling every ounce of love it's possible to summon, directing it to her. Come on, you can feel it. I know you can.

I don't know whether it'll help or even work, but it's all I can do.

As I breathe and focus, Rioyn continues to coax Falla with desperate words and promises.

"Wherever you are now, you can probably feel your family close by. And you miss them so much. But we're not ready to lose you yet, Falla. We won't agree to let you go, not so soon. I don't know if I can do this without you."

I surround the three of us in a warm purple glow. As calming as the energy is, it comes at a cost. Through the warmth, my mind groans with pain, demanding me to stop, feeling the poison threading through poor Falla like a living creature, moving between us like a trapped beast, thrashing and snarling. Heat flushes my skin, but I hold on.

A high, painful cry spills from my throat, rippling through the forest. The purple light breaks apart, my pain evaporating with it.

"I felt something!" Rioyn cries. "Her finger moved."

My eyes slide open. I felt it too. But do we just deceive ourselves? Is it wishful thinking, duping our helpless minds?

No! It is not. She's there, returning to us. Falla's face twists in discomfort, but I can feel her as her fingers flex and curl, and she starts to take progressively deeper breaths.

When her eyes finally open, her gaze swings wildly around, then settles on Rioyn.

"You," she wheezes, "never shut up."

A broken laugh shudders out of him as he drops his forehead to hers, tears coming, tracking down the side of his nose. "I'm sorry," he cries, shoulders shaking in relief.

"Always sorry," Falla groans. But this time, there is only softness in her words.

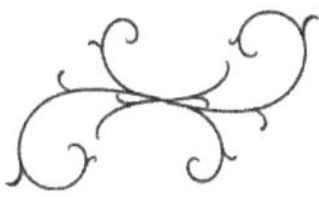

Night sets in as we eventually stumble out of the Carisan Forest.

Rioyn sets up camp and refuses to let Falla help, though it's clear she hates having to rely on others for assistance.

Eventually, Rioyn lies back beside the fire, Falla's head resting on his chest.

His arms looks as though they'll never let her go, wrapping her tight against the frigid air. And she does not wish to escape anyway, that much is clear.

I settle in and lie down, still charged with anxiety from this menacing day. I struggle to put my mind to ease, staring up at the dark night sky.

At first, I think there must be a light cloud covering the stars, then I realize the night is clear and bright as if some of the stars have winked out of existence.

My heart longs to feel Jax. I hope he's all right.

Exhausted, I fall into a broken slumber, to dream of a city in ruins.

Buildings have been leveled to rubble, mounds of trash littering the streets while the many small critters of the night are the only signs of life.

I can only wince at the sight of them feasting on the dead.

Up ahead sounds a child's voice, leading me toward the whimpering where a tall man is carrying the child in his arms. It's nighttime, the man moving cautiously from one shadow to the next. Jax. He carries the child through a broken door, down a corridor, and then a flight of steps to end at a room full of injured people, a makeshift hospital of sorts.

He places the child on a dirty cot, then speaks to a woman who looks red eyed and exhausted. He pulls a pack from his shoulder, handing her a parcel of some sort.

She clutches it to her chest as if it's the most precious thing she owns.

As he steps back outside, he pauses by the door, and slumps down against the wall, watching the street. I can see from the line of his shoulders he's barely able to stay awake.

I take his hand in mine, shocked by how cold and real it feels. My thumb grazes down his palm. He squeezes my hand, and with that, my eyes dart open, and I'm back in the woods where the fire is now just a pile of glowing embers.

Falla and Rioyn sleep peacefully.

Did that just happen?

I blink again, trying to grasp two distinct realities; it seemed so much like a dream, floating behind Jax like a drifting spirit. Yet it felt so real.

Impossible. Even though my Ascendance is of the mind, being able to physically touch him, feel him, is within the realm of possibility.

Cross-Ascendance is nearly unattainable, even for the most gifted masters but not impossible.

Also, how did I dream? We're not in Dremaria.

But then, earlier with Falla, it had felt as if my powers were healing her, or at least driving away the toxins. That too, should have been impossible, shouldn't it?

After all, I'm not a healant.

Riddled with guilt but desperate for connection, I tap our special pattern into the sayer cuff in my ear.

"Ayva?" Jax's voice is barely a whisper.

It's so good to hear his voice, I could almost cry. He asks me a few quick questions about Falla's injury, no doubt concerned by Mikel's updates. He continues to ramble. My body shakes with anxiety and I burst out of myself and ask, "How are you, Jax? Is everything alright?" I must know if what I saw and felt was real.

"I found an injured boy," he says. "I'm just getting home."

My face drops along with my stomach. I was there. "You took him to a sort of hospital, in a basement," I say as a half-question, half-statement.

"I felt you," he says softly. "Thought I might be going crazy, but I knew it was you."

We hold the tiny miracle between us, unsure what to do with it, or what it may mean.

"I don't think I could do it again," I say. "It was sort of an accident."

"Nothing is accidental, Ayva. You are more powerful than you can begin to know."

I hold his words deep inside me, needing them badly. After so many close calls today, there should be a greater sense of confidence in my abilities. Instead, this all terrifies me.

We almost lost Falla, and our trip has barely begun.

"Thank you, Jax. I … miss you."

We end the call, and I lie alone in the dark. Soon, the sun will rise, and with it a new day of challenges. Up to now, our little trio has been plagued by hurt and resentments, a fracture that almost killed us. I cling to the hope that if we work together, we might find a way to succeed and make it to the end.

Or at the very least, die knowing we did our best.

CHAPTER 26

THE BATTLE OF TRESCHERIA

The Past

SHIVANE

SYLON AND I ARE assigned different stations for battle. I stand with Mother and the other Ascendants– all women, Sylon and our father lead the charge at the helm.

My eyes scour the soldiers, looking for Coren.

Caya was injured during training and is in no shape to fight.

Though they both stepped forward without hesitation when asked if they wanted to join the ranks, Caya, with her broken leg, has been forced to sit this battle out.

It's such a shame since she so desperately wanted to fight and to test her new sword; for our birthdays, our parents gave us identical high carbon steelore swords, their hilts encrusted with glistening black crystals. Today, we are attired in our Dremarian Army issued armor, adorned with the Dremarian crest. Last night, the entire army marched to set up camp at the Restful Isles and I stirred in a restless sleep, contemplating my behavior regarding my parents. I hate what I did to Father, and also my behavior toward my mother.

No matter what has transpired between us, I love them more than life itself. After this battle is won, I vow to make amends with both of them.

205

The sun has yet to rise but I—along with the rest of the army—are already up, prepared to move out at first light.

My brother, mother and father appear resolute, none of them wavering in their conviction to invade a neighboring province then conquer the realm, an act blatantly defying the Laws of Seivan. If they had told me we were going to war prior to my time at Sansyre, I would've objected with everything inside of me. But I've seen beyond the comforts of my childhood home, now understanding the greater truth of our world.

For too long, resources have been stripped from deep within our soil and sold elsewhere, to line the pockets of people who have never even visited our lands.

Our people have been plagued by overcrowding, abysmal crops, and more recently, outbreaks of disease. If anyone from Dremaria leaves to seek a better life in another province, they are turned away and spat upon.

But why can someone be treated as lesser than others simply because of where they were born, something far beyond their own control? I thought peace and understanding would bring us together, but I've been proven wrong. They are for everyone but us.

Until the provinces see us as a legitimate threat, we have no leverage with which to demand the justice we so badly and fairly deserve.

The white sun breaks and the orders to move out erupt through the camp, every soldier falling in line. Swords shoot to the sky, boots stomping the ground. Swords lower, then shoot back up in a rhythmical pattern. Our battle-born cry is fierce.

With Father at the helm, Sylon at his side, and Coren closely behind them, we march across the isthmus and into Trescheria.

SYLON

WE STORM THE POOLS of Pearl, the capital city of Trescheria, my father giving the orders to leave innocent citizens out of this battle. We're to only fight the soldiers of the Trescherian Defense, those who fight with a righteous fervor.

We are the invaders, and therefore, the bad guys.

The frontlines clash in battle, bringing the heinous sound of metal clanging against metal. Fists pound into bones, crushing and crunching.

Our soldiers push through the capital city, pushing their soldiers through the Upside-Down Forest and into the fields lying before the Carisan Forest.

I swing my sword, slashing through shields and bodies.

Blood spills, splattering my face but I push harder and deeper into their lines, only adrenaline raging through me. My father battles at my side, Coren at my other.

Soldiers from both sides fall but we push harder, stronger. A surge of reserve soldiers barrels out of the Growla Station. We're outmatched by double.

Looking into the eyes of each soldier who fights with me—with Dremaria—brings a fierce hope. Not a single soldier allows a drop of fear to seep into their faces.

Soldiers, strong soldiers drop before me, their minds seized by the Ascendants.

"Come assist us!" my voice cries, seeking more of them to help but we don't have the numbers. The onslaught heads our way. It's time and I focus, channeling my Ascendance.

With every ounce of strength, I hurl an amber wave of energy toward the incoming soldiers and decimate them. A thick glow ripples through the battlefield, and I curl tendrils of death and destruction toward the cowards who run panicked and nearly whimpering, falling, their bodies crumpling down into the field.

A cheer explodes from our men as they witness the enemy's destruction.

The Trescherian Defense continues to collapse as our soldiers rip souls from bodies, and the remaining enemies begin to scatter. We've won. We have conquered the Pools of Pearls, the Upside-Down Forest and the northern section of the Carisan Forest.

"Reinforcements will come," my father barks. "Charge onward!"

We're pressing forward, farther into the northern edge of the Carisan Forest when two large shadows cast over us, the enormous dragolyons come soaring through the skies.

The heads of these beasts have flowing manes that cascade down their scales.

Scales that shine in the sun's rays as if they were made of crushed jewels.

The dragolyons soaring above us are the rarest of their kind.

When the sun shines on their scales, they appear to be a combination of blues and greens that pale to a reddish purple in the shadows. The only two people who ride these dragolyons are Monnaire and Arro Alore. Our entire army halts at their sight. In a wide, graceful arc, the dragolyons set down. Their wingspan extends forty feet, and their bodies are equally tall. Every soldier in the area stumbles backward, leery of their razor-sharp talons and massive paws, capable of ripping through a man like butter.

Monnaire and Arro take in the soldiers cowering before them, then slide gracefully off their dragolyon's backs and onto the ground. With a single nod, they command their beasts back into the sky while the wind from their wings feels like a small storm. The dragolyons hover high, carefully observing everything below. We all know that one command from Monnaire or Arro and the dragolyons will level this entire field with a single breath of blazing hot fire.

Arro marches toward us, his thunderous boots pounding through soil and blood. Monnaire follows behind him, daring any person to test her powers.

"Zianli," Arro commands in his deep baritone voice.

I rake through our crowd of soldiers, searching for my uncle, realizing I've not seen him on the battlefield once.

Slinking out from behind the trees, our valiant leader finally appears.

"Nice of you to join us, Arro," he calls. "Come to beg for a truce?"

Coren stands at my side, and we exchange concerned glances.

"I believe you were ordered to keep your army in Dremaria after you made your demands to the High Court."

My eyes narrow on Zianli. When did he go to the High Court?

It's a troubling development, meaning Monnaire, Arro and the other generals knew this attack was imminent. Zianli had promised us the element of surprise, but that had clearly been a lie. And for what?

So Zianli could follow through with a threat that none of us had known about?

I glance at my father and mother, catching sight of their eyes filled with similar confusion and anger. Father stomps forward.

"We fight for the rights of Dremaria and every citizen of our province. We will not go on waiting for justice. A justice that will never come unless we take it."

Arro's sharp shoulders lower at my father's words.

"General Greyea. You are a man who has earned the highest respect of your people. But you choose to follow the whims of a fool."

"Then our people must choose between a fool's fight and starving to death through the coming winter." The light in Arro's eyes dims at what Father has to say. "Our people would rather die fighting than die waiting."

I glance beyond Arro and into the incoming crowd of soldiers of the Grynndyre Command, who have formed in a solid line. My eyes meet General Orro's, boring through me.

Given the opportunity, I will battle him until one of us takes our last breath.

"For Dremaria," Coren shouts, echoing my father.

"FOR DREMARIA!" Every soldier of the Dremarian Army answers, their swords shooting to the skies as they pound their feet into the ground, rumbling our battle-born cry.

My snarled smirk focuses on General Orro when Monnaire unleashes her powerful Ascendance, forcing our army back with a wall of burning energy.

I summon my Ascendance to break through her wall, pushing my powers forward. The muscles in my legs burn from the weight of her energy, but her wall is faltering, failing. In her burning golden-brown eyes, her power is visibly fading.

I can hardly believe I have the power to defeat such a legend, but she's wilting under my attack, the realization flooding renewed power through my veins.

Sweat beads down Monnaire's face, her neck and into her golden battle armor made of the same impenetrable material as our own.

Then, with a sigh, the all-powerful Monnaire collapses. The Grynndyre Command surges forward, absorbing Monnaire and Arro into the protection of their ranks.

"CHARGE!" It is Zianli's command to give, but the voice is Father's.

Our army storms into the front lines of the Grynndyre Command. I battle my way through each soldier insulating General Orro, slashing my way closer.

Bodies fall, guts splayed open for the crows to peck at. Lifeless eyes stare up at me as I charge past the fallen, the crimson blood of others coating my armor top to toe.

General Orro is in my sights, so I raise my sword to slice it down again into his thick, armored battle suit. The direct hit sends him flying onto his back, but in a graceful roll, he returns to his feet with ease, immediately ready to spar again.

We go round for round, metal clanking each other's armor.

In one swift movement, my sword is knocked from my hand, so I lunge forward and pummel my fist into his face, bone cracking on bone.

He underestimates me. I will make sure you regret that misstep, I think, confident in my abilities against him. His punches are swift, his battle elegant like that of all highly trained fighters. Mine are brutal, relentless, fueled by sheer adrenaline and hatred.

General Orro lies gasping in the mud as I tower over him, lifting my sword.

"You'll die for that, Dremarian vermin."

My head slowly turns to meet the familiar voice. I almost laugh in joy at my discovery. Standing before me is my old nemesis, Xi Kai, alive and seemingly well.

He swings his sword toward me, but I dodge his pathetic attack. This sad excuse for a soldier wears the star of rank commander.

It will be an immense pleasure to rip it from his bloodied armor.

He continues to swing, and I bait him with a seemingly unbalanced swing of my own. He steps clumsily into the trap and moves his body to the side, ready to lunge forward.

The dagger on my hip is primed, slashing him chin to skull, claiming his right eye as my prize. He collapses to the dirt, crawling around like a lost child.

Just as I'm about to cleave his head from his body, a cry sounds behind me.

My father. I whirl to find him fighting Arro, alone.

Arro's sword doesn't penetrate Father's armor on the first try, luckily. I sprint across the battlefield as Arro's sword ignites with a white light in his hands and falls toward Father's torso. I swing with everything I have, knocking back the mighty Arro.

Together, father and son dance and weave, battling the legendary immortal.

His blows are what you might expect of a god. Bone shattering. It's clear even the two of us will be unable to bring the great man down, and it's only a matter of time before one of us falls. Then, there is my opening.

Arro's abdomen flashes before me, exposed as he lifts his arm and turns.

I lunge forward only to have him spin and catch me on my own unguarded side.

His enchanted sword lights and sizzles as it slices through my forearm. I stand there, sword at my feet, blood spilling from between my fingers.

Arro sheaths his sword through Father's heart.

"Father!"

Before I can take a step forward, energy curls around me. Monnaire has risen from her stupor, has trapped me in her powerful energy. When it feels as if the last tendrils of consciousness are slipping from my grasp, she releases me.

I crash to the ground, gasping for air.

Tears flood my cheeks for my slain father who lies in the mud, just beyond my reach. Boots stomp between us and my hand lifts, seeking just to touch his cheek, to let him know I am there as his life slips swiftly from his body.

But my hands are bound by Monnaire's powerful Ascendance.

I am nothing more than a cripple, left to watch this world burn to the ground. As Father gasps his last breath, his blank eyes cast to a brutal sky, something inside me dies as well.

The heart I never knew I had.

CHAPTER 27

BLACK FLAMES

The Past

SHIVANE

As the tide of the battle turns against us, Mother pulls me back from fighting to join her and the other Ascendants. Together, we channel our powers to create a wall of energy pushing the enemy soldiers back. Our combined powers are extraordinary, but even so, I can see it's not enough. There are too many of them.

A ripple moves through the wall of soldiers who begin to lift their swords in the air. Are they already claiming victory?

A moment later, the cause of their elation becomes apparent.

Monnaire parts the soldiers and sets her sights on us, or more specifically, on Mother. She walks through our wall of energy as if passing through a light breeze and stands before Mother, white hair whipping around her.

The two women stand, staring at one another. I'm surprised to hear Monnaire speak my mother's name with the same soft familiarity as an old friend.

"How many must die before reason prevails?" she wants to know.

"I'm not here to debate you, Monnaire. That time has passed."

"You could end this. Stop the madness before the men are consumed by their egos and hatred."

I channel my Ascendance to penetrate Monnaire's mind, trying to probe into her intentions. Perhaps even to show her some of our own, the real people and injustices we fight for. I've barely started when her bright golden eyes blaze in my direction.

"You dare to touch my mind, girl?"

With a single burst of energy, I'm sent stumbling backwards.

My mother lifts her hands and sends the same energy back to Monnaire; their battle of Ascendance unleashes. Both women are forces of nature as their power ripples through the air in strands of light, their feet hovering just above the ground.

I push myself up to my feet and try to launch my own attack.

My Ascendance feels electric as it explodes through every nerve and sinew. My deep purple eyes glow toward Monnaire when she hurls a dozen balls of energy toward Mother and me. I absorb every ball into a blanket of energy, sending daggers of lightning back.

Her wide eyes are telling. Ha! You didn't expect me to be this powerful, did you?

I summon every last bit of my Ascendance to try and break her with a final blow.

If Sylon did it, we can, too.

Raising my hands, I see our soldiers have begun to retreat from the front line, a group of them struggling to drag a warrior behind them. My brother.

His eyes are closed, and a rag has been tied around a large gash on his arm.

Another man is carried beside him, a sword protruding from his chest. Father.

"No!"

My desperate scream breaks through Mother's concentration, sending her gaze to the tragic spectacle unfolding across the field.

My mother emits a pained cry, a broken, hopeless sound I'll never forget.

The distraction proves fatal, Monnaire releasing a single dagger of light through Mother's heart. She is still staring toward my father and brother when the light in her eyes extinguishes, and she crumples to her side.

I'm not in control of the tidal wave of energy that explodes from my body to level every soldier still standing, enemy and ally alike. My knees buckle, crawling over to my mother, lowering my cheek against her chest. Not a breath, or a heartbeat. Only silence.

My face falls into my hands as my emotions constrict my lungs, my stomach, my heart. They're both gone. Perhaps Sylon, too. Though gasping, air refuses to come, as if my grief is so great, my body has forgotten how to live.

Monnaire bends down at my side, staring sadly at my mother.

"She was a noble woman and her death weighs heavily on me. But your mother was the first to understand that sometimes, death is the only way." Her cool eyes sweep over the chaos and destruction around us. "I let your brother live. Perhaps you will care to remember that as you consider your vengeance."

Her cool eyes study me, calculating.

"Yes, there is fire in your eyes, Shivane. A fire that can end worlds. If I were the cold-hearted creature you believe, I'd kill you now in one fell swoop. But great power can be a curse as much as a blessing, and there's been enough blood on my hands for one day."

She stands up and dusts off her pants as I lie silenced and humbled. Monnaire calls for her dragolyon, the beast landing with a ground-shaking thump close by.

"You and your brother are hereby banished to the confines of Dremaria," she says. "Along with your moronic uncle." Monnaire turns toward her dragolyon.

"You can't banish us!" I defiantly say, emphatic.

Monnaire whips around hard and marches up to me almost nose to nose.

"Actually, I can and just did. Anyone who fought in this battle is banished to live out their days in Dremaria. All your soldiers. All your commanders. Every. Single. Person."

My mouth has a habit of running itself. In this moment, I choose silence as Monnaire stares through me, waiting for me to flinch. I don't, standing down instead.

With a light step, Monnaire lifts herself onto the giant, scaly back of her dragolyon and waves at Arro atop his own beast across the field. As they lift into the sky with power and grace, I lie folded over Mother, protecting her corpse.

Monnaire might claim victory today, but she's made a fatal mistake, one that will ripple through the eons and touch more lives than she can ever imagine.

Victory and vengeance will be mine, no matter the cost.

CHAPTER 28

The White Fog

RIOYN

A CHILLED MIST DRAWS ME from my slumber. In the instant between sleeping and waking, it's easy to forget we are on this grueling journey. As the truth clears, the disappointment is crushing. Then my gaze falls upon Falla sleeping peacefully next to me.

Her warm breath tickles my cheek. She stayed tucked up close to me throughout the night. Because she's cold, I remind myself.

My hand itches to pull her closer and trace her curves. She's a woman of long lines and training-hardened muscles. Absolutely beautiful. But in sleep, she's soft and pliant. Her pillowed lips have lost their blue tint and are rosy once more, slightly open as she sleeps. I take a deep breath and force my mind to wander in a different direction.

Eventually, her eyes flutter open, and she pulls back, blinking.

"How'd you sleep?" I ask through my raspy voice.

"Fine."

I try my luck again. "Are you feeling better?"

"Getting there." I wait for her to elaborate. She doesn't.

Ayva wakes, cheerily calling, "Well, good morning!" Falla seems genuinely relieved to talk to my sister. It's petty and petulant, but resentment is swelling in me.

She may still be mad at me, but she acts as if I am solely responsible for ruining us. Sure, I screwed up, but isn't Falla the one who just vanished?

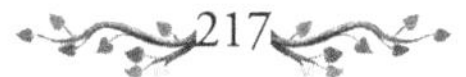

I tried to fix things. I tried to reach her, only to have her mother tell me she wasn't accepting my messages. Anger is one thing.

But Falla almost enjoys being angry at me, like a tired child who continues to scream and kick at the table leg at lunch time, hungry to find reason for a tantrum.

I stand up, my body groaning with the ache of holding Falla high off the cold ground throughout the night. I roll up my sleeping blankets, focusing on the task so my temper-laced emotions don't spill out onto either of them. The two girls continue talking, oblivious to my frustration, so I stomp my boots obnoxiously through the dried leaves to the edge of camp.

"Where are you going?" Ayva calls out.

"Finding food."

"Thank you, brother!"

Whatever.

AYVA

I'll take my chance while I have it, needing to know what Falla knows. She focuses on tying her pack, her movements sluggish. The tincture worked, but even so, it will take time for her to fully recover from the paralysis.

"I was wondering—"

"I don't want to talk about Rioyn." Falla's voice is curt but kind.

"I figured as much but it's not about him." Falla stops. "I was wondering if you've ever heard of anyone capable of cross-ascendance?"

Falla studies me.

"I'd always thought it was just a legend. But when Shivane and Sylon launched their attack, some of the soldiers I was fighting alongside claimed to have that ability. Why?"

My words stick in my throat. Do I tell her? I have nothing to hide but I'm also not sure what happened and if it's something I should share yet.

"Nothing. Just wondering what we might be up against." It's obvious in Falla's squinted stare that she doesn't believe me; my mouth should have remained shut.

"Thank you for not harping on about Rioyn," she says, changing the subject. "I'm grateful for what he—you—both did for me yesterday. But it's going to take time."

"I get it, Falla. But I just hope this war between you doesn't end up getting someone killed." We lock eyes and the message is clear. *If Rioyn gets hurt as a result of your anger, I'll never forgive you.* She nods once. *Message received.*

Boots crunch behind us then stop, fruit falling to my side.

As I swivel to thank my brother, there is only a pallor glazing his eyes. At the edge of our camp across the clearing, a thick white fog rolls slowly toward us.

Two clicks clatter in my ear. We each activate our sayer devices.

"Captain Mikel of the Iyanndyre Command," Mikel says, sounding officious. If the situation didn't suddenly feel so wretchedly dire, I might have laughed. "We have a problem. The White Fog is moving your way."

"It's already here. How far north are we?" Falla asks.

"You're half a mile from the territory of the White Fog, but it's moving and quick."

"So what?" I say. "We run back the way we came?"

"Go too far south and you're back in the Carisan Forest. Head east and you run into a regiment of the Starless Army."

"Our only option is west," I deduce.

"West leads you to the Onyx Ocean. You'll have no way north if you head that way. I'm sorry to say that the least of all the threats facing you is the White Fog."

"It's too late," Falla says as we scramble backwards. The fog rolls over the ashes of our fire, our bags and supplies. She looks at us in turn. "We can do this. Focus!"

We cut our connection with Mikel, and the fog slithers its tendrils into our nostrils. As soon as our breath takes the fog in, it has us.

The glimmer in our eyes dims to an ashen gray.

We all turn and march directly into the heart of the dense fog.

We dredge through the muddy terrain with spirals of fog corkscrewing around us, as if the fog has a mind and body of its own.

My thoughts sink into sullen despair, my gaze tracing the sparse and thin molten black trees hugged by a thick fogginess. Their leaves are black as night with burgundy red veins, while the dirt is covered with a thin layer of ash.

They say the White Fog is home to the souls who perished in this region during the Battle of Trescheria. These souls got lost on their path to crossover, then were left to be consumed by the White Fog which preys on those with weak minds.

It will penetrate your deepest thoughts and expose your deepest fears, leading you away from your intended path.

No one likes me. The thought circles through my mind. Every friend I ever had was delivered to me by my brother. Even Jax. No one sees me, not the way they see Rioyn. A bitter laugh curls through me. So pathetic. Why am I even on this journey?

I can't save anyone. I'm worthless.

As I wander ahead of Rioyn and Falla, they just don't care.

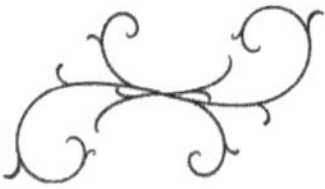

RIOYN

FALLA IS RIGHT, ANYONE who loves me is ultimately disappointed. My father knows that only too well. I push everyone away, thinking I'm something great but I'm just a boy with a sword and an empty head. But why does it matter anyway? Mom is gone.

Dad hates my guts. Everything has been burned to the ground…

We dredge through our hike for several hours, hoping we're not walking straight into the Starless Army, or an endless, thankless sea. No one speaks. No one turns. I'm stuck leading the way when a deep loneliness sinks in.

"Rioyn!" Falla shouts behind me like an echo in my mind. I stop, my body slow to turn.

Falla runs toward me.

"Rioyn, listen …" She shakes me but all I'm aware of is a dark, inescapable depression. All I want to do is sink into the slick ground and disappear, the smoke billowing from behind my eyes, keen to take its hold. It takes everything in me to fight.

"Ayva is gone."

"Where'd she go?" My gaze falls behind her. She smacks me. My head falls back. Nothing, I feel nothing. She smacks me again and again.

"Rioyn, focus on me." She cups my face, her hands so tender and warm. I close my eyes and she shakes me by the shoulders.

"Ayva's fine," I mumble. "Probably stopped to read one of her stupid books."

My eyes are closed and I'm swaying on my feet when warm lips press against mine. Smooth, soft lips, recognizable anywhere.

The kiss makes me feel nothing, oddly, even after craving it for such a long time.

Falla presses her body to mine, kisses me tighter, and there in her embrace, a slow steady warmth lights up my chest as if setting it aglow.

I wrap my arms around her and hold her to me, starting to kiss her back. As soon as I do, she shrinks back a touch. My eyes opening, her face is just inches from my own.

"Are you with me?" She peers into my eyes. "Ayva's gone. She's in trouble."

"How do you know?"

"Because she isn't with us, Rioyn. You and Ayva have a special connection. I need you to try and tap into it to help us find her."

A shiver of fear runs through me, the hair on my body standing at attention.

Closing my eyes, I'm straining to listen to my heart, searching for her in it.

Time and time again, the bond connecting Ayva and me has warned when one of us has been hurt or is in danger. Sometimes, just because she's sad, I feel her.

Through the veil of my own sadness, I feel her now too; it's faint, but I tune into it. It gets stronger and stronger, like a small light blinking through this foggy day.

She's behind us somewhere, but down and off to the left.

We glide over rocks and fallen trees as I lead us down a steep hill, our footing sliding in the wet ash that acts like mud. We reach the bottom, and there, I let my instincts lead us.

We approach two large boulders, then run right through the crevice to an opening with a large skull-shaped rock in the back of the clearing.

A dead, black tree shoots through the skull's crown, its thick black roots crawling up the base of the skull into a cavern with the appearance of rotten teeth.

Sticky red sap drips from the mouth, down the charred roots and into the festering dirt. A blue ambered fire glows in both eye sockets. Recognition dawns.

I've heard of this formation. Sancaro's Skull!

Yes, a dozen Sancaros, the spirits of lost and fallen soldiers, hiss in our direction.

Huddled in their midst is Ayva.

Falla and I assess our enemies, their rotting flesh seeming to float and glimmer as they're formed of ash and held together by an angry wind.

They appear to be disappearing in the air but disappear they do not.

Sancaros prey on those brave enough, or stupid enough, to attempt to cross the fog lands, preying on those with splintered confidences, those who don't believe in themselves. Once they have you, they make you believe that they're your salvation.

They will fight to keep you.

"Let her go," I command. Falla and I draw our swords, ready for battle.

The Sancaro standing before us is a half-rotted corpse that might once have been a Dremarian commander. "You're too late. Join us if you like or run for your lives."

I raise my sword and slice his head from his bony neck. Falla rushes to Ayva but is met with a handful of Sancaros standing in her way. Falla readies her stance.

A skeleton rushes forward. Falla waits … steady … steady. Just as the Sancaro takes his last step to close the gap, Falla slices her sword diagonally from the bottom up and then back down in the same diagonal pattern.

Her sword passes clean through his flesh-rotted bones.

I figure-eight my sword and run to slide on my knees, taking out several Sancaros in one fell swoop then finishing the last one by slicing his body in half.

His bones splinter at my sword's touch.

But when his upper half raises on his hands and crawls toward me, my body instinctively takes a leap backwards, then my sword slams through his already cracked skull, black blood draining from the wound. The corpse lies in his seeping pool of death.

Falla and I battle the Sancaros but are unmatched as more emerge. I focus my mind, channel my Ascendance, black smoke charring into tendrils. I launch them toward a Sancaro but the smoke crackles, sputters and dies before me.

A garbled laugh cackles behind me. "Your powers are nothing here."

Ayva takes the hand of a young girl who walks her toward the Sancaro's Skull. I pummel my way through the fog-ravaged bodies toward her, knocked back by more Sancaros through which I bulldoze my way. They claw at my back, pulling me to my knees, holding me down. I twist and writhe, but they hold me tight, my mind splintering with pain. I find Falla; they have her in their entrancement. "Falla, fight! Don't give in."

Her eyes, usually so bright in their anger, are now clouded over.

"You're one of us now," an oily voice wisps.

A master Sancaro emerges from the Sancaro's Skull, Ayva and Falla standing before him. He caresses them with a sharpened bone for a finger, and his touch lingers. He presses his bone blood lips to theirs and as he does so, their eyes turn from clouded to milky white. Their hair, their skin … their very essence floats among the air.

A passage from The Book of Legends echoes through my mind:

> *Beware the Sancaro's blood kiss.*
> *A kiss cursed with death.*
> *The blood with slit its hiss.*
> *Fear it not, break it not unless you possess the power of death.*

Fear seeps into my consciousness. There's not much time left after the Sancaro's blood kiss. All hope is ripped from them, and they're left with doubts of despair.

They'll never be able to break the cursed kiss.

Hands of multifarious flesh and bone hold me down, unable to move.

My sister and best friend—my love—slips into death's trance while fury ignites my veins. A deep fire has been set off and it rages through me, consuming every shred of my being as black smoke returns to my eyes. I feel it, see it but don't let it conquer me.

For once, it seems receptive, as if ready to be used and harnessed.

In any case, it's all I have to help me. If I don't use it, we're all dead.

Black smoke ripples beneath me and I form the smoke into tendrils, snaking them around the throats of the Sancaros holding me down, freeing their heads from their rotted necks. The master Sancaro whirls to me. I slam tendril after tendril toward him, but he deflects every single one. Tendrils shift to claws, daggers. Still, he deflects them all.

I don't have much control or strength, something he senses, whipping back to Ayva and Falla. I've run dry of the darkness. He reaches his arm down Ayva's throat, tearing at her soul. Grabbing the hilt of my sword, I charge toward him, black smoke beginning to snake around my blade. As if by its own volition, it slices the air, severing his arm from Ayva's soul, ripping decaying flesh from his bones.

"Release them," I command, forcing him back into the Sancaro's Skull.

"You can run, but we will come for you," the master Sancaro hisses.

"Is that so? I look forward to it." I wave my dagger-formed tendril as the master Sancaro dissolves in the White Fog. Ayva and Falla's trance is severed. The color in their eyes returns and with a shout, we start running, Falla holding Ayva's hand.

We run back up the embankment and along the ridge until we feel the warmth of the setting sun upon us, seeing the frosted blue sky overhead. We double over, gasping for air.

Once I can stand upright, I take Ayva by the shoulders and look into her eyes. Is she hurt? Is she … whole? She smiles, exhausted, but I'm quite sure the eyes staring back are my sister's. "Twins?" I ask softly.

"Twins," she rasps.

"The Cryar Bridge isn't much farther," Falla says. "Once we're over that bridge, then we'll be safe."

Safe. That's a word that seems to have lost its meaning. But we have no other option. We must go on. We quickly grab our packs and run until we're out of the White Fog.

CHAPTER 29

THE CRYAR BRIDGE

RIOYN

WE REACH THE OMINOUS Cryar Bridge, a mile long and shaped like a half-moon. Vines with vibrant flowers engulf the massive stone bridge that stands a mile high from the top of the Ruby River to the structure's center. As we approach the bridge to cross, there's a weather-worn wooden sign that has withstood the test of time:

ONLY HOPE WILL GET YOU ACROSS

ONLY HOPE WILL GUIDE YOU ON THE OTHER SIDE

Will I find it within myself to be the man I need to be to save our realm? Hopefully so. I breathe my hope in, absorbing and tethering it to my intentions.

"Ready?" I ask.

Falla and Ayva release the same breath, each having made their wish of hope. Falla doesn't hesitate. She leads the way.

Almost halfway across, courage comes. "Falla, about before—"

"It was nothing, just a case of doing what I had to do to save you and Ayva. Just returning the favor. That's all."

"You don't owe us any favors. I'd do anything for you, Falla, you know that. Surviving this nightmare will mean nothing if you and I aren't—" I

225

don't dare say together, even though that's what I'm thinking. "If we aren't friends anymore."

"Rioyn, you act as if you can do whatever you want regardless of who you hurt and the consequences. When it comes time to choose between me or you being the best, I don't trust you to choose me."

"Sometimes, people make mistakes, but good friends forgive one another. You gave up on me, on us."

"Because there isn't an us, only you. You couldn't stand the thought of losing to your cousin again, leaving me there like I was nothing more than an inconvenience to be erased."

My anger builds, even though there's truth to what she's said. My tone turns frigid as I say, "Then I'm sorry you lost and couldn't handle defeat."

I exhale a breath of regret as soon as the words escape but refuse to let her see it. Instead, my demeanor hardens, my forefinger picking at the callouses on my thumb. Falla seethes; are my false words the final nail in our dying relationship's coffin?

We're halfway across the bridge when she turns and punches me, hard, sending me stumbling back with a bloody lip. I don't dare to wipe it.

"Is that what you want, Falla? A fight?"

The bridge sways beneath our feet.

"I don't know," she says, eyes watering.

At that moment, our sayer devices click twice. We each activate the encryption.

"It's Mikel!" His voice is frantic. "They took Jax."

"What happened?"

"The Starless Army. He's gone."

In front of me, Ayva cries out and doubles over, still so weak from the encounter with the Sancaros. How much unwelcome news can she handle?

Falla puts her arm around her, leading her forward.

"Mikel, stay hidden, stay safe. We'll be at the Drone Mountains shortly. We'll talk again and discuss what might be done." I end the transmission, sprinting for Ayva.

What might be done? My best friend has been taken by evil despots and might at this moment be marching through the city with dead black eyes.

I can't do anything, trapped on this thankless journey to nowhere.

Just as I catch up to Ayva, the bridge shakes beneath us. Hope. My head shakes at the curse. Hope sustains the bridge, and hope is a resource on which we're running low.

We grab hold of the vines wrapped around the bridge's wall, using them to guide us as the bridge begins to crumble beneath our feet. It takes all our strength to avoid being tossed over the side and into the raging Ruby River.

Rocks pelt us, vines slash our hands, but we hold tight until we reach the end.

As soon as we claw our way to the other side, we are able to savor the crisp overgrown grass. Ayva is gripping her head in her hands.

"I have to save him."

"Ayva, Jax is one of the strongest people anyone could meet."

"He's gone, Rioyn! Our mother, our father, Bair, and now him. We need to go back."

"We can't. We have to continue," I whisper.

Ayva crushes into me, sobbing. Falla brushes a tear from her cheek. Behind her is another time-tested wooden sign with faded ivory paint:

THE HOPE YOU CARRY
WILL SHOW YOU WHO YOU REALLY ARE
HOPEFULLY, YOU HOPED RIGHT

Ayva pulls away with a spark in her eyes. "I can find him! I know how."

Falla rushes over. "You'd better not be talking about Cross-Ascendence, Ayva."

My brows furrow. "Ayva doesn't have that type of Ascendance."

Ayva's fury whips to Falla. "Do you have it, Ayva?"

My sister takes in both our worried faces, struck silent. Cross-Ascendence is a powerful gift but it's also a dangerous one. It means stepping into a world between worlds. One that can alert evil to where you are, and a place where forces can capture and destroy you, before you've even realized what's happened.

"Last night, I had a dream and found myself transported back to Casstell. I found Jax and … At first, I thought it was just a vision, but it turns out I could touch him. He felt it."

Our mouths drop.

Ayva's eyes dart between us. She knows the potential peril in which she's put us.

"I … If I could harness this power, it might be possible to find him. Even help him!" Ayva chokes on her words.

My arms wrap tight around her. "Or you become lost in the void and fall straight into the hands of Shivane and Sylon."

The pain in her heart is as palpable as if it were my own, her emotions barreling into me. "Think of what Jax would want," I whisper. "He's strong, Ayva. Have faith."

We press forward, heading toward the base of the Drone Mountains.

Once we arrive, Ayva plops down, hugging her knees. I wrap her blanket around her, then start a fire as quickly as possible.

After the fire has started blazing, Ayva just stares through its flames.

If only there were something I could do to ease her mind. Then it hits me.

How could I forget! I pluck an extra peach from my pack, stick a tiny stick into its top, and light the stick in the fire.

 I hold the peach to Ayva, whispering, "Happy birthday, twin."

She whips her gaze around, allowing a small flicker of a smile to emerge, and I match it. "Wish for a star."

She contemplates her wish then blows out the sad excuse for a candle.

After this, she digs out the stick and hands me the peach. "It's your birthday, too. You should enjoy it." She whips out her dagger, slicing the fruit in thirds before handing one part to me, and the other to Falla. A slice for each of us.

"Happy birthday, brother." Her smile fades as she sinks her teeth into the fruit. "We're eighteen now. You'll never need to forge Dad's signature again."

I can't help but burst out with laughter. It may not be true belly clutching laughter, but it's laughter mixed in with relief, exhaustion, fear. Whatever it is, I needed it.

"Here I am, fighting for Seivan. What a dream come true," I say with just a little bitterness.

"I'm sorry you didn't get to compete for FirstElite. Hopefully, we'll win this battle, and the university will still stand," Ayva says.

"Titles, trophies, and awards do not make a soldier. Nor do they make a man." My father was right. Actions have real consequences in the real world.

Ayva gazes into the darkness. There's a lot we've lost, university and the tournament being the least of it. But we still have each other. Falla's eyes meet mine across the fire, my lip still aching from her blow.

She watches me comforting my sister, a small smile passing across her lips.

I press a kiss to Ayva's temple and leave her to her thoughts.

CHAPTER 30

The Hypothesis

AYVA

Rioyn and Falla asleep as does the sun. I reach into my pack for my book, The Galilean Seivianian, and hold it up against the firelight.

The tome is a comprehensive guide to the various areas within each province, and I open the chapter titled, 'The Drone Mountains' and begin to read.

These curious geological features move and shift as they please, sometimes up to several miles in a single year. A pattern has not been discerned and its movements appear random, making it difficult to predict and interpret.

The mountains move? How can that be possible?

I tuck that book away, reaching for my journal to study the mountains, looking for any indication as to how they move. There has to be some rhyme to their reason. They appear to sit as still as the night and then off in the distance, a mountain peak shifts fifteen degrees to the left.

Outlining and drawing the shape of the mountain peaks on a blank page, I reference the first movement, then chart the other peaks that have shifted in position.

They appear to have stilled after a few realignments, and now, my gaze assesses the peaks to see if anything at the base of the range shifts.

My gaze raking left to right and back again, I see it.

Smaller boulders roll from side to side, rearranging themselves.

Smaller rocks will form at the base to create a path, and traveling on it will grow increasingly difficult. Your eyes will deceive you. Where to go once the path disappears, though? It's anyone's best guess. The Drone Mountains operate with a chaotic inconsistency unlike any place charted before.

Nature, at its most fundamental level, is random. However, for something to truly be considered random, its outcome must be absent of external influencing factors.

The Drone Mountain range is not free of external factors; there's plenty to influence it. It lives in a pattern, it has to. My eyes widen. There's a forming hypothesis which makes perfect sense, something read in a book long ago; it was a lost tome once belonging to Warriem, a studied mathematical sequence from her journal—The Journal of Warriem—in which each number equals the sum of the two preceding ones.

Could it really operate according to this sequence? Does it create a specific pattern using this sequence? Does the timing of its movements follow the sequence?

The mathematical calculations overwhelm me, instilling awe.

If this hypothesis holds true, then we have our way through.

I focus on the Drone Mountains, marking each movement, calculating the time lapse between each shift. The morning seem to bring more activity but as the day begins to warm, the mountains slow. Do they move based on the climate as well?

Only time will tell as we move forward.

Before I realize it, Rioyn and Falla stir awake as the rays of the early morning sun filter through the trees, creating a kaleidoscope of golden-green hues.

Eagerness roils in me, eagerness for them to drain the sleep from their eyes, finally seeing the excited smile plastered across my face. Rioyn finally notices.

"Everything okay? You seem … weirdly self-satisfied this morning if I may say so."

"Because I figured out how the Drone Mountains move."

Rioyn and Falla freeze.

"They move according to an ancient sequence from The Journal of Warriem, a fundamental sequence to which many aspects of nature adhere. This is it!"

Rioyn and Falla's cocked heads suggest I may have lost all sense of reality.

"The Galilean Seivanian believes the Drone Mountains' movements are purely random. That theory is false because several factors contribute, such as the climate and nature itself. Therefore, their movements aren't random. They're precise, like a calculation."

"And you believe the way through the Drone Mountains is based on that sequence?" Falla asks with an apprehensive curiosity.

"Yes, it makes logical sense and would explain why they're unpassable."

"Don't you think we should wait and test your hypothesis a little more? The Drone Mountains are dangerous enough with very few survivors," Rioyn retorts.

My blood instantly boils. "No, absolutely not. I watched them shifting this morning before you two woke up and the hypothesis has merit. I know what I'm talking about."

"But it's just a hypothesis. Don't you think we're better off pushing through the mountains and following the natural terrain while keeping north?" Rioyn suggests.

"Go your own way if you wish." I shrug. "I will travel according to my hypothesis."

Rioyn's mouth pops open. Falla chuckles. "Now you know how we all feel." She smacks him hard on the back of his shoulder.

I twist on my heels, digging into the soft dirt, then shove everything into my pack. Why are my frustrations so intense, and my patience so short with him?

My shoulders slouch, breathing in a deep exhale. I do know why and now I'm just lying to myself, frantically worried about Jax. I whirl around to face Rioyn.

"You're right. I'm sorry. There's no reason to be hasty. I want to get through these mountains, find the Iyanndyre Born and rescue everyone."

"Yes, and we all do. But we can't rush, especially through this mountain range. It's okay to admit you're wrong or need help."

"Putting anyone in harm's way is not something I'd ever do. I'm right. I've spent many nights studying the various books. Now seeing the movements in action, it's even more convincing."

Rioyn, for once, is speechless.

He nods then turns back to his camp to pack up.

"Bravo, Ayva. That was great to see you standing your ground and sticking to what you believe. I'm proud of you."

An invisible tug lifts my thin lips into a smile. "Thank you. I appreciate it, especially from you." A pause. "Would you be willing to teach me to spar?"

Falla flashes an eager grin. "Why Ayva Orro, do you want to fight someone?"

I chuckle. "Not my brother if that's what you're thinking." We share a laugh. "What happened yesterday in the White Fog opened my eyes. If it weren't for you and Rioyn, I would've been defenseless. I never want to be in a situation of being unable to defend and fight for myself. Even if I lose, I want to know I gave everything."

Falla nods, holding her smile. "It would be my honor." She places her hand over her heart, lunges her left foot back and bows, the Trescherian Bow.

"I don't deserve that bow. You're making me blush."

"Ayva, you saved my life. You deserve it all. Never, ever accept anything else." Falla lays her hand on my cold shoulder. "You ready for your first lesson?"

"Right now?"

Falla snorts a laugh. "The world isn't getting any safer."

"Where do we begin?" Standing straight, I flap my hands at my side.

To say I'm nervous is an understatement since I've never engaged in a fight, ever. Normally, I run from them and avoid any confrontation at all costs, but things are different now. Before I blink, Falla sweeps my legs, making me fall to my back. That hurt!

She stands over me, offering a hand up. My hand latches on to hers, pulling her down as I shoot up. She leaps to her feet, dusts herself off and grins, seemingly impressed.

"Good. First thing to remember is your stance. You never want to be caught off balance. Keep your feet shoulders' width apart, your knees slightly bent to lower your center of gravity. That will give stability. And keep your hands loose but ready."

Falla demonstrates, moving side to side, front to back. "Keep your hands up, ready to block and attack." She raises her hands, keeping them tucked in tight, protecting her face. I mimic her movements but must look clumsy and foolish in comparison.

We practice several rounds, teaching me a few hard lessons. My work is cut out for me and Falla will be a great trainer. I need to stay focused, to learn no matter how hard it may be at first; it will never get easier if the hard work isn't done right now.

We whip around at the sound of crunching leaves.

Rioyn has returned with breakfast, a quail he's no doubt hunted. My hands drop, stance straightening as Falla faces me with her hands on my shoulders.

"The most important thing to remember in any fight is to remain mentally strong. Don't let your opponent manipulate your mind and don't ever lead with your emotions."

Falla nods at Rioyn. I catch her hint, returning the honor of the Trescherian bow. She chuckles. Rioyn's curious brow arches.

"Am I interrupting something?" Neither of us answers him.

Rioyn's mouth parts as his voiceless words resonate.

He approaches Falla with trepidation.

She raises her pack and meets his eyes, then they stare at each other for a moment. Neither seems to know what to say. This awkward moment is intolerable!

"The sun has risen. We should move," Falla says, taking off.

CHAPTER 31

THE DRONE MOUNTAINS

AYVA

LEAD THE WAY AS we approach the base of the Drone Mountains.

"Is there anything specific we should be looking for?" Rioyn asks, curious about the plan. I stare up at the charcoal slate mountain range, mumbling introspectively.

"Ayva!" The wrinkle between his eyes is pronounced.

Falla stands next to him with her arms crossed, matching my glare.

"If anyone has a chance at getting us through this labyrinth of a mountain range, it's her. Give her the time she needs."

Falla's stern gaze softens Rioyn's. His nod is apologetic.

I stare at the obvious path ahead, the only area that hasn't adjusted and it's almost certainly our way in. A single, perfectly rounded symmetrical gray fieldstone with flecks of blue sits at the start of the path, sticking out in this rugged terrain as other rocks are naturally occurring, with an irregular shape.

My mind memorizes a mental image of this distinctive rock to draw in my journal later.

"We'll find the main trail through once we get into the mountains."

Looking at Rioyn and Falla, do their faces show confirmation?

"Is that a guess or are you telling us?" Falla's question forces me to find my confidence. My mouth chaps dry. If I'm wrong, who knows what imminent danger we'll face? If I'm right, then we'll be the first ones in known history to have ever traveled through the Drone Mountains in a single day. Mostly, voyants are the only ones who have ever made it through, but it took them months.

If we don't get through today, we won't have enough food and water to sustain us, and my fantasy of being the first to accomplish this will come to nothing. I can't get ahead of myself and chase an accolade. The Tournament of Galilei is one thing, but this is real life with real consequences, so all emotions need to be set aside.

Only science and logic from here on out.

"Ayva, you've studied the mountains. Trust your intuition." Rioyn places his warm hand on my shoulder. I ease into his grasp and close my eyes, searching for inner strength.

"This way."

Our boots crunch on the gravel path the Drone Mountains have laid before us.

I've never led the way, been in charge, or the one in control.

This terrifies me in the fear of failing but also, it's exhilarating, sending a surge of adrenaline to follow my instincts. It never seemed likely I'd be here on this journey but right now, there's nowhere better than to be here, leading my brother and friend, a sister.

We tread through a narrow opening at the mountain pass, the terrain unique, unlike at the other ranges across Seivan. Here, the trees are gnarled and twisted with brown-black trunks. Spiral crimson leaves dance in the slight breeze rustling from behind.

A low-rising fogs twists around our ankles, distorting the surreal rocky path. Dark purple flowers with ashen stems grow in the crevices of the slate rock.

About half a mile into the Drone Mountains, we come to a four-way fork in the road. The path thus far has been steep, almost vertical. Rioyn wants to forge straight ahead through an obvious clearing, but I consult my journal; if this is the start of the sequence, then there must be a numerical indication within the terrain.

Studying the four ways, none gives any indication of being the correct route.

A glimmer of inspiration sparks.

Consider all variables before reaching a conclusion. I twirl to examine the terrain behind and there it is, another perfectly symmetrical fieldstone.

In the Journal of Warriem, she makes mention of the various puzzles she and Everia concocted while creating this world. No wonder these mountains move as they do.

"This way," I say, smiling at the hidden wonderment created by Warriem and Everia all those years ago.

"We're backtracking if we go that way," Rioyn calls out.

At the splinter of an opening, I cross check my assessment, then repeat it at the fieldstone. There was one at the beginning and there's one here. This has to be the way.

"It follows the sequence. This way." I forge ahead, trusting Rioyn and Falla will follow. Rioyn huffs but doesn't deter my focus. He struggles with not being in control but right now, his struggling emotions are not my concern.

RIOYN

My sister is the smartest person I know. Smarter than most in the realm but not understanding where we're going or understanding what her plan is frays my patience. But second-guessing Ayva is a mistake.

I glance at Falla, curious of her thoughts, her kiss still humming against my lips.

"I was just doing what I had to, to save you."

She might say that, but deep down, it means more than she's willing to admit.

When faced with death and hopelessness, she chose to rekindle the feelings between us and spark us back to the land of the living.

If only she could understand that acknowledging the connection between us isn't just relevant to a life and death situation; we work better together in every situation.

I hurry a few extra steps and walk quietly at her side. She tries to ignore me, but it only takes roughly twenty feet for the silence to break.

"I still don't forgive you."

"No. You punched me in the face." I cock a brow and smirk. Falla snorts, but her smiles fades as she grapples with mixed feelings.

"I've been demanding you to be honest with me, so it's only fair I'm the same with you." She takes a long exhalation. "I've had a lot of time to reflect and think back about what happened. I understand why you did what you did. It just hurt because you did it to me."

"It doesn't matter why I did it. I never should've treated you—or anyone—with such disrespect."

"Then why'd you do it?" She searches my face for the answer. I sink into my heels, biting the inside of my cheek, lips pursing into a thin line.

"I couldn't stand the thought of you getting hurt." My eyes stay fixed on the ground. It's the truth but not the whole truth.

"I don't need you using some cheap move to protect me."

"No, you don't, and it wasn't one, Falla. I did it believing I was protecting you from my angry and bitter cousin." I reach for her hand, yanking her back to me, not letting go.

She pushes against my chest, breaking my grip.

"Look, you don't need anyone to protect you and what I did wasn't the right choice. But I'll never regret keeping you safe, ever. You may hate me for the rest of our lives but that will never change." I wait for her to push me away in outrage.

Instead, something in her softens as if a weight has lifted. Her shoulders release her tension. She holds my hand tighter, narrowing the gap between us. She can surely hear the pounding drum of my beating heart, beating for her as she leans in. She turns ever so slightly, her lips grazing the side of my cheek, leaving a soft kiss.

"Are you two coming or what?" Ayva yells.

Falla flashes me a smile but quickly hides it.

She turns to catch up to my pesky little sister.

Ayva hasn't wavered on her path we've been traveling for most of the day. Hunger now ravages my bile-laden stomach.

"Let's take a break. I could use a moment to refuel."

"Good idea," Falla seconds, flashing a quick smile. My cheeks burn with heat.

"Make it quick," Ayva adds. "Should we check in with Mikel?"

She tosses her tattered pack to the ground, keeping her journal close.

"Might not be a bad idea." Ayva is desperate to hear if there's any news about Jax being okay. Who could refuse her that?

"Don't chat too long. It's my turn to look for some food."

Ayva dashes off toward a group of clustered trees growing out of the side of the slate rock. I activate the sayer device.

Falla sits on a spindle trunk of a fallen, rotted black tree, so I take up position sitting next to her, leaving a few inches. Her leg gravitates toward mine.

Mine meets hers, an intense burning of desire washes over me, inching me closer. She hesitates then pulls away, leaving a void.

"Captain Vakor of the Iyanndyre Command at your service."

"Your title gets longer and longer each time we check in."

"Keep it brief, Orro. Where are you all now?"

"Somewhere in the middle of the Drone Mountains. Are you able to determine how much farther we have?"

"Hold. Calculating. Radar activated. Honing in now."

Falla's chuckle matches mine.

Mikel's ridiculousness has reached new levels, but he seems to be enjoying his new, self-titled position, gaining solace among the chaos.

"I assume Ayva deciphered the path?" he asks.

"Correct. Indeed. Hunch confirmed." Falla and I belt out roaring laughs. "Apologizes, Mikel. Couldn't help myself."

"Glad you two are in good spirits—and talking."

Falla and I share a satisfied curled lip.

She blushes, then shoots up to gain space. I should be upset that she doesn't want to be near me, but I'm satisfied that she's coming around.

Things aren't perfect between us, and there's still work to be done on my part but at least we're talking, like he said.

A loud explosion sounds in the distance of our sayer device.

"Mikel, are you okay?" Falla's tone is grave.

"Yes. Okay here."

"How's that radar looking?"

"My readings are getting worse the farther north you all head. I don't know what's causing this effect, but it's distorted. I'm going to try a quick recalibration based on your presumed altitude. That should give me a clearer picture."

I tense in this eerily quiet moment. "What do you have for us?" I eagerly ask.

"I'm getting a faint signal that I believe is the three of you. If Ayva's path stays true, then you all should be out of there before sunset. From there, you'll reach the Iyann Valley. The Iyanndyre is at the very northern tip of that and Grynndyre. It'll be at least a two-day walk. Keep your wits about you and stay close to each other. It's hard to say what's out there right now."

"Any news on Jax?"

The line goes quiet. Finally, Mikel chimes in. "No, they've captured more people. I should go. It's been too long."

We thank Mikel, rolling our eyes when he signs off with, "Captain Vakor, out."

We hike for another hour at a steady incline, powering through a layer of soft fog kissing the side of the mountain range.

Finally, we come to a high pass overlooking valleys on both sides.

To the north lies the Grynndyre province. Seeing the magnitude of the Drone Mountains and how far gives me a profound sense of achievement.

We still have a long way to go based on what Mikel told us but we're that much closer to finding the home of the Iyanndyre Born. Assuming he or she actually exists.

"This is the first time the Iyanndyre Born has been known and we'll be the first to meet this … hero," I offer.

"I hope Gran is right with her information. She's been wrong before," Ayva adds.

"You still won't let her live down not being able to find your missing stuffed bear. She speaks with the dead, not the dead stuffed animals." I chuckle. Ayva isn't amused.

"We should continue," I mention. We walk for several hours, always climbing higher, until our path leads us right to the edge of a cliff.

The views are beautiful, but panic floods in; there's no path down.

"There has to be a way."

Ayva scours the pages of her journal, finding nothing. Effectively, we've walked to the lip of a giant bowl that curves for miles left and right. We are at the lowest, gentlest part of the crest, but even so, trying to climb down would be suicidal.

Falla patiently waits for Ayva to figure it out.

Ayva's head falls into her hands. "I can't find it. I don't know."

Falla points down the hair-raising drop. "We descend here. It's the only way and it matches your path. Look down and see if you can pick up where to go."

With wide eyes, Ayva looks my way then back at Falla. She scoots her foot closer to the edge and keeps most of her body weight behind her, not letting her head come forward past her center of gravity. I squat down and inch forward, shuffling past, peering over the cliffside. Ayva, do the same, my thoughts beg her.

Falla follows my lead and finally, Ayva calms her breathing and joins us.

"See anything that looks like a marker to tell you where to go?" I whisper to keep Ayva calm as if my loud voice will send us over.

Ayva stares at the ground below us, searching through the electric green cover of the trees with crisp brown trunks weaving around the boulders below.

She points to a spot far down.

"There. There's where we pick it up." She swallows hard, pushing her fear down with it. "So … we climb … down."

Falla and I shoot to our feet, digging through our packs for rope, then we tie anchor points around a nearby boulder.

"You should go first," I tell Falla. She shoots me a dismissive look. "You get to the bottom then help Ayva down. I will stay up here and make sure the rope holds."

"What happens if the rope breaks before you go down?" Falla slams her hands on her cocked hip, her head tilted.

"Then I can free climb. I've done it before. I'll manage."

She scoffs but turns back to her ropes and starts tying them off, checking the knots.

I test their strength against the boulder and nod to Falla.

She straddles the rope, wraps one side up the side of her leg and across her body, then brings the rope behind her. "I'm ready."

Ayva trembles at the chasm below our feet. I wrap my arm around her shoulder, guiding her on what Falla is doing and how to move down the mountain.

By leaning back, Falla maintains a stronger connection with her feet. Engaging Ayva's mind has always been the surefire way to dwindle her fears and doubt. Falla makes it safely down the mountainside. I hoist the rope back up, then check it for any weaknesses before wrapping it around Ayva, reminding her of what to do.

I make her say it back to me. She's got it.

"I'll see you at the bottom." I step back and hold the rope.

"Slow and steady. Take your time. Don't let the rope rush through your hands. It'll burn you and most importantly, don't look down." I focus on Ayva's slow and steady movements. She's almost there. Ayva touches down and the rope slacks.

I jump to my feet and peer down at the ground. Ayva and Falla wave.

My turn. I check the rope, then wrap it around myself, telling myself what I told Ayva.

I take a deep inhale, release it and then rappel down.

"Keep talking so I can hear how much farther there is to go." Scaling the side of a mountain last time, I ended up in the healants' ward for a week. Slow and steady does it.

"Rioyn, hurry!" Ayva points up as the mountain begins to quake.

Rocks tumble around me, narrowly missing my body. I release my grip on the rope. It burns the palm of my hand as I scale down the mountainside.

All of a sudden, the rope snaps just as Falla foretold, sending me plummeting to the cold, hard ground and landing on my side. My wrist feels awkward, oddly cocked to the side. The bone moves! My shin, bludgeoned carrying Falla, also slammed into the mountain on the way down. Blood seeps from my pants.

Falla and Ayva help me to my feet.

"Are you okay? Can you walk?" Falla looks me over with dread in her eyes. "Your wrist, it's broken." Sure enough, it hangs there, limp, in a position it's not supposed to be in. Ayva doesn't look at it, possibly for fear of losing what she has left in her stomach.

Shuddering the pain from my mind as best I can, I grab my head. Falla yanks me forward, letting me steal a glance of Ayva's petrified shock.

"We have to keep moving. Who knows if there's more? Are you good to move?" Falla looks to my knee. I nod. "Rioyn?"

"I'll be fine. Let's go." I take one step before my leg collapses from the pain.

Falla props me up on my left side, sliding in under my arm while I balance my weight on my right leg. She wraps it with a scarf from her pack, the tightness helping with some of the pain, but it's difficult to remain conscious.

"Can you stand on it?" Falla questions.

I put weight back on the leg but hide my wince, simply nodding through the warming pain now taking hold of my entire body.

"Rioyn, you could ruin your leg." Ayva's pleading eyes don't quell my building worry.

"We have no other choice. We need to get as deep into the Iyann Valley as we can. Once we know we're not being followed then I'll rest, but not until then."

I take off at a hobbled pace through the softest, greenest grass ever to brush up against my skin. The rolling hills of the Iyann Valley glimmer in the afterglow of the setting sun.

Mists of blue and purple cast over the valley from the Sans of Sai in the east.

I focus on the beauty of our surroundings as opposed to the shooting pain radiating from both leg and wrist.

Ayva and Falla tuck into each side of me, propping me up using their shoulders.

I've never felt this broken, always being the one to protect everyone and help them in their times of need. Vulnerability overwhelms me.

We make it a little over a mile before my leg finally gives out, my body demanding I rest and who can blame it? Luckily, there's a large weeping Mulibarri tree roughly thirty feet wide and just as tall. Thin branches dangle from stronger, sturdy ones.

It will provide the perfect cover for the night.

Falla and Ayva help drag me to the tree and sit me up, Ayva examining my wrist while Falla rips my pants for a better look at my bleeding leg. My head rears in blinding pain.

"You're lucky. Your wrist is just dislocated," Ayva deducts.

Ayva shoves a stick in my mouth as panic floods my body. Falla dumps water on my leg. I wince from the burning cold as she cleans my wound.

Sweat beads form along my forehead, becoming lightheaded and dizzy. My stomach—even though it's empty—threatens to projectile acidic bile vomit.

Ayva nods to Falla. "Ready?" She presses down on my wrist. My bones crunch and pop. Searing pain electrifies my body like a bolt of lightning exploding inside me.

I lie there, breathing through the pain and feeling like a small, broken child.

If I can't harness my Ascendance, and can't use my body to fight, then what use am I? I'm only going to hold the girls back.

My eyes close, and I keep myself from releasing the accruing tears. Every second wasted, another soul is taken by the evil Starless Army. There's no time to waste.

If I'm not stronger by tomorrow, there'll be no other option but to force them to go on without me.

CHAPTER 32

THE IYANN VALLEY

AYVA

THE MARMALADE SUN SITS in the morning sky, taunting us with its warmth. Our day started hours ago before the sun dared to show its scorching flares.

We've been corralling thick branches and vines to create a makeshift stretcher for Rioyn. Falla fusses over it, tightening the vines and testing its strength.

He's not in a condition to move but we also can't stay here, needing to get to the Iyanndyre and find the Iyanndyre Born.

We're too close and have endured too much to give up or be captured now.

When Rioyn commanded us to go on without him, I laughed, and Falla looked ready to punch him. With all the gravity he could muster, Rioyn announced he was our leader, and that we had to listen to him; going on was a direct order.

That was enough to extract the rare laugh out of Falla.

After he passed out last night, Falla and I wrapped his knee and wrist with ripped clothes as tight as we could around his injuries, hoping to help lessen the pain. We were fortunate to find the Mulibarri tree in bloom with berries.

I stuff my pack with as many as possible.

"Mulibarri berries have a natural healing quality to help reduce inflammation while also providing some pain relief. It should also help him sleep."

Falla is smirking. "You might be the smartest Galilean around, but you'd almost make a great healant." I blush at her kind sentiment.

"I guess. It is all just science, and hope."

Falla drips with sweat. "It's as good as it's going to get. Are you ready to load him on it?" The crisp golden-green valley with sprawling rolling hills looks almost idyllic, but our trek will be anything but peaceful.

We lift Rioyn's shoulders and slide his torso onto the stretcher which creaks and settles as his weight bears into it. Falla places her hands on his hips, and I place mine under his damaged knee. She slides the rest of his backside onto the stretcher.

Rioyn grumbles, still annoyed at our refusal to obey his orders.

Falla carries his pack along with hers. She takes the helm and I the rear. On the count of three, we hoist him. I fumble with the weight of carrying him, then take another gander at the path ahead. Panic shudders throughout me, shaky hands giving my fear away.

"You okay to carry him?" Falla glances back.

"I'll manage." She nods, accepting my answer, aware that I don't have her strength but today, I'll find it. Today, I have to find every shred of strength inside of me because if I don't, the alternative is unthinkable.

No way am I leaving my brother behind in this thankless place.

My hands grip tighter around shards of wood splintering my fingers. I shut out the misery as the golden rays of the sun beat on my skin. I pray for a breeze, even a faint one, anything to wipe away the dripping sweat and provide reprieve. I glance to Falla to see how she's faring, but her emotions are steeled much better than mine.

She is stronger than me, stronger than most people, admirable in so many ways.

She's traversed the worst territories in Seivan and fought on this journey, after losing her entire family just days ago. She's survived near death, and worse—my brother. She's a master of her emotions and one hell of a soldier.

Today, I look to her for the courage to find the strength within myself.

WE'VE TRAVELED FOR TWO hours, and we are in desperate need of a break. We find refuge under a lone tree hugged by two hills.

Rioyn sleeps. I'm relieved he's getting the rest he needs. I mash up more Mulibarri berries into a paste and tuck a small amount under his tongue, hoping they'll provide him enough relief to stay in his restorative slumber.

Then I start about picking splinters from the palms of my hands. Falla rips more ribbons of torn clothing from her pack and wraps my hands with them.

Another couple of hours pass us by. The sun bears down on us without the glimmer of a cloud to break its scorching rays. I study Falla but she doesn't seem to need a break, so I tell myself I'm not in need of one either.

"What do you know of the Iyanndyre Born?" I huff at her back.

Falla chuckles, staring out ahead. "I would imagine they are strong, powerful. They are meant to represent all that is good in our people." Falla pauses, contemplating her next thought. "She's—"

"She?" I'm quick to question but cannot stop the smile that forms across my face.

Falla snorts through her laugh. "You act shocked, but do you think a man is capable of having all those virtues? It's gotta be a woman."

Falla revels in her thoughts and I laugh along, even as the vision of Shivane dashes through my mind, reminding me that the darkest evil is found in women, too.

"You're right, Falla. Look at this world that Warriem and Everia created. I wonder if the Iyanndyre Born is a studier of Galilean theories or the sciences."

"The Iyanndyre Born is a natural born warrior, trained and ready to fight in any moment. She was born to save us."

Falla is proud of her thought. I won't ruin it for her with semantics.

As we walk the ridge line between two rolling hills, we peer down into the empty valley where we spot a hollow tree. There, we seek refuge for the night under its canopy.

My hands rattle with anticipation to be relieved of grasping the stretcher. I sit next to Rioyn to check on him and rest my throbbing legs.

Falla dismounts both packs and says, "I'm going to hunt for our dinner. We could use some sustenance other than fruit."

Before I'm able to acknowledge her statement, she's off.

I pat Rioyn's head, wiping away his sweat. I tilt his head back slightly, dribbling water into his parched mouth. He tosses and flails in pain, but he's yet to break into a fever.

My all-powerful brother, the one who'd stand up to any man or thing foolish enough to get in his way ... has he really fallen to this?

My heart shreds in pain, forced to think about Jax and the horrors he must be living through. He's strong, incredibly strong like my brother but even the strongest warriors have their limits. I only hope Shivane and Sylon don't find his. My heart hurts with immense pain, desperate to believe that he's okay, refusing to believe the opposite.

A while later, Falla returns successful from her hunt. I have a fire ready and hot for the hare that she's caught, trying not to turn from the crimson stain on its large, furry head.

We roast the skinned hare over the open fire, mouths watering at the smell.

Once it's cooked through, Falla hands my meal across and we eat in weary silence, our hands too cut and bruised to be of much use.

Eventually, I nod at my brother, sleeping next to the fire.

"Our mighty commander. I doubt he ever imagined he'd be dragged to salvation by his little sister, and girlfriend." I throw her a quick smile. "Sorry, best friend."

I glance at Rioyn. His face stirs, eyelids forced shut.

"We should rest," she says, refusing to take my bait. "Hopefully, we only have one more day's journey before we reach the Iyanndyre."

Falla tucks into her camp opposite Rioyn. I don't blame her for the distance she feels she has to keep. I stay close to my brother in case he wakes disoriented.

The new day's sun rises again, yet Rioyn still sleeps. I envy his rest but worry that it's a sign he's falling into a more serious condition.

With our hands carefully strapped and a few small modifications to the stretcher, we continue on our way. My body feels heavier as if gravity is grasping for our bones the closer we get to the Iyanndyre. Its magnetic pull grows stronger by the minute.

"I read that Warriem and Everia created the Iyanndyre Born to protect this world if evil ever came to rip our peace away. They knew this time would come. The Iyanndyre Born is at the Iyanndyre. Our warrior has to be." They have to be, I whisper to myself.

Falla has been quiet most of the way. I respect her withdrawal, losing myself in my thoughts. Thoughts I wish I could block from my memory, and ones that leach the hope from my body with each grueling step.

Is our mother dead? Will we ever see our father again?

Was leaving Jax the worst mistake of my life?

Tears roll from the pain of my body or my heart, or both.

"Don't cry for me, big sis." Rioyn lies awake with a grin on his face.

At the sound of his voice, Falla comes to a halt, slowly lowering the front of the stretcher. Rioyn wobbles to his elbows to sit up and look around, as if just awoken to a fresh new day.

"The great commander awakes." I smile. "Thought you might sleep all the way back to Casstell."

Falla kneels down, her eyes solely focused on his knee. He reaches for her hand and takes it in his, waiting for Falla to look up at him. Finally, she does.

"Don't you say sorry," she grits. "I've been too worried about you to remain angry at you, but that could change."

Rioyn holds her hand tighter and pulls her to him.

She inches forward for him to wrap her in his arms. I give them space, wandering up a small rise to get a view of the landscape ahead.

Reaching the top, I lift my gaze from the wildflower speckled grass to find a massive metallic graphite gray structure gleaming in the sun.

The building is miles away, but the distance doesn't dwarf it. It has to be at least nine hundred feet tall, its intricate carvings glimmering with mystery. The Iyanndyre towers into the atmosphere with a glowing white polyhedron at its helm.

My hanging jaw matches my wide eyes. "Falla! Rioyn! We made it!"

I don't dare peel my eyes from the Iyanndyre, gazing at its glory as Falla helps Rioyn up the gentle slope. After everything we three have been through, we marinate in this moment, staring at the magnificent monolith structure known as the Iyanndyre. Inside its walls is a person we can only hope will save us all and put an end to this hateful war.

"We are the ones who must awaken the legend that is the Iyanndyre Born. We as true descendants of Warriem have shouldered this life-altering quest," Rioyn says, staring through the magnificent Iyanndyre.

I wrap my arm around Rioyn's waist; his is already around Falla who curls herself to hug me, our wild and raw emotions flowing freely through us.

"Shall we get going?" I squeeze out through my tears.

We travel another mile to reach the Iyanndyre but we're still a mile away, at least.

Rioyn fashions the thick branches of the stretcher into a crude crutch and hobbles along beside us, Falla carrying his pack.

The sun is almost ready to tuck in for the night as we keep our distance from the intricately ornate, solid tungstenore circular obelisk. The legendary Iyanndyre.

It's larger, much larger than I've ever imagined, its polyhedron top protected by a razor-sharp cage.

"I can't go any farther. Its force field or whatever won't allow me to," Falla says.

"No one is here," I shout, hoping maybe someone … the Iyanndyre Born hears me.

I wander until I'm close enough to see the Iyanndyre's detail. The force Falla felt, I haven't experienced yet but I also don't want to push that. The overly detailed carvings depict a chronicle of Seivan's history, up to perhaps a hundred years ago. I could study the images for weeks, but a more immediate feature captures our attention. As beautiful as the building is, there are no doors or windows. In fact, no sign of life at all.

Conflicting thoughts plague me as I dredge my way back to camp and rest for the night.

The sun sets and darkness spreads, but the night is deeper and darker than any I've seen before, especially so close to dusk. It's as if the moon and starlight have been extinguished, leaving … nothing.

The longer I stare into the night's depths, the more convinced I become that the night is not empty, after all. Something is out there, watching us.

"Come to me."

I'm not sure if I hear the words or only feel them, but they're there, then come again.

"Come, Ayva." The voice sounds hollow like a Sancaro, but they couldn't have followed us all this way, could they?

I'm snapped from my trance at Rioyn's touch. "Ayva, are you all right?"

I stare through him, barely hearing his words, both of his hands falling onto my shoulders. His slight shake and warmth of his palms reels me back, his hand grabbing for mine. "Ayva. Are you in there?"

His voice sounds like a distant echo in my head as a figure dressed in all black floats through the darkness toward me. Everything about him is black as night. His cloak, his hair, his skin, his eyes. Yet something about him is oddly familiar.

It's as if I've seen him. Seen him when I was young …

My memory snaps me out of it. I shake my head. "Yes. I'm fine. Sorry. I think I'm just exhausted." I rub my forehead, hiding the cold freeze pushing through my veins.

"We should rest and search for the Iyanndyre Born tomorrow," he says.

Rioyn walks with his arm draped around my shoulder as if terribly afraid to let me go. I lean into him. The comfort of my brother, my twin, eases my mind.

Falla builds a fire, leaving me struggling to get warm as if the chill has infected my bones and refuses to let me go.

Rioyn blows at the flames, seeing them lengthen and climb.

Within seconds of laying my head on my pack, a deep slumber consumes me.

CHAPTER 33

THE SHROUDED VEIL

Under the Shrouded Veil

ZOURA

I SWEEP THE DIRT, ONLY to uncover more below. With each monotonous stroke, feeling no hope of making anything clean, my movements merely keep my idle hands busy and my mind free from the clutches of madness. I pause and wipe my dirty hands on my equally filthy smock, the wool dress barely fit to serve as a mat for wiping grubby shoes.

But it's all I have. I loathe this place and everything about it.

Homes—if such a thing can even exist here—have been constructed from scraps people puzzle together as little more than a roof over their heads. Shacks are better fitting but even that term is too pretty a name for what we've been reduced to living in.

Our sky in this world is black as night without a single twinkling star above, a vast, never-ending emptiness. I search the void that stretches into the never-ending horizon, but there's nothing there. My skin used to sparkle under the stars. That sparkle is forever lost.

I've tried my luck wandering into the horizon, hoping there might be a way out through it, only to realize that if I stray too far from the feeble light of camp—or the sun—I might never find my way back. When I could no longer see my hands before my eyes, I sprinted back before the darkness swallowed me whole.

The sun rises but it's not the sun we know. This one is different. It's black and cold yet it will burn you if you stare at it too long. I desperately try to never let it touch my skin, having witnessed the blisters others have received from its wrath.

I continue sweeping until the sound of metal striking metal rings out behind me. The bell tolls thrice, meaning the Starless Army has arrived with their deposits for the day.

Deposits … Whoever they've captured throughout the realm will be passing through the sliver in the veil within a few moments. We're not people anymore, just some strange resource for the army to collect. To what end, no one knows.

Every day, I race to the sliver to see who they've captured but also to steal a glimpse of our old world. It's hard to remember what sunshine looks like, or how it feels.

The sound of birds chirping, or even a breeze rustling through the leaves; those things are gone now, reduced to a dreamlike state.

All the things we took for granted in our former lives.

I stand on a rubble of stone, my short legs not allowing me to see over the many heads crowding the sliver. Every day, fewer and fewer prisoners arrive.

There are so many people under this veil, I wonder if any were able to escape.

A family of four is paraded in, their faces smudged with soot. Their clothes are tattered, giving way to rips and holes. Next is a young boy, can't be more than seven, followed by a few more boys a little older.

The rest of the newly captured are being paraded in when—there he is.

My mouth drops. I recognize those piercing blue eyes anywhere. I leap from my stone perch, pushing my way through the crowd. "Jaxyon!"

His tired eyes meet mine, thin lips forming a genuine smile. To my great and pleasant surprise, he hugs me. I melt into this muscular chest, absorbing the heat of him, the smell of fresh air and sunlight. He pulls back before I'm ready to let go.

"I never thought I'd see you here. How'd they capture you?"

"They've started using children as bait. I was stupid enough to fall for their trap."

My heart swells. Of course, Jaxyon was out there, saving children. I'd expect nothing less. I just wish he'd been able to save me.

Jax looks around with grim stoicism. "What is this place?"

"Lord Shi and Lord Sy call it the Shrouded Veil. From the outside, from the real world, you can't see it. They say no one will ever be able to find us because they've hidden us in a world between worlds."

I take Jax through the central area of our downtrodden town, into the outskirts where makeshift homes struggle to stay upright. The muscles in his jaw flex at our newfound poverty, his nose crinkling at the stench of human waste. I lead him to the very edge of our encampment, moving a blanket covering the opening to a shack.

"This is—was—Kalli's place. You can stay here until you build your own."

"Where's Kalli? Won't she need to stay?"

I swallow hard to suppress my raw emotion, due to overspill. "They took her. She's in a place known as the in-between." I quickly lower my head to hide my swelling tears.

"Thank you. For this, for everything. I'm so sorry you've been trapped here." Jax reaches his stiff arm to my shoulder.

"If you need anything, I'm just across the way," I say.

"How do people get food here?"

"We've barely been given anything from the soldiers. Most of the food is scavenged from this barren land. Everyone here is starving."

I walk Jax through the depressing encampment.

Occasionally, we pass someone with lacquered black eyes, one of the drones left to walk among us, keeping watch. In a large central tent, some kind souls prepare donated meals for those who need them. Jax is given a half-full bowl of what I imagine to be lightly flavored warm water. An elderly woman with kind crinkled eyes hands Jax a piece of stale bread. He is kind and grateful to the weathered woman.

A young girl dressed in a dirty white nightgown tugs at my hand, my head whipping down at the strong jerk. She brushes her brown locks from shiny lacquered black eyes that narrow at my stare. Then she hands me a parchment scroll.

"Read now," she hisses.

"Who is this from?"

"The Lords."

I unravel the scroll. Once I finished reading it, the parchment singes to ash, making me wince with shock at the burning debris. Jax's concerned eyes acknowledge my alarm; I'm just relieved the scroll self-destructed and I don't have to show him what was written.

His concern doesn't deviate so I offer a smile to relieve any interest he retains in investigating what the scroll comprised.

OVER THE NEXT COUPLE of mornings, Jax rises before the sun, never returning to his shack until everyone is asleep. I look for him daily but haven't seen where he's wandered to.

I stare at myself in a broken shard of a mirror found in the large pile of trash that grows each day near my hovel. Lacking rouge or flower petals to color my cheeks or lips, instead, I pinch my cheeks, hoping for color to form from my pale complexion.

In the low light, it looks as if even my freckles have started to fade.

Meandering into the center of our village, I find people bartering and trading their few precious items. Gold watches are exchanged for moldy carrots, diamond earrings buying but a spoonful of herbs for a sickly child.

My gaze doesn't lock onto anyone or anything in particular. I wander farther to the outskirts but not so far that the darkness swallows me again.

My meandering gait is in no hurry to get anywhere, until I see him.

My heart pitter patters, joined by a hop skip in my step.

His sweaty, dirt-stained shirt clings to a toned, muscular body. I can't help but stare and fantasize about smothering myself in him, dirt and all. For the first time in a long while, even before we were trapped under this veil, I feel genuine happiness.

But my excitement evaporates at seeing him work.

He's digging holes into the pitch-black earth, deep ones, burying our dead.

I've heard others mention that the people who perished were piled up at the edge by the darkness. I never thought they had just been left there to rot and fester. My naivety I guess but here he is, doing something about it, shouldering the burden no one else bothers with.

He buries the people who fought for our freedom, even though they knew they were not powerful enough to win. People who have turned on each other.

People who let their grief and depression consume them into seeking a different kind of escape. There are people whose souls were too pure to be recruited into the Starless Army and were crushed in the process. Burying the bodies here under the Shrouded Veil, what happens to them all? Do their souls still find their eternal resting place?

When—if—we return to our normal world, will we ever be able to find these bodies and give them the proper burial they deserve?

Jax wipes the sweat from his brow. He glances my way and smiles, tossing aside the bucket he's been using as a shovel.

"Zoura."

A blush passes across my cheeks at the sound of my name on his tongue.

Guess I didn't need that rouge after all.

As he walks up and stands before me, I lean in. "I have a secret to tell you," I whisper. He offers me a single, arched brow. I return a grimace.

"You could use a bath," I gasp. "I can smell you from here."

We share a laugh, and he shoves me, playfully, sending a thrill through me at the contact, brief as it is.

Past him, the few remaining bodies are waiting to be buried. "Do you want help?"

Say no, say no … but I will help if he accepts.

"I'm almost finished. I appreciate the offer though."

Relief.

His gaunt yet still muscular frame draws my eyes. He's lost weight in the short time he's been here. "This is where you've been disappearing to, huh?"

"Souls need to be put to rest. We don't need the White Fog in here to add to everything else."

"I'll grab you some food. It's the least I can do." I turn but he grabs my hand.

"Listen, I don't have much longer. How about I meet you back at the shacks and we can have dinner then?" Jax's exhausted eyes flicker a smile.

My face lights up. "It's a date … deal." I blush hard. "Meet you there, okay?"

I walk away with what I hope seems like calm nonchalance, even though every part of me wants to skip in glee, reveling in the glimmer of happiness that never seemed possible in this place or in my life at all, here or back in our world.

I lay out a blanket by a fire pit, having already procured our meals. It looks like our cooks managed to find some root vegetables since our soup looks to be heartier than usual.

I keep it close to the fire so it's warm when Jax arrives.

My empty stare finds the darkness beyond our encampment, wondering what it is and what can be beyond it. A figure walks out from the darkness, casually gliding his fingers through his chestnut curls. His clothes are free from the dirt of his burden; how did he manage to wash up so well in this place? His blue eyes find mine.

Jax joins me on our blanket by the fire, and I hand him his soup. We eat in silence, his strong hand gently holding the twisted ironore spoon, taking the tiniest of sips as if hoping to make the meal last longer. Jaxyon Risor is a rare man, one who spares the souls of those who passed, so they might journey on to their next life.

It seems he is as good as he is handsome.

My thoughts flitter into my stomach, sending it into knots. My heavy head lowers as I set down my soup bowl. Damn that little girl and her parchment message. I suck in a breath to muster up the courage. "Are there many people left out there? In our world?"

"I'm sure there are some," he says slowly. "But I don't know how long they'll last. The Starless Army is relentless."

"Any of our friends?" I say, a touch too quickly. "I … I just thought I would have found everyone in here by now. I'm worried." I risk raising my eyes to search his; he's hesitant. Will he tell me anything? He resumes slurping his soup.

"Xylar and Mikel were able to escape to Windalai."

"Why didn't you go with them?"

"I wanted to help people here."

I hesitate to ask what I need to, but must do so, anxiety pulsing. "What about the Orro twins? Rioyn is your best friend, right? Were he and Ayva able to escape?"

Jax watches me closely. I swallow, and smile.

"Haven't seen them since the festival." He drops his spoon into his bowl and yawns. "It's been a long day. If you don't mind, I'm going to try and rest. Thank you for the meal." Jax rises to his feet, reaching to remove my empty bowl.

"I'll clean up." I take his bowl and watch the flex of his muscular back as he lifts himself from the blanket and trudges into his shack.

I clean up our date—our deal—that I suspect I botched, badly.

The night grows late. Soon, I peer out into the quiet encampment and tiptoe around the shack, careful not to make a sound. A slight noise makes me turn, then dirty hands cover my mouth, making me taste the filth encrusted in my captor's roughened skin.

He drags me back into my shack, throwing me to the unforgiving ground.

My eyes dare a glance at him, but he smacks me hard across my face. I open my eyes wide to ease the dizziness, cupping my sticky, throbbing cheek. Blood stains my hand. Before I realize what's happening the man grabs my ankles.

He's soon on his knees, yanking my legs apart, crudely ripping at my woolen dress. Realization dawns, and I kick at him with all I have. But it's not enough. He's much stronger and heavier. Choking on my disgust, I open my lips and bite down on his disgusting hand. He rips it away, cursing.

"Ah, a fighta." The grotesque man savors me with his red eyes, his rotten teeth curdling my insides. "I love a gal with spirit." He unbuttons his pants.

I have to escape. After everything that's happened, part of me imagines just giving up. What's one more cruelty, after everything else I've endured? I could just take it, perhaps spare myself more bruises and hurt. But my fighting spirit has been what's kept me alive this far. I can't give up now. And aside from that, he's just too disgusting to stomach. "Get off me, Roccali scum!" I scream, jabbing a thumb into his eye socket.

He squeals like a girl, then punches me once, twice and on the third time, sends me reeling back, barely conscious.

My vision goes in and out as a second man joins him. Please, not two of them…

A heavy grunt comes, the man's body moving atop mine. Then, the instant relief as he suddenly rolls off me, tugging me up off the ground.

"Please, don't hurt me," I cry.

"I have you, Zoura. You're safe." Jax carries me out of my shack and into his, settling me on the small pallet and fixing my dress.

His calloused hands brush the hair from my face, then he covers me in the blankets that smell like him—of sunlight and woodlands. I cry out, sensing him leaving the shack.

Where is he going?

"Eh now, I meant nothins by it." That horrid voice.

My skin crawls just at the sound and resonance of it.

A set of heavy thumps is followed by muffled pleas, then silence.

I don't fear for Jax, knowing that as strong as my attacker is, he's no match for the boy with ice blue eyes. The punishment sounds brutal, but the thug deserves it for what he did to me and likely to other women in this camp.

I'M JOSTLED AWAKE BY Jax lying down next to me. He keeps his space but still, his warmth is palpable, bringing a sense of peace lying next to him.

So much so that sleep quickly comes.

The next morning, my eyes open to see that Jax is already gone. Rushing out of the shack, I search for him high and low, terrified of crossing paths with that grotesque man.

Curling around the corner of the shack, I smack right into Jax, my hands bracing him upon impact. The feel of his warm, strong chest muscles under my palms feels a little like coming home.

"Glad to see you're awake. How're you feeling?"

My eyes glaze over, and I sink into him, effectively forcing him to hug me. I am not above forced hugs. "Thank you," I say, sounding about five years old.

"I'm heading out. Do you want to come with me or would you rather—"

"I'm coming with you. Give me a moment."

Darting into my shack, I clean myself up as best I can, careful to keep my eyes from the cot in the corner.

Jax and I walk through our makeshift city under the Shrouded Veil, my jaw still aching badly, my left eye also not opening fully. Even so, for a moment, I forget where we are, swept up in the delicious warmth of Jax's presence. He seems light-footed and happy today until we approach the pile of decomposing bodies, which has grown since yesterday.

The smell is enough to make me gag.

Jax hands me his scarf and grabs his shovel.

Anything vaguely resembling a weapon has been quickly confiscated by the Starless Army. But the encampment leaders have heard what Jax is doing and find for him an old shovel and hoe, a vast improvement on the rusty bucket.

"I can help," I say, muffled through the scarf. He shakes his head, but I insist. "Please. I want to." He offers a smile, handing the hoe across.

We work together, me doing my best to loosen the hard-packed dirt so that Jax can shovel it more easily. Instead of single graves, we opt to dig a large, solitary pit.

It isn't ideal, but we're eating starvation rations and have only so much energy to give in our weakened states.

Before we backfill the hole, Jax takes his time to whisper a prayer over each body, moving his hand in the traditional gesture to help guide them on.

Some will be fortunate to go to the upper world, while others will sink into the lower. At least, that is the belief of our people.

As the blackened day comes to an end, we grab our soup bowls, heading straight to the food tent, greedily finishing the little they offer us.

Eyeing him, so many words come to mind, but they never escape my lips; tiredness overwhelms me, and this isn't the time for small talk between us. We're too exhausted.

So, we walk back to our shacks, creaking with each step like an old married couple.

Jax pulls back the old piece of tin covering the entrance to his shack, then stops. He takes a moment, then faces me. "I think it's safer if you stay with me. Don't you?"

My cheeks flush, and I pinch my lips to stop from smiling ear to ear.

"Sure. I'm just going to change first."

Inside my shack, I peel off my dirty dress. Luckily, there's still some fresh water in my basin to try and clean off with, tying my hair up in a bun. When I've done the best I can, I pull on a slightly cleaner gown that belonged to Kalli, I've saved for sleeping.

Shortly, I find Jax where I left him, adjusting the blankets for me to lie down and I take my side. He lies on the opposite side of the blankets, farther from me than last night.

There, we lie in silence, breathing into the night; it's cool, a shivering noise escaping my lips, then I roll over to snuggle against his side.

He tenses, but I've come too far to stop now. With a yawn, I sling my arm over his chest, nestling my head on his shoulder.

He lies there beneath me, rigid and frozen as a block of wood.

Was this a mistake?

I'm about to slink back when his hand slides around my shoulders and tugs me into his side. In a world filled with nothing but darkness, Jax is my center. I will not let him go.

You will be mine, my mind says, drifting into blissful sleep.

The night is cool and quiet on waking a few hours later, remembering what needs doing. Gingerly, my arm pulls out from under Jax's own, tucking the blankets closer to him to nip the chill. With a single regretful glance back, my stealthy frame tiptoes out of his shack and into the night.

C H A P T E R   3 4

THE THRONEROOM

Under the Shrouded Veil

J A X Y O N

ZOURA SLINKS OUT OF my hut, jostling me awake from my light slumber. Where could she possibly be going at this hour?

I keep my distance, only just enough to track where she's heading.

Who knows why a vulnerable young woman would want to move through this dangerous wasteland in the middle of the night, especially after being attacked so recently? But I'm determined to find out, only hoping the answer doesn't confirm the creeping suspicion in my heart. She's been a little too inquisitive about our friends.

Slipping around a pile of rubble, I stare up at the vast, jagged building ahead, the only proper structure in this place, a monument that seems to have been pulled from the black soil and thrust into the black void of a sky.

Since arriving, I've been steering clear of this place. But here it is, the towering steelore door leading to the throne room of Shivane and Sylon.

My heart sinks. What is Zoura doing here?

My 'friend' walks up to one of the soldiers standing guard, darting a quick look over her shoulder, then leans in to say something.

The soldier disappears through the door, returning a moment later.

There's no need to know why she has chosen to go inside the very place all her fellow citizens fear more than death itself. The answer is apparent.

265

Zoura, either through desire or duress, is serving the enemy.

I remain hidden behind the rubble, breathing through my disappointment and anger. As furious as I am, I remind myself that in this place, people must do horrible things to survive. Who knows what evil threats Zoura might have met with?

It's a struggle to reserve my judgment until there's more information.

It doesn't take long before the creak of the door announces her return, and she's slinking back in my direction. I stay in the shadows, grabbing her arm and quickly covering her mouth as she passes.

When she realizes it's me, I release my hand, tugging her into the shadows.

"You're working with them?" I stare into her hazel eyes searching for the truth, finding only tears of despair.

"You wouldn't understand."

She squirms her arm from my grasp, but I hold her where she is.

"Try me. Unless you have other friends here, I'm all you got."

My arms fold across my chest.

"There's a place here that's worse than anything you've seen so far." She swallows. "They have Kalli in the in-between. I have to save her. They said if I get them information about the Orro twins, they'll let her go."

"Who is they?"

"Lord Shi and Lord Sy."

My heart sinks, a wave of panic blinding me. "Why do they want information about Ayva and Rioyn?"

"I don't know. Either way, I don't have the answers they want, and if I don't offer them something soon, they're going to turn her into one of those black-eyed monsters. Or kill her in the process because she's too good of heart to become one of them."

A tear tracks down her cheek. My finger catches it before it falls, brushing it away.

"I'm sorry about Kalli, Zoura, but—"

"You know where they are, don't you?" Her shoulders shudder. "I can tell. But you won't help me."

"I won't betray my friends. They might be our only hope—Kalli's too. I can't tell you anything more than that. But I have an idea that might just hold them off." I take a deep sigh, wondering if I'm about to make a huge mistake. It's a calculated risk. "I have to know you're with me on this. No more lies. This only works if we trust each other."

Zoura takes my hand, pressing it to her heart. "I swear, Jaxyon. I'll do anything. I just want to help my friend."

"Then let's go home and get to work."

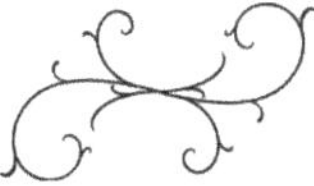

A FEW DAYS LATER, ZOURA is summoned back to 'Lord Shi and 'Lord Sy's' throneroom. This time, I accompany her, walking at her side.

The stench of sewage and rotting trash attacks my senses. Though breathing mostly from my mouth, the stench is so foul that its taste forms a slickness on my tongue.

Our captives apparently want to keep enough of us alive to force the remaining free leaders into capitulation, but they don't mind if the majority of us starve to death, or waste away. Slaughtering us all would have been a kindness.

Arriving at the entrance of the throneroom, Zoura stands with her eyes pinned to the ground as I address the soldiers, demanding entrance.

The guard disappears then returns a fleeting moment later. It doesn't take much searching to confirm we are unarmed. He allows our entry.

Zoura goes first and I follow behind.

She whips a look at me as if warning me to fall back. No way.

We pass by entrance after entrance to a plethora of dark chambers littering the dingy hallway. There's a pungent rotting smell, the stench of something lingering in the thick, choking and rancid air.

Every other second, a faint scream comes from one of the mysterious chambers; they seem to be torture rooms. Is this what's in store for us?

We come up to a door with no screams, no rotting smell emanating. The door is slightly ajar, inviting a peek inside. Bodies lie lifeless yet look as if they're sleeping.

Don't I know some of them? They seem familiar. But how can it be so?

One of the sleepers looks eerily similar to Rioyn's mother, killed before the veil came down. I inch closer for a better look when something forces me forward.

The hallway opens to a cavernous room just as dark as the hallway before us. Sprinkles of light streaming from above highlight the menacing thrones sitting atop the dais.

Shivane leans against her wild throne of spikes and thorns, covered in a blood-like rust.

Sylon sits against his cold steel throne, cast as a single, giant lightning bolt. He appears untamed and feral against the cold splendor of his sister.

"My dear Zoura, you've bought us a friend."

Shivane seems to slither, rather than speak.

I step forward. "When Zoura questioned me, I guessed at the reason. But if she is going to profit from my secrets, surely, I should have the opportunity to benefit as well?"

If they fall prey to my plan, then I can be the one to take them down, to infiltrate their inner keep. I keep my face neutral, even when longing to feel their blood hot and slick against my hands.

"You're bold," Shivane says, her eyes flashing. "And stupid."

I drop to my knee before the monster, hating myself more each moment. "No, Lord Shi, I'm just a man with nothing to lose."

"Humor me some more." Her dark purple eyes narrow, a devious grin sharply curling her lip as she raises her closed fist in front of my face.

C H A P T E R 3 5

WINTER'S BREAK

R I O Y N

WE CAMP UNDER THE comforting light of the rising moon, a raging fire keeping the cold at bay. Relief, even elation should set in, but instead, my stomach churns with worry as I sit watching over my sleeping sister.

What did she see in the dark?

Falla lays out her blanket next to me, warming me with her closeness. After a moment of fiddling, she shifts yet nearer to me, leaving me still wishing to be closer.

"That day, when you made me fall," she says, "I stared into your eyes, and you weren't there. Where did you go?"

My heart quickens as I reach for her hand. She doesn't move away at first, then uncomfortably shifts her own hand under her leg.

"They wouldn't have let you win," I whisper softly.

"I could've beaten him." She means it, judging by her confident tone.

"If it was a fair fight, yes, but they weren't going to let it be."

"You keep saying they. Who are they?" Falla studies my face for the truth. I struggle to find the words. "Rioyn, tell me."

"Hanri. Cartus and Niklon."

It's a truth she should've been told then, but I'll tell it all now even if it breaks my heart to do so. "The night before our challenge, they yanked

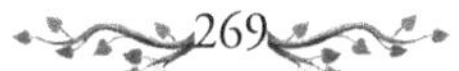

269

me from my bunk in the dead of night and told me to throw the fight and let you win.”

“Why?”

“They wouldn’t say, but my guess is they wanted you to pass to the final round to face off against Hanri. He would have loved to promote a final match between ‘Trescherian trash’ and a noble Grynndyre born. Especially if he could make some coin on all the bets.”

“I would have beaten him!” Her voice is full of righteous outrage. She wouldn’t have won.

“In a fair fight, perhaps,” I lie. “But a few days earlier, I had found him stashing herbs in his bag. The kind you use to make someone a little clumsy. My guess is that he planned on setting you up for a spectacular defeat.”

“So, why not tell me?”

“And start a war? We’d soon be in university together, and the last thing we needed was Hanri and his goons wanting to make life impossible for us. He might be a creep, but he’s a popular creep.”

“So, what, you just let him throw his weight around? Bow your head and look the other way?”

“If you beat me in the match, I planned on telling the commanders that Hanri was cheating. And if I beat you, I wouldn’t have to worry about being in the final round and meeting whatever Hanri wanted to throw at me. Didn’t think he’d risk upsetting my father by doing anything too drastic.”

I sigh. “My plan might have worked, if Hanri hadn’t realized I’d refuse to cooperate. At the very last minute, he switched the fighting pairs with you now facing a weaker opponent. You’d almost certainly make it through to the finals. I should have let you, and exposed Hanri’s plan. Instead, I decided to sabotage you. It was just a stupid camp competition. It hadn’t seemed important at the time.”

“So, when I was then matched up with Evon …” she begins.

“I had to make sure you lost against any opponent you could beat. I had to cheat you in that round, so you’d not be cheated in a later one. All because I’m afraid of my cousin.”

I drop my head in my hands. “I would say sorry, but it’s probably not what you want to hear right now.”

The crackle of flames fills the empty night.

"Imagine if you were fighting in a competition," she says, "and when no one was looking, I stepped forward and tripped you." I start to speak but she raises her hand, silencing me. "And if that weren't bad enough, I went on to win the entire competition. And when you asked me why I'd done that, I pretended not to know what you were talking about. Laughed with my friends and suggested I might need to learn to be a better loser. Imagine how confused and betrayed you'd feel."

"I'd be devastated," I admit. "And furious." Both are true. "The difference is, I wouldn't just walk away. Not from you, Falla, even after such a betrayal because I know you and your heart. I'd have given you a chance to explain. But I never got that chance, because when I came after you, you disappeared."

"I thought you sabotaged me because all you cared about was winning."

"I do care about winning, but I care about you more." It's the absolute truth I've been holding in, desperately waiting to tell her.

As we sit together, but not together. Something that ruptured inside of me that night begins knitting back together. Losing Falla's friendship and respect has cost me more than I ever could have ever guessed. I won't lose it again.

"It's funny," she says. "I always sensed that they judged me because I came from a different region. But I never fully realized how deep that hatred ran, until now."

"Shivane and Sylon are evil, but they also exploited fractures that were already there, and deepening."

"The colored wristbands people were forced to wear at the festival," Falla says. "Dividing us."

"The only division now is between good and evil. Light and dark." I stare up at the sky, only a few tiny dots of light remaining.

"Let's bring so much light into this world, those monsters are forever blinded by it," Falla murmurs.

I reach for her hand and this time, refuse to let her bury it away. I squeeze it, hoping we find a way to do just what she's described.

CHAPTER 36

THE IYANNDYRE

AYVA

"WE SHOULD SPLIT UP and each take a section," I say, staring at the giant structure.

"Don't get too close. Who knows what effects it has?" Falla says as she begins her trek. How close will we be able to get? Can we do it? What will the effects be?

I'm used to my brother questioning my directives, but today, he simply shrugs, offering to search the area around the north side of the Iyanndyre. He and Falla have been strangely calm all morning. It's hard not to feel a stab of jealousy. They have each other, whether they want to talk to one another or not. They're here together. Jax is probably suffering in some hellhole, wondering why he couldn't simply have come along. I wish he could've come. Did Gran know this would happen? Did she want it to?

"I'll meet you both back here, say two hours after high noon?" Rioyn says.

"Sure. I'll take the south."

With a huff of exasperation, I turn on my heels and stomp off, not entirely sure why I'm in such a grumpy mood, other than the fact that life sort of sucks. Majorly sucks.

Maybe it's this whole damned journey. We survived not just the Carisan Forest, the White Fog and the Cryar Bridge. We made it through the impossible Drone Mountains.

273

We also dragged Rioyn through the beautiful, seemingly never-ending Iyann Valley, and now we're here. We made it. But what is here, exactly? So far, a big fat nothing.

He or she has to be here. Somewhere. Anywhere. We have to find them. This legend.

After a few hours of feeling sorry for myself and allowing my frustrations to roam free, I trudge up another hill with the same velvet soft grass.

In the distance, the thunderous roar of waves crashes, then pulls out to sea.

If the answer to our prayers is here in the Iyanndyre, then we have to assume we're not the only ones with access to this information.

How long before the Starless Army finds its way here?

My eyes focus on the monstrosity of these crystal waves known as the Waves of Omaru, so powerful that if you're snarled in its riptide, you're likely never to return. You'll be lucky if they spit you out into Aquaria with hopes that someone might find you.

The Waves of Omaru pound the ambered crystal beach, clawing at the sand, taking out its tide then caressing it back in. The waves' sound soothes my frustrated anxiety, my eyes rolling with each successive one, coming and going, going and coming.

Gratitude rises inside me. These waves. The crystal sand beach of the Jesper Ocean—home to the Waves of Omaru—untouched by people throughout history.

It's selfish of me to sit and take it in when our mission is so urgent. But my heart is weary, needing a moment to steel myself for whatever awaits.

Settling into the soft grass, I let my palms rest on the tops of my knees, closing my eyes and listening, listening to the waves. Listening to what they might say. Almost unbeckoned, my Ascendance starts to rise and I let it warm its way through my bones, my muscles, through my heart, heat enrapturing my body as the glow spills from the depths of my soul, a purple light swirling around me.

Then I feel them. I feel Jax. I feel our father, our uncle. My heart skips with a joy unknown since standing on the stage at the Tournament of Galilei.

My eyes shoot open. I leap to my feet and sprint back to camp.

The forest of thick trees is denser than remembered, my sense of direction dramatically off. I push and wind through a collection of peeling birches where light pierces through the last set of hugging trees. Running toward the light, I wiggle through the small opening, my clothes catching on the peeling bark. Wrestling my way through the final tree, I spin around and come face to face with the Iyanndyre itself.

How did I get this close? I don't feel its effects.

My curiosity gets the better of me and I lurch forward, my foot catching on a raised root, stumbling, using the Iyanndyre as a brace.

My hand glows upon touching the tungstenore structure. Pulling back, my fingers lift to touch the Iyanndyre again, but this time slowly, watching what it does.

My hand hovering inches from the engraved surface, an image forms in the grayish, silvery metal.

It portrays two women hugging while a spherical object flies off out of sight.

The image is wiped away, replaced by another of the same women facing each other, holding hands. They're engulfed in flames. When they release their hands, the flames stop and their eyes glow. A ray of sunlight behind me filters through the foliage and onto the Iyanndyre, casting a golden hue over their glowing eyes.

"Did you find something?" Falla says, shouting at a distance.

"Maybe, I don't know. Did either of you find anything?"

Rioyn finds me. It doesn't affect him either.

"I haven't seen a single indication that anyone has set foot on these lands in a very, very long time," he says. An unspoken question hangs between us.

What if Gran'ama was wrong, or confused?

"What're our options? Should we contact Mikel? See if he has any information on his end?"

"Good idea." Rioyn enters the pattern into his sayer device.

A low, whispered voice comes through our transmission. "Hey … can you he … me?"

"Barely." Rioyn taps on his sayer device. "Can you hear us? Is everything okay?"

"They've launched more strikes. More search parties. I don't know how much longer I ha … until … You find the born?"

"No. No one is here," Rioyn clips. "The place is empty."

Through broken snippets of sound, we gather that Mikel has no other information to offer. Then, snippets of new sounds pop through the transmission. Broken as they are, the shift is noticeable. Mikel speaks urgently and fearfully, but we can't make out his words.

Rioyn and I exchange worried looks.

"Perhaps we should cut the transmission," I whisper. "It sounds like something is happening there."

We strain to hear as Mikel's broken voice is suddenly joined by others. We catch the crash of something breaking, and a final appeal from Mikel.

The line goes dead, his final words lingering in the air. Haunting, and horrifying.

Save me.

But we can do nothing, only stand here staring at one another in shock.

Falla rushes through the trees to reach us but an invisible force holds her ten feet back, closer than anyone thought they could get but not as close as we've gotten.

Rioyn rips his sayer device from his ear, throwing it as far as he can. He stomps to his pack and pulls out The Scroll of Alderon.

"Rioyn, wait!" I yell but it's all too late. He's unrolled the scroll, laying it on the ground. It shoots a blinding white light into the sky like a beacon.

"It's the only option we have left," he grits.

Rioyn searches the scroll, tracing our path to the Iyanndyre. Once his finger reaches the Iyanndyre, it comes alive. Dancing sparkled dust of gold, silver and rose hues creates the outline of the Iyanndyre before our eyes. The dust glimmers, floating in the air.

"Why is it connecting to Dremaria? Is that where we're supposed to go?"

Falla doesn't break her stare from the dust glistening as the light of the sun touches it.

It snaps into a hardened emerald line leading directly to Dremaria, but shows no path.

Rioyn traces his finger away from Dremaria, but the emerald line holds.

Then, as quickly as the dust flickered into existence, gravity snatches it back into the scroll and it's gone.

"Useless!" Rioyn roars, standing up and gripping his hair in frustration.

"The Iyanndyre could have more information. We have to look for it there," I offer.

Rioyn's head shoots up.

He charges to confront the Iyanndyre, with me chasing behind.

Rioyn and I stare at the magnitude of the Iyanndyre dwarfing us a thousand times over. Its sheer strength, fortitude and power are enough to send a strong man whimpering.

I reach out slowly, hovering it inches from the tungstenore structure. This time, there's a tug, a tether pulling my hand closer.

Without conscious thought, I signal for Rioyn to do the same.

He raises his hand.

Together, we lay our hands on the Iyanndyre. A bright golden light casts around us, whipping up the dust and dirt from around our feet. We're enraptured in a golden flame. As the dust settles, our reflections shimmer in the transformed tungstenore monolith. Our refections are mirrored with those of Warriem and Everia's.

The engravings are wiped away to a smoothed mirror finish.

Warriem and Everia's reflections fade and we are the only two reflecting in the mirror. Our eyes shimmering with a golden glow, and even that disappears in a flash.

"Argh!" I yank my hand off the Iyanndyre.

It burns and throbs.

Burned into my palm, two thin flames intertwine. The fire brand fades from seared ash to a deep red. Rioyn lifts his palm to reveal the same marking.

Dark, thick tendrils of smoke twine around Rioyn. Bigger, stronger, more powerful tendrils. Did the Iyanndyre do that?

My hand with my new fire brand rises in front of me to control a large group of rocks. I send them deep into the forest's spoils.

As we struggle to understand what just happened, Falla cries out, pointing. A dark crease forms in the air beside us. It ripples, then splits apart into a portal.

The wind howls as a tall, muscular man steps through, tall and broad, his hair slicked back like a helmet of gold. He's beautiful, and terrifying.

"Who are—" A long, thin needle carved from steelore is flung into Rioyn's chest. He falls to his knees, crumpling to his side.

Before Falla is able to reach the hilt of her sword, a needle pierces her from a distance as well. I freeze with a wide-eyed shock; looking down, there's a thin metal line protruding from my chest. It brings me to my hands and knees as my vision blurs.

It all happens so quickly. Surely, it can't end like this.

The black bloodstained boots come stepping my way as I close my eyes.

CHAPTER 37

THE DREAMSMAN

CHEST PAIN WAKES ME from a slumber so deep, I thought I was dead. I've only ever dreamt once before, but last night, my vivid dreams ran wild.

I assume they were dreams, anyway. People talk about living an alternate life when you sleep. That's exactly how it was.

I dreamt of a man, a beautiful, elusive, muscular man, so familiar as if I've known him for an eternity. His face, his features were all a blur.

I kept trying to see who he was, but my dream wouldn't allow it.

My thoughts race, trying to figure out who he is and where I know him from, coming up empty. The lingering tendrils of my feelings for him run deep within my subconscious, a desire so intense the dream and its residual feelings cannot be shaken. The man in my dreams said only, "I've finally found you." Whatever that means.

I wake more fully, my movements constrained by the tight binds of a coarse rope. Falla and Rioyn lie trussed up beside me.

A pull at my heart tells me we're still close to the Iyanndyre, but the fact I've been dreaming would suggest we're in Dremaria. Around us is a circle of dense green bushes. Color, which means we are not in Dremaria. Beyond that, I have no idea.

279

The crunch of leaves announces company, and a moment later, the golden man, our captor, steps through the bushes.

"Oh, lovely. You're awake. It's always tricky drugging children."

He squats before me, his long fingers pulling at my lower eyelids. He examines my eyes like a healant while I rip my head from his cold hands.

"What drug?" I demand, my words sluggish. "I'm not a child."

He twirls the thin needle. Up close, I'm able to see the intricate inscriptions of tiny stars twirling around the twisted steelore needle, a gasp freeing itself from my lips.

"This is dreamium, a drug so strong that even those who have lost the ability to dream may do so." He looks into my eyes again. "Did you dream?"

He taunts me with a flick of a brow.

"Are you the Iyanndyre Born?" Rioyn squeezes out through his dry throat.

The man's head falls back with a roaring laugh.

"Lower worlds, no. I'm a simple dreamsman. Nothing more."

"Liar." I don't know where the thought or impulse to hurl such an accusation came from but I don't release my angled brows from him. He is not a simple anything.

His face curls into a devilish grin. He leans into me.

"Which part?" He moves to examine Falla.

"What are you doing here?" Rioyn holds his stare, taut as he watches the man examine Falla, who is only just waking up.

"Looking for my sister."

"Liar," I snap again as a golden glow radiates around me, Rioyn's eyes becoming beacons of warning for me to extinguish harnessing my Ascendance.

"What's your name, then, Dreamsman?" Rioyn continues, though why does he trust a word the man says? Perhaps he's simply trying to lure him away from Falla.

"Coren. Coren Fakanery."

Never heard of him, but then again, I don't know anyone from Dremaria, let alone a dreamsman. Gran'ama's warning floods my mind. Trust no one.

"Coren, would you mind untying us? We aren't here to hurt you, or anyone," Rioyn says.

"Unfortunately, I would mind, so I won't be doing that. But you three do look hungry. I'll find something for you to eat. I may be a shrewd Dreamsman, but I'm not unkind."

The man disappears into the bushes.

"He's an enemy soldier," Falla says, apparently more awake than she's let on. "I can smell it on him, even without the uniform."

"This is all my fault," I say, filled with shame. "When I stumbled upon the Waves of Omaru, I practiced my Ascendance. It took me to a dark place. I felt them."

"Or they found us when I used the scroll," Rioyn offers. "Who knows?"

"Maybe. But they were all there: Rioyn, Jax, our father, Uncle. Even my friends."

Rioyn's gold-flecked, hazel eyes widen in surprise. And hope.

Coren returns. Rioyn breaks our stare and straightens, at least as much as he can while slouched on the ground. "Release us now."

Coren cackles an arrogant laugh, even as Rioyn's eyes close and the veins in his neck begin to bulge. But his laughter stops when those same veins begin turning black.

"Hey, stop it, kid. Open your eyes." Coren kicks Rioyn on the side of his injured leg. Rioyn grunts with pain but his eyes stay sealed.

Coren slaps him across his face, but this only seems to channel Rioyn's dark fury.

Behind Coren, the black portal opens again, the wind kicking up dust and dirt. A couple dozen soldiers of the Starless Army march out of the darkened sliver.

I cower my head to brace myself for whatever Ascendance Rioyn is channeling. After what I saw when he touched the Iyanndyre, it's hard to know what will be unleashed from him because of this unpredictable dark energy living inside of him.

"I will drive my sword through your heart!" Coren warns.

Blinding blackness impales everything around us.

My ears ring with a high vibration, then silence. Black filaments scatter across the land. I blink furiously, trying to regain focus.

Rioyn stands over Coren's body, fists clenched. Veins protrude through every muscle in his body, his searing rage thickening his breath. More bodies lie lifeless all around, and never have I seen such an angered rage through Rioyn, ever.

"Rioyn. Rioyn!" He blinks, looking around us.

He falls to my side, hands ripping at my binds. "What just happened?"

"The portal to Dremaria is closing," Falla points out, cutting herself free with a small blade. "That's where the scroll wanted to send us. Let's go!"

"But the Iyanndyre!" I hover, wanting to study the monolith and better understand it. But there's no time, and Falla is right that Dremaria is our best lead.

I yank the onyx platinumore portal ring from Coren's limp finger, reaching up under my shirt and stuffing it into the middle of my brassiere. We grab our packs, haring through the black hole one by one, the portal lacing itself up behind us.

Dark cyclones swirl and consume us, then our bodies seem to merge with the environment and become one with the air. After a few bizarre seconds, we find ourselves spit out of the portal onto the shore of a black and white beach.

These must be the Restful Isles of Dremaria, which means we're lying on the silvery sands of the Onyx Ocean.

Waves caress our sides, gently pulling us toward the water's edge. Falla and I get up and drag Rioyn up shore, under a sand bank with tall, spar-kling white grass.

I've only ever heard about the monochromatic tones of Dremaria.

Apparently, the only time you see rich, vibrant colors is when you dream. For now, the white sun lingers in a depressing gray sky.

Falla smacks Rioyn's face hard, but he doesn't wake. "Rioyn! We need to move before someone finds us."

I claw the sand bank to see past the high white grass. "How far is Nighamaire?"

Falla's head whips up to find me. "Why would we go there?"

"That's where the Castle of Everia is, right?"

"Yes, but again, why?"

A hunch? A guess? Answers Falla will struggle to accept.

I pause, trying to understand the impulse tugging me in that direction. "It's where Shivane and Sylon likely plotted their war. Why else would The Scroll of Alderon tell us to go to Dremaria?" I pause, deciding if I should be honest. "It's also just a hunch I have, and so far, those hunches have proven to be right."

Falla looks to the departing sun.

"Night will be here soon. We won't be able to move swiftly through Dremaria dragging him along, and I don't want to roam with the dreamers."

In the distance, we find a shack, so rotten and full of mildew we have to assume no one has lived there for some time. Still, it's shelter from prying eyes, and a place for Rioyn to rest and regain his strength.

Falla curls up next to Rioyn, forcing him to drink some water and wash his face.

I opt for the other end of the shack with my back turned to them. Maybe it's to give Falla privacy or maybe because my conflicting desire for something I don't understand—and can't have at this moment—leaves me feeling hopelessly lonely.

Lonely for Jax. Lonely for the mysterious man of my dreams who have ignited this burning desire inside of me.

We finally, miraculously made it to the Iyanndyre, only to leave empty-handed and more confused than when we started.

Now, we're in enemy lands, with nothing more than a hunch on which to pin our hopes.

I had imagined this night to be one of celebration and triumph.

Now, the best I can wish for is a damp night's sleep on cool sand, and the bitter promise of better luck tomorrow.

CHAPTER 38

NIGHAMAIRE

RIOYN

KNEEL ON TOP OF Ayva, grabbing her shoulders, shaking until the slumber loosens its grip. She's dreaming, and I can't help feeling a touch of jealousy.

What does she see right now? Something happy, I hope.

Even so, we have to go. Every second we wait here, our chance of being discovered increases. Her groggy eyes find mine, realizing I've pinned her between my knees. She pushes me off her.

"Sorry, but you weren't waking up."

Ayva jolts to her feet, stuffing her blanket into her pack without a care for what else might be lingering in there.

"I don't see anyone," Falla says, peeking out of one of the broken windows. "Luck may be on our side. The dreamers aren't up yet. We should make it to Nighamaire by high noon."

"Why are we going to Nighamaire?" I ask. It was a big enough surprise waking in Dremaria.

"It's what was decided last night after you passed out from your … Ascendance," Ayva snaps.

"Why are you so snappy with me? What did I do this time?"

Ayva doesn't stop cramming her pack.

I grab her hand for her to stop. She yanks it back.

285

"I'm sorry. This journey is—it's … it's breaking me down bit by bit. I don't know how much more I can take. I was mentally prepared to find the Iyanndyre, whatever it took. Then when we got there and the Iyanndyre Born wasn't there, something in me just broke. And then last night, I had this dream of fire, and Jax, and burning …"

She wipes her eyes, and I hold her until her uneven breaths settle.

Even without dreaming, I know how she feels. "You're not alone, my sister. We're all in this together," I soothe.

Or at least, try to soothe.

"Twins," she whispers, falling into a hug.

An hour later, we've moved out of the dilapidated shack, continuing to trudge through the silvery soft, sinking sand, leaving the isles to carve through the trail between hills with the black blades of grass, white-hot sun bearing down on us through grayish colored sky.

I survey my arms, wondering, is there an effect on us here like in the Carisan Forest? My deep golden skin is dark gray here, all of our coloring monochromatic.

It's an odd sight to get accustomed to.

Up ahead, two people walk toward us.

Their heads hang, and they're dragging their feet as they shuffle forward. We pull our hoods as far over our heads as we can, shielding anyone from glimpsing our features.

The man and a woman pass by without even registering our presence.

So far, their province is quiet—depressed but nearly silent.

Shivane and Sylon haven't yet stepped out of a portal or sent their minions, so I'm hopeful they don't yet know we're here.

We wind through the final turn of the Black Hills and stare at the mouth of Nighamaire.

Black wrought ironore gates fifteen feet high hold the capital city of Dremaria hostage while the area outside of the gate is littered with dilapidated, makeshift shacks.

The stench of human waste lingers with a pungent heaviness in the humid salted air.

Whatever resources their leadership had for their people has since been diverted to their military.

"Keep your wits about you," I warn before we weave through the cleared pathway, heading for the black gates of Nighamaire.

We pass by droves of Dremarians whose eyes don't bother acknowledging us. The people here are dirty, dreary, drugged, even in their wakefulness. They suffer the lingering effects of the dreamsman's needle. Is this what happens to you when your dreams fail, and you have to turn to a drug to ease your mind? Do Shivane and Sylon even care that their people are in this dire of a condition? They're so keen on righting the injustices of our realm, but what have they done to end their own people's struggle?

We approach the towering, threatening gates when a woman cries, "Please! Please. I need more dreamium. Please. I'll do whatever you want."

We pass the last shack to find her on hands and knees, begging a man in fine clothing.

He stands before the begging woman in flowing black silk pants that billow out, then tighten at the ankles. His black silk tunic fits his slender body, his skin as silver as the sands of the Onyx Coast. He taunts the woman as he twirls a long, thin needle, and I begin to wonder, was Coren a dreamsman, after all?

We pass the open doorway, leaving the woman to her bitter fate.

"You said last night that we needed to go to the Castle of Everia," Falla says. "That something was tugging you, telling you to come here. Do you still feel it?"

Ayva emphatically nods.

"Then let's do this," Falla says, staring at the massive castle.

The sounds of marching boots echo against the stone walls and pavement. I draw the girls behind the trunk of an ancient, gnarled tree, watching as the soldiers approach. A breath hitches in my throat in recognition of their tattered uniforms. They are from our province, local soldiers, possessed by evil. And leading them all is our cousin, Hanri.

A deep, dark rage simmers within me. Hanri might be possessed, but he seems to have embraced his possession with a special relish. As the soldiers pass us, the desperate woman stumbles from the dreamsman's door, and into their path.

With a brutal kick, Hanri sends her sprawling.

She collapses with a desperate cry, bowing her head as they march past.

My hand clenches the pommel of my sword, but I hold myself back.

He's my cousin. He's possessed, I remind myself, having to focus on the task at hand. "What are we looking for once we're in the Castle of Everia?"

"I don't know," Ayva admits. "But I sense there's something deep in that castle. Something that tugs on me as well but has been tucked away and kept protected."

"Before we go gallivanting about in a dark, strange castle, we should figure out if there's a method to their guard rotation. See who comes in and out."

Falla has a point.

She takes the first watch over the guards stationed in the makeshift city outside the gates of Nighamaire. Ayva and I study the Castle of Everia, once erected from the essence of Dremaria. Now what remains is a sorry ruin of mud and ash.

Behind the monstrosity of the castle is a hillside where the wealthier Dremarians reside. Dreamsmen, the Drems Courtiers, and the Dreacoms don't live amongst the chaos of the city and its downtrodden dreamers.

These are the people who do Shivane and Sylon's bidding, while their citizens rot.

My eyes are drawn to a commotion at the castle's entrance where soldiers of the Starless Army drag a beaten, bloody body along the stoned pavement.

The man doesn't flinch as his body is raked over the harsh pathway.

As they pass the people of the makeshift city, boos and curses rumble through the streets. The shouts grow louder, and a woman cries, "Death to Shivane and Sylon, and their cursed army!" More slurs are hurled the soldiers' way.

The Starless Army unsheathe their swords, jabbing at anyone stupid enough to get too close. "Do not speak ill of those who rule your dreams!" a soldier shouts.

"Please!" A woman breaks from the crowd. "I know this man. He's not a thief, only hungry!"

This draws more people toward the spectacle, and the soldiers shift uncomfortably. Shouts begin to increase as the crowd grows even larger.

The disturbance draws Hanri from the bowels of the castle; he comes strutting out, leading a dozen heavily armed soldiers. Most of them are blank-faced, and nothing more than black lacquered eyed drones, driven by evil and dead inside.

Not Hanri though. It's as if the curse has only emboldened who he really is.

He stalks over to the group, the crowd of townsfolk parting before him as if escaping the plague. He raises his hand for silence. The people of the makeshift city rumble to a stilted hush, crawling away from the gates, cowering among themselves.

Hanri peers at the unconscious man through his black-as-night lacquered eyes, curling his fingers around the hilt of his sword, whipping it from its sheath.

He takes the sword in both of his hands, raising it above his head.

"Shall we spare this man? A petty thief who dared to steal from our great leaders?"

Looking sidelong, the crowd is hushed, tears streaking their dirt-crusted cheeks. Not a single person dares shout now, not even the woman who knows him. They are terrified of Hanri. "Apparently not," he mutters, and plunges his sword into the man's heart.

As blood paints the street and spreads beneath his boots, Hanri addresses the crowd.

"Anyone else wish to protest?"

He meets with silence.

Hanri bends, carefully wiping the blood off his sword with the dead man's shirt. The woman falls beside the lifeless man, holding his head in her hands.

Hanri watches this display of grief and drops his hand to caress her wet cheek.

The woman recoils from his touch, then realizes her mistake.

She kneels before him. "My apologies, sir."

"Never mind," he says generously. He leans down and pats her on the head, like a faithful dog. His other hand lightly clasps her cheek. With a quick, sharp flick of his wrist, a crack tears through the air, and the woman slumps to the ground.

Beside me, Ayva gasps. "He … He broke her neck!"

I take her hand, trying to contain my fury, no longer able to decipher if it's my temper that's grabbing hold of me, or the black smoke entwining with my Ascendance, burning through every fiber of my body to attack Hanri.

For some, failing to release or channel the energy of their Ascendance causes them to go mad. For others, a hole literally burns through them from the inside out.

My hand tightens so hard on Ayva's that she lets out a yelp.

"Sorry," I mutter. I hope I haven't hurt her. "We need to move. Now. Before another uproar breaks out." Briefly, my gaze scouts our surroundings.

"I hate to say it, but we'll be safest in the slums. The people there don't seem to care about strangers."

Falla sighs but agrees. "Then let's go."

CHAPTER 39

THE CASTLE OF EVERIA

RIOYN

WE MAKE IT THROUGH the slums and around the side of a menacing wrought ironore fence. Ahead, a Residents' Gate blocks the entrance to a restricted internal area. Flanking the gate are black stone walls soaring high above our heads, stretching farther than the eye can see.

The walls seem to have been recently erected.

For military defense, or against the threat of their own rioting citizens? I wonder.

Stepping into a shadow, I see a short, husky man striding up to the Residents' Gate. He places his palm on an iridiumore plaque, the gate clicking in response.

The husky man flings it open as if he has not a second to spare.

As soon as he's through, I lunge forward to stop it slamming, yet the heavy metal bangs into my palm, the same side as my injured wrist. A white-hot pain flickers through me, but I bite my cheek and wave Falla and Ayva over.

They tug the gate open, relieving my throbbing limb. Falla nudges me forward and we slink into a steelore side door at the edge of the castle.

291

Here, we meet a flight of stone stairs leading to an intricately carved stone archway, opening into a vacant hallway. I snatch a polished silverore candelabra.

Ayva creeps forward, leading the way, clutching on to her left wrist. The golden-red flame brand on her palm glows in the low light.

I look down at mine, seeing its flame dark now, almost flush with my skin.

We hustle down a long, dark empty hallway. No portraits. No curtains. No furniture. Nothing but a single door thirty feet ahead.

"There. That door," Ayva whispers.

The castle is dead quiet. The metal door is smooth as silk. I push down on the latch, shoving forward the heavy door. It whispers as it glides.

The faint ivory light of the candles glows throughout the room, and Ayva beelines for the black stained oak desk, rifling through papers. Falla and I spread out, searching for what, we don't know. Mainly, we are here to protect and defend Ayva. My pounding heart slams into the ribs of my chest, palms turned sweaty. The candelabra slips in my grasp.

"Look at this!" Ayva whispers. She holds a correspondence letter in her shivering hands. I hold the light over it:

Dear Lord Shivane,

Thank you for your desire to align your incredible Starless Army with ours. It is a great relief to finally meet someone of equal mind to bridge the centuries-long rift existing between Drycour and Seivan.

We look forward to receiving word regarding your successful conquest.

With our alliances forged, we will bring forth the powers of the Iyanndyre to expand our Empire.

We're also pleased to hear that you plan to find the Iyanndyre Born. We have waited for this resurrection for a long time and have developed a honing tool to aid in your successful capture. Our ships will be ready to depart our shores once we receive word of your conquest.

We will dock at the shores of the Daiyaman Ocean within three months' time. By then, we trust you will have successfully disabled the forcefield around Seiwan, allowing our safe passage.

Until then, may your conquest be swift and your reign infinite.

Your Drycour Allegiant,

Lord Qaxion

P.S.: Lordess Heiliana sends her warmest regards.

"They made a deal with the Lord of an Outer Realm?" It's outrageous, but even more annoying to have been unable to guess the truth myself. It explains the scope of their invasion. "And what do they want with the Iyanndyre Born?"

Falla snatches the letter out of Ayva's hand in sheer disbelief. "The same as us, obviously. To control a powerful weapon."

Ayva takes the letter from Falla, folding it and sliding it into the slit of her pants. The information is enlightening, but it's not why we're here.

We leave the study chamber the same way we came, the intricately carved stone archway within our sights. As we rush down the hallway, I notice a small flickering light.

Hanri stares out of the window, hands clasped at his lower back.

"Hm. I thought I smelt you sniffing around outside Nighamaire," Hanri says in his usual slithering manner.

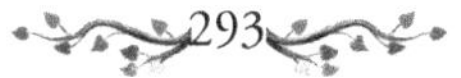

I freeze. He slowly turns to face us.

"Cousin," I snarl. "I see you've taken to your new personality with admirable gusto."

Hanri's head tilts, chuckling. "It's certainly brought a sense of clarity." His black eyes flash when he spots Falla. "Ah, still cavorting with Trescherian trash, I see."

Hanri moves closer. I hold my position.

Falla falls back, pushing Ayva behind her. "Rioyn. We're leaving. Now."

"You should listen, although you won't get far. You can run, you can fight, or hide, dear cousin. It's just too bad you just won't get to live."

"Let's go." Falla seethes. "He's trying to bait you. Don't be a fool."

My cousin and I stand there, facing off. I should end him now before he hurts more innocent people, and before he announces our location to the fellow devil spawn he calls his comrades. But Falla is right. There's no time. We have to move.

Still, the anger inside me refuses to let him go. We have a bitter vengeance that's far from over. I step forward, my hand on my sword.

"Rioyn!" Ayva cries out. I turn and freeze.

"No sudden moves." A woman with black lacquered eyes stands beside my sister, a knife to her throat. A horde of soldiers lines up behind her. To my shocked surprise, Xylar stands among them. "If you want your sister to live." Her eyes motion to my hand resting on my sword.

Fool. I allowed Hanri to distract me, just long enough for them to gain the upper hand.

I study the soldiers, trying to gauge our chances of fighting our way out of this. My gaze stops upon a single figure in the middle.

It's Xylar, his eyes as black as the rest of them.

Ayva keeps her chin held high, even as a faint line of blood appears at her throat. A single tear falls from her cheek, though it's not a tear of sadness. It's a tear of hatred, the black knowing rippling between us.

Slowly, painfully, I lower myself to my knees, raising both hands.

"That's more like it. Cuff him."

Black crystal cuffs slam closed around my wrists, Falla and Ayva receiving the same treatment. Ayva forms her hand into a fist, concealing her branded palm. I follow suit.

The woman saunters over to me, tall and wiry, as strong as any man. "Now that's a good soldier." She leans down, lifting my chin with one calloused finger, thumbing the black crusted gouge on my forehead. "Interesting."

She cocks her head, studying me anew.

"I'm Caya Fakanery. You met my brother earlier." With a flick of her wrist, she scratches fingernails across my face, almost taking my eye. "He sends his warmest regards."

They drag us down the dark, desolate hallway, their heavy boots marching in echo.

I can't dare look at Ayva and Falla, too steeped in shame to meet their eyes.

Once more, I fell prey to my bitter desire to best my cousin instead of listening to my friend and true family.

I've failed them, perhaps for the final time.

PART III

The VEILS of INTERMUNDIUM

CHAPTER 40

The Return from Xaeria

The Past

SHIVANE

I SLINK INTO MY COOL ironore throne, cast in the image of burning stars across the universe. Mindless people relegate stars as beacons of hope and happiness. If I could extinguish every single one, I would leap at the opportunity to rip them from existence to live in the pure and unrequited emptiness of the dark. Darkness that harnesses the true side of humanity's deepest, blackest hidden desires.

Barely a breeze ripples through our throne room on this hot spring morning.

Blinding white light from the pointed arched windows illuminates Sylon and Coren sparring in the middle of the room, glistening salty sweat cascades down their rippled, muscular bodies. I devour Coren's chiseled physique with hungry eyes. When was the last time someone touched me, held my hand or ran their trailing fingers along my skin? I can't even remember. Far too long for my desires to go unsatisfied.

"Would you stop? We're trying to concentrate." Sylon throws a disgusted grunt over his shoulder, and I snap my mind shut.

Coren looks between us, bemused by our silent communication.

At that moment, Caya struts into the throne room, walking right between Sylon and Coren without so much as a glance to either. I can't help but smirk at her odd relationship with men—or rather, with people in general. She stops right in front of me and drops a thick, leather-bound book at my feet, with her typical flare for the dramatic.

My brows narrow. "What's this?"

"The answer to your prayers."

I lower to pick it up, opening the stiff leather cover and thumbing through the delicate parchment.

"I have plenty of dusty old books already. I don't share the enthusiasm for this one."

Caya's grin widens. "It's The Book of Everia."

And? I think. "I got my first copy at four years of age."

"Not this version, you didn't." Her smile turns slightly sinister. "Everyone has read about her and Warriem's early days in Seivan. The book you hold in your hands is the one she penned after she banished her Ascendance powers into the crystals. Before Warriem and her mindless drone of a husband, Alderon, could take them from her."

My eyes leap from the book to her, lit with intrigue.

"I thought it was only a rumor, a legend."

Sylon steps to the dais and sits on his throne beside me, leaning over for a glimpse of the prize.

"Most rumors have some grain of truth. When there were whispers that the Scribe of Echolyne had a secret vault, I decided to pay her a visit."

"Oh, please tell me you didn't venture into Xaeria."

"Ah, well, I most certainly did." That devious grin of hers is always dangerous. "I charmed my way into her library and was kind enough to only deprive her of a single title. She may or may not come looking for it." I chuckle at Caya's casual indifference.

I adorned her with the title of Drem Courtier to bridge the gap between our province and the others. She was the only one among us who didn't fight at the Battle of Trescheria and is therefore free to roam the realm.

It quickly became apparent she was less interested in diplomacy, and more suited to serve as our spymaster and mercenary. A lion shepherding lambs to slaughter.

Caya's eyes chastise Sylon. "Would you mind clothing yourself?"

Sylon taunts her. "You're the only woman to have ever complained about my half-naked body."

I swivel to him. "Am I not also a woman?"

"Yes, just how many women are there, Sylon?" Caya continues with her playful jabs.

"I should ask you the same question." He flicks his fallen curls from his sweaty forehead. "And It's Lord Sylon to you."

He dismisses her with a flick of his wrist, inciting a rippling laugh through us.

We discuss the possibilities the old book might hold, and I set it aside to study later.

The boys leave and Caya and I spar for the next several hours; when we tire of it, we turn our sights to the poor souls in the training court.

After the Battle of Trescheria almost ten years ago, Sylon and I returned from the bloody catastrophe and stepped up as the rulers of Dremaria. We appointed Coren and Caya as the generals of our Dremarian Army, relegating Zianli to nothing more than a figurehead to the people—who despise and wish him an early death. He's perfectly suited to take the brunt of their hatred while we're free to plot our conquer of this blasted realm.

I usually enjoy watching our soldiers fight. They become more dangerous, more brutal each day. But today, I'm distracted. The dusty old book calls out to me. I stalk off to my study chamber, Caya hot on my heels. Once ensconced in the room and totally alone, I place the book on my desk and fall into my chair. "So, what is it about this musty old thing? What're we looking for?" No doubt she's already digested it cover to cover.

Caya leans forward and braces her palms on my desk. "The second-to-last chapter. It explains how Everia regained her powers by using the Iyann crystals, formed deep inside the trenches of the Iyanndyre."

"Interesting," I muse, flipping to the back of the book.

"It's said that the crystals grow in power with time, and it's been centuries since Everia first found them. But that's just the start. Guess where she's kept them hidden?"

I shrug. She could have picked anywhere in the realm.

Caya's eyes glitter with excitement. "The Dungeon Lair."

"Right here in this castle?" My head shoots up. "Under us this entire time?"

I try to fully absorb what she's saying. The very dark power of the Iyanndyre, right below our feet! "Surely, we would have felt something, sensed it somehow."

She laughs. "This whole place has always felt like a bomb waiting to explode. I just thought it was the magic of the dark twins at work."

"Funny," I bite. "So, you're telling me we just sparred for three hours, while you sat on this information?"

"Patience is a virtue, friend."

Exactly fourteen minutes later, digging commences. Caya, Coren, Sylon, and I watch the progress of the twenty-four Befouled as they attack the floor of the Dungeon Lair, Caya selecting a far corner as the first place to search. I have no idea of the size of these crystals, and whether we are looking for a barrel in a room, or a needle in a haystack.

The Befouled are young men and women who have entered into their teenage years and wish to one day fight for the Dremarian Army.

Upon their initiation, they are beaten and broken to see how much they're willing to bleed for Dremaria. Many cannot take the initiation but those who do earn their place among the Befouled until they turn eighteen and graduate into the Dremarian Army.

With our past university dismissal still fresh in our minds, Sylon and I have a single rule for the recruits: if you are caught betraying Dremaria, you are killed. If you break, you leave in disgrace. But no person is barred because of who they are or what they've done. Murderer or thief, every man, woman, and monster is welcomed in this fight.

Several hours pass and my patience is thinning when one of the Befouled suddenly cries out. He's scrambled out of the hole and is crouching, staring at his hands.

"They're burning," he cries like a child.

I push past him, jumping down into the hole. Black dirt coats my fine clothes as I dig into the earth with bare hands. The moment my nails scrape against something both smooth and jagged, I bark at the Befouled, "Get. Out."

Sylon orders them to take the injured boy to the infirmary, issuing four guards at the door.

I raise the crystals from their centuries-long resting place.

They are wrapped in a thick fabric of some sort that's mostly rotted away. Buried below them is a small tungstenore box which I unearth as well, handing everything to Sylon before climbing out of the hole. I can't help noting that the crystals don't burn my hands, only offering a sort of warm hum. But as my brother's fingertips lightly graze them, his skin glows and the purple in his eyes glimmers.

He opens the tungstenore box to reveal two rings and a folded piece of parchment.

"These are the prized portal rings," he says, almost breathless, "of Warriem and Alderon. When they took my powers, I helped myself to their beloved rings."

"Portal rings?" I eye my brother in sheer disbelief at the gift to move at whim anywhere in the realm in a mere instant. To shift between worlds.

Coren leans in, studying the crystal's large razor-sharp clusters before moving away. It seems they make most people uncomfortable, but not me. Something draws me closer, and I abide, raising my eyes to Sylon's. His pupils have dilated, his violet eyes now turned almost entirely black. "Your eyes are wild," I tell my brother.

"So are yours."

Without even discussing it, we reach out our hands for the crystals, wrapping our fingers around their sharp points, squeezing. Our blood runs red, then black, but neither of us lets go. We couldn't, even if we wanted to. The vibration of the crystals increases, then in an instant, they implode in our hands until all we're holding is a fistful of black dust.

My brother's eyes are slowly returning to normal.

At least it might appear so, but the enormous power of the black Iyann crystals runs through me, electrifying, probably doing the same to my brother too.

"Hold out your hand," I request him, and he does, while I first slide the onyx portal ring onto my finger, then place the other on my brother's pointer finger. Both fit perfectly, as if all preordained.

But preordained for what, exactly?

Delicious anticipation swirls through me at the possibilities—the raw, unstoppable, power. Coren and Caya look between us in awe, and with just a touch of terror.

We will soon find out.

CHAPTER 41

THE SCRIBE OF ECHOLYNE

The Past

SYLON

STROLLING DOWN THE STONE spiral staircase, my hands dangle close to the coldness of the stone wall which I don't dare touch, not touching anything as I enter the Dungeon Lair.

The bleak stone floor has already been replaced by the Befouled, and the prisoners reinstated. The foul tang of human waste ripens the thick, heavy air.

I lead with my lifted chin to the very last cell, and there, to my surprise, I discover that Shivane has beaten me down here. Perhaps I shouldn't be taken back by that; my sister is the most motivated person ever. She stands before the kneeling Scribe of Echolyne.

"Witch!" she spits out. "Liar. Deceiver. Traitor. I could kill you for just one. But I will annihilate you for all four."

"Careful, Shi." The Scribe looks like a helpless woman, but I am not fooled. The question is, what has the scribe done to anger my sister so profusely?

Her soft brown curls hang from the front of her black hood. She kneels on the hard stones but appears completely relaxed, her eyes fixed on the floor before her.

A thick, green and black serpent is visible through the gap in her robe, curled around the scribe's shoulders and throat. Disgusting.

"You will rot here for the rest of your days."

Shivane turns on her heels and marches from the Dungeon Lair. I follow her with my eyes until she disappears into the shadows. Before I can speak, the Scribe of Echolyne's quiet voice echoes through the stone. "I've come for my book."

"What did you say to my sister?"

The scribe huffs, "I merely showed her who she is. I thought she'd appreciate the truth."

"Showed how?"

"Would you like to find out as well, sir?"

My sister's white face and trembling hands suggest it might not be a pleasant experience. "I'll pass, thank you."

"Very well. Then I will only say this once more. I've come for my book."

My arms sheath across my chest. "Then your trip has been wasted, Scribe."

"I figured as much." She snaps her fingers, and an object appears on the stone floor before her. I straighten to move closer to the bars of her cell.

"If you have such powers, why deign to come here at all?" Anger sears into me and I'm betrayed by my own voice.

"Because I wanted to meet the famous twins and sniff out the reason why you needed my book. Now that I know, I'll be going." She wraps her long, delicate hands around the leather-bound book, edging closer to the cell bars.

I back up, embarrassed by my own caution.

"Interesting," she says. "I need not show you your soul's image. Simply look around into the eyes of the ones you've enslaved to a life down here; therein lies your answer."

My eyes narrow. There's no interest in carrying on with her games. "What other books are you hiding in your library?" I cut to the chase. "Assuming Shivane hasn't already burned it to the ground."

She laughs. "I would burn the books myself before allowing them into your hands, again."

"How about a bargain? An alliance?"

"Here's a bargain for you to consider. If your spy ever comes to Xaeria again under false pretenses, I will not hesitate to skin her alive."

She runs her tongue over her jagged teeth.

The Scribe of Echolyne is something different, something of pure evil hiding behind an Archivant's non-threatening exterior. She's not from this world but first appeared shortly after Warriem and Everia. She possesses powers not of this realm or world.

In short, I like her.

"You think you like me for the darkness I possess because it reflects your own. But we are two quite different creatures. The chosen one will come, and then you will see the truth of what you are, whether you wish to or not. Might come as a surprise."

The scribe cackles to herself under the hood of her velvet robe. With a quick snap of her fingers, she disappears into a thin plume of gray smoke.

I race up the circular stone staircase and charge into the study chamber where Shivane, Caya, and Coren pore over battle plans. "We need to push our plans forward. Now!"

Shivane stands up tall. "Why? What did you do?"

"The scribe is gone. She knows our plans and will surely tell whoever she feels needs to know. We'll lose the element of surprise if we don't act right away."

Shivane moves closer to me. "Why did you tell her?"

"I didn't. She somehow knew just by looking at me—us. It seems we stirred a hornet's nest," I snap, throwing a look at Caya.

"If you want great power, there is always a price to pay," Caya says with hardened eyes. "You know the scribe is from an ancient world just like Monnaire and Arro, though she's been here as long. Did you expect her to send you cookies and a thank you note?"

"She's something different from them and has no allegiance to us. Though I offered her an alliance to join us," I explain.

Shivane shifts back in her stance with a flicker of disappointment. I shrug her off. At least I tried. Shivane only hurtled abuse at the woman, insulting her further.

"We need to act," I urge again, pushing my way to the desk.

Shivane shifts her frazzled gaze to Caya. "Are you ready?" Caya faces her, nodding. If there's any doubt inside of her, it's not visible.

"What are you doing?" I demand.

"If the black Iyann crystals gave Everia her powers back, then they'll give Caya powers she's never had," Shivane explains.

Shivane grabs her black velvet pouch and stands before Caya. She reaches into her pouch, then blows the black Iyann crystal dust in Caya's face.

Caya's visage contorts and when her eyes open, they roll forward, metamorphosed to a solid lacquered black. Shivane is grinning from ear to ear.

"Welcome, General to the Starless Army." Caya's lip curls into a smirk that sneers from a dark place inside of her. She snatches the pouch from Shivane's hand and goes storming out of the study chamber. "Her battle begins now."

"What is the Starless Army?" I ask.

"People who live with hate, darkness, emptiness inside of them. They'll be freed to unleash who they really are, to live in unrequited freedom. Caya will share this gift with our fighters, now to be known as the Starless Army. We will portal them into the Pools of Pearl at first light. From there, the infestation will spread outward across the realm."

Shivane saunters to Coren, her long finger stroking his chiseled face. "You will be our dreamsman, roaming the realm and hunting down important or inaccessible targets."

Coren accepts his mission, snaps his back straight.

"None will escape my needle," he says and smiles.

Shivane's eyes don't waver from his, studying him. "Stay close to Nighamaire. The dreamers seem to have an awareness of things amiss around the realm. If they dream of anything, then you'll be right here to pick up their whispers."

"Whispers of the Iyanndyre Born, perhaps?"

"Potentially. We have a present gifted to us by an ally. It will aid us in finding this Iyanndyre Born, and we have reason to believe they're already in Casstell. We will trap them and drain their powers with the black Iyann crystals—a fate none could resist. Then we'll keep them under the Shrouded Veil."

"Let the mayhem begin." Coren glides up to my sister, his finger now stroking the side of her cheek and down her throat. "But are you sure you don't want me at your side? Bent to your will?"

I feel slightly ill. "Perhaps you need to be bent to my will, Coren."

Shivane flicks her wrist, dismissing me. "Leave us."

"This is my study chamber, too. I'd prefer it not be defiled."

"Too late." Coren smirks, more for my sister than for me.

"Go sharpen your sword, brother." She turns for a slight second to flash her glowing purple eyes at me.

I slam the door shut, all too glad to get away from there.

CHAPTER 42

The Dungeon Lair

AYVA

XYLAR'S ICY HAND HOLDS my arm in his clenched grip. I yank it as hard as I can, but his long nails threaten to break through my skin. An amused grin tugs at his lips. This isn't like him. Who is he now?

It takes three soldiers to hold Falla captive, and even then, they struggle.

We were so close to making our way deeper into the castle but to find what, I'm not sure. But we've now lost all chance of finding out.

If only Rioyn hadn't fallen so easily into Hanri's trap. It's hard not to be angry at my brother. Falla and I had stood there, yelling at him to leave.

We should just have continued on without him. Perhaps we were the stupid ones, risking the mission by remaining loyally blind at his side. But then how could we just leave him? We're in this together. I must always remember that, no matter how hard things get. As my anger calms, it becomes clear that it's hard to blame him.

Chains clack, dragging against the stone floors.

Rioyn is marching behind me; there are not only the black cuffs around his wrist, but also, a large, black metal collar sits tight around his neck and a black hood has been pulled low over his head. For all my empathy, a flicker of resentment rolls through me too.

You did this.

The Starless Army surrounds us on every side, coming to an abrupt stop at a thick, steelore door. A soldier drags it open and right away, the foulest, most gut-wrenching stench of human waste and rotting flesh ignites my gag reflex. It's the most disgusting air I've ever inhaled. I turn my breathing shallow, preventing the acidic bile from rising anymore.

They take us down a steep, dark spiral staircase.

Ancient lights flicker, splintering the view of our new confines. I lose my footing on the last step. Xylar's grip keeping me from falling face first into a pool of rotted vomit.

We descend into the death-marred prison known as the Dungeon Lair.

Falla keeps fighting to break free even though we've no way to escape our heavily out-numbered escorts.

As for Rioyn, he's given up from what I can tell. He was ready to rip Coren's head off at the Iyanndyre, vaporize the Sancaros, and was ready to kill Hanri. But now, he's the one to thank for our damnation in this dungeon and now he gives up?

What happened to his forever fight to always be the best?

The soldiers hurl us all into a grimy cell, its smooth, timeworn stone floors are wet with urine and who knows what else. They rip the cloak off Rioyn's head.

He staggers to regain his balance, then submits to a dark corner.

Falla slams into the cell door as it closes behind us. "I will kill every last one of you."

Caya cackles at Falla's threat. "I'd love to see you try!"

She strokes Falla's flustered cheeks, but Falla rips her head away.

"So fiery." Caya's gaze rakes over Falla. "I wonder if that mouth is as spicy as it spits."

Howls and grunts from the other prisoners erupt at her lustful tone.

"Who are you?"

Caya seems to love any invitation to speak about herself. I exploit her giddy narcissism to learn more, and draw her attention back from Falla, who seems ready to combust.

"The General of the Starless Army." She mocks me with a deep bow. "At your service."

"What do you want with us?"

How much does she know of who we are, and the threat we represent?

"As soon as you disappeared into my brother's portal, he alerted me to your intrusion. I was intrigued. Few can escape my brother's clutches, and I just had to meet the ones searching for the Iyanndyre Born."

I wrap myself in my arms, shielding myself from Caya's disturbing gaze.

"Anything else your heart desires to know, darling?" she asks.

I shake my head.

"Good. Search them." She snaps her fingers and at once, the steelore doors fly open.

Rioyn allows the soldiers to search him without a fight while Falla lands several kicks and punches but is met with a bone-crunching retribution, sending her to her knees.

"Falla, stop," I say, falling into my own state of acceptance. "Please."

I wait as Xylar begins searching me, clearly enjoying my discomfort. "I don't have anything," I snap, staring through furrowed brows.

Caya walks over, hefting Xylar to one side, her warm whisper chilling my spine worse than Xylar. "Liar." She grazes her lips over my earlobe.

The hair on my body rises.

She mandates, "Hold her arms out."

Xylar and another soldier pin my arms straight against the stone wall. Ever so briefly, I glance at Rioyn, expecting him to stand, make threats, or do some other foolish impulsive thing to protect me, his twin. But that brother is seemingly gone.

Caya runs her hand down my body, violating every inch of me with her invasive touch. Her lacquered black eyes don't hide her desire.

Her hand is close to my brassiere.

I close my eyes, willing her, please don't find the ring. Please don't …

Now, she is running the palm of her hand underneath my right breast, halting in the middle before continuing. She grazes past the ring, and I release a relieved exhale, no doubt fully revealing my tell. And sure enough, she stops.

Her eyes flicker to mine with her signature arrogant grin.

She cups my left breast, pushing me further into the wall. Falla surges toward me but the soldiers slam her into the ground, pinning her down.

Caya's lips float over my heated cheek, then she grazes the tip of her nose on my flushed and mottled skin, her warm lips hovering a millimeter over mine as she reaches up my shirt and finds the hidden portal ring.

She digs into my brassiere, freeing the ring which she holds in front of me.

"This. Doesn't belong to you." Lit with brazen hatred, I spit in her face.

She chuckles along with the other soldiers while I release an exhale, her fury unleashing. She backhands me. Raw pain exploding across my lip.

The soldiers release their grasp, letting my body sink to the cold, damp floor.

Caya turns on her heels. "We're done here."

The black steelore door slams shut once again and now, they're all gone except for Hanri who stalks the hallway beyond our cell, reveling in our captivity.

"Nice to see you three are where you belong." He spits on the stone.

I'm surprised to see Rioyn's head lift finally. There's an expression on his face I've never seen before. At first, I think he's sitting in a dark corner of the cell, but then I realize the shadow is moving while the weighty blackness lingers behind him, pulsing and shifting. Tendrils of pitch-black smoke curl in toward Hanri, who begins to back away.

Falla and I are struck into silence, seeing the smoke curling into our cousin's nostrils. Terror floods Hanri's lacquered black eyes.

What is happening?

I stare at my brother and gasp. In the blink of an eye, his whole face has blackened, as if he himself has become a shadow. "Rioyn!" I cry, my voice fractured with fear.

Hanri stumbles backward, severing the trance. That's not supposed to happen. Without another word, he's running down the hall, desperate to flee, a desperation I've never, ever seen in my cousin before.

Rioyn is gasping for air.

"What. Was. That?" Falla demands, caught somewhere between awe and terror.

"I don't know." My brother shrugs. "Whatever it is, it wants to get out of me."

"The black dust Shivane blew into your face. Is it controlling you? It took over your eyes, and then your face. Just like those monsters, but worse."

Rioyn's clear hazel eyes glitter with rage. "What do you want from me, sister? Do you want me to fight them? Or roll over and do nothing? I never asked for any of this!"

His anger turns on me, but I won't break his stare, won't let him turn this around on me. "Neither did we!"

"You weren't complaining when I harnessed my power to save you from the Sancaros. Or when I used it to help us flee the dreamsman. I was in control of it, but it's magnified."

"Guys, a little discretion?" Falla juts her chin at the cells around.

She's right, anyone could be listening in.

We stand there, staring at one another with our lips sealed, so much left unsaid.

When Falla finally speaks again, her voice is quiet, intense. "Don't you understand, Rioyn?" He stares back at her, eyes simmering from under his hood. "You've doomed us. All so you could fight Hanri." Is she angry at Rioyn or does she pity him? "Every time you allow your anger to control you, you lose sight of what you're sacrificing in the process. All you care about is whatever desire to win has you in its grip."

Rioyn's face drops, hidden behind the hood. He can't deny what is clearly true.

Falla lies in her corner facing away, and in the silence that follows, it takes everything in me have not to open my mouth wide and scream.

I sit in the last unoccupied corner, hands around my knees, rocking. In the gloom, it feels as though something is staring, eyeing me through the bars.

From the adjoining cell, sure enough, two golden-brown eyes glow back, offering a mere split second to register their beauty. And then they're gone.

IT IS IMPOSSIBLE TO tell how many hours have passed by the time cacophonous thumping steps make my head lift from my knees. A man is trudges down the stone staircase carrying a steelore pot, his stinking clothes rotting off an equally putrefied frame.

His greasy half-head of hair is slicked back against his skin. "Stick ye bowls out." He speaks the words as if they are all he can utter, words spoken so frequently, they pour free.

The other prisoners shove arms and bowls through the prison bars while my eyes desperately search our cell for one, finding a pile of them lying in the corner. I flip them over, then squeal like a little girl when a rat darts out and scurries across the cell.

The bowls are filthy, perhaps even moldy. The man reaches our cell. Neither Rioyn nor Falla feigns interest in whatever meal stews in his pot.

"Get ye bowl, girl. I don't gots all day."

The bowl looks less than appealing; am I hungry enough to eat from among the disgusting remnants? Can we even trust the food hasn't been poisoned or drugged?

I'm starving, but for now, it's better for my guts to eat their own selves.

The man stares me down with his one straight eye, then hobbles to the next cell as I slump back to the floor, head on my knees.

"You need to eat." A man's voice behind makes me swivel quickly. "Sorry, didn't mean to scare you. It's just that some days, we get no food at all, and what we do get is barely enough to keep a flea alive. So, when you got it, eat it."

A man sits in the shadowed corner of his cell, hands and feet all shackled just like Rioyn's. "Who are you?"

"If I told you, you wouldn't believe me."

The man chuckles, but where's the joke?

"Try me."

My face doesn't mirror his peculiar joviality.

With a grunt, he leans forward into the half-light, offering high, proud cheeks and a sharp, severe nose as if for inspection, features that would be recognizable anywhere.

In fact, a portrait of him hangs in our abandoned home, all over our dejected city.

This man looks about a century older, ragged and scarred, but his identity is undeniable. The fact he is here, imprisoned, is unthinkable.

"Is it really you?" I can't believe it. He leans back into the darkness. "Rioyn, wake up!" I kick out, striking his bad leg. He winces from the pain.

"Sorry," I say, even though he deserves far worse.

"Leave me be," he snaps.

Sadly, that's not an option. "Arro is here!"

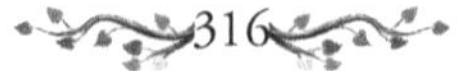

With a cagey cynicism never witnessed in my brother before, he looks past me to the man lounging in the dark.

"I only see another sad prisoner." Rioyn lies back. "Stop bothering me and let me be."

"Rioyn Orro, Son of Durran Orro."

The deep baritone voice rumbles through the darkness, a voice that could command a hundred thousand men and has. "General of the Grynndyre Command."

Rioyn slowly rolls over and rises to his feet. With faltering steps, he walks to the bars of the adjoining cell, his chains click-clack-click-clacking along with him.

Rioyn stands hunched before the bars while at the same time, Arro's head moves in the darkness, scanning Rioyn up and down. "It sounds like you have an unquenchable desire to win, my boy. One that's led you and your friends into trouble."

"I don't need a lecture. Even from you."

My brother turns his back on Arro, but the older man won't have it.

"Turn and face me."

He hesitates, a small flame of hope starting up when he musters the last of his strength to stand tall and turn back.

Arro pushes himself to his knees and slowly stands. He's always been a handsome man, strong and heroic, especially for how old he is. And just how old is he? No one has a definitive answer. Eleven hundred years, maybe more. He comes from a world with which we lost contact a long time ago, one where people are immortal or so we've been told.

As he shuffles into the light, his dark, crimson hair reveals itself in desperate need of a trim. His beard is long, shaggy, his face stained with dirt and soot.

He's draped in a tattered cloth shirt and ripped pants, a stark contrast to his normal Xearian flight armor.

"Giving up is a luxury you can't afford, Rioyn."

I wait for Rioyn to speak but he's still too broken or something to utter a single word.

"We don't want to give up. But there's no way out," I chime in, speaking for us both.

"Ayva Orro. The star academic of Galilei."

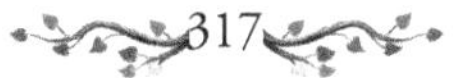

I was shocked that he knew Rioyn's name. But mine? I blink in surprise.

"Now," he continues, lowering his voice, "did these hooligans take The Scroll of Alderon from you? You were to bring it to me."

Rioyn and I exchange a look at this new, inexplicable revelation.

Either we are sorely ignorant or being deceived.

Neither is optimal. "Gran'ama never said anything about giving you the scroll," I say warily. "Or that we would find you in this dungeon."

"Sometimes, a soldier is only told what they need to know. Some secrets are too great to be risked."

None of this makes sense. Even if Gran'ama couldn't tell us we were seeking Arro, how could she know that going to the Iyanndyre would in fact lead us here, to Dremaria, where he was being held? Unless she suspected that sending us to the Iyanndyre was a surefire way of having us captured. A chill runs down my spine.

She had called it a suicide mission …

"The time will come when you cross the path of a trusted person, and the scroll must change hands," Rioyn recites. I stare at him, confused.

He turns to me. "Gran told me before we left."

Then he turns to Arro. "They took our packs, so I've no way of giving it to you."

"Those powerful chains may hamper you, but they've underestimated your sister and left her unshackled." Arro's grin sharpens as he turns to me. "The answer lies in your palm, Ayva. The guards might not have noticed, but my eyes are sharp as a hawk's."

I open my clenched fist and stare at my throbbing brand. "How am I supposed to get The Scroll of Alderon using my palm?"

"Both of you look at me and understand this."

Rioyn and I nod, hanging on every word.

"You're true descendants of Warriem," he says, and we deflate.

"We already know," Rioyn clips.

"Good. And now you have the insignia on your palms to prove it."

Rioyn and I exchange glances. What does this insignia truly mean and why have we never heard anything about it?

"It's not a truth Warriem wanted known among the masses. You both were able to touch the Iyanndyre, something no one has ever been able to do. There's a reason why Grynndyre Command has placed a boundary around the Iyanndyre.

"If anyone gets close, they face the same suffrage as when one gets too close to the Infinite Void, except worse."

"Wait, are we the Iyanndyre Born?" I ask.

Arro studies us for a long moment as if looking through us, into our souls. He shakes his head. "Wish I could say you were. Your Gran'ama thought you might be given that you each check off a lot of the criteria to fulfill the prophecy of the Iyanndyre Born. The Iyanndyre must've heightened your Ascendance's but that seems to be it."

"So, Gran sent us on this death-ridden journey because she thought we might be the Iyanndyre Born? Then why didn't she tell us?" I demand.

"Sometimes, a soldier is only—"

I raise my hand to stop Arro from reciting what he's already told us.

At this point, my irritation is ripe, rising to the surface.

"So, we need to get the scroll," I say, taking a deep breath. "How?"

"How have you overcome all other impossible challenges thrown in your path, child?"

It's a good question.

At times, my powers have arisen almost entirely accidentally, such as on the evening I traveled through the veil to reach Jax. At other times, they've been triggered by extreme hatred or fear. I think of Mother's gentle voice, encouraging me to calm myself and focus.

"Your mind is powerful, Ayva. Use it to control another and get them to do what you want. What you need. It's the same feeling as when you did it before, except this time, you'll be entering their mind, controlling them."

CHAPTER 43

THE SCROLL OF ALDERON

AYVA

WHAT ARRO IS SUGGESTING sounds wildly violating of someone's privacy and an overuse of my Ascendance.

"It is." I jump back at Arro's statement. He's obviously reading my thoughts.

"I am. You need to learn how to guard your own mind. Until then, you have a choice. Do what is absolutely necessary to get out of this cell so that we all can fight to live another day or choose to stay here to rot and die."

My mouth hangs but he's right. These are not simple times relying on simple answers. We—I—must do what is necessary to save us so that we have a hope of saving our realm.

I can do this, I chant to myself over and over, hoping it resonates.

There's also no time to argue and go back and forth with a man who obviously knows more about myself than I do.

I sit cross-legged in the back of the cell.

Rioyn crouches next to Falla, who is only now waking up and staring at Arro in wide-eyed recognition, scrambling into a deep bow. Rioyn speaks softly into her ear, bringing her up to speed. She seems too awestruck to remember she's mad at him.

I root myself into the chilled stone floor, hands resting atop my knees. I stare ahead and my gaze climbs to find the piercing golden-brown ones of Arro. He nods.

On a deep inhalation, I close my eyes and focus with a sharp intensity.

My mind travels through immense darkness until there are stars, an abundance of stars, my heart twisting at the sight. Are these the stars we've lost since the Starless Army consumed them? I reach out to touch them, feel them, to see if they glimmer back in recognition. Friends, family—who am I gliding past? But my longing goes unanswered as I'm pulled forward by an invisible force. The stars converge to glimmering straight lines that consume me and then, I'm standing outside the cell.

My head turns, gazing back into our prison. I see me, us as we are. Arro, Rioyn, and Falla stare intently at my sitting form. The foul stench of the Dungeon Lair is slightly less pungent but still lingering in this in-between space.

Running up the stone encased spiral staircase, my feet are light in their touch.

There's no need to actively walk through the door, only to think about passing through and in the next moment, I'm in the stone-encased hallway. I follow my intuition and the tug on my gut to return to the study chamber we found yesterday.

I picture myself walking through the door and into the room.

The first thing I notice is Caya sitting splayed across the high leather wingback chair at the desk, facing Xylar and Hanri. I freeze but they don't see me.

Our packs sit at the opposite end of the study chamber. No time to waste. But how long can I maintain this degree of focus? I study the three of them, seeking to determine who is the best candidate to control. Then it hits me. Xylar!

I focus harder, mulling over all of the times he's tried to get close to me, but I refused him … and then I'm inside his mind, feeling him go cold yet warming to me at the same time. His feelings for me are palpable, guilt immediately riddling through me. I should not be in his mind, should not be aware of what he thinks and feels like this.

Forcing myself to focus on the task at hand, I won't give up now.

"Why don't you guys head down for dinner? I'll check on our prisoners," I command Xylar to say, hoping it's the right utterance at the right moment.

Hanri stands. "We have a lot more to discuss but I could use some food."

Caya squints at Xylar as if studying to determine if his behavior is odd. Her lacquered black eyes dart back and forth between Xylar and Hanri. She's on to him, knowing somehow. She stands and walks around the desk, then looks up at Hanri.

"Your turn to cook." Caya smacks Hanri on the arm and they depart the study chamber.

As soon as the door shuts behind them, I give my command to Xylar.

"Reach into Rioyn's pack and find the rolled-up scroll."

Xylar moves to the back of the study chamber, immediately going for Rioyn's pack.

He must know which one is which without looking after spending many summers with Rioyn.

Xylar reaches into the pack. As he does, I see his memories of me and all the accompanying feelings. I never thought he actually liked me, believing women were nothing more than a sport to him.

My moral compass spins, my guilt continuing to rip my heart to shreds.

Xylar claims the scroll. He stands and just stares at it.

"Walk out of the study chamber and into the Dungeon Lair." Xylar doesn't move.

Loud voices resonate, walking by the study chamber. "We should kill them."

Xylar whips around to face the door, hiding the scroll behind his back. Somehow, I'm separated from his consciousness and fall through a wall. Except that I'm not in the wall.

I'm now in a room with no doors and scour the area, trying to figure out what it is.

A map of our entire world, inner and outer realms, fills the giant wall area.

A glass table with clawed feet sits in the middle of the room with two large worn leather chairs. Is this a secret study chamber of Shivane and Sylon?

How do they get in here? The same way I did? I feel myself slipping.

Focus, Ayva.

I study the map as best I can in the limited time, agog at such a detailed representation.

Clearly, Shivane and Sylon have been researching, spying, and scheming for years. Drycour and its neighboring realm, Stielmaire, are marked with red flags.

The route is also mapped out, all the way from Drycour to the shores of the Daiyaman Ocean here in Seivan. It looks to pass around the treacherous Cape of Tryndai and through the Middle Ocean—under the Starless Divide. This must be the route Drycour will take to get here.

At least this is what I assume based on Shivane's letter from Lord Zaxion.

The other realms also warrant inspection.

Barony allies with Drycour but Sairu, Myenndore, Quairland, and Assoria don't bear the same marked flags. Maybe. Hopefully, they aren't siding with Drycour and Shivane.

And equally hopefully, they're still our allies.

Allies we haven't visited or welcomed in over four hundred years.

I glance at the realm of Nabbula, home of the savages.

It seems they have no interest in either of us but that doesn't mean they won't join in one way or the other for their own self-interest.

The language written on the map is ancient, archaic, something not of our world but I've seen it before in my studies.

I whirl my head around at the sound of strained voices nearby, moving through the wall and into the main study chamber. I can't take the chance of someone going into the Dungeon Lair and seeing me in my Ascendance position.

Reconnecting to Xylar, we rush out of the study chamber and down into the Dungeon Lair which goes silent once Xylar's presence is known. He stalks up to our cell door.

I'm eager to relinquish my hold on his mind, not feeling good for once, being this deep into his mind. My final command is for him to free us from our rotting cells.

Once the doors to the cell are unlocked, my physical eyes fly open and I'm back in my body and out of his mind. Leaping to my feet, I rush toward Xylar, staring into his crystal-clear eyes. His rich amber tone has returned. Gone is the deep void of the lacquered black. He is free of the Starless Army curse. If this is the good that comes from me infiltrating his mind, then my mind is at ease somewhat.

"How did you all get down here?" Xylar asks.

Through squinted eyes, I reply, "You don't remember capturing us and throwing us into this putrid cell?"

With shock and awe, Xylar shakes his head.

"We don't have much time," Arro says. "Ayva, you must channel your elemental Ascendance. Sure, you haven't used it before, but the Iyanndyre not only heightens your main Ascendance, but it also unlocks the other one within. You need to break our chains."

I'm dumbfounded by all of these monumental revelations but like Arro said, there's no time to dwell on my sweltering thoughts. Arro stands in front of me with his shackles hoisted in front of him. I raise my hands, placing them over his confines.

Focusing my mind is a great struggle but I push through my racing thoughts to focus on decimating these chains to dust, the heat rising within me, transferring to his chains.

It becomes unbearable just before they incinerate into a million speckles of black dust.

He's free! Rioyn rushes over and I do the same for him.

Arro extends his hand, palm up in front of Xylar, requesting The Scroll of Alderon. With wide eyes, Xylar gingerly lays it in Arro's hand. The scroll glows at Arro's touch.

"I will travel back to Xaeria and find the Scribe of Echolyne. I will return The Scroll of Alderon to her."

"Why give it to her?" I ask.

"As good faith. The scribe will never give you anything without sacrificing something of importance to her first. She has the ability to resurrect the Army of Turmine."

"The Army of Turmine? You can't be serious! That outer realm army is the deadliest to have ever plagued this world. Leaving them dead and buried is the best thing for everyone. They won't just kill the Starless Army, they'll kill everyone else," Rioyn explains.

He's studied every war and battle, as well as who fought in them.

"You're not wrong and it's impressive you know about that army but we're out of options. We can only hope the scribe has the control over the army that she believes she does."

"Are we to follow you there?" Rioyn asks.

"No. Get back to Casstell but on the way, you must find the Omniscient of Haven Hill. She is the gatekeeper of knowledge, the only one who can help us find the Iyanndyre Born now."

CHAPTER 44

The Dreamers

RIOYN

ANOTHER PLACE WE HAVE to go. Another person we must find. When will this end? No one seems to have any understanding of the Iyanndyre Born. Those to whom we look for guidance and from whom we seek understanding seem as lost as we are. They have thoughts of who and what should happen, but no one knows. Was this how it was always supposed to be? Was this the plan Warriem and Everia had when trouble was afoot?

"What do I do?" Xylar asks. All eyes whip to Arro.

"You come with me. The journey they're on only requires three. We must leave now." Arro leads up toward the stairs that deliver us into this miserable place.

I follow behind Falla, feeling Ayva stop.

"We must go now. Why are you stopping?" I ask. She looks around the Dungeon Lair. What she's about to say is obvious.

"We have to save them."

"We don't have time."

"Are our lives worth more than theirs? If we don't have the time to save them, then we don't have the time to save ourselves." Ayva's stare burns a hole straight through me. "You know these dreamers were put in here unfairly. Who are we to leave them behind? We're on this mission to save the people of Seivan. That doesn't mean we get to pick and choose who. If we don't save them, we're no better than the ones we seek to destroy."

My head shifts back into my shoulders, looking to Arro, Falla and Xylar, seeing it in each of them. She's right. Ayva is right.

She doesn't wait for my delayed agreeance in any case, beginning to unlock all their cells one by one. Falla, Xylar, Arro and I quickly jump in to the dreamers—at least I assume they're all dreamers. The hollow, vacant eyes give most of them away, but they can be anyone. They all congregate to the middle and huddle around Ayva.

Immediately, I brace for any attack that might come our way.

Anxiety laced tension whistles through me as one dreary-eyed dreamer stammers to Ayva. "You saved us. You didn't have to, but you did. We will never forget what did for us here. We will tell all of Dremaria. We thank you indeed." The dreary-eyed dreamer gets down on one knee. With his hands draped at his side, he lowers his head.

"I merely did what was right," Ayva says.

"You are a heroine to us. We will never forget today and—" Just then, Caya, Hanri and the rest of their Starless Army make their way into the depths of the Dungeon Lair.

The dreary-eyed dreamer shoves Ayva behind him, the rest mounting a frontline stance.

"Well, well, well! What turn of fortune do we have here? Setting pathetic dreamers free, I see," Caya says.

The dreary-eyed dreamer whips around to face Ayva.

"Bigger battles are ahead of you to fight. We'll fend them off. You all go. Now."

"We're not leaving you here to fight them alone. They're awful and will make you suffer terribly just for fighting for us."

"If you get stuck here, then no one will have a chance. Go."

Just as Ayva is about to relinquish her pride and allow the dreamers to fight for us, something stops her. She moves forward. I grab her arm, spinning her to face me.

"We need to go."

"Not without that portal ring." The look in Ayva's eyes tells me there's no point in arguing with her. She turns to face Caya, her hazel eyes glowing.

I stammer back and whip my curiosity to Arro. He too is intrigued.

All at once, the dreamers enter a trance-like state—seemingly at Ayva's command, just like Xylar— and push forward to attack the Starless Army. Our army of dreamers. Ayva sets her sights on Caya.

Falla, Arro and I push with the dreamers, ready to fight.

Ayva extends her hand to Caya. "I'll take that ring now."

Caya's head falls back as she lets out a prolonged and loud cackle. "Try and pry it from my finger. I'll enjoy you being close enough to taste."

My head pushes back into my shoulders at the searing rage that pulses through my sister at Caya's lewd comment. Never in our eighteen years on this planet have I ever seen my sister this angry at anyone or anything. Even I'm a little nervous for the pain she's about to inflict on this wretched excuse for a woman.

Ayva focuses on Caya using her mental Ascendance to penetrate the Starless Army trance and get into her head.

Ayva's face turns purple as she tries forcing her way into Caya's mind.

Caya ridicules Ayva with her taunts. Ayva seemingly had an easier time penetrating Xylar's mind, probably because she and Xylar were already familiar with each other.

Caya's eyes glimmer from the black lacquered void back to the purple for a flash, and then it's gone. When her eyes return, Caya has had enough of Ayva.

She unleashes her Ascendancy of shadows onto the Starless Army.

We all hesitate, jumping back at the new-to-us powers that Caya possesses.

The Starless Army pummels its way through the dreamers who have chosen to fight with us. The dreamers—and even we—are no match for the strength with which Caya is impregnating the Starless Army.

Then it hits me! If Caya can give the Starless Army strength through her shadows, then I, in theory, should be able to do the same. I summon every last ounce of strength and channel it into my shadows, then release those shadows onto the dreamers. As soon as my shadows touch them, they're ignited with the strength they need to fight and win.

Arro, Falla and Xylar fight valiantly alongside each and every dreamer.

Now that the dreamers and Starless Army face off in more of a fair fight, Ayva unleashes her newfound elemental Ascendance on Caya. Ayva doesn't hold back.

She slams Caya into the bruising stone wall behind her. Ayva holds Caya against the wall by her neck as she slides the portal ring from her finger.

"This … doesn't belong to you anymore," Ayva taunts.

Caya is unable to speak, dropping to her knees when Ayva releases her grip from Caya's bruised neck. Ayva spins on her heels as Caya gasps for air.

The dreary-eyed dreamer stops Ayva. "Get on now. We will finish this fight here."

"I can't thank you enough for what you've all done."

"No, no dearie. It's us who thank you. Proud we are to fight for such a true-hearted leader." The dreary-eyed dreamer whips back around and unleashes years of pent-up fury onto his Starless Army victims with the help of my strength.

Arro, Falla, Xylar and I clamor to Ayva.

"Where do we go now?" Ayva asks.

Arro turns to address her. "Open a portal to Xaeria. Xylar and I will head there. Once we're through, open another one to the Omniscient of Haven Hill. You'll be taken straight to her."

Ayva slides the ring over her pointer finger and rotates her hand in a circle. A black hole of a portal opens, through which Arro and Xylar disappear. Once that portal closes up, Ayva opens another. This time, the portal is bright white.

We each jump through it, disappearing too.

CHAPTER 45

HAVEN HILL

AYVA

THIS PORTAL JUMP IS different than the last, surrounding us in a white light, surrounding us in warmth, peace. The calming essence of the light radiates from me.

Moments later, we're standing on the caramel shores of Haven Hill where the whitewashed landscape comes into crystal clear view.

Cascading blue skies kiss the tall grass flowing in the ocean's breeze. Beautiful hard oak trees line the border from the grass to the sand.

Haven Hill is not on any known maps. To be granted access here, someone must have a true purpose for their visit. Normally, an invitation or summons is needed; however, since we have the portal ring, finding this place has proved so much easier for us.

Haven Hill has a mystical property much like the Labyrinth Brick, shrouded in extreme mystery. I've yet to ever meet or to hear of someone who has been here before.

At least, I haven't heard of it directly from anyone who has lived to tell the tale.

The Omniscient of Haven Hill is another enigma roaming these beautiful shores, providing insight when the dire need arrives. A few sayer scrolls have appeared to provide guidance during challenging times but otherwise, this Omniscient has never been seen.

Standing before us under the shade of two immense oaks is a woman dressed in a white linen dress that dances in the tender breeze, her silvery blonde hair glistening from the ocean's rippled light. Her gentle smile is young, contrary to her highly advanced age.

Falla leans in to whisper, "Are you sure we should trust her? Gran'ama said to not trust anyone."

"Arro told us to come here. His word is as good as Gran's."

I sense that Falla isn't buying my trust in this woman, or in Arro for that matter.

"My name is Atheyl, and I'm the Omniscient of Haven Hill. Welcome."

"Arro of Xaeria sent—" Atheyl kindly raises her palm, her hand fire branded with an ancient script outlined in red, just like mine and Rioyn's except for the fact that hers covers her entire hand and wraps up her wrist too, only stopping at her elbow.

"I know why you're here. Come." She snaps her fingers.

A bright, white light engulfs us and, in a flash, we're inside of her house.

The three of us are seated on her light mint green sofa with the departing sun basking upon us through her large, clear window.

"Have some tea. It will heal the injuries you have."

Atheyl floats her hand with the fire brand in an infinity swish. We look down and a tray with a crystal tea kettle and three delicate teacups with saucers appear before us.

Her knowing eyes seem to be encouraging us to drink.

My trembling hands reach for the tea kettle and pour the tea for us, the kettle rattling from my pent-up nerves.

"You three are safe. You will be safe while you're here. Relax."

Easier said than done but I gather she already knows that.

I center myself with my breathing, continuing to pour the tea which we each sip, finding it the perfect temperature.

"Where did you get those fire brands on your hand?" I can't help but pry, again lifting the delicate teacup to my lips.

"The same place you did, dear."

"How did we get them simply by touching the Iyanndyre?" She obviously has the answers we desperately seek. This journey has relentlessly pressed down on us to the point of shattering. I want to know what everyone seems to be hiding.

Atheyl's eyes narrow, crinkling her brows.

"When Warriem and Alderon threatened to trap Everia's powers in the Iyann crystals, they were trying to protect her from herself. They believed that no one person should have the ability to destroy what they had created. That such power would eventually drive a person mad. But it broke their hearts, and Warriem could only inflict this pain upon her sister if she condemned her own powers to the crystals as well." Atheyl sips her tea.

"The crystals that held Everia's powers turned black. Warriem's turned the crystals white. Light and dark. Opposites, yet balanced."

Light and dark. I think of my brother, and of the new powers now residing within him and me. His born of Everia's loss.

"Warriem hid her white crystals at the top of the Iyanndyre in the polyhedron—which is why it's surrounded by the cage—knowing that only a person of the purest heart could access them." Atheyl places her teacup down, staring at both Rioyn and me.

"Where do we find the Iyanndyre Born?" Rioyn hastily asks.

"Who told you that you aren't the Iyanndyre Born?"

"Arro."

Atheyl raps her fingers against the ornately carved wooden armrest of her chair. "Interesting. A hot shower, fresh clothes and a cozy bed await the three of you. We'll continue this discussion in the morning."

Falla and Rioyn jump up at the invitation, both awkwardly bowing and leaving the room. I long to follow, but too many unanswered questions simply won't allow it.

I am not done with this conversation, not by a long shot.

My face scrunches, staring at Atheyl.

"Wondering where you've seen me before?" she asks.

I nod. She does seem familiar.

"I am your Gran'ama's great-great-great gran'ama."

Atheyl smiles bright as the realization dawns.

"Wait, I've been here before, haven't I?" The revelation that I do in fact know this place and that I've been here before and not at the Dara'Ana Station like I previously thought sends a radiating shock through my entire body.

"You have. When you and your brother were sick all those years ago as children."

"That sickness. What was it? I remember it was unusual and odd. Rioyn ended up being carried away on a healants' emergency bed. I think about that day constantly, wondering what caused him to get so sick that he had to come here and not the Dara'Ana Station."

Atheyl's chest raises with her deep inhalation. I don't break her eye contact.

"It was odd. It was an illness not of our realm but of our enemies'."

I sit up, giving her my full attention.

"Something got in. The Outer Realms used the dragolyons—"

"The same ones Arro and Monnaire have in their Xaerian Fleet?"

Atheyl nods. "The very same. At the time, it was the only way to bypass our defenses of the Infinite Void." Atheyl smooths the ripples in her dress.

"There's a lot of good in your brother that has kept the darkness at bay. The same goodness that's inside of you."

"You said that Everia was dark and Warriem was light. Are Rioyn and I the same? Was he born with the darkness that the black crystals … awakened?"

"He was and the darkness isn't a bad thing like most people are driven to believe. It is simply the opposite of the light and together, they create a balance. It's important to know how to use both and not let either consume you."

"What about the dragolyons? Do the Outer Realms still have them?"

"No. Arro and Monnaire confiscated them from the Outer Realms and their eggs by order of the Iyann Treaty." Atheyl tucks a sliver of her ice-blonde hair behind her ear. "The Outer Realms are dangerous and powerful. Given the opportunity, they will do worse things than what Shivane and Sylon have already done and plan to do."

I sit back in the comfort of her sofa but comfort I do not feel. Drycour will be coming for Seivan. My head falls back, eyes rapt on the ceiling, lost in my thoughts that shift me into the sweetest and deepest of slumbers.

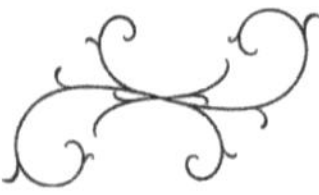

MORNING HAS ARRIVED. THE sun dances on my face through the lace curtains flowing in the soft, salty breeze. I awake in the most comfortable bed ever, stretching my arms out wide to help rid my body of its sleep. To my surprise, nothing aches. There is no pain.

The aroma of cinnamon and cloves tickle my senses, bringing a blissful smile, studying the yellow-painted walls until I realize where I am and the mission still before us.

Leaping from the sumptuous bed, I'm soon running, hurtling down the tight hallways and into the living room where Rioyn and Falla sit with Atheyl.

"How long have you all been up? Why didn't you wake me?"

Rioyn says, "We don't have much time before we need to leave, so we need to finish our discussion about the Iyanndyre Born. Where can we find this person who's supposed to save us all?"

Atheyl studies his eyes.

"As much as I've enjoyed our conjoined time, you're right; your leave is now."

"We were told you have the information to help us find the Iyanndyre Born. Tell us what you know," Rioyn presses.

"I do know, and where you are headed is where you'll find the information."

"Where are we going? Did I miss something?"

"You're going to the Labyrinth Brick."

I feel Rioyn and Falla's eyes whip to my pale face. "The Labyrinth Brick is a world between worlds. The only way to get there is …" I hesitate, all eyes falling on me.

"To die." My pulse quickens, sweat beading along my hairline.

How are we supposed to go to the Labyrinth Brick and then come back with the Iyanndyre Born to save our world?

The sound of Falla unsheathing her sword breaks the silence. "We're not dying. Not today."

"Is there a way to come back? If we die?" Rioyn asks.

"Coming back is up to you. To get to a world between worlds requires the ultimate sacrifice.

Atheyl snorts a chuckle. Falla readies her stance along with Rioyn, and I keep my focus locked on Atheyl. She offers up a silverore tray with three teacups.

"Drink this and pass through to the Labyrinth Brick. Find out how to find the Iyanndyre Born and save Seivan. Or don't and die anyways when you face Shivane and Sylon."

"We're not drinking that," Falla says.

"She's right. Without the Iyanndyre Born, we will die. If anyone knows what the right answer is, it's her. And we're all out of other choices," I say, pushing by Rioyn and Falla to grab a teacup. Before Rioyn can stop me, I fully drain the liquid poison.

My body immediately becomes weak, the effects of the drink sending me stumbling backward. In the distance, a man emerges from around the corner.

Wait … he's the odd vendor from the opening ceremony. Why is he here?

My vision blurs, a sweet goodbye whispering forth from my lips.

The world turns black.

CHAPTER 46

THE IN-BETWEEN

Under the Shrouded Veil

JAX

Zoura and I stand at attention next to Shivane and Sylon as if we're somehow a part of their Starless Army. Continually, I remind myself that I am nothing like them, certainly not their mindless drone. Except that I am.

My eyes have become the Starless Army's signature lacquered black.

Slowly, I look at Zoura who glances up in sheer disappointment through her deep green hazel eyes that she still possesses.

A rumbling knot of guilt chews away at my stomach at what I've done to my friend.

I thought these sorts of feelings were extinguished when my soul was converted to the Starless Army's. It was the only way, so it has to be. But convincing myself of this fabricated truth is harder than ever imagined. My body suddenly relaxes, my mind numbing. I did what I had to do, did what I should've. Why should he be free?

Why should he hold the secrets Lord Shi and Lord Sy desire?

My attention comes again into crisp focus when chains bang against the unforgiving stone floors. Mikel may not be much of a fighter, but he has a fighter's heart. A part of me desperately hopes he'll be able to break

337

free and escape, but I also know that wish is but a mere dream. The other part of me is relieved that he has to suffer here along with me.

The large ironore doors to the throneroom slowly edge open.

A full squad of Starless Army soldiers drag Mikel in, hurling him to the ground before a prideful Shivane and Sylon. His lack of grace and coordination grates on Shivane.

Her noticeable side-eye is not lost on me.

My attention snaps back to Mikel struggling to stand, his thick legs betraying him.

Just as he's about to get his feet under him, one of the black lacquered-eye soldiers knocks him back down to his knees.

I lunge forward to help him up but find myself frozen in place by Shivane, every fiber in my body seized. It's not possible to break her immensely strong control over my mind.

The fury in Mikel's eyes fire daggers aimed right for me.

Shivane descends from her throne, gliding down step by step.

With an empathetic reach, she extends long fingers to lift Mikel's chin, though his eyes still refuse to meet hers.

The Starless Army soldier who knocked him down takes a step forward to attack again. This time, however, Shivane brings the soldier to his knees in excruciating pain.

He grabs his head, his visceral screech sending shivers down everyone's spines.

"Rise, Cadet Valkor. You are a guest in our home."

Mikel peers up through furrowed brows. If he had any sort of Ascendance, he would annihilate her with that death-laced stare alone.

"We have invited you here as we need your esteemed expertise. You've proven yourself to be exceptionally valuable to us."

"Invited? Strange phraseology since you dragged me here against my will," Mikel lashes out. I've never seen him this mad in the ten years of knowing him. He needs to rein in his anger. Shivane won't take kindly to his blatant disdain, but what do I care?

Shivane huffs.

"You kidnapped and brought me here for a reason. Stop wasting what little time you're granting me and get on with it. Because no matter what you say, I'll not do a single thing for you. I am not a traitor." Mikel's pointed jab aimed right for me does the damage he intended. I crumble internally yet compose myself quickly; if he knew the truth, that sentiment might ring different from him.

The intense heat of irritation seeping from Shivane glistens her skin.

My lacquered eye remains focused on Mikel, emotions of caring and indifference battling inside of me. I need him to play along, otherwise my plan will not work.

My plan. My plan? Is that what I still want?

"So, you'd rather die than give me one small piece of information?"

"If it's to tell you where my friends are, then yes, yes I would." Mikel swivels his head to sear disdain toward me. I mouth, tell them. The wheels turn in Mikel's head.

Just when I think he might actually consider it, he spits at my feet.

Shivane arrogantly cackles to Sylon, her head whipping back to me with a ferocity I've only seen once before. My eyes peel wide, glancing at Mikel, hoping he will change his tune. Instead, he seems to be enjoying my impending punishment.

Shivane's long fingers extend for me but in a flash, I disappear.

Mikel and I reappear into adjoining jail cells. Before I'm able to blink, Mikel lunges his chunky arm through the ironore cell bars, reaching for me.

I lean back, escaping his furious grasp, my voided eyes slowly sweeping him up and down. Why am I stuck down here?

"How could you do this to me? How could you do this to Rioyn and Ayva! Luckily, they don't know about Falla. You're a disgrace. I never would've guessed you'd be the one to help our enemies."

Mikel's anger gradually gives way to a deep sadness. I, however, feel nothing.

"You don't understand. I needed to give them information to gain their trust. To get close to them. It's all a part of my plan."

"If giving up your friends is in your plan, then you don't have a plan. Look at your eyes. Look at who they've turned you into. There's no gaining their trust." Mikel studies every single defeated prisoner banished to these cells. "Where's Zoura?"

My lips part, giving way to share an answer to his question, but I find myself at a loss for words, not belonging here with these prisoners. Where is Zoura?

"Zoura is probably being punished because you won't cooperate. Kalli is stuck in the in-between. We were trying to save her and anyone else they banished there."

"What is the 'in-between'?"

"We're not entirely sure. But what we do know is that there's no way back from it unless Shivane and Sylon say so. It's a prison worse than this."

"Explain your reasoning for giving up Rioyn and Ayva. The two people, mind you, who are risking everything to save you, to save everyone. The two people—along with Falla—who are our only hope at restoring peace to our realm. How does giving them up justify saving Kalli? When they find the Iyanndyre Born, he can save Kalli and everyone else. But if they don't find the Iyanndyre Born, then saving Kalli doesn't matter."

Mikel's explanation is valid and I'm ashamed to say I didn't think about it like that. "I did this to gain access to them and help a friend …"

"But there's a flaw in that argument. Kalli isn't your friend. Zoura isn't your friend."

"I need to get Shivane and Sylon to trust me though."

"Why would you ever think they would trust you? You're not stupid, Jax."

I lean in to whisper to Mikel. "Because if I can get close enough to them, then I have a great shot at killing them myself."

Mikel's head cocks back as he lets out a loud roar of laughter.

"Quiet. You don't want to wake everyone up in here."

"That's your big plan? You risk all of your friends' lives to be the hero? To kill the two most powerful people in our world? You're delirious, at best. Do you really think Shivane doesn't already know this? She can read your mind, you fool."

My face pales at the realization that Mikel just might be right. He is right.

Now, I'm just their lacquered black-eye drone.

"It's funny. Everyone always thought Rioyn was the one driven by his need to be the best. To be the one everyone revered. I thought his drive for always being number one would cloud his judgment. Yet here we are. You're the one betraying everyone for glory."

"I did what I had to do to defeat evil. Yet I've realized that maybe Shivane and Sylon are right. Maybe this isn't a world to save. Maybe we're better off with them at the helm."

"When Rioyn and Ayva's Gran'ama said to not trust anyone, I guess she meant you."

Out of nowhere, Zoura appears in our cell. I reach for her, hold her tight. She pulls away, slinking to a dark corner of our cell.

"Get close all right. It all makes sense," Mikel states.

"You have no idea what you're talking about," I retort.

Mikel's head swivels to stare me down. "All's fair in love and war, right?"

Mikel retreats to the dark corner of his damp cell, making me call out for him, but he refuses to look my way. He'll understand once I'm able to carry out my plan.

It'll all be back to normal. I will take out Shivane and Sylon. I will rule this realm.

First thing the next morning, Mikel, Zoura, and I are ripped from our jail cells. Mikel thrusts his weight into the soldier but his brave attempt at escaping is thwarted when several more soldiers rush to contain him effortlessly.

They drag us into the throneroom where Shivane and Sylon calmly wait in their obnoxiously oversized thrones. Shivane's nails slowly screech against the metal armrest.

The Starless Army soldiers heartlessly throw us to the cold stone ground.

"Tell us, Cadet Valkor, have you had time to reconsider?"

Mikel glares up through his furrowed brow.

With a pronounced hop in his step, he leaps to his feet. "I won't give you a shred of information. I will never give up information about my friends. You will not win. They will find the Iyanndyre Born. So, do what you must. You'll get nothing from me."

Shivane gasps an arrogant laugh. "They won't find the Iyanndyre Born. She is with your friend, Kalli. And we figured you'd continue with your pathetic allegiance, which is why we recovered the device you used to track your friends ourselves. Thanks to our new loyal soldier."

Shivane drags her long nail under my chin. My grin curls with deviousness as soldiers drag in the radar machine we took from Grynndyre Command. Mikel's mouth drops.

"You can't force me to …" Shivane's temper flares at Mikel's defiance.

She mentally clenches his head. He crumples to his knees, his face violently red.

"Let him go," Zoura demands, tears streaming.

Shivane orders the soldiers to hold her down.

"Watch your friend suffer." Shivane's eyes close, her face twitching as if she's searching for something in her mind. As her eyes whip open, I realize what she's doing.

She releases her grip on Mikel. He flops to the ground, exhausted from the pain. A wicked grin tickles her lips.

"I have the information I need. You've proved to be useless. I hope you enjoy your time in the in-between."

Mikel feebly rises to his feet.

Shivane clenches her fist and Mikel crumples back to the floor like a heavy sack. I leap to check what I already know but the soldier's grasp on my shoulder is too tight.

Mikel's chest does not rise, filling with air. She has killed him.

Shivane snaps her fingers, soldiers stepping forward to carry his lifeless body away. I wipe my cheek, finding it's dry.

Zoura backs away when I reach for her.

Shivane waves her hand, and the Starless Army snatches her, dragging her from the throneroom. Then Shivane circles me. "Your heart has changed."

My gaze stays true to the unforgiving ground in front of me.

"The one you think you love. Do you still?"

I take a deep breath. "Don't know what you mean."

Shivane huffs a laugh. "Stop being a child. Be honest with yourself. You're in love with the one who's in front of you. The one who will have you. The one who is here. Doesn't matter what package she comes in, does it?"

Shame devours me whole, the first real emotion since the transformation. But is it shame, or realization of the truth? I've betrayed Ayva for my desperate need to not be alone … for my desire to be the hero. I will be the one who triumphs in the end.

Shivane circles me. "What shall we do with you now? Shall you join the frontline ranks?" Her fingers rap along her chin. "No, you shall be mine. At my every need and beckoning call."

Shivane snaps her fingers, and her Starless Army surrounds us.

She leads us out of her throneroom.

CHAPTER 47

THE LABYRINTH BRICK

RIOYN

As my eyes fly open, I'm lying on my back as the world beneath me feels as if it's rotating into the correct position. Slowly, I sit up using my elbows as braces, glancing around this world between worlds to which we've been committed. Ayva and Falla painstakingly roll up to a seated position, gandering along with me at this odd place.

The sky is misted with waves of gray, distorting the landscape, the void of vibrant colors and energy resembling Dremaria far too closely for my comfort.

As my vision focuses, I gaze upon the shimmering goldenore gates that seem to be the entrance into the Labyrinth Brick, a world between worlds.

These gates flow into a solid wall covered in thick curved vines, freckled with colorless flowers. As we step closer to them, hints of jasmine and rose tickle my nose.

Falla steps up to the immaculate, ornate gate, glancing first to her left, noticing a copperore plaque on the wall, its outline inscribed with stargazer lilies. It reads:

Behind these gates lie the secrets of the realm.
To your heart. To your soul. To your mind.
Enter at your own risk, with your heart at the helm.

I take a moment to take in the shapeshifting sights, the sounds, the sheer awe of what I stand before, pondering what awaits beyond these perfectly crafted goldenore gates.

The copperore plaque stares back as I absorb its words, envisioning the goodness and peace for which Seivan is known … The love, the harmony, and kind hearts.

That is what I want my heart and mind to know before I enter.

The darkness Arro said lives inside of me mustn't be allowed to hinder what lies beyond these gates and what lies ahead for me in my future.

We push on the goldenore gates, stepping into an oasis with rich green grass leading to an orchard of weeping Mulberry trees. The long hanging branches tickle the petals of oversized ground-dwelling flowers swaying in a tantalizing breeze. The colors beyond the golden gates are a far cry from the world between worlds on the outside.

This is pure harmony of nature.

A woman drenched in light—as if the sun follows her and only her—walks toward us, her golden amber hair flowing in the soft breeze.

Her lilac-colored gown kisses the wheaten pathway of crushed pebbles.

Falla and Ayva fall in line next to me as we wait for the woman's approach, her arms open wide to us. Her soft hazel eyes are aglow as she meets each of our anticipating stares.

She barely looks a few years older than us, radiant in her youth.

"Welcome to the Labyrinth Brick. We're excited about your arrival. I am Dorranna Xall. It's an honor for you to join us. Follow me." Dorranna escorts us along the path, the light following her illuminating her gloriously sun-kissed skin.

"The Labyrinth Brick is a sanctuary for the Spirits of Old, a world between the physical and spiritual universes that was forged several millennia ago."

She sweeps her arm in a graceful arc, taking in the landscape. "You see, there is more at stake than just saving the people of Seivan." Dorranna bats a wink.

We follow her down the path, past more illustrious flowers and ancient trees not found anywhere else in Seivan. I could spend a lifetime charting and indulging my senses in this mystical bridge between universes.

Next, Dorranna leads us through waist-level stone hedges opening into a large circle with a dais nestled in the back. Behind this stands a large, roughly round building covered in vines and moss with opal blue windows. The crest of the building comes to a crystal-pointed peak shooting twenty feet into the atmosphere.

She leads us into the middle of the circle.

And she waits.

Her hazel eyes lift to the sky. We follow her gaze, enraptured to see the white puffs of clouds parting as three rays of light shine down onto the heather gray dais.

Ayva stands tall in the middle, Falla and I at her side.

Through the rays of light, three figures float to the dais, promptly molding into their human forms. A strong, muscular man with wavy light golden hair and amber brown eyes stands next to two tall, beautiful women with scorched red hair and crystal hazel eyes.

They're each dressed in blue-black form-fitting fighting armor, two long swords running down the length of their spines. Fighting knives are sheathed on their thighs and ribs; undoubtedly, they are each dressed for battle.

"I recognize them from the Iyanndyre," Ayva whispers. "That's Warriem and Everia. He must be Alderon."

"Alderon is Warriem's husband, right? There's little ever written about him other than he was the first voyant and the one who created that order, right?" Falla asks.

"And The Scroll of Alderon, of course," I add.

At this, Falla rolls her eyes, silently telling me I'm ridiculous for even stating the obvious.

Dorranna turns to us with an impressed smile, confirming our theories.

My hand raises to cover my gaping mouth. Ayva and Falla, far more gracefully, drop to their knees, their right forearms balanced across them.

Feet stumbling, I follow, all three of us dropping our heads into the Grynndyre bow.

"I take it you know who we are?" Warriem stands tall. Leading with her strong chin, she steps forward from her middle position.

Ayva rises and steps forward as well. "We do, Holy One. It's an honor."

The warmth of Warriem's smile befalls us. "As you know, we were the first to inhabit this realm and plant the seeds of creation for what it is today. During our time here, we discovered this sort of 'in-between'." She motions to the air around her.

My gaze darts from Warriem to Everia, who stands with her feet shoulder width apart, hands in her pockets. What about the rift between the siblings?

Did they manage to overcome it and live together for all eternity?

It gives me hope, hope to carry with me for those times of quarreling with Ayva.

"We had the Omniscient send you here," Warriem continues. "As your Gran'ama told you, there is more at stake in this war than just the continuation of your tiny province."

I hang on to Warriem's every word, but as much as I long for the truth, it's also frightening, something to fear. The fate of our home is enough of a crushing responsibility. I can't say I wish for more.

"What is more at stake than the peace we're fighting to protect is the peace you brought to this world?" Ayva asks.

"The Iyanndyre."

All of our eyes fly open wide at Warriem's disclosure. No one really knows what the Iyanndyre is and why it's there. "It is the most important structure in the known universe."

"What is the Iyanndyre?" Ayva continues with her brave questioning.

"It's protection. We built the Iyanndyre to conceal a door we forged, a thick tungstenore door hiding the primary dark matter bridge. This single bridge connects to every dark matter bridge, which connects to every galaxy and every universe on our plane of existence."

I look at Ayva for understanding. Her eyes are bright and calculating. "Are you saying it's possible to travel through those bridges to other galaxies and universes?"

"It's possible, theoretically. But we've not found any galaxy or universe with the level of advanced technology required to do such a thing, not yet. We certainly don't possess those abilities here, though it hasn't stopped people from trying at all costs. Technology aside, it is possible some possess powers strong enough to travel through the gate."

"What does all this mean in our fight against Shivane and Sylon?" Ayva presses.

"You three are the key to saving Seivan and to protecting this gateway. However, none of you are ready to fight. We need to train you, so that Seivan has a fighting chance."

At this, Falla pipes up, "Surely, we'd have a better chance if you were fighting at our sides." She drops her eyes. "Excuse my impertinence."

"It's impossible for us to fight," Alderon sharply explains with his arms still folded over his chest.

"So then, why help at all?" Falla flashes.

"We have no desire to save you," he says heavily. "We are only interested in your continued evolution. You are a grand experiment. Of limitless potential."

"And some experiments fail," Everia adds with a dark smirk.

I can't help but laugh to release my nerves.

This whole encounter is so otherworldly, I might be losing my mind!

Everia catches my eye and winks. Falla looks a lot less impressed. "And this training. How long will this take?" she asks.

"Three months."

Warriem, Everia, and Alderon chuckle at our gaping mouths. "But remember that time is a construct. Entire days in the ripple are mere minutes on the outside."

While this revelation delivers a cooling wave of relief, Falla and Ayva seem to be getting more frustrated with every passing moment.

"And what about the legendary Iyanndyre Born?" Ayva presses. "Do they even exist? You could've saved us all a lot of headaches by just bringing us here in the first place. That journey was cruel."

Alderon steps forward. "You aren't wrong. It was a cruel journey that each of you experienced. Strategy is one thing, and destiny another. We speak of the exact coincidences, experiences, and failures that led you to this moment. This innate wisdom exceeds the limitations of your young minds—and our ancient ones, too."

Everia's cool, calm voice, silences any further questions from Falla.

"This evening, you say your goodbyes and begin your training individually." She juts her chin in my direction. "You, child, will be with me."

Warriem smiles at my sister. "Ayva."

Alderon nods at Falla, and just like that, our fates have been sealed for the next three months. With a flash, the three disappear back into the lights from which they came.

It leaves the three of us standing here newly enlightened, yet more confused than ever.

Falla studies the ground in front of her, stirring circles with her boot. This is good news, a miracle quite literally sent from above that might give us our only chance to make a true difference in this war. So why does it feel as though I've just been hit by a boulder?

Three months apart.

The period looms before us like a prison sentence.

This is not how I'm going to leave things. I will not spend these next three months wishing I'd done more to make things right between us all.

Falla is now attacking the ground with a vengeance.

I love her.

I've never said those words to her or myself, smart enough to know that now isn't the time. Even so, I close the gap to her fast before she has time to think, wrapping her in my arms and holding her. She tries to back away, but I hold her tighter. Slowly, she curls her arms around my back, and when she looks up, I kiss the salty tears from her cheek.

An insatiable urge to kiss her burns in me, but I won't. Right now, I'm here as I've always been for her, as her friend. I will earn back her trust, fighting to restore what we could have been. I don't want to just kiss or hold her. I want all of her, every bit of her.

But mostly, it's her heart, her soul that I crave.

"We'll get through this," I whisper in her ear as my lips graze it lightly. "I promise."

The tip of my nose traces her cheek.

She lifts her emotion-laced icy blue eyes to meet mine, then steps back, hugging my sister. A moment later, she's walking away with Dorranna.

"Please don't read my thoughts," I groan, turning to my sister. "I felt you in there, rifling around."

"I don't need to read your thoughts," she cuts back. "I just need to look at your sad, lovelorn face."

I huff a much-needed laugh, but it sounds hollow.

"I can't help but think about the competition for FirstElite," I say, sighing, "and how embarrassingly stupid it seems now. I ruined my relationship with our father, and for what? A children's game."

"Or you revealed the kind of stubborn fighting spirit needed to save the world."

"Hey, it's a step up from 'arrogant jerk who only wants to win'."

Ayva smiles, even as we both seem on the verge of spilling tears. "Twins."

"Twins." I pull her into a hug. "You've got this."

As I squeeze her tight, it hits me. I haven't asked her—

"How are you dealing with Jax being captured?" I gingerly ask, tears welling in Ayva's eyes.

"I think about him all the time but also shove him out of my mind, just so I don't break. I don't talk about him or about what happened because it's too hard. My emotions keep flooding through me."

I pull her into another hug until she pulls away to head down the path.

She has the shoulders of a young girl, yet all the swagger of a confident young fighter. For all of Alderon's talk of destiny, I can't deny this journey has changed us in ways that could never be taught in school.

I only hope it will be enough for whatever trials come next.

CHAPTER 48

EVERIA

RIOYN

A SOFT LIGHT WAKES ME. I've never slept better in my life than I did last night. The bandage on my wrist is gone, so I lift my pants leg to check the state of my knee.

It is no longer black and blue. Both have been healed.

I don't know how or why but I'd be a lying fool not to admit I'm beyond relieved, having been worried how my injuries would hold up if in any fight during this training.

Surely, fighting will be a large aspect of it.

On the desk rests a neatly stacked set of clothes together with a note:

Get dressed. We start soon.

Unfolding my new blue-black battle armor, I lay it out on the bed, noting it's stiff and rigidness, my hands running down the jacket sleeve. The armor's impenetrable material is the same as all our militaries wear. However, this feels stronger, thicker, with built-in sheaths on the thighs and the ribs. The jacket's back has been designed to hold short swords, just like Warriem, Everia, and Alderon wore at our greeting.

On the left breast of the jacket is a branded insignia, identical to the platinumore clasp on The Scroll of Alderon, an infinity symbol woven through a star, Warriem and Everia's crest of honor. This is a battle suit, one I will wear with pride.

In the bathing room, I prepare for whatever today and the next three months will bring, buttoning the stiff, thick armored pants and tightly adjusting the leg straps.

Then I do the same with the jacket.

"I'm ready," I call out, disappearing in an instant.

"That armor looks good on you."

Whipping around, I find Everia leaning against a tree with her arms folded across her chest. She's adorned with the same armor from yesterday, the same that I wear today. Her scorched red hair that matches mine is braided in a thick, tight braid, reaching her mid-back. She smirks with a crested brow.

My stares turn furious, charting my surroundings. Lake Lo is one place in Seivan that I avoid at all costs since its memories are crushing. "Why have you brought me here?"

She kicks off the tree, stalking toward me.

"To elicit that exact reaction from you, of course."

Her hazel eyes flicker with a quick golden glow.

Before I can react, she lands a punch across my face, sending me stumbling back, keeping my hands at my side. She rounds another punch, striking me again. "Are you even going to attempt to fight back?"

"I'm not going to—"

I gape. I'm not going to what? Fight a goddess? A superior? A hero? A girl?

"Wrong answer." Everia unleashes a barrage of punches, jabs, and kicks. By the time she's done with me, I'm on my back, gasping for air and holding my broken ribs. At least I'm pretty sure they're broken. Every inch of my sides hurts so much, and sitting up, I'm spitting blood. Yeah, they're broken.

"War knows no gender, nor mercy. Hesitation is for the weak. Now fight me!"

"I can't fight a ghost."

"On your feet, you pathetic wimp. You child."

I can't help but laugh in her stern face. "You might be a creator of worlds, but I fear my father more than I fear you."

"Because you love your father."

"Sure."

She walks around me, twirling a dagger with her dainty fingers. "It's too bad he could never love you. Only his control of you, and what he might turn you into. A miniature version of himself."

A scoff escapes, even as a flicker of anger lights my chest. She's trying to bait me, but I won't let her. If this journey has taught me anything, it is to cool my reactions and give myself a chance to think through the scenario.

"I would be proud to grow into a man like my father."

She pauses, tapping the tip of the blade against her lip. "Well, he hates you."

Not true. If she wants me to get angry, she'll have to do better than that.

"Warriem and I created your world, and in essence, every being in it. We know the innermost heart of each creation. So, trust me, Rioyn, when I say your father hates you because he fears you, seeing the endless potential in you long before anyone else. He saw what you could become, and it terrified him."

He saw the darkness. Deep down, it's apparent she's right.

I stare into her eyes, embarrassed by the hurt and rage flaring through my own.

She is manipulating me, but the staunch plummet of my stomach makes me wonder if she's even speaking the truth.

"Can't blame the man," I say. "He was right."

Anger swirls through my body like a living thing, something she can see and smell on me. When she charges, I block her punch and the next one. She's swift, quick. Quicker than I am, her boot crunching into my back.

I spit blood, again. If my ribs were broken before, they're shattered now. My breathing is shallow, but still I fight, focusing on channeling my anger and using it to propel me to block out the sharp shooting pain radiating through every bone and muscle in my body, thanks to her. But I will not give in, even while wondering, how is it possible to handle three months of this abuse?

She knows I'm hurting but doesn't stop, only fighting harder.

So must I then, not backing down.

"Going to cry, little one?"

She rounds a punch, and I block it, knocking her on her back. The wind escapes her chest. She looks up with wide hazel eyes. I reach a hand down. She takes it.

"Good. That was better."

"Better? I knocked you on your ass."

"It was a good move, but never underestimate your opponent until they're down and done."

"Understood."

Everia takes up residence on a log, motioning for me to join her. Finally, a moment to relax. She hands me her water sack, but I struggle to sip the desperately needed water. The adrenaline subsides and I feel every bit of my body that she broke in no time.

"Your wounds will be healed by tomorrow—or the next day. I haven't decided yet." She winks. "They won't heal like this on the battlefield. If you aren't strong enough and you're injured, you'll have to suffer through the pain to keep fighting. You have to steel your body, your mind, and fight."

Everia twists the tip of her knife on her calloused finger.

"What was it like fighting in the Great War of the Realms?" I ask.

"Heart wrenchingly horrible. You fight like hell to watch your fellow man die in front of you. That war broke us. It changed us. It changed me."

It changed her. There's more meaning to that statement. There's a longing to know what changed in her because this war could do the very same to me. "How?"

Everia slowly turns to face me with a cocked brow.

"I thought Warriem and I were the same, equals, but we're not. I realized it during the ultimate battle when we almost lost. When we had no other options left."

Everia pauses as if the memory of what happened still pains her all these centuries later. Then she adds quietly, "I knew in that moment that Warriem was the only one who could truly save us, but she wasn't powerful enough."

"Why her and not you? What made you decide that?"

"Evil cannot defeat evil. It will only give way to more darkness. You need light to be able to pierce through it. Warriem's heart is as pure as they come. It was obvious we were going to lose. There was no other option, so I made the conscious choice to give her my powers then and there. Darkness is more powerful than light so when the dark combines with light, her unstoppable powers were born, making her invincible."

What Everia just told me is the most heroic thing to ever imagine anyone doing. To give up something so important to you for the better of mankind is incredible.

"Sometimes, I wonder if I'll eventually stop feeling anything. This dark power—" I sigh, suddenly feeling awkward, it robs me of every feeling; pain, joy, empathy, and leaves nothing but rage in its place. But saying that aloud feels like spitting in her face. After all, that dark power did come from her.

"Don't look at it like it's a curse," she says. "Take it from me, it's a blessing."

"It seems like a curse for Shivane and Sylon. Or whatever's left of them."

Everia gazes into the glass-like lake. "Yes. It can destroy you if you allow it. But it's always been a part of you. The Iyann crystal dust that Shivane blew in your face simply woke it up. How it takes hold depends on you."

We sit in silence for a few moments. Should I dare to ask her more questions about the realm or just keep my damn mouth shut? It's a quandary.

"Go ahead. Ask whatever you want."

Of course, she can read my mind. She winks, skinning her apple with her throwing knife.

"We'll work on tactics for protecting your mind another day."

"It's not a pleasant feeling."

"You can't even begin to imagine. Shivane's one of the most powerful mind crawlers I've seen."

Wonderful.

"Over the next three months, I'll train you to fight, teach you how to use your rage using the dark side of your Ascendance for good. You'll learn more with me over these next three months than you would in ten years at Sansyre. I'll also teach you how to harness your Ascendance and bring out every bit of the power that resides within you. I've never seen it so strong within anyone before. You have a gift, Orro."

I hold her hazel eyes, waiting to see if she's going to say it.

She breaks my stare, and I dance back and forth within my thoughts. Dare I ask?

"Out with it already," she beckons, reading me again like a book.

My mouth opens but the words don't follow. Everia stares.

"Am I …" I exhale hard to control my breathing. "Am I the Iyanndyre Born?" She stares with her big hazel eyes that are almost translucent when the sun hits them exactly right. She stares at me as if looking through me, into my soul.

"No." Her words sink my heart. I never said it to myself or dared to say it to Falla or Ayva but deep down, I … I'd started to wonder. To hope.

She doesn't blink, holding my stare. "But you sure fight like you are."

I turn to stare out at the calmness of Lake Lo, unable to decide if I'm disappointed, relieved, or something else.

"So, how do we find the Iyanndyre Born?"

"Trust in yourselves and let go of what you know." Disappointment at her quandary of words destroys my previously calm demeanor.

"It's not all it's cracked up to be. Trust me." Everia stands. I stand to meet her. "I think that's enough for today. I'll show you a shred of mercy just this once. You will heal overnight, and you better come prepared tomorrow."

She reaches out for my shoulder, and just like that, I'm back in my cement room.

There's another note:

> *Train your mind to be a steelore wall.*
> *I will climb your thoughts and steal what I can—if you let me.*

With those comforting words of encouragement, I clean up and change. For the rest of the night, I do exactly as she says, building the strongest walls possible around my mind when I sense her lingering. My body aches and I'm exhausted, but I promised Ayva I'd succeed. And I'll do so, not willing to let her down, not failing either of them or Seivan.

I'll die before that happens.

CHAPTER 49

ALDERON

FALLA

ALDERON, THAT SMUG YET annoyingly handsome bastard—something I will never give him the satisfaction of hearing—leans on the same tree he's always perched against, picking the remains of his breakfast from his teeth.

Meanwhile, I'm drenched in sweat, engaged in a sword fight against a beast of a man. A man two heads taller than me and ten times as strong.

This has been my life for the past month and a half.

"You can't even fight me yourself. You had to summon this demon to bring me down?"

"It's more fun to watch you suffer. Plus, seems like you're doing just fine."

"You're a cruel bastard."

"Am I though?"

I want to punch that smug smile right off his face. I can't lose, can't give him any more pleasure in my pain.

Over the last month and a half, he has taught me how to wield my sword with expert precision and cunning moves.

He has taught me more than I ever thought possible and for that, I truly am grateful.

He is a master at fighting, and it's clear why I was paired with him even if I want to run my sword through his arrogant neck, not that it would do any harm to him if I did anyway.

He is strong, smart, and calculating just like me and I'm proud to learn from him, especially since neither of us possesses an Ascendance.

When our time comes to fight Shivane and Sylon, I will be ready.

I've had enough of this fight, having toyed with this beast of a man for way too long.

I unleash the fight within my soul, the fury that Alderon helped me channel and that I use when necessary, a skill I've desired to master.

Metal clangs against metal as we go blow for blow. I set him up, calculate my next moves like a game of chess. I dance but keep my stance strong and balanced. Then, when the beast is in my grasp, I release a killing blow, eviscerating him back into thin air.

Alderon kicks off his perch, clapping. He reaches into his pocket and tosses me an apple. We each sit on a rock opposite each other.

"You're becoming quite the fighter."

Notably, he utters it with slightly less condescension than in previous days.

"I already was quite the fighter," I lob back, a snarled laugh curling his lip.

"Now you're unbeatable. Almost. We still have another month and a half to go. By then, you'll be leading whatever military branch you want, if not all of them."

"Did you fight in the war? The Great War of the Realms?"

Alderon leans back, nodding. "I did. Valiantly, I might add." So arrogant. He can't ever let a moment of vulnerability peek through.

"What was it like?"

"Brutal. Painful. Heart wrenching to watch your fellow soldiers, realmsmen, brothers, and sisters fall in battle … it has its own sets of wounds, leaving scars unable to fully heal." For the first time, he allows me to see the pain he went through, to see him for who he is—or was.

"When you fight to save Seivan, remember the love that exists in your heart. Your enemies, especially Shivane and Sylon, will try to use it against you. So, you have to protect it and keep it safe no matter what, but you can't ever forget it's there. If you do, you'll lose yourself and when it's all done, you'll have no clue who you are in the end."

"On our first day here, Warriem said the three of us were the key to saving Seivan's future. I can see why Rioyn and even Ayva are but why me? I don't have an Ascendance or connection to Warriem and Everia like they do."

I pick at my apple.

Alderon sits forward, leaning his elbows on his knees. "Ayva and Rioyn are very powerful, and they're learning how to use, channel, and control their Ascendance but there needs to be someone in between them, a voice of reason that can re-center them both, so they don't tear each other apart. That center is you."

"Is that what you were to Warriem and Everia?"

A reminiscent chuckle loosens his lips.

"Indeed, I was. Things between them could turn volatile at a moment's notice. If one of them glanced wrong at the other, they could launch into war just because of that one wrong look. They have a great love for each other but they're also strong-willed, hard-headed women who seem to love riling each other up for their own entertainment."

"That had to be … fun for you." I flick him a mirror of his own smug snarl.

"Sometimes, yes. But there was a dark period toward the end, very dark. That was not fun." His eyes stalk the dirt between us. Something stirs in his mind, so I wait for him to continue with what he's calculating to say. What he'll disclose.

"You've seen the darkness living inside of Rioyn?" he asks.

I nod, not that it was entirely a question.

"Part of it was there the day he was born. It's the yin to Ayva's yang. But it was manipulated when he was young to become something darker than it should have been. Everia is teaching him how to use and control it, which he will, but there will be times when Ayva's light won't be enough to save him from it. That's when you'll need to. It won't be easy for you, which is why you must always keep that love in your heart. Don't ever let it harden. Don't ever let it fade."

Alderon's pointed words stick in my throat which bobs, choking on my apple.

"May I give you another piece of advice?" Alderon asks, deftly skinning his pear.

"You've never held back before from inserting your opinion when I didn't ask."

He shakes his head, letting out a low chuckle.

"Let yourself feel. Let yourself live. Let people in. Let love in. Let him in."

My eyes narrow. "Why are you giving me lessons on love? Stick to the fighting."

Alderon chuckles. "If it were possible, I'd swear you were my daughter. You and I are almost identical."

"If I'd been your daughter, I'd have run away."

Alderon's head falls back, letting loose a roaring laugh.

"I told my father I'd do the same. Then I did. I fled here, to this world. But I never forgot the words Mother told me before she died."

Alderon shifts his gaze to me. His golden hair reflects the sun.

He continues, "The same thing I just told you, it changed my life. I came here closed off from my former world, even this new world. Then I met my soul's mate."

"Warriem?" I ask. He nods. My moment where he's softened and slightly vulnerable has finally arrived. I strike, the moment unexpectedly hot. "Is Rioyn the Iyanndyre Born?"

Alderon squints as if looking for something.

He replies, "You will become useful. More useful than you know. It will require sacrifice and trust that you're on the right path to protect those you love."

"What does that have to do with my question? Will you stop speaking to me in riddles and answer in plain English for a change?"

Alderon smirks. "A bargain. If you beat me, I'll answer your question."

"I'm so grateful for these lessons." A devious smile curls both our lips.

"Before I beat you into submission." I pause for dramatic effects. "At least tell me if we'll find the Iyanndyre Born. Whether it's Rioyn or not."

Alderon's face elongates, the glimmer in his eyes shifting but not dulling.

Now I'm the one who is lost in thoughts, my jaw hanging open like a damn fool. Has this quest been all for naught?

Alderon is swift to shatter the tension and moody atmosphere we've created. He lunges to his feet and draws his sword. I snap out of my head and follow.

Our fighting stances are identical, and the blows begin. I remember every lesson and direction he's given me over this last month and a half.

He's strong but I'm quick.

He has the experience of a few centuries on me, but my stubborn naivety won't let an old man best me.

He's quick and cunning, far more than I give him credit for. I must focus, taunting him with strategies from his own game, wielding my first chess piece, a pawn for him to cackle at. Then a few more blows and blocks to lure him in.

When he's right where I want him, I make my next move, letting him think he has me. He's quick to take the bait as I bare my teeth, mimicking his arrogant smug smile and striking, sending him to his back. I have him in a kill shot, then we disappear.

I'm returned to the comfort of my stale room.

A note has been left on my bed with a single word:

No.

No, what? No Rioyn isn't the Iyanndyre Born? Or no, we won't find the Iyanndyre Born? Disappointment floods through my veins like a vicious virus.

CHAPTER 50

WARRIEM

AYVA

As I awake on the final day of training, I glance over at the clothes lying on my desk, different to the ones issued over the last three months.

My curiosity pulls me to my feet, holding the simple, long-sleeved shirt and pants before me. These are not my usual battle armor. Since time doesn't particularly matter here, I take my time in the bathing room as we'll be departing soon.

Though ready to leave the Labyrinth Brick and resume our mission, something inside of me wants to hold onto this place for a moment longer. This isn't a place that is easy to visit. It's not every day that you die and wind up in a hidden world.

After dressing and braiding my hair, I disappear just like on every other day.

Opening my eyes, they peel wider.

I'm standing in the living room of my home, the one I haven't seen in almost four months. It's dark, quiet, embedded in the aftermath of when it was ravaged by the Starless Army, after they took Mikel. Chairs have been knocked over, destroyed, fabrics ripped into shreds. It's caked in rubble and garbage.

Even though my house—my home—is a mess, I can't help but feel at ease for the first time since we left.

I take in the dust-laced air, searching for any scent reminiscent of the days past, remaining in the darkness, still and calm as Warriem appears. She snaps her fingers and the house illuminates, my breathing intensifying as memories of home flood my senses. My home has changed back to how it was before this war began, the aroma of cinnamon and cloves igniting my desire for Mother's breakfast rolls.

"You've come a long way in your training. Better than I could've ever hoped."

Warriem twists an oversized copperore coin between her fingers, then sets it on the glossed mahogany table next to her.

I could say so much to this woman, a world creator who has also become a mentor, friend, and drill sergeant to me. But no long speech could fully convey sufficient gratitude for what she's given me. My words are feeble and inadequate, but they're all I have.

"Thank you, Warriem. For everything."

"My sister and I poured our hearts and souls into this world, and in turn, it became woven into the fabric of our being."

She means it; that much is clear. I feel the love they have for this realm through her. "Know that when you fight for this land, you fight for us as well. If you ever want to read about our history, then see yourself into our first home in Casstell. There, you'll find the information to satiate your indelible palate of knowledge." Warriem sits back in her chair.

"I thought the museum, your home, was permanently closed?"

Warriem huffs. "It's only closed to those not welcome. Everia thought it funny to encase it in an Ascendance technique she created, banning anyone not worthy enough to enter. Only those seeking knowledge for the betterment of our kind and who are smart enough to recognize her encasement are able to enter. You, my dear Ayva, possess both. Simply walk up to the front door and you'll figure it out. If you don't, then I guess you're not as gifted as we all think."

A blush claims my cheeks, anticipation and curiosity of what knowledge I'd find in their former home filtering into me.

Warriem can't help but taunt me with her devious grin.

"We've trained for three months now, and I've done everything you asked, including not asking all of my nosey questions and respecting your orders. However, this could very well be the last time I get the chance; I'd be remiss not to ask."

I wait for her to object. She doesn't so I continue.

"If Seivan was meant to be a place of peace and harmony, then why did you create places like the Carisan Forest, the White Fog, and those awful Drone Mountains? I feel the negativity of those areas has given way to the disturbance in harmony we now face."

Warriem chokes on her laugh.

"We didn't, well, not with the intention of what they've become." I flash her a furrowed brow, questioning. "This world, like all the rest, is a living, breathing creature all to itself. We laid the groundwork but what it has turned into is the result of the people who have come and gone through those years. Creatures that have come and gone."

Warriem turns the ring on her left ring finger around and around.

"We hoped evil would never find roots here, but they did a long time ago once we were gone. At first, it was quiet and unassuming and then those roots grew, spread, and became deeper and stronger. It spawned and created things like the Fayrilynds and the Sancaros, who leech the evilness of the realm from the very dirt they inhabit. It's how they grow stronger. That very evil found roots within the citizens of the realm as well."

Warriem catches on her words. "You can never truly rid a world of evil. All you can do is lead with your heart and hope that the hearts of those who possess evil are open enough to let love in and allow them to see a better way."

"How did Shivane and Sylon come to be as evil as they are?"

"Shivane's always struggled to walk the line between being good and giving in to her deeply rooted anger. Her brother, Sylon, however ... there is something different about him. Something we can't even see through. The darkness inside him is so profound."

"It will take a magnificent light to crack through it. There's great love inside of him, a great man, too but ..." Warriem's face twitches as if she's trying to make sense of who he is and what he's plagued with.

"So, there's no good in him at all?"

"There's good in every soul, somewhere, until it's snuffed out by one's own thoughts. His soul, from where his darkness comes, is not of our universe. We believe he made a bargain a long time ago, and until those terms are satisfied, that darkness has a hold of him. We think he might be trying to free himself of this curse. A curse I believe was cast upon him from the Souls of the Dark."

My eyes flare wide at her quandary, and revelation.

"So, he's here to destroy everything?"

Warriem shrugs with a flexed jaw. It's not that she can't or won't tell me. She doesn't know. Something bothers her about him.

"Is Rioyn the Iyanndyre Born?" I change the subject.

"No," Warriem states emphatically.

My chin pushes back into my shoulders at her quick response, shocked. Disappointed really. Something inside of me thought that maybe it was him, hoping it might be. It would certainly be an easy solution to end this battle.

"So, the Iyanndyre Born will really be there in Casstell when we go back?"

"The Iyanndyre Born will make themself known. It's up to you to fully embrace who the Iyanndyre Born is and don't immediately dismiss who they are or could be."

Warriem stares, frowning.

"Why would I not embrace the Iyanndyre Born? It's the one we've been seeking."

"Finding something and embracing it are two different things. You must accept the Iyanndyre Born in order for the Iyanndyre Born to be realized."

More mind-numbing riddles.

Warriem sits up with a smirk. "There will come a time, Ayva, when you will have to make the hardest decision you'll ever face. And when that time comes, you must choose with your heart, not your mind. For it will be not only the hardest but also the most crucial decision ever."

My mouth parts, at a loss for words, finding this all more than I bargained for.

More than I ever could've dreamt of confronting.

"What are you thinking?" Warriem's sharp gaze softens as it lands on me.

"Look, why are you asking me all these questions? Telling me all this?"

Warriem sits up with a smirk. "Ask me what you really want to know, Ayva."

I observe her beautiful hazel eyes in stark contrast to her scorching red hair. I don't know what that question is. But I do have one. "Will we win?"

She chuckles and leans forward, resting her forearms on her knees.

"After everything I just told you, that's what you want to ask me?" She waits for my answer. I shrug and nod. She tilts her head, accepting what I've asked.

"We chose you for a reason. You have prepared as best you can. You all have. That's all you can do."

She studies me, studies the twists of my face grappling with my thoughts.

I don't sense her snooping around my mind the way she did when she trained me to strengthen the walls to protect it.

"Your brother loves you with every muscle in his heart and you love him the same. You two are the same yet different. Learn to love the differences."

"He's infuriating. He's impulsive. He never stops trying to best … everyone!" My face reddens without warning. Is that what has always bothered me about him?

Rioyn wants to be better than everyone, including me.

Warriem chuckles. She knows all too well with Everia.

"Yes, but that's also what makes him who he is." She pauses for a moment. "You can embrace, accept, and love him for who he is. Or you can constantly battle against him and further drive that wedge between you."

Her voice is soft and comfortable but a punch to my already twisted stomach.

"I don't know if I can fully trust him to forgo his desire to always be number one. He seems to always put that need over his better judgment, and over me."

"That is something you will need to figure out, and soon. Be the leader you were born to be. Don't hide behind the facade of the different masks you put on to hide from who you really are." I nod. There's nothing left to ask.

"Your heart hurts but not for your brother. Who?"

Her question jostles me. I stare through Warriem.

She knows the answer but why is she asking?

"I miss the guy I was just starting to get to know. The guy I have longed for, for a very long time. I miss him very much." It's the absolute truth.

"Everything will all work out in the end. What's meant for you will always be for you."

Warriem sits back in the chair, confident in her generic statement.

She means to provide solace, but it doesn't work.

I'm ready, having prepared the best I could over these months here, like she said. So, we will fight with everything we have. Will it be enough?

Warriem places her hand on my shoulder.

"Tomorrow, you will leave with your brother and friend. Tomorrow, you will make the journey back to Casstell and face Shivane and Sylon." I suck in a large inhale. "You're strong, Ayva, and incredibly powerful. It's been an honor to be here and train you."

A spontaneous tear shatters my gaze.

With a snap of her fingers, we disappear into thin air.

CHAPTER 51

A Dinner with Family

RIOYN

EVERIA PORTALS ME BACK to my room, announcing, "Rioyn, you need to freshen up; you stink worse than a rotting carcass in the scorching summer sun."

After that, I head straight for the bathing room and cleanse myself, although for what specifically I don't know, nor will she even say.

Upon emerging from the bathing room dressed only in undergarments, an outfit has been laid out on the bed. I pick up the silk shirt, like velvet in my calloused hands. I pull my arms through the sleeves and button up, leaving the last one undone.

The pants are made from a fine cotton that hugs my thick thighs. My legs have become more muscular and toned during these months from all the intense and grueling training. I tuck my arms into the sleeves of the jacket, its lapels stiff and peaked. The jacket sits tight around my chest and stops right at my waist. Its delicate black fabric is lined with silver threads and brassore buttons, fit for a general—one like Father.

I take a large inhale and, on the exhalation, disappear.

When I appear again, Falla and Ayva are standing next to me. Smiles tickle our faces as we all open our arms for a long-awaited embrace.

We pull back from each other to notice we are all dressed in the same formal attire.

"Ahem." A voice turns us around. Warriem, Everia, and Alderon stand side by side with their arms folded across their chests, also dressed in the same attire.

"Please join us for your final meal in the Labyrinth Brick."

Alderon smiles, showing off his bright white teeth.

We march together toward the table under the cover of trees. The mahogany table behind them is long, dressed with fine linens and delicate tableware.

Glass orbs hanging from the trees above are filled with lightning bugs.

As we meander closer, the three of them part to reveal our other dinner guests, the three of us stopping dead in our tracks. My head whips around to Falla as she fights her tears.

Her father, mother, brother, and two sisters rise from their seats as Falla runs to her slain family. The family of six engulfs each other tight through their free flowing tears.

Ayva leans into me. I don't need to look at her to know what she's feeling. Wrapping my arm around her shoulder, I pull her into my side.

Another "ahem" as Alderon pulls our attention toward him, then moves out of the way. Standing behind him is our Gran'apa. Ayva and I rush to him.

He kneels with his arms open wide and we lunge into him, falling to our knees.

"Gran'apa!" Ayva gushes over the old patriarch of our family. They'd been close when he was alive, the reason Ayva became so transfixed with her studies of Galilei and how the world worked. It crushed her when he passed away several years ago.

"I wouldn't have missed this for anything, my darlings."

"What's it like? Your universe?" Ayva can't help but inquire. I smile at her curiosity.

"Aye, my dear. There isn't much within them I'm allowed to reveal to you."

As Gran'apa stands, a figure appears behind him, a sad smile immediately tugging at his lips. Ayva and I stare at the figure. Who else is here? Then the figure comes into form, my heart simultaneously plummeting into my gut.

I feel Ayva shudder beside me as our Gran'ama walks up to us.

"Please tell me this is one of your abilities, that you're able to use your image to cross in between worlds," I say.

"I'm afraid not, my dear boy."

Immense heartbreak shatters the peace I've found in the Labyrinth Brick.

"How?" Ayva asks, tearing up.

"The Starless Army came, escorting Shivane. I was too much of a threat to her alive, so here I am now."

Ayva immediately rushes to Gran'ama, smothering her with a constricting hug.

"If you will all please take your seats. Dinner will begin."

Dorranna appears out of nowhere, her dainty wrist motioning for us to take our seats at the exquisitely decorated table.

Once everyone is situated, Warriem raises a carved crystal glass. "Please join me in a toast." Our crystal glasses fill with an amber liquid. I palm mine, bringing it to my nose.

"There's no alcohol in it." Everia cocks a smirked brow. I hold my glass out to toast.

Warriem continues, "We have all come together from different universes to be gathered here where they align. This gathering is to celebrate our three young warriors as they embark on a mission to destroy those who threaten this beautiful world. We gather here to remember the things in life worth fighting for. Each other."

Our glasses raise higher, and we each drink the mystery liquid from our carved crystal glasses. As each empty glass returns to the table, silverore domes appear over our plates.

"Everyone please eat, enjoy," Dorranna instructs then disappears again.

"So Gran'apa, tell us. What were Ayva and Rioyn like as kids?" Warriem poses the invasive question.

Gran'apa roars with delight. "They were hellions. Both of them."

He smirks at our appall.

"We were most certainly not!" Ayva snaps.

Gran'apa turns, smirking.

I lean back in my seat, crystal glass in hand, arms folded, playing into the silence of all eyes on me. "I was, too." I laugh—for the first time in a while, a good laugh.

Being here with family members we're not able to see in our physical world is an immense treat. Especially since we didn't get to even say goodbye, nor did we know that our Gran'ama had passed on. This is a treat that I do feel guilty to indulge.

The rest of our realm suffers while we feast, celebrating good times from the past.

Falla's laugh is the first to fade. "I'm sorry. I'm sorry I wasn't able to save all of you" She exhales hard. "But I will have our revenge. I will fight to destroy those who took your lives." The eyes of Falla's family dart to Xan who keeps his gaze glued to Falla.

"My darling, fearless daughter. Revenge is nothing but a fool's bargain."

"But that's not—"

He holds up a finger. "Revenge fills your heart with hate. It should never be chosen as your means to an end. I would never want that for you, or anyone. However, you do have an enemy to defeat and defeat you must, through your training, your skills, and your sheer will for good to triumph over evil. Leading that charge with revenge will poison your mind, your heart, and you won't clearly see the task at hand."

Falla's face pales, sequestering her emotions with a bowed head. "Thank you, Father. I will never dishonor you, this family. I will represent you with pride."

The night carries on, the food continuing to appear and disappear into our ever-expanding bellies. Most of the night is spent laughing until the muscles on our faces have given way to their exhaustion.

I take a long moment to take in every single person at this table, starting with Warriem. When she was alive in the physical world, she was the woman who held back armies of a thousand men and women to protect her people, her family, and the Iyanndyre.

My thoughts move to Everia, who has an incredibly kind heart but also a devilish dark side to her. When things were too tough and required too much sacrifice for Warriem, she stepped up and handled whatever was needed.

Then to Alderon, a man of incredible strength and abilities. A man without any sort of Ascendance but who still fought as if he were the most powerful man in the universe.

These three individuals are gods among mortals, then and now.

My sights move to Falla's family. A noble family who sacrificed their lives for the lives of others.

Then to our Gran'ama and Gran'apa, two people who always gave me the courage to be the best person I could find within myself.

I promise myself right here and now that I will aspire to live in their honor every single day.

Warriem stands. "It is time." Everyone else stands, followed by me, Ayva, and Falla. We follow Warriem around the table. "Please say your goodbyes."

Immediately, I turn to Falla's father. "High Rank Kai?" Xan turns to face me with a soft smile. "I promise to always look after and take care of your daughter, sir."

I witness Falla's jaw drop out of the corner of my eye as if to tell me, how dare you! I shake her father's hand. He pulls me into him, whispering a soft message for my ears only.

I smile brightly, then hug him one last time.

Falla takes her moment to bid her family farewell. Ayva and I stand before our Gran'apa and Gran'ama.

"You two hellions be good now, you hear?"

Ayva and I smile through our tears. "We'll miss you both more than you could ever know," Ayva says.

Before we go, I must know, "Is Bair in whatever world you're in?"

Gran'apa and Gran'ama share a knowing smile then shake their heads.

Finally, a piece of good news. Relief floods through me.

Gran'ama, Gran'apa, and all of Falla's family disappear as if they've become one with the air. Ayva, Falla, and I rein in our heavy emotions, standing next to each other before Warriem, Alderon, and Everia.

Falla kisses me quickly on my cheek. I blush, hard.

"What was that for?" I ask without a thought.

"I couldn't imagine this journey … life … without you. You're everything to me."

My heart flutters with joy. The most I've felt in a long time. The most I've felt … ever. Before I can get the words out of my throat, Ayva is quick to get back to our mission.

"What do we do when we get back to Casstell?" Ayva stands tall with her question.

"Take down the Shrouded Veil. That's how you will find Shivane and Sylon along with the rest of your world."

"How do we find the Shrouded Veil?"

"Look for the ripples." Warriem dances the riddle off her tongue.

Alderon and Everia chuckle.

They sure do enjoy their frustrating riddles of the universes.

"What about the Iyanndyre Born?" Falla interjects.

"Take down the veil. The rest will reveal itself." Alderon smirks.

Falla rolls her eyes, throwing her arms up.

Warriem and Everia hold hands, Warriem placing her other hand on Ayva's shoulder. Everia's rests on mine. Alderon places his hand on Falla's shoulder.

Something catches my attention behind Everia. Two figures appear. They hold on to each other, staring right at us. Somehow, I feel the pain and guilt in their eyes, recognizing them as General Daun and Evon Greyea. My heart skips a beat as it falls into the twisted pit of my stomach. I glance over to Ayva who feels the same thing.

I steal another glance but this time I see someone else lingering behind them. He looks oddly similar to … Mikel? It can't be. Can it?

Warriem rips my gaze away to face her. "You two will return to Casstell."

"What do you mean 'you two'," Falla asks with a snap to her tone.

"Shivane must be stopped. There is no room for failure," Warriem states.

"Once we find the Iyanndyre Born, then she will be," Ayva says.

"We aren't willing to take any chances. Until you return to the Labyrinth Brick with her as your captor, Falla will be remaining here with us."

I reach out to grab Falla.

"I absolutely will—"

Falla's words dims as a bright white light engulfs Ayva and me. We're immediately transported out of the Labyrinth Brick.

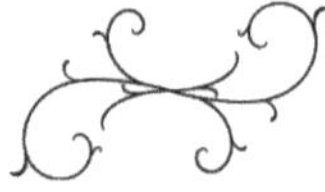

We wake from our comatose slumber back in Haven Hill, with Atheyl waiting by our side.

Our bodies have been resting in her comfortable beds until our return.

Falla's body remains asleep.

I leap out of the bed and pull Falla into me, her body warm but lifeless. I shake her, somehow thinking it'll wake her from her slumber.

"Don't worry, I will keep her safe here until you're able to return and free her."

Anger burns through me like I've never felt before. Atheyl knew this would happen, knew what their plan was. I rush to separate her head from her body, but a force of wind stops me in my tracks, holding me in place.

Her Ascendance is strong and right now, as much as I despise this manipulative woman, our fight isn't with her. So, I rein in my throbbing anger.

"This is what had to happen. Accept it, let it go and fight to save our realm. You two are our only hope now."

There are no words for the immense betrayal I feel, glancing over at Ayva who seethes with a reddened anger as well, her restraint impressive.

There surely has to be some solace in this bitter moment.

"We'll be leaving now." Ayva uses the portal ring. Neither of us wastes another moment. We leap into the bright, white portal light and disappear again.

The Iyanndyre Born

AYVA

OUR TOWN, OUR HOME, sits in the darkness of the starless night sky. Lightning bugs flutter through the air, offering us their comforting, familiar light and escort. The night is quiet, eerily so. Nothing stirs, nothing croons, nothing croaks.

"We have to capture Shivane at all costs. We have to save Falla," Rioyn frantically says as he grabs my arm and whips me around to face him.

"Of course, we'll save Falla. We have to save her and everyone else."

"Promise me, Ayva. We cannot leave her rotting in the Labyrinth Brick."

Rioyn's worrisome eyes bring mine to tears. I force them back and remain focused on the mission before us, surveilling the landscape. Nothing here feels right.

Nothing feels like home—at least the home we remember.

"We need to find the ripple, whatever that is. Do you have any idea what it could be?"

Rioyn stares into the vast darkness, then nods. "I saw something like it the night the veil came down. I didn't know what it could be. And it was gone as fast as it came."

"What did it look like? And where was it?"

"It looked like … a ripple. As if the very fabric of air was tearing against itself. I got a glimpse of the awful world underneath the Shrouded Veil. It was for a split moment, then it was gone but I was able to feel it, sending a tendril of my shadow through the ripple.”

“So, you think you can find it again?” My voice rises a few octaves in excitement, the first ounce of it I’ve felt through this entire journey.

“Let’s head into Circle Park. That’s where the veil went down. If the ripple is anywhere, I think it’d be there. Hopefully, then we’ll find the Iyanndyre Born.”

“Won’t Shivane and Sylon know we’re here if we go snooping around so close?”

“Honestly, I don’t know. But I think it’s worth the risk. We don’t have time to waste searching the air throughout the city, hoping to find this mysterious ripple. If we can get to the source of where it came down, that’s got to be our best bet.”

I hate to admit it, but Rioyn’s logic is right. We need to maximize our time and find the ripple—any ripple as soon as possible.

We charge through the destroyed, desolate city we still call home.

Nothing stirs except the litterbugs and rodents feasting on the carcass that used to be Casstell. Buildings lie in ruins, garbage littering every inch of every street. The only light we have is from the bright moon; however, we stick to the shadows. The shadows!

“Think you’re strong enough to form into shadows when we get to Circle Park?”

“What’s your reasoning for that?”

“We don’t know how the Shrouded Veil works or if just by being in Circle Park sets off some alarm alerting Shivane and Sylon to our presence. Your shadows give us an edge to stay hidden and buy us time to find this ripple.”

Rioyn’s logic is on point tonight. Whatever training he had with Everia has centered and grounded him. He isn’t thinking how he can win. He’s thinking how we can.

My confidence in him and this journey has never been higher.

We pick up our pace and race through the quiet streets. After several miles of running through heartbreaking devastation, we come to the edge of Circle Park. Immediately, we both crouch, clinging to the darkness of the shadows.

Rioyn, confident, looks right at me and nods.

His eyes slam shut, and he shifts into shadow form.

I'm able to follow him for a moment but then lose him to the darkness, eagerly watching for any glimmer of him, but seeing nothing. Many agonizing moments go by while I wait, not knowing if he's okay or was found out.

Time drags on and then finally, ripples of smoke race through the charred trees.

I stand ready for anything.

Rioyn converts back to his normal form. "RUN!"

I do not wait, do not ask, simply turning, both sprinting as far out of Circle Park and into the depravity of Casstell as fast as we can.

Except that we're not fast enough. A large, smoky shadow two stories tall takes form ahead, the shadow condensing to form a large, powerful man.

"Sylon."

My head whips around in shock at Rioyn's disclaimer.

Sylon's menacing face comes into the light of the moon, an indulgent smirk raising the corner of his thick red lips.

Rioyn shape shifts into a shadow and flies toward Sylon, who does the same.

Focusing my Ascendance, I'm trying to hinder Sylon's mental ability to hold his shadow form when sharp claws scrape against my mind, eager to get in.

I force them from my mind, whipping on my heels to find Shivane stalking me with an animalistic mindset. I try to force my way into her mind, but she is too strong, too powerful. There must be another way to stop her and Sylon.

Soldiers of the Starless Army emerge from almost thin air. Then I see it.

"Rioyn! There it is." I point to a ripple in the air. Rioyn's shadow dissipates from Sylon's grasp and flies toward the ripple.

Somehow, I have to buy him time as Sylon is on his heels.

I use my mental Ascendance to harness the powers of my elemental Ascendance and launch a pile of rubble at Sylon, knocking him off his trajectory.

Shivane does the same, launching a charred tree branch, knocking me back.

Sylon, however, is too powerful to be stopped by mere bricks.

But it gives Rioyn just enough time to find the ripple. Shivane charges toward me but I evade her grasp, helping Rioyn.

The Starless Army charges toward us, making me think back to what I was able to do in the Dungeon Lair. So, I summon my Ascendance and infiltrate their minds.

Some immediately break free of their entrancement but some of their lacquered black eyes remain. Those who are freed immediately turn on Shivane and Sylon, intent on helping us in our fight; however, they're not enough.

We're not enough.

Rioyn latches onto the ripple with every fury of strength he has.

I hold control of the Starless Army as best I can, losing ground.

Finally, Rioyn is able to take down the Shrouded Veil just as Sylon tackles him.

Gray dust fizzles from the air, coating everything in a thick coat of ash. People that weren't there before emerge from their hidden world. There's not time to take into account who is there and if everyone is okay.

I rush to save Rioyn when a sharp energy wraps around my mind, collapsing me to my knees. Shivane and Sylon have us in their grip.

There's no way out of this, no way to win.

Fellow citizens flood from the depths of the Shrouded Veil and aid us in fighting the battle but they're weak, starved.

Shivane bears down on me.

My mind screams in pain, unable to focus, unable to think of how to free myself when I see a vast army marching our way. Shivane follows my line of sight to see what I see. Her grip loosens and I fall forward, gasping for air. After a few moments, I am able to rise to my feet, drawing my sword and slashing through her thick armor, drawing blood.

She whips around, grabbing her arm, ripe with freshly freed blood. My eyes glow, racing my way through her mind, into the depths of her innermost thoughts, seeing the death, destruction, and total control she desires for our realm. She doesn't just want to conquer Seivan, she wants to destroy every bit of our home, her true intentions rooted in pure evil. She will enslave everyone and murder anyone who will not bend to her will as she raises incendiary fires across Seivan, burning everything to the ground.

Shivane rips my grasp from her mind. Her intense stare turns into a devious smile as if she revels in me knowing the depths of her planned depravity to our home.

I chance a look behind to see who the army is that marches toward us, then I see Arro and Xylar leading the way. They actually convinced the Scribe of Echolyne to raise the Army of Turmine and they're here. They've arrived to help us!

Shivane leaps to grab me, but I swiftly move out of her grasp and knock her to the ground. She's surprised by my quickness, only angering her more.

Glancing to my side, I watch Rioyn battle Sylon.

Arro, Xylar, and the army grow closer by the second.

"Hold him off, Rioyn. Help is here," I shout.

Sylon whips around and sees the vast army moving his way.

Worry strikes his deep violet eyes.

Shivane commands the Starless Army to charge and charge they do.

Dust kicks up, soldiers barreling past, heading toward their new target. I'm careful not to harm them as they're helpless to their entrancement.

However, the Army of Turmine isn't so kind. They are ruthless in their bloody carnage. Heads are separated from bodies, limbs sliced off at a merciless pace. The army barrels through anyone and everything in its way, leaving behind a wreckage of bodies.

Rioyn, Xylar, Arro, and I battle alongside our new army, metal clanging against metal. Bodies fall, collapsing on top of each other.

I rush to Rioyn's side. "Where is the Iyanndyre Born? Is he going to help us?"

"We don't have time to worry about that. We have an army now. We can win, Ayva. Believe and fight like hell." And fight like hell we do.

Swords flail. Punches land. Bones crunch and break. Some men run, some standing to fight, even though their fight is close to coming to an end. I can't help but take in this fight, this unnecessary battle. No one's life is worth losing over someone else's greed, yet here we are. We fight together, fighting each other.

As we battle for our lives, large shadows cast overhead. Dragolyons emerge from the clouds and rain down fire around those opposed to us.

Monnaire leads the charge, and for the first time, it seems we have a fighting chance.

Sylon shifts into a shadow and shoots to the sky, Rioyn following suit. He won't let Sylon out of his grasp and seeks to destroy him. I must do the same and find Shivane.

I weave through the sea of soldiers and find her attacking the innocent citizens who have chosen to fight for Seivan. She is despicable in the fact that she preys on the weak first. I infiltrate the minds of the ones over whom she has a hold, severing the connection.

"Pick on someone who can fight you back."

Shivane's annoyance at my presence is not lost on her expression. My cold demeanor turns devious as I've gotten under her skin and now have the upper hand.

Shivane looks to Sylon who goes blow for blow with Rioyn. Neither backs down. Neither gives in. Then Sylon's gaze whips to Shivane's. She nods and Sylon turns into his shadow. Rioyn also converts to a shadow, pursuing them both.

Around us, bodies litter the grounds, long strings of guts splayed in the open fields. The battlefield is soaked with deep, deep red blood. And all the while, our enemy gains on us.

From behind, the large shadow known as Sylon casts over the bodies of the fallen, Shivane's purple eyes glowing with a disturbing force.

Their power combines, channeling between them.

One by one, the fallen rise and fight against us. It doesn't matter who they fought for when they were living. They all now fight for Shivane and Sylon.

Sylon maintains his shadow form as he flies high in the sky, chasing after the dragolyons. Rioyn is nipping at his heels but can't keep up anymore.

Sylon rips the dragolyons from the sky one by one, the rest retreating while they still can.

The undead army slaughters more and more people at an alarming rate. Watching this many perish is heartbreaking.

I can't help but have horrible haunting flashbacks of being attacked by the Sancaros.

"We can't win this war," I shout to Rioyn, who's stopped in his tracks, staring at the resurrected army of the undead. He reaches his fire-branded hand for mine.

I look down at his hand, unsure of what it is he wants me to do.

There's no intent to run from this fight. No, it can take everything I have to give.

RIOYN

FOR A MOMENT, FEAR confines me in its grip. We're losing, but what can we do?

Bodies fall and then rise again, only to turn on one another.

Shivane now controls both the living and the dead.

This can't be how our world ends! Evil has no place here and cannot win. Then like a burst of lightning, it hits me. I remember my training with Everia.

I remember how Warriem's powers that saved the realm were born.

I reach for Ayva's hand. She's frozen, staring, wondering what I'm doing. "Take my hand, Ayva." She hesitates. I stretch it out harder. "Twins."

Her shoulders relax. Through the chaos and death surrounding us, this moment is still. I see the fight in her, seeing the peace, the good … the light. This is the only way.

Finally, she takes my hand in hers. As soon as our palms with the thin flame fire brand connect, I release my powers to her, able to feel them drain from me ounce by ounce and flow into her, her light absorbing my darkness. I feel how pure she really is.

Releasing my hand from hers, all that I am left with is the darkness. Why did that stay with me? I thought she'd be able to absorb that and harness it with hers. How am I going to defeat the darkness inside of me without having the power to do so?

A heaviness settles in me, but I cannot let it take hold. I cannot let it win.

We have to win this war. I must fight, must save Falla.

AYVA

A BLANKET OF WHITE LIGHT energy surrounds me, a surge of incredible power electrifying every fiber of my being. My powers grow at an increasing rate. This sudden change is profound, every piece of me feeling strong, invincible.

I glance up and there he is, my brother, my twin.

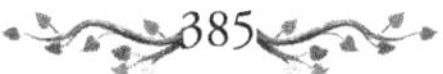

The pain and sorrow in his eyes pierce my heart. What did he do?

"My powers are now born into you. You are the Iyanndyre Born, Ayva. Now go win this war."

"What do you mean? How can that be?"

"You have all three Ascendances now, rendering you the most powerful person in the world. You are our guiding light."

"What about you?" He notices my hesitation.

"Twins," is all he says.

Warriem's words flood my mind. Be the leader you were born to be.

The anger I've carried with me over these last months for what they did to my family, my friends, and my fellow realmsmen simmers to a peace inside of me, a peace that is focused, sharp. I summon and unleash this new, incredible power that burns in me.

I feel Shivane's claws scraping to enter my mind, clamoring at my shields that are impenetrable to everyone, including her. I cast her mental attack back on her, crippling her to her knees, trying to fight through the excruciating pain. The palms of my hand open, summoning balls of fire-filled fury toward her. A white glow radiates around me.

Sylon unleashes a fury of fire-breathing wind toward Rioyn and Arro. I shield them with a blanket of ice water evaporating the flames. I return his fire, igniting my hands and sending a thousand thin needles of burning pain into his chest. He crumbles to his feet.

I stop the army of the dead and incinerate them so that they may pass on to their eternal resting place. We do not need the White Fog spreading to Casstell.

Do it or they'll die. My hands glow with crimson, launching balls of fire at every undead soldier who dares to challenge me.

I march for Sylon as he grapples to stand, his legs betraying his strength. My eyes fixate on him, on his tall, muscular body that struggles to stand. A figure emerges from behind him, a man I recognize. It's Jax!

A scream resounds behind me. "AYVA! Watch out."

Sylon whips his gaze to meet mine. My brows twitch at Sylon's. The way he's looking at me, it's as though he knows me.

"Ayva?" His voice—my name—sends a frisson of electricity through me, stopping me dead in my tracks, mouth parting.

What is it about him? The familiarity. Does he know me somehow?

I glance at Jax, who races through the other soldiers to be at my side. He watches Sylon gaze at me and it stops him dead.

"AYVA!" Rioyn's screech jostles me enough to stop Shivane from her blindsiding attack. I launch claws of air toward her, crippling her, bringing her to her knees.

I turn back to face Sylon. He stands, hands at his side, palms open. He walks toward me and I don't move. He's not trying to attack me. My lips part.

I don't realize that my clamp on Shivane goes limp and she opens a portal. "Sylon!" she barks at him.

He's unable to peel his mesmerizing, deep violet eyes from me.

His lips part too, struggling to find his words.

Shivane disappears into the portal and I snap from my trance; I've let her escape.

"NO!" Rioyn screams as he races toward the portal. Arro runs to tackle him to the ground, otherwise Rioyn would've jumped into the portal himself.

I launch a wind-formed dagger at Sylon, striking him in his chest. He falls back into the portal, grabbing hold of my Ascendance in him, wrapping his fingers around my dagger stuck in his chest. He too disappears into the darkness of the portal.

His heartbeat is in time with mine. The portal closes but I still feel this tether that now connects us. Me to him. Him to me.

I feel him, mentally tugging on it. I tug. He tugs back. I stumble backward.

With eyes wide open, I watch the portal slam shut, Shivane and Sylon now gone. We didn't capture Shivane. We have no way to save Falla now.

Arro rushes over and studies the air where Shivane and Sylon escaped through the portal. His curious brow is alarming. Does he know where they went? I can only hope.

I pay little attention to them, or anyone around me as my left forearm throbs in pain. I clench it hard, lifting my sleeve to find another red flamed brand in the shape of an arrow connecting to the thin red flame on the palm of my hand. Are both connected?

Jax rushes to my side, deep concern splayed across his face. Does he detect this force that has tethered me to Sylon?

"Are you hurt? Are you alright?" Jax wraps me in a crushingly tight hug as I cry into his chest. My emotions have overrun me—relief, happiness. I don't know what to feel right now, so I simply cry. His finger laces through my hair, holding the back of my head.

As I pull back from him, he gently caresses the side of my face. I settle into his embrace until I see Zoura, whose face is laced with a shocked expression of … betrayal?

My brow furrows, unease curling through my stomach.

She's always had a thing for Jax, but did something happen under the veil?

Jax traces my stoned trance, seeing who I'm glaring at. With a reddened face, Zoura stomps her way over and I brace for the venom that will undoubtedly leak from her mouth, unsure if it'll be for me or Jax. She stares Jax down. He lowers his head, hiding his eyes. Something definitely happened between them. Then she turns to face me.

"We … I need your help."

My head zips back, aligned with my shoulders.

"Kalli is stuck in the in-between. We have no idea how to rescue her. She needs our help." Zoura stares through Jax's eyes.

"What is the 'in-between'?" I ask, trying to break her stare.

"We don't know," Jax concedes, eyeing Zoura. Does she have more information?

"All we know is that's what they called it. A world between worlds."

Fear sends a fluttering shock through me, my mouth dropping as their eyes widen at this telling response.

"You know where that is?" a teary-eyed Zoura asks.

I slowly nod, forcing down a dry-mouthed swallow. "She's in the Labyrinth Brick. Who else is down there?"

Zoura's face turns furious as she whips it to Jax, who sinks into himself.

"Jax. Who else is down there?"

Through his parched swallow, he edges out, "Mikel".

"How'd they both get there?" I ask.

Zoura waits for Jax to explain. Irritated by his closed-mouth cowardice, she says. "Kalli tried to form a coup against Shivane and Sylon. She along with others were banished to the in-between as Shivane and Sylon called it."

"What about Mikel?" I look to Jax. Zoura continues.

"Mikel wouldn't give up your location to Shivane and Sylon."

"How did they know that he knew where we were?"

Zoura slowly turns to Jax.

"We," Zoura clears her throat at Jax's choice of pronoun. "I told Shivane and Sylon that he had information that would help them. I did it to try and save Kalli in the belief it would save both of them but when he wouldn't give them anything, they sent him to the in-between—the Labyrinth Brick, too."

My heart stops, plummeting into my gut at what Jax did. I brace myself against a crumbling statue to withstand the dizziness overtaking me. Would Jax really put Mikel in harm's way? Not only that but he intentionally plotted to use his friend as a pawn to give up information about where Rioyn, Falla, and I were. Even if Mikel were spared from harm and Kalli were to be released, he was willing to give up me, Rioyn, and Falla.

The dizziness takes over and my knees buckle. Jax tries to catch me but the immense rage inside of me ignites. I'm enraptured in a burst of flames.

Jax burns his hand trying to lift me back up.

While the flames subside, the fire still burns inside of me.

"I can't believe you did that. After everything, you were willing to give us up? For what? What would you gain from it?"

My eyes travel to Zoura, who takes a few steps back from the line of fire.

"Ayva, I'm so sorry—" Jax's apology is interrupted.

Citizens emerge from their hidden areas. With wide-eyed stares, they wander over to me in pure shock. I stand still in this moment. A moment I never would've thought could be mine. But it's not all mine. If Rioyn hadn't done what he did, then we would not be standing here. We would not have won. He gave me everything he had so that I could save us. Not him. He chose not to claim victory for himself.

I search for Rioyn through the crowd, needing him to not only help me navigate this attention that is very new to me, but also to be a buffer between me and Jax. Although he won't be much of a buffer once he finds out what Jax did.

I find Rioyn kneeling where the portal was, sobbing into his bloody hands.

My heart breaks with his. Whatever it takes, we will find a way to save Falla. She will not be banished to the Labyrinth Brick.

"To the Iyanndyre Born!" Arro's voice howls from the back. I whip around to find the entire crowd joins in the chant. "To the Iyanndyre Born. Hooray! Hooray!"

"The Iyanndyre Born is the one who is good beyond reproach. Born from the selflessness of their equal yet opposite for the greater good," Monnaire shares.

"We have to go through the portal. We have to capture Shivane!" Rioyn shouts as he rises to his feet and pushes through the crowd.

His beet-red face reveals the fury that burns through him.

Rioyn confronts Arro. "You know where they are. Take me there. NOW." Rioyn pushes Arro back.

Pushing through the crowd, our father and uncle rush to Rioyn's side, seeing him push a calm and collected Arro backward.

It takes both of them to hold Rioyn back from attacking Arro or anyone else.

"I know what they are in but how we get there, I don't have a definitive answer. Once I do, we can craft a plan to go after them but it will take some time to confidently know where exactly they are within the world they're in."

Rioyn may have lost all his powers, but he is still incredibly strong.

Stronger than our father and uncle originally believed. Their shocked wide eyes water for the pain Rioyn endures.

"We cannot let them escape. We have to capture them, otherwise, this war isn't over."

Arro studies the air of the portal through which Shivane and Sylon disappeared again. "I may not be entirely sure where they are but the one thing I do know is that they are trapped. Once we figure out where they are, we can go after them."

Rioyn whips around to face me. "This is all your fault. You let her escape."

My mouth drops along with my heart into the pit of my stomach.

How could he think that?

Before I'm able to say something I'll undoubtedly regret, Monnaire uses her Ascendance to coax Rioyn into a comatose-like state. He slumps into our father's arms.

"Don't for one second believe what he said. His heart is in deep pain," Monnaire explains.

I nod. She's right but is Rioyn right too? Did I let Shivane escape by being far too fixated on Sylon? Is this all my fault?

Monnaire steps forward from the crowd.

"The war is far from over. But for right now, you all are free. Go. Celebrate with your friends and family. Cherish this moment you have right here, right now. And trust that when the battle continues, we will be victorious for the prophecy is true. The Iyanndyre Born is here, alive, and fighting for Seivan!"

Monnaire grabs my wrist, raising my arm high above my head.

Cheers rip roar through the crowd as others drop to their knees in their own Grynndyre bows of respect.

The next hour or so is almost dreamlike as people reunite, others falling into despair as they learn who didn't make it. There are shouts of joy and grief, hope and disbelief. It will take time for our people to heal, but at least that journey can finally begin.

We've lost several people. I search the crowd for our mother, but she seems to be one of those we've lost. I guess Shivane really did kill her, then.

My heart crumbles into a million pieces of rubble.

C H A P T E R 5 3

DRAGOLYONS

R I O Y N

Two months have passed. Two months since we won, and I lost Falla. No one seems to care. They say they do but their actions tell the real truth.

The crowd celebrates our victory, worshiping at the feet of my tiny, miraculous sister. Still, I feel nothing. The day we won, Monnaire used her Ascendance to rid my mind of my heart's destroyed emotions. Every day since, I've demanded she keep me in this state, a shell of nothing, watching my sister bask in her fake glory. Glory that I handed her.

As I stare at the ground before me swaying back and forth, Father whips around.

"When are you going to stop feeling sorry for yourself?"

I barely look up at him. What's the point?

"This is the last day Monnaire uses her Ascendance to dull your pain." He searches my downtrodden eyes for something. A glimmer? Hope? I don't know why he bothers.

"What would Falla think of you right now, huh, you not fighting for her? Not fighting to find a way to save her. She would be embarrassed for you, that's what."

Monnaire's Ascendance tries to extinguish the rage ignited inside of me.

I fought for everyone. We fought for everyone.

"What am I supposed to do, Dad? Huh? If I did fight and get in your way or Ayva's way, then I'd just be the same old Rioyn. You can't have it both ways."

His incredibly strong fists grab hold of my shirt collar. "Shivane escaping is no one's fault. Falla getting trapped in the Labyrinth Brick is no one's fault but what is your fault is you not trying. Is you giving up. Is you blaming everyone else."

As he lets go of my now wrinkled shirt, Arro rushes over to us.

"I figured it out. I know where they are."

My entire body tingles with excitement. "Finally!" I feel something. Hope.

"That's great news. Where are they?" Father asks.

Arro's eyes dart between us. "Before I tell you, I don't want you to get your hopes up. I know where they are but just don't know how to get there … yet."

"We have confidence that you'll undoubtedly figure it out. Please, give Rioyn and the rest of us some much-needed hope."

Arro sucks in a large breath. "The Infinite Void."

My eyes, along with my father's, open wide. How can that be?

How can anyone be in the Infinite Void?

As I struggle to comprehend this mysterious quandary, two large shadows cast down on us, everyone's head shoots to the sky. Ayva and Jax rush to our side.

Everyone else within the vicinity clamors around.

The two large dragolyons that are circling us are almost twice the size of any I've ever seen before. What I wouldn't do to be free like them!

They soar as if weightless through the pale blue sky.

Dust swirls around us. The two dragolyons prepare to land.

Ayva and I move backward.

We gaze into the sun as the dragolyons set down, shaking the ground beneath us. We're blinded by the sun to see who the riders are as they make their descent.

Whispers of 'betrayers' cry out behind us, my brows rising to a high arch, curious about what the whispers mean and the riders for whom they are meant.

Both riders slide down their dragolyon's back as if surfing a wave at Omaru.

They jump the last part, both of their feet reaching the dirt with helmets in hand. My eyes open as wide as the horizon before us.

"My son." The dragolyon-riding woman directs her comment to Jax. Her deep blue eyes contrast her braided golden-brown hair. She's dressed in Xaerian golden flight armor.

Jax's jaw is on the floor. It takes him a moment to realize his mother—Cyanda Risor, for whom he's longed since she disappeared—is standing before him. He rushes to her.

I rip my gaze from Cyanda to the next rider. Ayva grips my hand and squeezes tight. He is dressed in the same golden Xaerian flight armor, helmet in hand.

"Hey, little brother. Hey, little sister. Now that you have finally figured out who you are, Ayva, we have work to do. A war is coming and Drycour will be at our shores soon."

Bair!

EPILOGUE

THE FIERCE WINDS GROWL around us as Henri, Coren and I stand at the very peak of the Castle of Everia. Southeast plumes of smoke billow into the skies originating from the heart of Casstell.

My entire body inside and out feels lighter but the rage still boils inside me.

I turn to my brothers in arms, seeing what I feared.

Our lacquered black eyes have returned to their original hue.

Coren and Hanri gasp with wide eyes at the shared realization.

"Shivane and Sylon are in trouble," I state.

"Command the army. They'll all still fight for us and if they don't, we'll kill them all. We must storm Casstell," Hanri asserts.

My sharp gaze turns to my brother, his attention staying true. "No. We'd be fools to."

"Then what do you suggest? We just sit and wait for them to attack us?"

Coren's demeanor doesn't shift from his continual calm. His head cocks. "They found the true Iyanndyre Born, which means we won't be able to stop them. Storming Casstell will only result in an immediate sentence to the Prison of Xall."

My brother is right. "So, what do we do?" I ask.

Coren's calculated silence infuriates Hanri. "We fight. We have to. We …"

Hanri stops at Coren's raised finger. "We break into the Prison of Xall."

"That's your brilliant idea? Why would we do that? Why not just let them throw us in there with the rest?" Hanri isn't one to handle his emotions well, obviously.

"Break in to do what, exactly?" I ask.

"The worst of the worst inhabit the Prison of Xall. Some of the worst in all of the realms, I might add."

"If we want to defeat the Iyanndyre Born, we need the one person who can do just that," Coren continues.

"And who might that be?" Hanri snaps.

Coren slow turns to face us with a proud, sinister grin, proclaiming, "The Assihilator." Devious grins consume our faces.

THE END

ACKNOWLEDGMENTS

Four years ago, I embarked on a writing journey with a story that was vastly different from what it has become today. This book would not have been possible without the incredible support, guidance, and inspiration of so many wonderful people, and I want to take a moment to express my heartfelt gratitude.

To Cate Hogan, the very first person I trusted with my early manuscript. Despite its very—and I mean VERY—rough state, your kindness and generous feedback gave me the confidence to keep going. Through every step of this process, you helped refine and shape this story into what it is today. Your in-depth wisdom and insightful advice have been truly invaluable, and I am forever grateful for your encouragement.

To Annie Jenkinson, my brilliant editor, who took this almost-finished book and transformed it into the beautifully crafted story you hold in your hands. Your sharply tuned editing skills and remarkable ability to bring clarity and cohesion to my writing are unmatched. This book wouldn't be what it is without your exceptional talent.

To Rena Violet, my incredibly gifted cover artist, map-maker, and interior illustrator. Your eye for detail and your unparalleled creativity brought my world to life in ways I never imagined. From my rough ideas, you created artwork that elevated this story to another level entirely. Thank you for sharing your visionary talent with me.

To my best friend Brigette, you kept me going through it all. Whether it was keeping tabs on my progress, listening to my wild ideas over countless cocktails and tacos, or simply reminding me that I could do this—you've always had my back. I couldn't have done this without you.

To Jonathan—you may not be a reader at heart, but that never mattered. You believed in me not just for what I was creating, but for who I am. Your unwavering support and faith in my dream gave me the courage to keep going, even when the road felt impossible. Thank you for standing by me.

To my amazing family—my parents, brothers, cousins, aunts, uncles, and my godfather—your unwavering support and belief in me made all the difference. There were times when you had more faith in me than I had in myself, and that kept me pushing forward to write the best story I possibly could.

And finally, to you, dear reader, thank you for taking a chance on an unknown writer and her debut novel. Your decision to pick up this book fills me with gratitude beyond words.

Thank you, from the bottom of my heart, to everyone who helped make this dream a reality.

ABOUT ANNE SOSTMAN

Anne Sostman is a Las Vegas native who spent her childhood shooting hoops and perfecting her game on the basketball court. She graduated from Cal State Fullerton with a degree in marketing, and now resides in sunny Scottsdale, AZ, where she enjoys the company of her two perpetually cheerful Pomeranians. When she's not working, Anne loves exploring new adventures, traveling, and crafting new, deliciously fun recipes.

Find me online!

www.AnneSostman.com

@annesostman